The door of the café swung open just then and a man came in. He was tall, with fairish floppy hair, a moustache and a lounging way of walking as if he had all the time in the world. It was impossible not to see he was English. His bearing, his colouring, the fine tweed suit, the shirt – there wasn't a French thread of cotton in him. Nelly's eyes fairly blazed. The last time she'd seen him, he had been carrying a dead girl in his arms.

Lovers

SUZANNE GOODWIN

SPHERE BOOKS LIMITED

A SPHERE BOOK

First published in Great Britain by Michael Joseph Ltd 1988
Published by Sphere Books Ltd 1989

Printed and bound in Great Britain by
Richard Clay Ltd, Bungay, Suffolk

Sphere Books Ltd
A Division of
Macdonald & Co (Publishers) Ltd
66/73 Shoe Lane, London EC4P 4AB
A member of Maxwell Pergamon Publishing Corporation plc

ORSINO: For, such as I am, all true lovers are;
    Unstaid and skittish in all motions else,
    Save in the constant image of the creature
    That is belov'd. – How dost thou like this tune?

Twelfth Night (II iv)

Part I

CHAPTER ONE

The servants' entrance to the house was in a deserted alley lit by one gas lamp at its further end. Nelly blessed the shadows as she went down a certain flight of area steps, guarded by high spiked railings. It would not do for Madam to catch sight of her before she had changed her clothes. Madam wasn't the sort to understand that elbows would stick out of sleeves and toes begin to pop out of boots, thought Nelly. I'd better hurry in case I'm rung for.

After three months Nelly was still in a state of elation at working in the toffs' world of St James's. Fifteen years old, she looked younger, a thin perky Cockney whose only beauty was a mass of brown curling hair. It was so thick that in her previous work the porters had wiped their fishy hands on the top of her head.

Slipping down the steps, she opened the basement door of Granville House. A wave of warmth and the smell of expensive food came to her and she sniffed with pleasure. Five minutes later the ragged girl was transformed. A spotless starched grey dress reached to her ankles, neat patent shoes, and an apron edged with lace.

'There you are,' said Mrs Maxton, the housekeeper, appearing at the door of the cloakroom where Nelly was pulling a comb through her hair. 'Madam wants you in the salon. I can't think why she doesn't call one of the footmen. Hurry, girl. And stop looking in the glass or you'll crack it.'

Putting out her tongue at Mrs Maxton's angular back, Nelly went quickly up the stairs. At the top was a green baize door, studded with brass-topped nails.

Beyond was a further door to ensure that not a hint of cooking, let alone noise, could penetrate from the lower world into paradise.

Nelly had become accustomed to the heaven on the other side of the baize doors. And had been too sensible, even when she first arrived, to do more than stare a little. It was a very extraordinary place. The owner's taste ran to everything French. Enormous looking-glasses edged with gilt laurel leaves hung on the walls and were fixed to the ceilings. The crimson carpets were patterned with fleur-de-lis, the floors in the entrance hall were of veined marble. A golden staircase resembling one in the Paris Opera curved up to the first floor, and at its foot a fountain bubbled scented water into a silver basin. In every room were huge paintings of naked goddesses sprawling upon clouds, ogled by gods or bearded glaring satyrs.

The corridors from the entrance hall to the three reception rooms were lit with branched golden candelabra, and one of Nelly's tasks was to replace the candles every few hours. Their radiance, more gentle than gaslight, shone upon flocks of young women who dallied in rooms murmuring with music and their own soft voices. Eventually, the girls climbed the golden staircase to bedrooms on the upper floors.

Nelly was a servant in one of the best-run brothels in Europe.

Three months ago it had been a different story. She had been at Billingsgate Market, starting work at five in the morning. She'd rushed to and fro hawking cods' tails which hung, long and limp, dangling from her fish-smelling canvas apron. Porters pushed by, wearing white smocks and the round iron-hard hats which cushioned the heavy trays on their heads. Oozy trickles ran from the boxes of fish on to their faces. And the noise in the market was deafening.

'Had-had-haddock, all alive, alive oh!'

'Here you are, turbot, turbot, fat turbot. Splendid whiting just the right sort?'

'Glass of peppermint this cold morning?'

'Crabs, fine cock crabs, hello, hello!'

4

The bellies of the fish shone, children younger than Nelly sold huge baskets of brown shrimps, the air was filled with the seaweed odours of the sea. And Nelly smelled of fish from the top of her head wiped over by the slimy hands of the porters to the soles of her feet, slimy too from fish heads thrown down on the cobbles.

Walking home from the market when it closed at midday one wet summer morning – summer had been rainy for weeks – a cab had pulled up near her at Ludgate Circus. The cab door opened and a big woman, taking a false step, fell heavily into a filthy, brimming gutter.

Nelly put out a strong hand and tugged her to her feet. Then spun round to hurl insults at the cabby.

It was his ★ ★ ★ fault the lady had fallen over, what did he ★ ★ ★ think he was ★ ★ ★ doing? Why didn't he ★ ★ ★ look after his fares, eh? Eh? Nelly stood, hands on hips, using obscenities as fresh as the Billingsgate fish. The lady, who weighed at least fifteen stone and was shaken by the fall, gave the surprised girl half-a-crown. She must have been impressed by her young champion, for she also gave her something even better: her address.

'Come and see me, child.'

And Nelly did.

Now an accepted member of Granville House, Nelly went down the corridor to the big salon, dropping her eyes modestly whenever a man sauntered past her. She'd been told this was the rule. It was scarcely six in the evening and what she called high jinks would not start for a while. Most of the girls were upstairs, dressing or asleep. The orchestra had not yet arrived, although below-stairs the wonderful food was almost ready and two uniformed commissionaires were on duty at the main door.

It was the time of evening when Madam relaxed and chatted with favoured clients. She probably, thought Nelly, wants her usual brandy and ginger cake.

Madam Ruth had been radiantly beautiful thirty years ago, and had posed naked in the *tableaux vivants* which were still

5

popular in the London backstreets of the 1860s. But whores, like jockeys, must keep thin. They must 'waste', and Ruth was no good at self-denial. When her youth and figure left her, she took up the long-respected tradition of brothel-keeping. She flourished, moved to larger premises and a few years later bought the 18th-century mansion off St James's. She grew rich and refined, and so did her stable of girls.

Nelly knocked and went quietly into the salon. Her employer was stretched upon a divan near the tall windows overlooking the park. Nelly gave a bob curtsey and looked inquiring. Madam smiled. She never forgot a good turn, nor the reverse.

Ruth Waterford was wondrously fat, a mountain of a woman, with a broad face like a plate, black eyes and a slow way of talking. She was religious, and although Nelly's obscenities from Blackfriars had repelled her (Madam's girls were forbidden to swear) she had been touched by her ragged champion. She was accustomed to more highly born knights errant. Ruth was a snob. She knew the English nobility and the European nobility, too. Burke and the *Almanach de Gotha* were beside her bed with her Bible. She entertained the titled, the fabulously wealthy and a high percentage of the Brigade of Guards. Granville House was select and Ruth kept it that way. She had a peep-hole in the front door in case of trouble, and she picked her girls as a millionaire owner picks horses. As for Nelly, when she was older and filled out . . . Ruth had not made up her mind.

'Champagne, Lord Leckford?' asked Ruth.

A dark young man on her right muttered something about vintages and Ruth agreed. A second young man, fairish, with a moustache, who was sitting nearby, said in a drawling voice that he would join his brother in a glass of champagne.

'Child, fetch the Viscount's champagne right away. Mrs Maxton knows his choice. And bring something nice for me.' It was Madam's way of describing the brandy and cake.

With another bob, Nelly turned to go, giving a lightning look under her lashes at both men. It was a trial not being

6

allowed to gawp. Toffs weren't like any men she had known in her short crowded life. They never shouted, or hit people when they were drunk. One had even said 'Thank you'. Old or young, handsome or ugly, fat or thin, they had in common a kind of elegant behaviour which awed her – though most of them looked straight through her as if she were a pane of glass.

As she left the room she heard the fair man say, 'She might do. What do you think, Ruth?'

Whisking down the corridor and through the baize doors, Nelly said a loud 'Cripes'.

She wasn't a virgin. Curiosity and Blackfriars had seen to that. But she was as far removed from one of the Granville House racehorses as it was possible to be, and the notion of a toff fancying *her* made her giggle. Madam would never allow it.

It was midweek and early in September and London was reasonably full of the grandees who patronised Granville House, although some were still away in Scotland. Soon the front door bell pealed and clients began to arrive for an evening in a place they regarded as a hospitable and decorous club.

To the strains of familiar waltzes the girls drifted down the stairs. They were exquisitely dressed in gowns sewn with coral beads or frothing with white lace; they were seductive and creamy and young as new roses. Visitors sought out this girl or that and sat flirting and drinking. The girls listened and smiled, furling and unfurling their fans. Only one couple as yet went up the stairs towards a bedroom. The fountain bubbled. The air smelled of scent and cigars.

Down in the kitchens champagne and wine bottles were lined up in rows like soldiers. Silver trays covered with lace cloths were carried away by footmen, who returned later with empty glasses and empty bottles.

Nelly, having delivered the champagne, brandy and cake, was told to polish glasses. She wished she could do more tray-carrying but Mrs Maxton wouldn't allow it. If she could turn me into a skivvy in the scullery she would, thought Nelly, who knew she was a favourite and that Mrs Maxton resented it. Arranging the gleaming glasses, Nelly had a sense of anticlimax. No astounding message had required her presence above-stairs. The toff had said she 'might do'. Madam must have offered him one of the girls instead. As if she wouldn't, thought Nelly, treating herself to a thimbleful of discarded lukewarm champagne. She thought it tasted disgusting.

Up in the salon, Matthew Ayrton was thinking about Nelly at just the time she was thinking about him. The salon was filling up, the music playing. Ruth had changed from a tea gown into a magnificent black velvet, with ropes of pearls and a ruby brooch the size of an egg. She sat on a slight stage at the far end of the salon, a Guards officer on either side; when visitors arrived, they went over to bow to her, to be treated to a stately acknowledgement. It might have been a royal levée. Matthew recognised many of her clientele. Elderly noblemen who had known his father. Cabinet ministers. One or two high-rankers from the French Embassy. Some of his own and his brother's friends. Matthew himself had never visited Granville House until tonight. It was amusing that the brothel was like a richly endowed club. The girls, far prettier than debutantes, were just as modestly behaved. No doubt they shed all that in the bedrooms, but here in the salon respectability was paramount. Even the Old Queen could not have faulted the behaviour of Elsie, sitting beside Matthew and looking at him so charmingly.

He wondered where his brother Robert was. Robert had arrived in a filthy mood and Matthew hoped he had recovered. Looking round, Matthew saw him at the far end of the room, seated in an alcove with the girl he preferred, a very young, very fair creature called Gertie Jewell.

It was entirely due to his brother's particular tastes in sex that Matthew was there, for brothels had never been his line. Matthew, moving in Society, had many discreet affairs but had never been with a whore in his life. He enjoyed the excitement of the chase – in his world it was usually months before he successfully bedded some glorious married woman.

8

Apart from that, his interest was in painting, and he had taken a studio in Chelsea where he worked during the months he remained in London.

His brother had called there that afternoon.

'How's the painting?' Robert said, roaming about. He had the air of not giving fourpence for Matthew's reply.

'Not good. I've used the same model too often.'

'That one? Where did you dig him up?'

Robert indicated a charcoal drawing of a craggy man in sailor's cap and muffler.

'He works on the river. Takes people to and fro on Hamerton's Ferry to Marble Hill. I talked him into sitting for me. Now that battered face has become too familiar. I've begun to look at him as if I were a passenger in his boat rather than as a painter.'

Robert wasn't listening. He continued to stroll about, picking up canvases and putting them down.

'I don't know how you stand this place. It stinks of turps. Come out with me tonight. We'll go to Granville House. I've told you about it often enough. Ruth will find you twenty girls to paint. Or to do something else with if you feel like it.'

Matthew was looking at the drawing.

'I might.'

Robert sat down, repeating his remark that he didn't know how Matthew stuck it here.

'I quite like it, old fellow.'

'I still think you should get out. I tell you, you've never seen such wenches as those on parade at Ruth's.'

Matthew had heard all this before. He was devoted to his elder brother, loved and disapproved of him. Conventionally good-looking, resembling a portrait of the young Berlioz, Robert had inherited the Viscountcy and the estate very young. He was spoiled to death by their mother, was introspective and selfish and liked only the sex he paid for. Years ago, when they were nineteen and seventeen respectively, he confessed to Matthew, 'I can't do it, old chap, unless I'm with a whore.'

'That'll wear off. You will have to marry eventually, Bob.'

'I can't imagine doing so. Some frigid virgin!'

'Why not begin,' said Matthew, already older than his years, 'with one of those married women who devour you at dinner?'

'Can't abide them. Give me an evening in a well-run brothel. You can take your pick of the best-looking bits of fluff in the capital. Just you wait, Matt. You'll see what corkers they are. That's what I like. To pick out some charmer and squeeze her until she squeaks!'

His long handsome face had relaxed into a reminiscent grin, the expression it wore when he went to the tuck shop as a small boy and bought marshmallows.

When Matthew, from good nature, had agreed to accompany him this evening, Robert's spirits had revived. He would show Matthew 'what a swagger of a place' it was. Matthew had the impression that his brother rather wanted to make his tastes go in the same direction as his own.

Now Matthew sat watching the girls and listening to the music. The air was heavy with sex, and Elsie, whose face was like a flower, sat closer. I suppose I shall have to take her upstairs, he thought. He wasn't feeling sexy. It was probably because the atmosphere was deliberately created to arouse: it worked in the opposite way for him. And while the girl at his side offered herself in every look, he found himself thinking about the little servant he had seen earlier, whose impudent face might be interesting to paint . . .

It grew late. Matthew had supper, played a little baccarat and returned to the salon to sit about, watching the shifting colours of rich dresses. Elsie had left him and he was relieved. The panorama of the crowded rooms amused him. There had been a parade of girls earlier, and the men had picked out the girls of their choice. Matthew thought how smiling, how complaisant, how *possible* the girls were. And when couples strolled from the room they were as casual as people at a garden party.

Matthew supposed his brother had also gone upstairs for an

10

evening helping of sex. But he saw, glancing again across the room, that Robert hadn't stirred. He was still talking to Gertie Jewell. Matthew noticed with dismay that his brother seemed angry, he was arguing and the girl was nervously shaking her head. Finally, she stood up and walked away. The swaying, provocative movement acted as a goad to the man left behind, who sprang up and followed her. Matthew, slightly alarmed, went after them.

Outside the salon was the big open hallway, floored in black and white marble like a giant chessboard. It was deserted except for a footman who went through the door into the Baccarat Room. Gertie Jewell had reached the staircase when Robert caught up with her, saying loudly, 'You shan't go to that bastard!'

'Bobsy, I've told you and told you. Madam's fixed me with him from now on. I've got to go. He's waiting.'

'To hell with him. Ruth knows you're for me!'

Robert's face was ashen.

'Oh Bobsy, Bobsy, get another girl. It can't be me any more. It doesn't have to be me,' she cried tearfully. 'You're a sweet boy but we can't be together any more. *Please leave me be.*'

Robert grabbed at her and Matthew involuntarily exclaimed, 'Stop!'

'What are you doing here?' Robert shouted, turning round. 'Go away.'

Gertie Jewell's sweet vacant face altered from alarm to relief.

'You're his brother, aren't you? Tell him to let me go, oh do! Madam's arranged with Mr Arnott and he's paid such a lot, hundreds, and maybe he'll buy a house and put me there. I daren't go with Bobsy when Mr Arnott's waiting upstairs.'

'Bob,' began Matthew, taking in the whole sordid mess – his brother's white face, the girl with her whore's obedience, and the invisible ominous presence of the next man to own her. 'Let her go. You can't force yourself on a woman who doesn't – '

'Want me? She wants me all right, don't you, Gertie?' said Robert viciously, catching the girl's jewelled wrist. 'She wants it five times a night with me, she told me so. Do you know how old Arnott is? Seventy. My God, do you think I'll let him have her – '

He twisted her wrist, she gave a cry of pain and Matthew, shocked, gripped his arm. Robert's anger transferred itself for a moment to his brother. As he spun round, swearing, he unconsciously let go of Gertie who gathered her skirts and sped up the stairs, stumbling in haste. The moment she began to move, Robert rushed after her, reaching up to clutch at her dress. There was a tearing sound, one shoulder of the dress was ripped down, exposing a full pink-nippled breast. Gertie began to sob.

'I hate you. I hate you. Leave me alone.'

As she reached the landing, Matthew cried out: 'Let her go, for Christ's sake.'

But Robert heard and saw nothing but his prey escaping, and lunged at her as she stood, holding the torn dress up to cover her breast and still weeping, 'I hate you, get off me –'

Then it happened. Matthew, outraged at his brother's behaviour, had almost reached the top of the stairs. He was ready to knock him down. In the next there was a hideous scream. Gertie, backing away from Robert and unconscious of how near she was to the balustrade, toppled backwards, made a sort of helpless movement to right herself and fell in a heap of white skirts, landing with a dull thud on the marble floor twenty feet below.

For one frozen second Matthew saw the scene in horrifying detail: the figure crumpled and still, a trickle of blood on marble, the aghast face of a little servant who had come through the baize door and must have witnessed everything.

'Oh God. Oh God,' Robert groaned. The brothers threw themselves down the stairs in violent haste as Nelly fell on her knees beside Gertie.

'Gawd. She's dead,' gasped Nelly. She had seen dead people

half-a-dozen times and knew the look. She picked up the girl's hand. It was warm.

Ignoring her, the men bent over the still figure. Matthew felt the pulse. Robert choked out, 'Gertie, open your eyes, don't frighten me. Open your eyes.'

Matthew gently put down the young hand.

He said in a low voice, 'It's no good. She's dead.'

He paused for scarcely a moment.

'There is just time. *Go.*'

His brother lifted an anguished face.

'What do you mean?'

'Go, for God's sake. Think of the consequences if you don't. Robert, *go now.*'

To Nelly's astonishment the dark young man stood up, swaying as if he were drunk, and his brother took him by the shoulders and literally dragged him away from the dead girl. He said rapidly to Nelly, 'Are the servants' quarters through that door?'

'Straight down the stairs, Mister.'

Opening the door, Matthew pushed his brother through it and the further door and slammed both. He returned to kneel by Gertie, just as Ruth appeared.

'Trouble?' she said, coolly. Then she saw the figure's dreadful stillness, and the blood.

'She's dead,' said Matthew.

With a swiftness rare in somebody so fat, Ruth turned to the two girls who stood aghast beside her.

'Back into the salon both of you, and keep people away. Off with you. Quickly.'

She walked over to the body with a swashing stride and contemplated it for a moment. Then said, as if she had known him all her life, 'Matthew. Take Gertie into my study yonder. You, girl, help.'

Matthew picked up the dead girl, whose head lolled like the head of a puppet. Nelly shovelled up the trailing skirts and retrieved two satin shoes. Madam walked over to a sunburst clock on the wall. It was a quarter to two.

'Listen,' she said, and at that moment there was the peal of the bell. 'It's the police. The usual Wednesday raid. I didn't bargain for a dead body.'

The story of what was dubbed 'Death in Mayfair' made a considerable stir in the newspapers. The British public relished scandal and this had the best ingredients. High Society in a nasty mess. Beautiful girl of easy virtue killed in questionable circumstances. The most notable Madam in the business giving evidence (in sables worth a king's ransom). Finally, the younger brother of a Viscount in the box. The affair was discussed in every public house in London. The girl's dress had been torn off, mother naked she'd been, poor trollop, only seventeen and deep in a life of vice. She'd fallen forty feet from the fourth floor, wasn't it? Of course they *said* she'd fallen. They weren't going to admit she'd been pushed.

The judge was hard on the Honourable Matthew Ayrton. There was no evidence whatsoever that he had pushed the girl over the banisters. (That would have been murder, said the public regretfully.) The Honourable Matthew admitted there had been a violent quarrel. The judge spoke of 'frequenting the cesspools of evil'. More newspapers than usual were sold and small crowds gathered outside Granville House to look at 'the scene of the crime'.

Society itself was sickened. Matthew Ayrton had not merely quarrelled with a whore and been connected with her accidental death, he'd brought the dirt of low reality into the exalted world. He had dragged his reputation, and thus the repute of the entire privileged class, into the mud. He had damaged *them*. The sooner he was removed the better.

Young Viscount Leckford, the brother, was treated with delicate sympathy and no mention of the affair was made to him during the distressing days when the case was being heard. There was also no comment by his friends on the verdict that Gertrude Jewell's death had been from accidental causes.

Although nobody spoke about him, it soon got about that

Matthew Ayrton had left the country. There was a mute sigh of relief.

Matthew Ayrton was not the only one whose life was destined to change after Gertie Jewell's death. Another victim of that fatal moment was Nelly Briggs. She also left England.

She and Matthew had no sooner laid the crumpled body on to a chaise longue in Madam's private study than the noise of the police raid silenced the music in Granville House. Hearing voices, Matthew and Nelly unconsciously looked towards each other. Matthew's face wore the look of an acrobat about to perform some perilous leap without a net. As for Nelly, she was simply scared. She had the Cockney mixture of contempt and fear of the police. When the door opened silently, she nearly jumped out of her skin.

Madam shut the door and leaned against it. The rouge stood out on her cheeks. She crossed the room, lifted a plush curtain and unlocked a small hidden door. It led to a flight of stairs.

'Nelly, straight down to the servants' hall and get some work. Any work. You weren't up here. You were in the scullery or pantry. *Move.*'

Nelly fled. The door was locked behind her.

Police raids at Granville House were a regular formality, a mere check to ensure the licensing laws which forbade drinking and dancing after midnight were being kept. The chief inspector and Ruth were old friends. She always knew the time of the raid in advance, and when the police appeared at the front door the commissionaire sounded an alarm bell. Glasses and drink were stowed away in secret cupboards in the walls or under floorboards. The police were admitted in a leisurely fashion, walked through the crowded rooms where men and girls sedately talked over cups of coffee. (The police never went upstairs.) It might have been a vicarage party.

Not tonight. With Nelly out of the way, Madam fetched the inspector and a constable and took them to the study. Matthew was waiting. He answered the questions with cold upper-class politeness and was asked 'to accompany us, if you please, Sir, to the station.'

Below-stairs, polishing silver and holding her tongue, Nelly listened to confused, excited and ghoulish talk. Had Gertie been throttled? 'You never know with men,' said a scullery maid with eyes like lollipops. Nelly managed to be seen in three or four places. In the kitchens and sculleries, the butler's pantry and the servants' hall. When time was up, she changed into her patched clothes, pinned on a raggle-taggle hat and went up the area steps. The police vans had gone.

She took the tramcar home. It stopped on the south side of Blackfriars Bridge, still brilliantly lit and making the riverside streets seem darker. A huddle of vagrants were sleeping against a wall. The coffee stall lit by naphthalene flares looked cheerful enough, but Nelly kept clear of it for there were dangerous loafers there at night, as well as dockers, some stupid with drink, returning from night work or going on dawn shifts. Nelly crossed the road and dived down a passage with high, blackened walls on either side. She'd once seen a man kill a woman along there. He'd knocked her down, she'd hit her head on a stone, and he'd picked her up senseless, still swearing at her. Nelly had taken to her heels. Over the water it wasn't wise to interfere.

Turning into a gaping doorway, climbing a stair stinking of dirt and mildew, Nelly thought – I suppose she'll be drunk as per yuge. Whether the bundle of rags who called herself her mother was so in actual fact, Nelly had no idea. A woman who lived next door, not quite so drunken, not quite so filthy as the so-called Mrs Briggs, had once told Nelly she was a foundling.

'Thass wot you were. Found somewheres. Anny Briggs she took you and nobody the wiser. Oughter be grateful, you ought.'

Nelly wasn't sure she believed the story, and the idea of gratitude was pitiful. She'd spent her fifteen years grateful to nobody until Madam tumbled into the gutter. Nelly resembled the flowering plants which sometimes peer out of the dirt.

She knew every alley and dockside, every warehouse and

rotting tenement within two miles of the slum she called home. She knew the life of kerbside London to the south, where Ma Briggs sometimes hung about selling trays of stolen shirt studs. There were weighing-chairs there, and the doll seller, and you could buy a penny map of London and a penny history of England. The kerbs were a sort of fair – with the comic-song vendor, the try-your-strength machine and the man who sold groundsel for canaries. Not that Ma Briggs ever owned a singing bird. The only live creatures where she and Nelly lived were the occasional scuttling rats. Nelly dodged them after a boy told her they went for your throat.

She had spent her childhood dodging things. The Ragged Schools, for instance. And the Salvation Army lassies with bonnets and Bibles. Nelly didn't want to be caught by any of them, although she didn't disapprove of the Sally Army, who had shelters where men and boys she knew had nightly bunks for twopence. In Blackfriars, too, was the cheapest lodging of all: the Penny Sit-Up, a large shed with rows of benches crowded every night by homeless men who couldn't afford twopence for a shelter. Nelly went to the Penny Sit-Up one night, looking for an old boatman who had been kind to her. Among all the men sleeping with heads bent forward or lying drearily back against the benches, she never found her old friend.

Since she was eight years old, Nelly had done her best to earn food for herself and brandy for her mother. When sober, Anny Briggs sold at the kerbside. Lately she had stopped doing even that and had stolen some of Nelly's clothes to sell for the drink. When that happened Nelly made up her mind she'd done her fair share of keeping the old bag. Well, thought Nelly climbing the stairs, she can't sell no more of my things. That's a blessing. The day before, Nelly had fixed a padlock on her door the size of a tea-cup.

On the following day, with a thin rain falling on filthy pavements, every newspaper carried reports of the tragedy at Granville House. It gave Nelly a queer feeling in her stomach to see people on the tram reading about it. Over and over in her thoughts, she tried to puzzle out why one of those two gentlemen, the fair one, had forced the other to run away. She couldn't make sense of it. She'd never known anybody who didn't 'look out for hisself'. It was her own philosophy. She was kind-hearted but not an idiot, and taking the blame for that poor girl's death, well, that was the action of a lunatic. She didn't understand the toffs and decided, drumming her muddy heels absently against the wooden base of the seat, that she didn't want to.

Granville House had something different about it that evening. There didn't seem to be any lights shining through the thickly curtained windows and, when she went into the scullery passage and the cloakroom to take off her mud-splashed clothes, she noticed a most curious silence. She buttoned on her dress, gave her hair a quick dab, examined her face – clean – and went into the kitchen.

Mrs Maxton, with the elderly butler and only two of the footmen, was having a late tea. She was deep in conversation, but broke off to give Nelly an odd look.

'You're here, are you?'

'Large as life and twice as natural.'

Like a dog, Nelly smelt danger.

'Madam wants to see you. Look sharp.'

Mrs Maxton's tone alarmed Nelly even more. Streuth, I'm being given the boot 'cos of last night. Her mood suddenly switched from fear to outrage. What had *she* done? Only picked up Gertie's feet and helped carry her into the study. Only tried to help. Nelly's naturally pale face, with a few freckles on a short, upturned nose, blushed. She marched up the stairs and down the passage, averting her eyes from the place where a large unfamiliar Turkish rug was thrown across the marble. Instinct told her why.

She knocked at the salon door.

Madam was sitting by a large fire, for the evening was cold. She wore deep black. When she looked across at Nelly, the girl's alarm returned.

'Come here, child.'

18

To Nelly's surprise the voice was kind. She stood facing her employer, the blush ebbing.

'You behaved well last night. You spoke to nobody.'

'How do you –'

'Know? Never mind. Now, Nelly. You told me when I said you could work for me that you were glad to come here.'

'Oh, Madam, I am!'

'You also said your mother drinks.'

'She's a sot. I have to lock up me clothes.'

'So you would not mind leaving her?'

'Mind! But how can I? Gotter live somewhere until I make me fortune,' said Nelly with an urchin's grin.

But Ruth's big face, painted and set, was as stern as a judge.

'I have found another employment for you where the wages will be higher. No, don't thank me. Just listen. I have not much time this evening.'

As coolly as if telling Nelly to fetch some brandy, Madam said there was a vacancy as lady's maid with a friend of hers. The lady in question was leaving tonight, however. For Paris.

Nelly was too stunned even to speak.

An hour later, rigged up in a coat and hat Madam fetched from among the girls' clothes upstairs, Nelly made her way to Victoria Station. The lady, Madam said, would be waiting under the clock and would recognise her as Nelly was carrying a Gladstone bag with a yellow label. Nelly was given the bag, which had nothing in it, and enough money for her omnibus fare.

Rain was still falling; smoke from the engines mingled with the remains of last month's fog under the glass roofing of the station, which echoed with noise. Porters went by with luggage on hand carts. People hurried on their way to Sydenham and Sutton and other country places, pouring into the station and elbowing each other into stuffy trains. Nelly had never been to Victoria before in her life. All her experience of London was bounded between Bermondsey Wall and Blackfriars on the south of the river, Billingsgate and (recently) posh St James's to the north, and the four bridges spanning the Thames which she'd known since she had learned to walk.

This great deafening hastening place with its sense of travel was new. She was excited. She was going to earn more money and do new work. Go to a foreign country. And escape from the drunkard who hadn't give her a kind word in her life and whom, mother or no mother, she detested. Standing under the huge four-faced clock, she looked keenly round, grasping the Gladstone bag and hoping its label was showing.

'Good evening.'

A woman in sober navy-blue clothes with a serious hat was standing beside her.

'I take it you are Ellen?'

Nelly said she was. The lady introduced herself as Miss Fisher and waved imperiously at a porter. Before they boarded the Dover train, Miss Fisher counted her trunks and valises twice – there were six – and reproved the porter for clumsiness. When she tipped him he didn't swear, so Nelly decided Miss Fisher wasn't mean. They entered a First Class compartment, the lady looked it over, and moved to a further compartment marked Ladies Only.

On a night of gathering mist, Nelly stood on the deck of the steamer watching England disappear. Her heart beat with delight. This, thought fifteen-year-old Nelly, is the life. It did not upset her that her future had been altered by death. Drunkards were found dead in the river. Dockers were killed in brawls. Girls fell from golden staircases. You were just lucky if you weren't one of them.

CHAPTER TWO

As companions, Miss Mabel Fisher and Nelly Briggs were as unsuited as an elderly spaniel and a tattered mongrel pup on a double lead. Miss Fisher had agreed to take the girl as a favour to somebody useful to her but when she saw Nelly under the clock her heart had sunk to her patent leather boots. And so, for a moment, had Nelly's. Miss Fisher looked the sort who carried Bibles to Blackfriars.

Mabel Fisher was tallish and not unhandsome and had she wished could have been what men called a fine woman. Her strong olive-coloured face had a certain nobility, she had steady grey eyes and frizzy hair which gave a lightness to her gravity. She was reserved and respectable.

She had been reared in a Superior Orphanage – both parents had died in India – and from her earliest youth had shown some artistic talent. After a sketchy education the girl evolved, first working for other people, later for herself, a curious employment. She had an eye for what was fashionably opulent and theatres began to hire her 'to dress up the foyer a bit', or to smarten the theatre boxes. The aristocracy knew nothing of Mabel Fisher, but their well-born bodies reclined on sofas she'd bought in Paris, and draughts were kept away from their shoulders by curtains she'd ordered in Lyons. She bought furniture, fabrics, porcelain, glass and great trembling chandeliers. Many of these came from France and her purchases were shipped back to England, always with Miss Fisher supervising the packing cases. At Dover, Mabel took a room in a hotel and settled down to discussions with Customs. Her severity, reasonableness, sales dockets and, in the end, willingness to pay always brought success. Customs men liked her and served her cups of stewed tea.

Among her clients were two or three owners of the richest London brothels. It was Mabel who had decorated Granville House's salon and some of its elaborate bedrooms, and she had such excellent taste that Ruth recommended her to friends. Mabel soon had more work than she could manage to cope with and could pick and choose.

It had caused her an hour's struggle with her conscience when she was first offered the task of buying curtains for a bordel. She'd left Granville House, walked down St James's into a quiet patisserie to have some coffee and a bun. She sat and looked at the morality of what she'd been asked to do. Would buying new velvets for Madam Ruth encourage vice? Would choosing one of those pretty flower-painted Louis XV beds mean some young girl would take the primrose path? Mabel avoided thinking of what would actually happen on the bed she planned to buy in the Rue de Seine. The point was – would she be doing wrong to purchase it at all? Eating the bun, she decided not. All *she* was doing was creating pleasant rooms and earning her living. The colour of the curtains, the style of furniture or looking-glasses wouldn't make a straw of difference to the behaviour, or indeed the nature of girls willing to do what they did.

Mabel Fisher didn't pretend that comfortable settings would do any actual good. But she refused to accept that they did harm either. She couldn't change the world, and used the worn argument to herself that if she didn't work for Madam Ruth someone else would.

But she groaned inwardly when Madam asked her to take a young Cockney servant with her to Paris. She knew Madam was in difficulties over the death of one of her prostitutes, although neither of them mentioned it. Ruth was an excellent customer: it wasn't possible to refuse. Particularly when the girl's fare and a salary for the entire six months of Mabel's Paris stay were paid in advance.

22

'There is the problem of when I return to London, Madam,' Miss Fisher had said.

'Oh, the trouble will be ancient history by then. And the girl will find something else to do. She's that kind. Besides, six months with you will give her some polish,' said Ruth, with a note of flattery.

Nelly was quiet on the train and the steamer. If her blue eyes shone with surprise when she first heard French spoken, she saved Mabel Fisher the torture of Cockney exclamations. Not a 'Coo' or a 'Cor' were heard.

Miss Fisher's small apartment in the Rue des Martyrs was let every year for the period that she was away. It had been vacated by tenants recently, and was clean and provided adequate comfort. The carpets and furniture were on the shabby side, but Miss Fisher's interest was the luxury of other people. The apartment was within easy reach of antique shops, the district round the Opéra, and some of the auction houses. This saved fares.

Nelly was given a poky bedroom but she thought it a palace, with its rose-trellised wallpaper, washstand and basin and jug patterned with pansies. Her room at Blackfriars had been dark, reeking, hung with thick cobwebs and a broken bedstead had been propped up with filthy newspaper. Ma Briggs used a tin can for a teapot.

In a bed with real sheets, Nelly slept like a log.

It took Mabel less than twenty-four hours to realise that Nelly would never make a lady's maid. The girl had never seen a goffering iron, couldn't dress hair, and, standing on one leg behind Miss Fisher obediently handing hairpins, she gave the silent impression of a bird tied by a string. She did not say she was bored but it was in the air. She was cheerful and wonderfully energetic. She was never tired. But Miss Fisher did not approve of the repressed but bubbling high spirits, the angle of her nose or the mop of thick curls. She dressed Nelly in brown with a lace collar, but somehow the girl's figure seemed to burst out from under the buttons, and her womanly hips were prominent even under the fullest skirts, indicating lascivious curves . . .

Miss Fisher feared for her virtue, ruled that Ellen should be home from shopping or taking a walk by six every night, and gave her a moralistic homily. Nelly listened with respect. Miss Fisher herself liked men well enough and enjoyed doing business with them – Frenchmen in particular. She knew she was admired as a lady who drove a hard bargain. She had one or two men friends in Paris who took her out to restaurants or occasionally to the Opéra. She had never been to bed with a man in her life, nor wished to know about what she termed in her thoughts '*Les grosses pattes des hommes.*' The brocades and gilded furniture, the huge silver looking-glasses and the cash in Coutts Bank were her pleasures. Men and women had coupled since the world began. She herself was the result of such antics by two strangers. Her handsome face never darkened with sorrow at the thought of parents she'd never known, or love she'd never experienced. The girls who flocked like doves up the stairs at Madam Ruth's were nothing to do with her, save that one had been killed in an accident and Ellen, as she would call Nelly, had been a witness. She perfectly understood why Madam had hustled the young servant out of England.

Miss Fisher gave the girl a host of simple tasks. To clean the apartment. To fetch and carry. To do the shopping.

'But I can't speak the lingo, Miss.'

'Miss Fisher or Ma'am, please, Ellen. Never just "Miss". I know you cannot speak French. Try.'

The advice was not as idiotic as it would have been for anybody without Nelly's nature. Philosophically, she slung an enormous basket on her arm and clattered downstairs into the *boulevard*. She began to pick up French words that morning by pointing and laughing. She knew phrases in a week. In four she could chatter nineteen to the dozen. She had a natural aptitude for languages, a perfect memory, and a good ear. When she sang, in a pretty voice, she had perfect pitch. Miss Fisher couldn't help being impressed with Nelly's French, but she was shocked to hear her exchanging insults with the fishmonger.

24

'Call that a *hake*!' shouted Nelly. Miss Fisher had been passing the stall and stopped to remind Nelly of some forgotten purchase. 'You can sole your boot with it. Just look at it! Stinking it is. If your ★ ★ ★ fish isn't ★ ★ ★ fresh, you can forget me as a customer.'

She added more French argot Miss Fisher wished she did not understand.

Nelly settled in Paris as if she'd been born there. She liked scrubbing Miss Fisher's kitchen table until the wood was white as flour. She liked the deafening market, struggling through the crowds and using her elbows as the Frenchwomen did. She enjoyed selecting cheeses and feeling the ripeness of fruit; in London you'd be yelled at. Nelly learned to speak French in the idiom but didn't attempt the French lilt. From the start men seemed to like her accent. And even Mabel Fisher couldn't miss the fact that Nelly liked men.

She developed followers. There was Julian, a waiter in Montmartre, dark, short and nervous. He took Nelly for walks in the richest streets, showed her Maxim's and the Ritz and described the food they served. He had friends who worked among the wealthy 'who eat so many courses it would make you sick' said Julian, thin as a piece of string. He was ambitious, 'To be a great chef?' inquired Nelly.

'I have not the flair. I want to own a restaurant. Be *le patron*,' he said, sighing. 'But I need money to achieve my dream.' They were walking up the street leading to the Paris Bourse.

'Look,' he said, pointing at its noble pillars. 'As Théophile Gautier said, "the religion of money is the only one which has no unbelievers".'

'Waiters read books,' remarked Nelly to her employer later, 'but they're bags of nerves. Do you know why, Miss? Sorry, Miss Fisher. They gamble. Chronic, isn't it? Waiters gamble all their tips, and that's why he looks so pale. Gambling and losing, see? I told him he was crazy but all he did was pay me compliments. These Frenchies!'

It was winter now and Nelly's rounded cheeks were red

with the cold wind in the streets. She had had her sixteenth birthday. Miss Fisher noticed with concern that the girl was becoming quite good-looking. It boded ill for the future. And there were more followers now. A clerk called Laurent who developed the habit, appalling to Miss Fisher and to a groaning Nelly, of writing to her every day. Nelly had never been to school and read one word at a time until the impatient Miss Fisher gave her lessons. Poor Laurent would have wept to see how many letters of love were pitched unopened into the stove.

Nelly's latest follower was Patrice Jacob. She met him on top of an omnibus. The conversation had been one-sided, the big young Jewish man springing up to help her with her baskets, Nelly raying smiles and beginning to chat. Patrice listened, fixing her with brown eyes which had a melting brilliance: they were his best feature, although his bony sallow face and beaked nose were impressive. He resembled a young patriarch about to lead his people through the desert. But he was so silent. He spoke, as it were, only with his eyes. Nelly knew he thought her attractive, he listened and looked at her with such passionate attention. He jumped up again when she reached her destination, said, 'It is my direction, Mademoiselle,' and carried her baskets all the way to Miss Fisher's.

She liked him from the moment she'd sat down beside him and he soon became her favourite follower.

It was a bitterly cold winter, the rich Parisians were swathed in furs. Miss Fisher's forays to warehouses, auction rooms, the great spreading markets selling everything from tallboys to coal scuttles, were going well. Nelly's presence in the Rue des Martyrs turned out useful after all. The girl had a sort of tact, for all her unspeakable origins. She was, for instance, either too busy or too clever to broach the subject of her own removal from London.

Miss Fisher decided Nelly's lack of curiosity came from her attitude to life, which was to take things as she found them, keeping a wary eye open. Nelly was somewhat changed from the girl in clothes too large for her who had waited at Victoria

Station. She was rosier and plumper, seemed to have lost her Cockney whine. She'd picked up some of Miss Fisher's ways, some of her manners, including a daily bath. She washed the deplorably curly hair and Miss Fisher suspected that on her afternoons off she used scent.

The blessing is, thought Mabel Fisher one morning in bed at half-past six, warm under thick blankets, the blessing is that I am sure she is doing nothing immoral. Mademoiselle Besson (the old concierge) would never allow men here during the day.

As it happened Nelly had been to bed with Patrice Jacob a number of times. They'd gone to his rickety barn of a studio to have bread and cheese. It was up the hill and innumerable muddy steps in the vast dilapidated track of land above La Butte in Montmartre. His studio in summer, he said, was covered with ivy. Nelly thought when the leaves came out it must look like a kind of square tree. In winter the bricks were criss-crossed with a network of dry stems and indoors was cold as charity. After their meal and some disgusting coffee, they kissed. And that was it.

Nelly liked him, and was moved by the way he looked at her. He proved an experienced lover, strong, potent, energetic and perfectly silent. His face was filled with gratefulness, even with love, before and after sex. She felt good about him. Of all her French followers she preferred him although he never said a ★ ★ ★ word. I suppose I ought to stop swearing in my head. Don't expect I will, though.

Nelly had lost her virginity, or, to be exact, had arranged to give it away, when she was just fourteen. She had been born into a world without innocence or chastity and although she was quick and strong, she had lived in a dangerous place. She was never a match for the hulking longshoremen and labourers who lunged at women in Blackfriars. When she countered the grabs of some lecherous drunk, she swore at him with a mouth showing charming white teeth, and her bright eyes blazing with contempt were a dark blue. She was a spitfire. But to know about sex was essential and the sooner the better. She decided upon a boy of sixteen who was cleanish and kind-hearted. They made love in a deserted warehouse overlooking the filthy, fast-flowing Thames, doing it regularly for a few months until he moved away to work at the Chatham docks. When they first slept together, Nelly was nervous of becoming pregnant. But the boy Sydney was proud of his experience.

'Don't get in a fuss. Me Dad taught me the necessary,' he said, emerging in skilful time from Nelly's moist body.

All this seemed a long time ago to Nelly when she decided to lie in Patrice's muscular arms. She enjoyed his love-making. One afternoon, after a particularly energetic time in bed, she returned home in good spirits, and busied herself getting Miss Fisher's tea. Her employer, to her surprise, asked her to sit down and join her.

'Tea, Ellen?'

Nelly accepted a cup of China dish-wash and didn't even grimace. She sipped daintily, wondering what was coming.

'You have never asked me exactly why Madam wanted you to come to Paris,' said Miss Fisher.

'Because of that poor girl, I suppose.'

'You didn't ask yourself more than that?'

Nelly looked at her rather shrewdly. She had thought about the tragedy too often. Although she had seen violence, and death too, since she was a child there had been something strange about that night. It hadn't been in some filthy street brought about by a man and mad with raw gin. But in a world of music and flowers and beautiful women.

'I did think something . . .'

Miss Fisher waited.

Nelly rubbed her nose.

'Well, Miss – sorry, Miss Fisher. The fact is there were two men with Gertie Jewell on the stairs. I came through the basement door, see? I saw both of them. A dark one raging at that poor girl, *she* was haring up the stairs away from him and he caught at her and ripped off her dress, nearly. The other, the tall one, tried to stop him. And then – '

'Then?'

'Then she fell. Horrible it was. Her skull cracked like an egg.'

'Yes, yes, there's no need to go into that,' said Miss Fisher hurriedly. She was weak stomached.

'The tall fair one told the dark one to scarper. To go. The dark one didn't want to, but somehow the other made him. And it was the tall one who stayed and carried her into the study with me. And waited for the police, I suppose.'

'Did you read the newspapers next morning?'

'How would I do that, Miss Fisher? I couldn't read more'n a few words then, not like now. I'm getting quite quick. In French, of course. But I did hear the newsboys shouting "Death in Mayfair", and "Peer's Brother" or some such. Then all of a sudden I seemed to be on the train with you.'

Mabel Fisher paused.

'There are times, Ellen, when somebody does something brave. Rashly brave, I consider. But I can understand why. The tall one as you call him is the Honourable Matthew Ayrton, his brother is Viscount Leckford, heir to a famous name hundreds of years old, and a great estate too. He is the one you call the dark one. Both young men are noblemen. People of privilege.'

'Rich,' said Nelly.

'Yes, of course, but that is not what we are talking about. They have great responsibilities. People like Viscount Leckford and his kind have made the history of our country. They are leaders, patrons. The best of ourselves. You don't understand, do you? The point is that if scandal touches them, it touches *all* Society and undermines the way things should be. It is very terrible.'

Nelly said nothing but her face was eloquent. She was thinking this was so much twaddle. It was the dark man's fault the poor girl toppled to her death. Why should the tall one take the blame?

'The Honourable Matthew persuaded his brother to leave Granville House just in time.'

'And the police nicked the Honourable Matthew because he said it was him who'd been with the poor girl.'

'Yes.'

'What good did that do? He's upper class too.'

'But the *younger* brother. It is not the same. Society certainly blamed him. But the Leckford name was protected, thank heaven,' said Miss Fisher, who revered the idea of the nobility. Their enormous houses. Their wealth. Their rudeness.

'Madam got rid of me because of what I saw, then?'

'You were the key witness. But happily nobody knew you were present. And you were very discreet.'

'She still wanted me out of the way double-quick. But all those lies. They beat me.'

'You will perhaps understand one day. Will you bring more hot water, if you please?'

The subject was closed. The winter went by satisfactorily for both of them. Miss Fisher's haul included satin chaise longues, glass-topped tables, the inevitable looking-glasses supported by cherubs, console tables of delicate design, and paintings of ripe young women floating on clouds and showing their rounded stomachs and pink nipples.

As for Nelly, she was busy with three followers.

March came. Parma violets surrounded by ivy leaves were sold in great baskets at the corner of the Rue des Martyrs. The trees in the Place Blanche looked as if they wanted to bud. Nelly returned punctually from an afternoon with Patrice, wearing the swimming look of a woman who has had a good hour's loving. Miss Fisher was already home doing her accounts. She looked up, regarded Nelly somewhat penetratingly, and said, 'I wish to talk to you.'

'Oh ★ ★ ★ ,' thought Nelly, 'she's rumbled. But how can she? She wouldn't be seen dead on the Butte . . .'

'I am making arrangements for our return in two weeks' time. I have told you we are soon due home.'

Nelly paused for a moment and then said, 'I thought maybe I'd stay.'

She looked at her employer with a bright face. In the six

months they had lived together Mabel Fisher had never seen her gloomy.

'Indeed?'

'It's not half – I mean it's quite nice here.'

There was a speaking pause.

Miss Fisher thinned her lips.

'Paris is scarcely the place for a girl only just sixteen, unless, as you are at present, she is under the care of an adult. In her guardianship.'

Silence.

Nelly looked at her with frank blue eyes. The look was polite but said as loudly as if she'd shouted that Mabel Fisher had no jurisdiction over her.

Nelly twisted her feet round the legs of the chair.

'You think I'll get taken up by somebody like Madam and work in a *maison de tolérance*,' she said.

The phrase had a certain irony.

'The thought had occurred to me. I don't think you have a notion of the dangers of staying alone in Paris.'

It did not occur to Miss Fisher, friend of Madam Ruth's and supplier of looking-glasses for ceilings, as being paradoxical to outline the fate of 'fallen women', the degradation and the poverty at the end even if, for a while, you are kept by a rich man.

'Yes, Ma'am, I know,' said Nelly when her employer ran out of steam. 'Honestly, I shan't become one of those. I don't fancy the life. I'm not saying I don't fancy men because we all do,' she added, with a comradely look at Mabel. 'But not some chap who pays ten francs for a go.'

'You say that now,' said Miss Fisher, wincing at Nelly's description of immortal love.

'And with you out of the way, you think there's nothing else for me. Well, that's not what I plan. Not for a minute.'

Mabel Fisher was disturbed. She did not particularly like the girl although she respected her talent for French, her indomitable good humour, and at times was even amused by her. Conscience, however, pricked. 'My God,' thought Mabel

31

Fisher, who rarely called on the Almighty unless directly addressing Him. 'How young she is. I can't leave her on her own.'

'You realise I have to leave this apartment, Ellen. It is let in two weeks' time.'

'You told me. It's all right, Miss Fisher. It's nice of you to worry about me but yesterday I found myself a little *pied à terre*. Rue de la Mire near the Place Clérissy. Bit cramped but not a cockroach in sight.'

Miss Fisher shuddered.

'It's true. I know the smell,' Nelly assured her. Feeling more was needed she added she would miss her employer and Paris wouldn't be the same without her.

'It certainly won't,' said Miss Fisher with feeling.

'I'll be on my own,' said Nelly.

Not for long, thought Miss Fisher, and gave a sigh.

'How do you propose to pay the rent for this *pied à terre* of yours?'

She wondered if the girl were going to ask for money and if so whether she would give her any. Madam Ruth's cheque would have covered, by the time Mabel Fisher left Paris, the meagre wages, the food and the extra trouble of putting up with Nelly. But her return fare had not been spent. Mabel Fisher also wondered if she was willing to give the girl any cash. Probably not.

'I've got some work, Ma'am. In the Atelier Guelle. Maître Guelle is quite a success, you know. He has ever so many students. And real painters go there, too, to work so they can use the models. It's in one of the old houses in the Clérissy.'

She did not say it was Patrice who had found the work for her, or that Maître Guelle had only agreed after Nelly had obligingly stripped to show him what she termed her shape.

Miss Fisher sighed more deeply.

'Without your clothes, I suppose. Ellen, Ellen, I despair. How will you get a husband if you are willing to appear *like that* for a few francs?'

'But it's very respectable, being an artist's model. Some of the artists get famous. One Italian girl who posed for an Englishman called Whistler has opened an Académie herself in the Rue Stanislas. And Monsieur Renoir married his model, you know. Maybe I'll be lucky too!'

Nelly's apparent familiarity with a world Mabel Fisher preferred to know nothing about left her flummoxed. She was aware of Montmartre, a poverty-stricken gimcrack place above Rochechouart where the very poor lived, whether they were artists, poets or pimps. It was filled with rough people who drank absinthe, danced like madmen, frequented run-down brothels and obscene shows of naked women. Madam Ruth's was an embassy compared to Montmartre. As for painting, Mabel's taste was for goddesses and cherubs and the new-fangled art of the last twenty years repelled her. She looked at the young girl in silence.

'I got something else,' said Nelly, with a note of glee, 'I'm going to sing at night.'

Her employer's mouth actually fell open.

'*Sing?*'

'Good, isn't it? You know Julian, well, 'course you do. He was here on Monday, took me to the Cirque Fernando to see the clowns. He spoke to Monsieur Moréas who has a *café-concert* near where Julian works. It's called Chez Paul-Marc. Monsieur Moréas has got a pianist, a dear old thing called Louis, fat but plays like a good 'un. Louis can pick up any tune you sing. Well, Monsieur wants a singer and said he doesn't mind English songs. So I gave him "Henery the Eighth" and "Brown Boots", and "Heaven will protect an honest girl".'

'Did you?' said Miss Fisher faintly.

'Yes, and he says I'll do. I'm to sing at the caf-conc' every evening and twice Saturdays. It's closed Mondays. He's paying ten francs a week *and* me dinner.'

Miss Fisher threw in her hand.

The morning of their departure, Nelly was up hours earlier than usual, packing, cleaning and shrilly whistling. She was her quick obliging self and there wasn't a chore she didn't carry out at once, including going out to fetch Miss Fisher fresh croissants for breakfast and cutting ham sandwiches for the journey. She gave the kitchen floor a final scrub, and accompanied her employer in the cab to the Gare du Nord. Then stood on the platform as the train puffed out, waving and smiling . . .

Nelly left the station. She walked into the Paris of a March morning, alone for the first time. The streets had just been washed, the paling sky presaged sunshine. She sniffed the air like a young animal. Her first day free of Miss Fisher. Liberty. In the land which had invented it.

Walking along the Boulevard de Magenta, she felt she had lived in Paris all her life. The air was noisy with the clip-clopping of horses' hooves; smart carriages and omnibuses and carts went by and in every blessed one, she thought, they're talking or thinking in French. And so can I. She looked at the passers-by, the top-hatted men, white-bonneted servants with baskets. She'd been carrying one of those yesterday. She gazed up at the wrought-iron balconies. She was in an excellent mood.

Laurent, mathematically inclined, had pointed out on her sixteenth birthday that Nelly had been in Paris a twentieth of her life if you counted from the age of six. Nelly agreed because before six she only remembered the dirt and the cold. '*Ma pauvrette*,' muttered Laurent who found her tales of the slums erotic. This twentieth, Nelly decided, was the best so far.

First there was her childhood with her drunkard mother. Then Billingsgate where at least she'd had pennies in her pocket. The market had faded in her mind into a sea-smelling dream. Her thoughts moved on to Madam Ruth's – a house like a palace, clean clothes and more pay. The scent of rich food. And all those lovely women. Well, here she was now, an artists' model and a singer. She grinned in satisfaction.

She had taken a fancy to Montmartre the first time Patrice walked her up those muddy steps to the studio where he lived. When not at Les Halles as a porter, Patrice painted every spare minute. She liked the bare room, the whitewashed walls, the very smell of paint and Patrice's clothes. She liked the drinking-trough further down the hill where horses dipped their chins into the water. She felt at home in Montmartre. City born and bred, she thought it was like the country. There was fresh air and a wind sometimes which until a few years ago had made the windmills spin. The little shops sold fresh milk and apples. The ascending streets and alleys, the endless flights of steps, climbed by the walls of old cottages whose gardens spilled over, their branches touching Nelly's arms. Grass grew between the cobbles. The children were the sort of impudent urchins she herself had been; and the most practised beggars.

The Place Clérissy was scarcely a *place* at all, it was not far from the Montmartre cemetery where she and Julian sometimes went for a walk. Gloomy Julian liked cemeteries and said they were educational.

'There's Berlioz,' he said, halting at a pretentious tomb on which somebody had placed a wreath of laurel leaves. 'Such a handsome man. Such dramatic sentiment in his work. He is buried between his two wives.'

'There'll be trouble on the Last Day,' said Nelly, laughing.

'Henri Murger – *he* understands us of the Bohemian life,' said Julian, wearing his respectable black waiter's coat.

When Julian had enough money he took her to the café on the corner of Clérissy. It was called La Vache Enragée and was decorated with two ceramics of the furious cow. In one, the animal angrily chewed its own tail; in the other, rearing upright, it attacked a thistle. Nobody knew the origin of the café's name. But it was in the Montmartre style . . . like the Lapin Agile, with its sign of a rabbit jumping out of a pot, or Le Chat Noir, with a devilish black cat against a hellish background.

La Vache had none of the fame or infamy of the Chat Noir. It was a good-smelling café with a garden and weatherbeaten wooden tables and benches outside for the fine weather. Trellised alcoves were intimate places in summer for lovers.

Nelly was early for her first morning's work and was also hungry. It seemed hours since her hurried breakfast with Miss Fisher. She went into La Vache and was greeted by Edouard, who wore a white apron to his feet and who brightened at the sight of her.

'Croissants, Mademoiselle?'

'Bread and *confiture* is cheaper.'

'That is true,' agreed Edouard. And served her double portions without charging for them.

The café had begun to fill up. There were burly workmen in blue overalls called *bleu du travail*, who drank small brandies and large bowls of coffee. There were middle-aged men in frock coats who looked like diplomats and were not. They had waxed moustaches and neat beards. Nelly's dark blue eyes ranged round. She savoured the scent of coffee, the stronger smell of freedom. Miss Fisher was on the train, dozing and rocking her way back to London. Nelly smiled disloyally.

The door of the café swung open just then and a man came in. He was tall, with fairish floppy hair, a moustache and a lounging way of walking as if he had all the time in the world. It was impossible not to see he was English. His bearing, his colouring, the fine tweed suit, the shirt – there wasn't a French thread of cotton in him. Nelly's eyes fairly blazed. The last time she'd seen him, he had been carrying a dead girl in his arms.

What's *he* doing here, she thought. Why isn't he in the Ritz? I suppose he thinks he's slumming. While she polished off her bread and jam, she debated whether to speak to him. She decided not. She paid her bill and collected her shawl and basket, avoiding the corner where the Englishman sat reading his newspaper. Unexpectedly he put it down – and saw her. He stood up at once.

'Why, it's you.'

'Thought you hadn't seen me,' said Nelly jauntily.

Then, 'What are you doing in Paris?' they both said at the same time. And laughed. Nelly had forgotten how tall he was. She was used to compact Frenchmen, even Patrice was much shorter than this man. She had to lift her head to look up at him.

'Are you on holiday?' she asked.

'No, I live in Paris. I'm going to the Atelier Guelle this morning.'

'I'm – I'm blessed,' said Nelly, swallowing another word. 'That's where I'm off to.'

'I haven't seen you there before. Are you studying with Guelle?'

'Starting as one of his models. Today,' said Nelly.

Matthew Ayrton murmured politely and lingered, asking her if she would have some coffee. Nelly wanted to accept. It was a treat to speak English with a man, she hadn't done so since London. But time was flying.

'Thanks, but I've got to skedaddle. I must be in the Atelier before the others, you see.' She added in a friendly way, 'I didn't know you were a painter.'

'Not much of one. I'm glad I'll see you at Guelle's.'

You'll be seeing a deal more of me than you're doing at present, thought Nelly, saying goodbye.

Maître Guelle's house in the Place Clérissy was of good solid stone and stood out from the rest by reason of having three floors. He had enlarged the windows, put in skylights and built a model's stage. The Atelier was successful and economically priced, and students who would never be accepted by the École des Beaux Arts were eager to enrol under Guelle.

The students were a noisy bunch like a flock of starlings, gathering, circling, dispersing, only to gather again. They were silent at work, but when it was over poured out of the Atelier to their favourite cafés, which they filled with talk and no money.

Nelly's employer, François Guelle, was a painter as well as a teacher. His works were large and romantic, well executed and overtly sexy. He went in for harems and slave markets which were popular with the wealthy bourgeoisie. Guelle's Eastern beauties lay about in his pictures like scented fruit, their flesh so real that a buyer felt he could lean right through the frame and touch it.

Part of the studio was fitted up with carved screens, rich-coloured and dusty silks, piles of cushions and a pierced metal lamp of the kind which summoned the genii in *Aladdin*. When Nelly entered the studio, the Maître was alone. His class had not yet arrived. He was standing by the stove, under the high skylight, studying one of his own paintings of two young women lying in shuttered sunlight. The lamp in the painting actually hung above Maître Guelle, and the cushions, dirty but recognisable, were in a corner by a wall inches thick with the scrapings from palettes.

'Good morning, Mademoiselle.'

Nelly greeted him respectfully. Her new employer had hair like black wire, a curly black beard and eyes like currants. He rather liked the young English girl. But he liked all his models, indiscriminately calling them '*ma belle*'.

'You may prepare yourself in the *grand placard*,' he said. Nelly looked inquiringly through the forest of easels. He was pointing at a gigantic cupboard at the far end of the studio. She would find, he said, some robes in there to keep her warm until the work began.

The *grand placard* was not dark when she shut its door. The ceiling had a circular window in the roof, and in the pale light, stripped naked, Nelly looped her garters on a nail, put her clothes on a tin trunk which she rubbed beforehand, finding it coated with dust. Garments hung on hooks like the row of Bluebeard's dead wives. A turquoise velvet edged with moth-eaten fur. Dark red silk with medieval sleeves. A white monk's habit, the moth had been at that, too. Velvet, black, banded with braid, gold. Nelly chose the turquoise which looked the warmest, and emerged barefoot.

'Come to the stove, *ma belle*,' said Maître Guelle. 'Keep warm as long as you can.'

He glanced at her. He had been relieved when Patrice Jacob, not a student of his but an acquaintance, had called in with this English girl. Guelle's favourite model, Marie-Flore, had deserted him. She'd left to model for Gustave Moreau at the Beaux Arts, where she was busy now, posing in one of those fantasies Moreau went in for, princesses and unicorns. Guelle had been affronted at Marie-Flore's treachery, and regarded the new girl, thinking the students would approve. But for himself? Alas, that nose was too impudent for a houri, and the eyes were not languorous enough. Could one improve them with belladonna and kohl? The hair was a good colour but there was too much of it. He remembered, with a pang, Marie-Flore's fine fair hair and a face which melted, so to speak, with the paintbrush.

Fifteen minutes later the studio was crammed. Nelly was placed in a standing pose conveniently near the stove, its heat pleasant on her bare bottom. Round the stage the students were grouped, each with his canvas on an easel scarcely three feet from the ground. They squatted on low stools, looking upward at the glowing girl, full-breasted, slender-waisted, pink-nippled. Her skin seemed opalescent, her hair took on chestnut lights from the strong daylight overhead. There was silence except for shuffling feet or easels being shifted slightly. The air was blue with dust and cigarette smoke.

Maître Guelle passed from one student to another, commenting or explaining. Sometimes he encouraged, sometimes shook his head. Once he took the student's brush from him 'to show you the architecture of the body'. He did not speak to the Englishman at the back of the studio, sitting where the floor was slightly raised, painting steadily. Nelly remained like a statue, her buttocks growing rosier from the heat of the stove.

When the class broke at midday for luncheon, she thought her neck would never move again. She wrapped the velvet robe round herself and padded off to the *grand placard* to dress. An hour-and-a-half's freedom. She'd buy some bread and eat it in the Place. The sun was out.

Released, the students thundered down the stairs, talking and laughing loudly. Maître Guelle vanished to his own living quarters two floors below, where his wife must be a good cook judging from the scent of food floating up the staircase. Nelly heard one student say, 'Lucky pig. Going to put his head in the trough again.'

When she came out of the cupboard the only person left in the studio was Matthew Ayrton. He was leaning against the paint-encrusted wall.

'I hope you are not tired after the long morning stint?' he said, with an unfamiliar, concerned politeness. Nelly said she was never tired, but she was certainly hungry. She gave him an impartial smile.

'I agree,' he said, 'I wondered if you would do me the honour of having luncheon with me.'

Nelly rubbed her nose at the formal invitation. Her followers put their hands in their pockets, spread out a handful of francs and sous, and calculated what they could afford. Once she'd tried to add a franc and Julian shouted, 'A woman pay? Are you insane?'

She looked at Matthew without speaking. He supposed she was trying to find a way to refuse.

'I quite understand. You are having luncheon with friends.'

'I'm not eating with anybody. I'm going to buy a *batard* and cheese and have it in the *place*. Why not come too?'

'That is kind. But if you are free, you would be doing me the greatest favour to have luncheon.'

To Nelly's doubtful surprise she found herself walking with him towards the *grands boulevards*. They stopped at a small restaurant, the Coq Hardi, where, apparently Matthew was known. They were squeezed into a recently vacated table. The room was full of people eating and drinking and talking vivaciously.

Matthew ordered omelettes and salads. Nelly refused any wine. She had the dislike of alcohol which comes to drunkards' children.

When the meal was served, her doubts about her presence there vanished. An omelette sizzled in a silver dish. The salad was shiny with olive oil and freckled with black pepper. A *batard* of fresh bread, which would have been her whole meal, was broken into golden pieces in a basket. The square of butter would have lasted her a week.

'How are you liking Paris?' asked Matthew in his formal way.

'A lot. Had to get used to it, though. The French doing things the opposite from us.'

'Do they? I hadn't noticed.'

'But you must have done! Like they sweep their chimneys starting at the top, and drive on the wrong side of the road, and in French they say "*blanc et noir*" and *we* say "black and white".'

'So we do.' He looked at her and smiled.

'I knew you had left London. Madam Ruth mentioned it. But not that you had come to Paris. How did that happen?'

'She got me a post as lady's maid. I wasn't no good at that. Well, imagine!' said Nelly, sharing the joke. 'But I soon picked up some French and got useful to the lady, she buys furniture and that. She went back to London today. Now I have some new work. Not so dusty.'

'You're a very good model.'

'I am, aren't I? I've always been able to keep still. As a kid down the docks I used to play Statues. Well. Now and then we did,' she said. Playtimes had been rare.

'Did you mind being packed off to Paris?'

'I was like a duck in thunder – couldn't believe it. Turned out good, though.'

She buttered a piece of crust and looked straight at him. She remembered what Miss Fisher had told her.

'I suppose you're here same as me, Mister Ayrton.'

'I suppose I am.'

It was the right moment for him to speak. She forestalled him.

'The lady I worked for explained why I was hustled off. 'Cos of being a witness. Apart from you two I was the only one who saw what happened. But it was your brother who done – did it, and that's the truth, Mister Ayrton.'

He was taken aback by the matter-of-factness and lack of delicacy.

'He never meant to,' was all he said.

'I know. He was beside himself when he pelted after her like that. I seen the same thing in Blackfriars. Men go mad when they're jealous. They can kill a girl. Poor thing, it wasn't his fault.'

There was a pause. Then she said, 'You didn't half move quickly, making him run. He didn't want to.'

'You've thought a great deal about this. It's very natural.'

'No, I haven't, Mister Ayrton. I put it out of my head. I do with things if they're nasty. It's just that Miss Fisher explained why you took the blame. She said you were right.'

He poured her some mineral water, thinking this conversation was between people each speaking a language incomprehensible to the other. No, that wasn't it. *He* understood her. But Nelly, Miss Fisher or no Miss Fisher, wouldn't grasp a word he said. And she must.

'You don't think I did the right thing, then?'

She shrugged.

'How can I? Miss Fisher said about family and that, I still think taking the blame for somebody else getting killed is plain daft. But it's your life. You chose it.'

He waited for her cruel truth to turn on Robert. But it seemed that his brother was of no interest to her. He himself was because he happened to be here. With this girl, he thought, it's out of sight out of mind.

'Nelly. May I call you Nelly?'

'Everybody does.'

'Thank you. Nelly, what you say is perfectly true, I did choose to take my brother's place which is why I'm in Paris, just as you are. Madam Ruth was right to send you away. I'm sure you wouldn't have managed a lie in the witness box. And it would have been wrong to expect it of you.'

An expression of irony far older than her sixteen years went across Nelly's face.

'Scandal, that kind of scandal, shocks many people,' he said. 'And it is vitally important that what we *said* happened is believed. Will you promise me you will never reveal the truth to anyone?'

Ah, thought Nelly, as a trolley of puddings was wheeled up, now I understand the meal. Nothing is for nothing and why should it be.

'I'll promise if you like. It still beats me why you took the knock.'

'My brother is the head of our family. He is the one who – well – represents us. I do not matter. He does.'

'But he done it. I mean did it.'

'It was a tragic accident.'

Nelly was silent for a moment. She was thinking that although his brother hadn't meant to kill the girl or even hurt her, he'd frightened her silly and torn off half her dress.

'He chased after her and he was half crazy,' she said. 'He scared her and she fell and split open her skull.'

Matthew paused. The poor dead girl lying like a broken doll on the marble floor, the unspeakable fact of somebody young and beautiful, alive one moment, a corpse the next, all this was in his thoughts. But so was Robert. And in his heart, too. Could he trust the girl opposite him? She was so naive. Almost a child. So insouciant. I shouldn't think she gives a damn, he thought. But her knowledge is dangerous.

'Don't fret,' said Nelly, reading part of his thoughts in his face. 'I swear.'

She licked a finger and traced a cross on her swelling bosom.

'A promise is a promise, Mister Ayrton.'

CHAPTER THREE

Pinned on the wall in Matthew's Montmartre studio was a small watercolour of a house. A rose-pink Jacobean vision, with fanciful pepperpot chimneys, cupolas, weather vanes. An enormous row of ancient yews clipped into dark circles stood nearby. The house, the trees, had been there for hundreds of years. Matthew rarely painted landscapes or used watercolour, and had done the picture on a whim one afternoon years ago. Never knowing that in the future it would be all he had left of his home.

He could not have imagined for a single moment that he would suffer the catastrophe of social ostracism, be the centre of a scandal, and meted out to him would be the 'Just rewards of sin'. Yet he had known perfectly well what he was doing, the night Gertie Jewell died.

The morning after the tragedy, so quickly does bad news travel, it had begun. Messages came to the Chelsea studio, to Leckford Court, and to Belgrave Square. In every one of them, the invitations – to dinner, weekends, parties – were cancelled. His friends were so sorry but . . . there followed transparent excuses. It was as if he stood in the centre of his world and heard, one after the other, the great doors slam.

On the night the girl died, he had been interviewed at length by the police, but was then told it would be in order for him to return to Dorset; they knew his address, of course. The words 'accidental death' were in the air; there was no talk of a crime or the necessity for bail. Travelling home, Matthew chose the slowest, emptiest train. He had a compartment to

44

himself. Long legs outstretched, he reviewed what had happened.

His first instinct had been to get his brother out of the way. If the truth had come out, a fatal blow would have been struck at the family. English Society was surrounded by a high wall, and the rules, rigidly kept, held its members in a magical thrall. It was curious how, when wealthy Americans or people of the middle classes with new money stormed over the wall, they became as keen as any lord to keep the unbreakable laws.

Whatever happened behind bedroom doors in noble houses or for that matter in rich brothels, appearances must be kept up. Society was always loyal to its class, and therein lay its strength, its power over the common people. A man who became entangled in any kind of scandal, like the caste of the Untouchables in India, was beyond the pale.

The Leckfords were an ancient family which had flourished in Dorset for centuries. The original title had been bought by an ambitious John Ayrton from Henry VII, never averse to putting good money in the royal purse. The Ayrtons had been wool merchants, and the newly entitled Leckfords chose good sheep land and plenty of it.

During the Reformation, the family, like the more noble Norfolks, somehow managed to remain Catholic. They became recusants, which meant that they refused to belong to the new Church of England. For that they were at times persecuted, and regularly fined huge sums of money. When Charles I came to the throne with his Catholic wife, the Leckfords found themselves in the sun again. A beautiful house had already been planned and now rose upon the remains of the old one. They spent lavishly. Fines or not, they were still rich.

But with the Civil War, they were again eclipsed; the house withstood a siege by Cromwell himself and had cannonball marks to prove it. For two hundred years, the Leckfords were excluded from public life. But they had their eye on the main chance. They bought land and they married heiresses, one of

45

whom owned broad acres upon which a coal mine was discovered.

Yet the strain had thinned. There were Viscounts fond of the arts, others fond of the chase. They bought costly treasures, they hunted, their vast inheritance began to shrink. Robert and Matthew's father, Aubrey Leckford, had been of the hunting kind, a stocky man who wore an eyeglass on a black ribbon, and peppered his talk with 'Hey?'

He was handsome when young, and Honoria Forrest, a considerable heiress, fell in love with him. To marry Aubrey, Honoria became a convert to Catholicism. In the way of people new to a strong Faith, she was soon far more pious and strict than her husband.

The marriage was approved by Society who liked the Leckfords, but it bored Aubrey. And was a matter of secret grief to Honoria until she bore her first son. Honoria had been an eager girl, smallish, neat-featured, sensibly aware of her own wealth, and spoiled by her brothers. She was proud, and all her married life never admitted to a soul, scarcely to herself, that sex with her husband was brief and repulsive, that he was unfeeling and profoundly selfish. All her love was showered on her first born.

Robert was an enchanting child. He was everything Honoria could want – handsome, biddable, quaint, even his looks were like her own brothers', dark and classic. When her second boy arrived, she scarcely bothered to glance into the cot. She handed him over to her old nurse who welcomed him eagerly. If she could have managed it, Honoria would have sent only for Robert every afternoon at tea-time. But Nurse wouldn't allow such a thing and when the old woman was about Honoria had to pretend an interest in her fair, tiresome, clever second son.

The Viscountess did not have a gleam of self-criticism in her nature. In her upper-class way she was as uncomplicated as a child. If an archangel had appeared at her bed and told Honoria that the way she treated Matthew was a grave sin, that she was a worse mother than a woman in a slum who kissed and beat her child, that there was not one mitigating circumstance for her behaviour, Honoria would have been furious. She would have argued at the gates of Heaven.

Aubrey Leckford did not even pretend to be interested in his sons. Leckford Court was in its mid-Victorian heyday. The place filled every weekend, sometimes for months at a time, with relations and friends, soldiers home from the Colonies, Cabinet ministers. With artists now and then, actors never. Viscount Leckford, who was Master of the Hunt, often declared he 'loved the singing sound of the pack' and was out every day, riding across the countryside. He and his wife went to London for the Season. Their sons were packed off to the Catholic school, Stonyhurst. Aubrey vaguely noticed that they were gone.

He died when Robert was at Cambridge, Matthew still at Stonyhurst. He was ill a very short time, succumbing to a virulent pneumonia. He left the ancient Catholic title, the magnificent house and a not-so-well-run estate. The fortunes of the past had been squandered and the bulk of the Leckford money now belonged to Honoria. Matthew inherited a pittance from his father.

On her husband's death Honoria went into black silk and had worn nothing else since.

'There's Mother,' Matthew once remarked, seeing a figure black as a crow on the terrace.

'Doesn't mourning suit her?' said Robert affectionately. 'Much better than the Old Queen.'

Matthew raised his eyebrows and said nothing.

From a very young age he had somehow known that his mother had no idea she behaved badly to him. He accepted injustice with a child's philosophy, accustomed to her face brilliant with love for Robert, then turning to cold impatience for himself. Once as a small boy he had been with friends and had been astounded to see a lady kiss her second son as fondly as her eldest.

If Honoria's indifference verging on dislike had not damaged the boy, it was due to his old Nurse, a large elderly

47

woman who talked with a Dorset accent and loved him dearly. When he went to boarding-school, she cried. She wrote to him every week, with bands of kisses at the bottom of the letters, and once she posted him a big cardboard box filled with primroses and wild violets.

Matthew took lessons in painting at Stonyhurst, he had an excellent teacher. After their father's death he did not go to University, but to London where he worked for three years at the Slade.

Honoria thought a son 'who painted' was contemptible. An aberration. Robert rode like a champion, played skilful tennis, was good with the tenants and had a sense of duty about the estate. It only remained, thought his mother, for him to marry.

To the disappointment of Society matrons with single daughters, and to the envy of their own men friends, neither of the Leckford brothers had yet married. Robert was thirty-two, Matthew thirty, and both were as necessary to a hostess's lists as good champagne. During the Season they were invited everywhere. They were popular, sought-after, eligible. And they danced with each new batch of debutantes who appeared, like the spring, crowned with wreaths of flowers.

'It's absurd that Bob and Matt stay bachelors. It isn't as if they don't love the gals,' said somebody.

There was a difference in the way Society saw the two young men. Robert was conventional and agreeable, but one felt that in his heart – or was it his thoughts? – he was absorbed in other things. Matthew was quite another story; he was discreetly dissolute and most people knew of his quietly conducted affairs.

Society had sex on its mind: the very air in drawing-rooms quivered with it. It permeated the scent of damp earth and tropical blossoms of conservatories. The act itself, the longed-for sexual delight, was rarely achieved for weeks or even months. Young married women sighed and blushed, they kept secret assignations while trembling with nerves. At last the lovers joined. Matthew enjoyed his women. But he enjoyed almost as much the challenge and the chase.

All Matthew's friends knew that the old Viscountess kept him disgracefully short of money and that it was only his brother's affectionate generosity which stopped him from getting into debt. It was a humiliating position for a man of character. Yet there was a charm and gaiety about Matthew. He seemed to have mastered the art of living. He was friendly, easily amused. He was lazily attractive.

But Robert, charming, perhaps rather shy, had another darker side to his life. Only whores excited him, the girls he paid for and who would do anything he wanted. Robert was only at home in Ruth's sexually overheated house where the girls paraded for him. He picked one. Then another. Until the first time he saw Gertie Jewell, and after that he wanted nobody else.

He did not know he had fallen in love with her, only that he couldn't keep away. She was very fair, her hair so blonde it was almost white, her skin like thick pale velvet. She was blank-faced, silly, big-breasted, swaying-hipped, her voice squeaky like a little girl's. She rolled his cigarettes, made him Turkish coffee. In sex there was nothing she wouldn't do, giggling, sinuous, thrilling. Sometimes she laughed when they made love. After they reached their climax, she lay and slept in his arms. During the year he'd known her, Robert went to Ruth's almost every night. It had been simply a whim to persuade Matthew to come with him to Granville House.

But it was Matthew's life, not his, which was ruined.

Matthew stared through the train window at the green vales and low hills of the Dorset country. A grey stone village with the ruins of a castle on a rise of grass. A hare scampering across a meadow. The haystacks were thatched now. The lovely soft country was his no longer. It was lost, as his friends now were, and all the lovely women who had smiled at him in enchanted rooms. He saw that the trees were beginning to turn and the year was dying. Where shall I go, he thought, with dreary resignation.

Before tragedy struck, Matthew had often wished he could afford to live in Paris – for to anyone interested in painting, it was the place to be. Extraordinary things had been happening there for the last twenty years, it was the very heart of new movements, controversy, violent and passionate debate. The Impressionists had fascinated him since he'd been at school. They had changed the very heart of painting. Their vision was the air and water, the breaking and fusion and scintillating movement of light. When he'd seen a few of their pictures in a gallery two years ago, they had filled him with uneasy emotion.

He did not want to imitate or join them, his own absorption was with the human figure. But it would be good to be in the city where painters had created so profound a revolution. I have lost my world, he thought. Could I go towards theirs? Even to stand upon its edge.

The brief time of thinking about a possible future left him again, he sank back into misery. It was curious to accept his fate, literally make it happen, and still suffer. They were making him an outcast. The cruel laws of Society were no different from the ancient custom of banishment when a man, forbidden his own country, was condemned to wander the world.

The train drew up at last at the tiny station of Leckford Magna. The old porter touched his cap.

'The victoria hasn't been and come from the Court for you, Sirr.'

'I'm not expected, Harry. I shall walk.'

'Rain's held off, Sirr. T'wont be back until dark.'

The old man forgot to take his ticket.

The lights of the house shone in the misty autumn dusk when he walked up the drive. The enormous old yews clipped into dark rounds like so many green balloons stood where a Leckford had planted them in 1700. The manor was a single mass, a sort of Jacobean hymn of glory to its owners.

Deciding to get the worst over, Matthew went straight to the Yellow Drawing-room where his mother sat in the early evening. A fire sparkled in the huge fireplace, giving the stately room a turn-of-the-season gaiety which told on his nerves.

Honoria sat in a high-backed chair studying the flames. She suited the age and formality of the room, wearing her eternal black and a lace cap. The firelight caught the gleam of silk. When she heard him come in, she turned, glanced at him, then resumed her study of the fire.

For the mother of so tall a man, she was as small as the Old Queen. But whereas Victoria was stout, Honoria Leckford was thin and dry as a fallen leaf. Her pale wrinkled face had never known powder or paint, her mouth was thinned by the years, her eyes were Matthew's colour, dark grey. She looked frail and formidable.

He sat down facing her.

'Good evening, Mother.'

She gave a slight shudder and said nothing.

'You have heard what happened, I see. Did Robert tell you? I believe he came down earlier today.'

'What has your brother to do with it?'

'I thought perhaps he had broken the news.'

She was silent again. Then, in a thin voice, 'He would never speak of such – such things to me. And you shall not. I do not intend to tell you,' forestalling him, 'how I learned of your unspeakable actions. It astonishes me that you dare show your face here.'

'Oh, I realise I shan't be exactly *persona grata* in the future.' He was angry in spite of himself. Usually he managed to accept her treatment with sour amusement: parody had nothing to add to a mother so besotted of her elder, so disliking her younger son.

But although he'd been ready for icy rejection, for shuddering disgust at any mention of sex and crime, he had underestimated her. He now perceived in her a sort of triumph. As if her own maternal cruelty were at last proved right. It had not occurred to him what a favour he'd done her by becoming the black sheep.

'*Persona grata?*' she suddenly repeated and gave a laugh. 'Here? Do you imagine I shall ever consent to see you again? That you will be allowed at Leckford? That your brother will exchange another word with you? I cannot continue this conversation. Ask your manservant to pack your possessions and arrange for your trunks to be sent,' she shrugged, 'wherever you are going.'

A weaker man would have quailed at the speech and the enmity which underlined it. At the haggard, unforgiving old face. But something in its way as pitiless to her as she was to him kept Matthew where he was. She attempted to stare him out, looking like some fierce bird. But it was she who eventually looked away.

'There is a small matter of money,' he said. 'I mean to go abroad.'

Silence.

'Mother. Do you expect me to live in Europe without anything financial being arranged?'

'It is of no interest where you live or upon what.'

He made a noise like a growl.

'You know very well what a farcical amount was left me by Father. Not sufficient to live if I am to leave this country and my home.'

'It is no longer your home.'

'For Christ's sake.'

'Do not take the name of the Lord in vain.'

This was too much. He stood up, pushing the chair aside. It fell over heavily and he did not stoop to right it.

'I repeat, for Christ's sake, stop being so hideously self-righteous. So disgustingly pious. You call yourself a Catholic. Don't you? Don't you?'

No reply.

'Have you never heard of forgiveness? Not seven times, but seventy times seven times. Do you think I'm idiot enough to believe I can stay in England? I don't want to! But if you could just stop being so –'

She had never disliked, almost hated him as much as now with this filthy story enveloping him like a miasma. She wouldn't soil her mind by thinking about it. She could scarcely bear him in the house, let alone here in this room.

52

And he had the unspeakable effrontery to ask *for money*. She would not give him a shilling and nor would Robert.

He had stopped speaking, leaving the sentence unfinished. Despite her age and character, she was a woman. She was filled with a disgusted curiosity to know what he had been going to say of her. The fallen chair lay between them.

'What, pray, do you think I am?'

'*Pleased*,' he said between his teeth, and strode out, slamming the door.

Up in his rooms he did not ring for his servant but sat on the bed, looking at his shoes which were muddy from the walk home. He was still studying them when his brother came in.

'Hello,' Matthew said.

Robert shut the door and burst out in a shaking voice.

'I can't stand it! I've got to tell her the truth.'

'*No, you will not.*'

Robert seemed not to hear, he began to walk up and down the room.

'I tell you I can't stand it. How can I let everybody believe it was you? You who quarrelled with her and frightened her? It's a nightmare, I feel so sick. So sick. I keep seeing her face when she went backwards, her mouth was open, she was trying to scream –'

Matthew saw with incredulity that his brother was on the verge of tears.

'Bob, shut up! Don't let go. Don't wallow and look back. It won't do. I suppose you've spent all day thinking about her and me. What the hell is the use of that? Gertie Jewell is dead, and I'm gong away. You'll have to grin and bear both those things.'

Matthew's voice was hard but it had no effect. Robert was bent on self-pity. He continued to walk up and down, talking in a monotone.

'I'm to blame. I've always been to blame for going with whores. I wish I was like you. I've never wanted sex with respectable women, I couldn't do it with any of them. Mother is waiting for me to marry and I can't. It's all my fault, everything is my fault, you only came to Ruth's last night because I asked you to.'

'I was looking for a new model to paint. I told you so.'

This did penetrate Robert's miserable egotism.

'Yes. Yes, you did, I remember.'

'Bob, for God's sake stop walking about like a tiger in a cage. *Sit down.*'

Because Matthew shouted, Robert obeyed. Matthew stood looking at him.

'You're done in.'

'I haven't slept. I went back to Granville House –'

'You didn't!'

'It was all shut up and there was a policeman at the door. Then I caught the train. I don't know how I got through today. Where have you been? Why weren't you here?'

'I was at the police station.'

'God.'

'No, no, it wasn't too bad, they were reasonable and the inspector was quite sympathetic. I remember he said something about "It could happen to anybody" as if girls fall down staircases like ninepins. Perhaps they do. I had the impression that he wasn't displeased to find somebody of our kind in a mess.'

Robert wasn't listening again. He sat huddled, his handsome looks smeared with fatigue.

'What – what about Gertie?'

'Her skull was cracked. One mercy. She died instantly.'

Then the tears welled up in Robert's brown eyes.

'I suppose I loved her in an awful kind of way. I couldn't be without her, had to have her all the time. The idea of that old man doing it with her drove me out of my mind. Poor love. Poor little love. She was only doing what Ruth told her. If only I hadn't rushed at her . . .'

' "If only" are the two most useless words in the English language.'

Matthew wanted to reach him. Bully him. Get him back to normal. The self-pitying monotone got on his nerves. He loved and pitied him and wanted to hit him. They said nothing for a while.

Matthew began to think about packing, what train he should take, and whether all his sketchbooks would fit into a cabin trunk. Could Bob perhaps have them forwarded? A sudden pain took his breath away when he looked up at his brother's exhausted face and saw how he was struggling with his grief for that pretty harlot. Shall I ever see you again? he thought. A terrible sadness swept over him. All their boyhood lay between them like a shared and gleaming treasure. In Robert's memory and in his were the years of their growing up. He loved Robert more than anybody in the world, his brother's very faults made him lovable. He was such a bad loser, such an egotist, so selfish and curiously clumsy, he never seemed aware of another person at his side. But which of us has no faults? Matthew disliked his own more than his brother's. Robert had a sense of right, a fairness which had shared every blessed thing poured over him by their mother. He would wait with a secret wink for Honoria to leave the room before cutting even a stick of chocolate into exact halves. Robert was funny and kind and vulnerable. His very need for support was endearing. But not now.

'We must go and dress. That's the dinner gong.' Robert finally dragged him out of a swamp of thought.

'Bob, be realistic. Do you imagine our revered mother would sit at a table with me?'

'Oh, Christ.'

'As you say. I've no doubt she's been in the chapel praying for my soul a good deal today. Am I right?'

'I – I did see her go there twice this afternoon.'

Matthew couldn't help laughing and Robert, hearing the chuckle, looked at him with passionate gratitude.

'I'll have some cold meat sent up here,' Matthew said. 'By the by, I spoke to Mother and got it over. She just about brought herself to speak directly *to* me, and said you hadn't mentioned the matter. She appeared intensely grateful to you for that.'

'I was waiting until you were here. I wanted to tell her the truth.'

'I repeat, *shut up*. You will not confess all. You will not mess up the things I've arranged. You're the head of the family and your task is to keep our name nice and clean. One thing . . . Mother threatened not to give me any cash. The old parental weapon. So, could you very kindly?'

'God, Matt, do you need to ask?'

'No. I'm sorry I did.'

Robert came over and gave his brother's shoulder a convulsive squeeze. And Matthew knew, he could sense, that he had given in. He would accept the sacrifice and carry on as the stainless Viscount with a reprobate brother. He would be wrapped about by the great cloak of his mother's awesome love. Matthew went with him to the door, and gripped both his hands.

'I know it's worse for you. But best for us both if we think of this,' looking round, 'and the family and all that rot. You agree?'

'If you say so.'

'Come on, Bob, *you* say so as well. And don't look back, old fellow. You know what happens when one does that.'

It was clear that Robert did not understand.

'You turn into a pillar of salt,' Matthew said.

CHAPTER FOUR

The air was soft and Nelly no longer needed to heat her carpetless room in the Rue de la Mire. The problem of how to afford a stove and wood to burn hadn't been easy but Nelly's optimism had solved it. She had bought blankets at the Marché des Puces, took its name literally and soaked them in disinfectant before hanging them for a good blow out of the window. She bought a two-handled coffee cup and made her coffee in a biscuit tin with a ship on the lid. In a corner near her bed her clothes hung on a piece of string pinned to the walls. It fell down now and then. She had one good meal a day. Free.

Chez Paul-Marc was primarily a café-bar but the owner, Monsieur Moréas, provided a hot dish every evening – there was no choice – and after doing her songs Nelly had a large plateful of whatever was chalked on the blackboard outside: pigeon casserole, *coq au vin*, *choucroute*. But before she was allowed to eat, her patron was pitiless about encores.

'One more song please, *ma belle*.' He had adopted the Guelle name for her.

'I die of hunger, Monsieur.'

'Your customers have need of you,' was the flinty reply. Nelly, in the basement kitchen, could hear feet thundering on the café floor. The clientele liked the young foreigner and her incomprehensible songs. One or two of the regulars decided they might pursue her. She looked juicy.

So Nelly sang a few more songs from her repertoire, adding 'Waiting at the Church', did a bob curtsey, and at last found herself at the kitchen table, settling down to a soup-plate full of *boeuf bourguignonne*. She refused the raw red wine.

Nelly was now thoroughly at home in Montmartre. Miss Fisher's apartment in the Rue des Martyrs had been the usual tall shuttered house not far from the *grands boulevards*. The distance between it and Montmartre was short enough: half-an-hour's walk took one to the top of the Butte. But the difference between the two *quartiers* was as riches to poverty, corsets to naked flesh.

Studios had grown steadily up the hill towards the two domes of the unfinished basilica of the Sacré Coeur. They had been cottages or stables or barns once upon a time, with here and there a stone house in a wild garden. In summer, women sat in the doorways peeling the vegetables. In winter the steep roads were impassable to horses. La Butte was a place of hope and despair, of shanties made from the doors of lost houses, washing stretched to dry on toppling fences, and the thick plumes of lilac nodding in waste land. There were old cattle sheds and a tiny stone chapel which had been a shrine. A vast Benedictine abbey had once covered the whole of the Butte. The chapel and vestiges of stone walls were all that was left. In huts and stables and barns, painters stored their canvases, packing them away with bright hope, and leaving them to a mildewed future.

Nelly was part of the *quartier*. She belonged in Chez Paul-Marc, and she belonged in the Atelier Guelle. She learned to spend hours remaining stock-still except when the weather was piercingly cold and even the stove couldn't keep her warm. Then it was hard not to shiver. Once or twice a student shouted 'Belle Nelly, keep still for the love of the holy saints.'

'I'm cold.'

'Then sit on the stove. We like your backside a good rich red.'

On the whole, Nelly posed without strain, developing the gift of going into a pleasant trance. There was an impersonal feeling between her and the Atelier full of young men. She stood. She sat. She lay on a chaise longue on her back, on her front with legs outstretched or one leg bent. Her opalescent body belonged to the students who painted her. They used her for their art. Once, when she lay naked, she'd happened to glance up at the skylight where she saw the figure of a workman mending the roof. She gave a shriek and seized a shawl.

'Help! There's a man!'

When the sessions were over, the students swept Nelly out with them to La Vache Enragée. They told her they adored her ridiculous English accent. They treated her as a mascot, a pet, enjoying her high spirits. She was kind to the shy ones, bold with the rowdy ones, lavish when she'd been paid. Any student could borrow from her and she always forgot to ask for repayment. It was lucky for Patrice that he did not go to Maître Guelle's. He would have suffered pangs of hell from jealousy.

One of the students, Charles Tigli, who came from Provence, was a devoted admirer of Nelly's. Scarcely five feet tall, he was nicknamed Le P'tit. His face was narrow, like a friendly water rat, he had heavy, sexy eyes, adored women, and Nelly most of all. The students competed for her attention. Even Le Père Fabri.

He was a very old man who was also a model, with an emaciated body, deep-set eyes and a white beard floating to his chest. Maître Guelle and other painters found him very useful. He posed as Elijah or Job, a Roman senator, a Renaissance noble, a Spanish beggar.

Le Père had appeared in famous canvases of the past and one midday he met Nelly in the Place Clérissy and spoke of his triumphs.

'Even as a young man, I sat as model for a prophet. I was always thin, d'you see. Monsieur Delacroix used me in his great mural painting in Saint-Sulpice. I was Moses. What an honour . . .'

He fell into a pose, imaginary staff in his hands, rheumy blue eyes looking skywards.

He talked of the differences between the *ateliers* where students were taught by professors from the Beaux Arts, and the 'real' studios where painters worked among their friends.

He had been a model at the Académie Suisse. 'Cézanne and Pissaro met there,' he said reverently. 'The Count Toulouse-Lautrec, of course, entertains his friends in the Avenue Frochot. Never go there, Mademoiselle Nelly, you will find the dregs of Paris drinking their brains out.'

Nelly wanted to know why real painters (she was thinking of Matthew Ayrton) worked among a pack of students.

'I know it's to use the model, but wouldn't they be better to choose their own?'

'Money, Mademoiselle. They cannot afford a model for themselves.'

The old man had lived on the Butte all his life. He had watched the Impressionist movement begin, remembered when Eugène Boudin first took the young Claude Monet to Le Havre. 'They came back with such paintings! Sea and sky and sand all melted and misty like a dream.' There was nothing he didn't remember about the early days when the young painters had fallen in love with light.

'Alas, I have rarely been of use to them. They use the trees of Almighty God and the waters of the Seine. Lovers in the distance. White sails or white dresses . . .'

He pulled at his beard.

'But I revere them. I revere them. They've all left Paris now, you know,' he added in a brisk change of tone.

'But I thought everybody was here,' Nelly said, with a Parisian gesture of her thumb.

Le Père Fabri said no. Now that the Impressionists were almost accepted, the close friendships had broken, some with terrible bitterness. They were gone . . . Cézanne to Aix, Monet to Giverny, Sisley to Moret.

'And we are the poorer,' said the old man.

Nelly patted the freckled hand. She thought a few painters more or less wouldn't make much difference in a place teeming with them. People lived and breathed paint, practically ate and drank it.

Just as she had learned French with ease, Nelly picked up the students' talk, hearing about the Neo-Impressionists in the

Avenue Clichy and the 'Nabis' – a new movement named after the Hebrew word for prophet.

'They won't employ us,' said Le Père. 'They say they're the antidote to naturalism.'

He smiled at her. Nelly's ripe body, his scrawny one were natural enough. As it happened Nelly met one of the Nabis, a young man with a face as rough as a bricklayer, who noticed her in La Vache and asked her to model for him. She had to refuse: he offered half the hourly sum she earned with Maître Guelle.

Once she met, or nearly collided with, a real Impressionist. She persuaded Patrice to take her dancing to the Moulin de la Galette, she loved the rowdy place. As they crossed a room packed with dancers, she almost walked into Auguste Renoir. Patrice muttered his name in her ear as the peasantish-looking man went by. A beautiful girl was hanging on his arm, but as he passed Nelly he gave her a very obvious up-and-down stare. Patrice quickened his step and pulled her with him.

'I might have been in one of his paintings,' complained Nelly as they started to dance.

'That's what I was afraid of.'

She chuckled and then forgot everything but the pleasure of dancing. She and Patrice often went to the Café Variétés to dance with the servant girls and their lovers, but her favourite was always the Galette where the dancing was crazier, the boys rougher, everybody young and merry. Couples played tag in between the tables or flew in and out of the place like swallows. In warm weather, gas chandeliers glowing among green leaves, there were hidden places to kiss and cuddle. It was noisy and vulgar and teeming with life. Nelly could scarcely bear to leave when, Cinderella-like, she had to race down the hill to Chez Paul-Marc.

Montmartre was home. She knew all the alleys and flights of steps, the steep hill which everybody called 'La Butte', where once the draught horses had toiled to fetch grain from the windmills. There was always a breeze on the Butte, more air than in the *grands boulevards*. Not a soul had any money.

People wandered in and out of each other's studios or overflowed into dusty squares to talk. I don't expect there's anywhere on earth, thought Nelly, where people talk so much.

She was part of the *quartier*, sitting in the cafés listening to the young men who amused her. Their theories, however, didn't and she'd heard most of them before. After an absinthe or two, the talk became incomprehensible. The students talked of intensity of expression, the danger of too much knowledge, colour 'straight from the tube'. Nelly grew restive when the subject of beauty cropped up. She considered that so much tosh. She was also puzzled at what they called 'serenity under tension', and the problems of painting movement on something as stock-still as a piece of canvas.

Sometimes interrupting, often laughing, occasionally making a joke, Nelly was the students' companion. She drank only coffee or mineral water and did not care when her friends drank too much beer. But absinthe bothered her. Beer had come to Paris from Germany with the French soldiers returning after the victorious campaigns under Napoleon. But that now-familiar drink was being replaced by something more potent, romantic, and more fatal. They called it the 'Green Fairy'. Nelly was afraid of absinthe. There was a dazed half-mad look on the faces of absinthe drinkers which made her feel sick. It reminded her of her so-called mother.

Singing every night except Mondays at Chez Paul-Marc, posing every day but Sundays for Maître Guelle, Nelly still had time to enjoy herself. She and Patrice went for walks through the city, watching the fishermen by the Seine. Once, by the Pont de la Concorde they saw a man catch an immense barbel.

Nelly knew, although Patrice didn't say, that he hoped she would leave the Rue de la Mire and live with him. But she preferred freedom and the first room she'd ever paid for out of her own pocket. Its bare boards, white plaster, the view of crooked French chimney pots, the rag mat and home-made blue curtains which she herself had bought, they delighted her. When a student gave her a few cheap flowers, she carried them home in triumph, arranging them in a multi-coloured vase in front of the looking-glass. In that way five roses turned into ten. She kept her clothes folded on a chair, and her best hat wrapped in tissue paper.

She relished her Montmartre life. She realised from the first that Montmartre was not the friendly, poor and crowded place it looked at first glance. There were darker parts on the Butte. In the steep narrow streets were the *hôtels de passe*, not exactly brothels, where the girls pretended to be dancers or seamstresses, singers or even schoolgirls. Nelly passed these places daily and scarcely gave them a thought, until in La Vache she saw a girl who looked very ill. The girl was eating dry bread and Nelly wondered if she could offer to pay for a good breakfast. But she was afraid to hurt her feelings and when she murmured to Edouard, he looked at the girl and shook his head. Mortality among such girls was high. Some died by the fatal wand of the Green Fairy. Some from syphilis. Some committed suicide because of love and sorrow.

The most infamous place on the edge of the Butte was the Moulin-Rouge in the Boulevard de Clichy. Unlike the Galette, it had never been a windmill, it was a cheap dance-hall 'as big as the Gare du Nord' Nelly said. An enormous stucco elephant, with crossed and baggy legs and sad eyes with huge rings under them, commanded the garden, looking over the pavilion where ballets were performed. In front of the pavilion the crowded tables were occupied by rows of prostitutes waiting for trade. Everything about the Moulin-Rouge was disliked by Nelly. The reproductions of a Normandy farmhouse and a Spanish palace. Even the sails of the windmill were false, and the poor little monkeys were kept on chains to amuse the customers. As well as the now famous Can-can, with its flourish of white knickers, there was a new dance called the Cakewalk. The shows were loud and exotic and garishly sexy, and vice had begun to be big business there. Beneath the deafening music was a market in women, and corruption with the police. The customers all seemed foreign: South Americans, Russians, Rumanians, even Englishmen.

After one afternoon there, Nelly turned up her nose and said, 'Let's go back to our own Galette.'

Sometimes instead of sitting in cafés or dancing, Nelly posed for Patrice. She didn't like his paintings at all. Their colours were fierce and dark, their shapes brutal, and when he painted a nude of her she was too polite to say she wouldn't have recognised herself. Patrice painted himself a good deal, staring into a mirror and frowning in a trance of concentration.

Of all her Parisian friends, her lover was the one she was fondest of. Over the months, by coaxing, she had learned something of his life, although it had been difficult to get the mute young man to speak at all. He would merely say, 'You don't want to hear all that.'

'Oh I do!'

He laughed helplessly.

Patrice was twenty-four, and came from a little place called Crèvecœur, the name made Nelly smile. Patrice's father was a corn merchant, and Patrice had never shown a moment's interest in painting until at fifteen he caught pneumonia. To cheer him during his convalescence, his mother bought him a cheap box of paints.

He copied the only picture in his bedroom, a badly reproduced print of the Raphael cartoon, *The Miraculous Draught of Fishes*. He painted the curved boat weighed down with new-caught fish, the sons of Zebedee bent over the nets, the profiles of Christ and St Peter. He painted them over and over again.

'I began to live then,' he said.

After that he drew and painted in every spare moment, covering his schoolbooks with sketches. His parents were anxious and unsurprised when the big gawky lad said he wanted to go to Paris 'and maybe paint'.

His father gave him a small allowance, 'so I wouldn't starve', Patrice told Nelly. But he had got work in Les Halles as a porter. The first time he returned to Crèvecœur he repaid every sou his father had given him.

'Papa wept,' said Patrice.

'He was proud of you,' said Nelly, wondering if Monsieur Jacob had perhaps wept with relief at seeing his cash again.

'So here you are in Paris,' said Nelly, putting her arms round his neck. They were lying in bed. 'You came like all the rest, I suppose, because of the Impressionists.'

'No. Not them. I don't know why I came. Because it's the best place.'

'I think so,' said Nelly, laughing.

'Le P'tit says the Impressionists want to catch the very moment, the very second that they see,' she remarked. She was wondering (he never *said*) if they were going to make love again. She rather fancied some more.

'Cézanne paints stone quarries. He has solidity,' said Patrice.

Nelly was out of her depth. She had seen a Cézanne of a man in his bathing-suit. Not her kind, as solid as the rocks he appeared to be fond of.

But Patrice was looking at her with heavy eyes. He did not want to talk any more. He pushed her down flat and covered her.

With Patrice as her regular lover, and Le P'tit and other Guelle students as admirers and friends, Nelly's life was filled with men. But she did lose her two earliest followers, Julian and Laurent. Julian had always been jealous and somehow discovered about her affair with Patrice. One night when she was trotting down the hill to Chez Paul-Marc he came looking for her. He made a furious scene in the street.

'I hate women! My life is in ruins!' he shouted, shoving her away when she tried to calm him. He rushed off down the hill, while Nelly stood watching helplessly. But as she preferred Patrice physically, there was nothing to be done. And she wasn't surprised to see Julian the following week, dancing at the Galette with a blonde girl whose large bosoms wobbled like jellies.

Nelly's clerk-admirer Laurent, who had buried her in letters when she lived with Miss Fisher, left for a different reason. He had to go home to Abbeville as his father was ill.

'My family own a little hotel, as I told you, *ma chère*. I shall take command until he recovers. Perhaps I must be patron permanently. I feel I shall never come back to Paris.'

He took Nelly for a farewell evening to the Cirque Fernando, and held her hand in the old sexy way, fitting his fingernails into hers. This trick had always stirred her and she'd often thought when he did it that it might be nice to go to bed with Laurent. She felt melting when they said goodbye near the kitchen entrance of the café. Laurent took her in his arms, pressed his open mouth to hers, exploring her teeth with his tongue. His kiss tasted bitter. At that moment, while Nelly returned the embrace, Patrice loomed out of the shadows. The kiss stopped. Nelly thought, as Laurent said goodbye, that he knew they'd lost an opportunity . . .

But when he was gone, and Julian too, she scarcely missed them. She was busy and cheerful and each day turning more into a Parisian.

The Englishman Matthew Ayrton was at the Atelier three times a week, and whenever she saw his lanky figure, the reserved face with the fair moustache, she thought – there's that chap. As if she were not surrounded by them.

Le P'tit, her most passionate and hopeless admirer, had a success with Nelly when he said he would teach her to bicycle. It was the new craze in Paris, everybody was on wheels.

'We will have a glorious time spinning in the Bois,' said Le P'tit.

'That sounds all right,' said Nelly, wondering what to wear. Parisians were all in cycling knickers or divided skirts, showing their ankles or even their legs to excited male companions. When Le P'tit called for her at the Rue de la Mire, Nelly was wearing some second-hand bloomers she'd bought in the flea market. Le P'tit had always admired her. Now he fell in love with her.

They had a wonderful day. Nelly screamed and fell off all the time, and Le P'tit had the exquisite joy of shovelling her to her feet, his small figure pressed against her curves.

Her sexual attraction for men was universal. Students

shouted to her to join them at La Vache and threw looks of hatred at Patrice when they saw him with her at the Galette. They elbowed each other out of the way to get her attention, borrowed and sometimes paid back her few francs. The other artists' models at Maître Guelle's did not like her. They were of a variety chosen for different styles of work – dark girls like blackbirds, plump goddesses, a blazing redhead. One and all they disliked the foreigner and cut her dead. Being disliked was new to Nelly. It surprised her. In Blackfriars she had been too young and dirty to deserve it. In Granville House a skivvy was invisible in the world of beauties for sale. Now she was being treated as a dislikable equal.

The spring weather was warm and one Sunday Le P'tit again took her cycling in the Bois. A glorious day and Nelly's bloomers freshly ironed, she was more irresistible than ever. She was wobbling her first ten yards along the pathway used by the cyclists, Le P'tit's arm was round her, when someone shouted.

'Coo-ee!'

'Who's that?' gasped Nelly, swerving.

'Take no notice. Concentrate, *ma chérie*.'

He held her firmly. He could smell the tarry shampoo she used to wash her hair.

'Coo-ee,' called the voice again, Nelly turned round, forgetting the handlebars, tried to save her hat and fell straight into the tan-ride for the horses. The bicycle fell on top of her.

With a shout of dismay, Le P'tit dropped to his knees.

'Don't move! Something may be broken. Oh, it is my fault, my fault, I was not holding you closely.'

Nelly burst out laughing, saying she was perfectly all right. A girl in a brown dress, a man in a check suit, came up to them.

'Are you hurt?' exclaimed the girl in French.

'Of course I'm not and you're English,' said Nelly, smacking at her bloomers – Le P'tit nearly fainted with lust – to get rid of the clinging tan.

'Why, yes, I am. How do you do? I'm Edith Holden and you must be Miss Briggs. Le P'tit has told us about you.'

Introductions were made. Mademoiselle Holden. Réné Filliol. Réné lifted his curly-brimmed bowler and Edith Holden gave a slow impartial smile. When Nelly had retrieved her hat and repinned it to her back hair, she and the English girl fell into step while Le P'tit, wheeling Nelly's bicycle as well as his own, talked to the young man.

'You're the first English girl I've met since I came to Paris,' said Nelly in their own language. 'What a treat.'

'How long have you been here?'

'Six months. Seems longer.'

'It's surprising you haven't seen any of our compatriots. You would if you went to the English bookshop.'

Nelly looked impressed. Miss Fisher had never been to bookshops.

'You work *chez* Guelle, don't you?' said Miss Holden. 'I wish I could come to his classes but he's rather expensive. I go to old Mademoiselle Quercy. She's three francs cheaper and good with landscape but rather disagreeable. It's her rheumatism, poor thing.'

They paused and the young men's conversation reached them. It would soon be time to submit canvases to the Salon at the Académie des Beaux Arts. If you were accepted for the exhibition it was your own chance of success. The judges were supreme arbiters of all popular taste.

'At it again,' said Nelly. 'They ought to talk less and paint more.'

Edith Holden gave her a curious smile. She was short, scarcely five feet, with corn-coloured hair rippling down like the waves of the sea. It was not worn in the usual chignon but down her back, and falling from under her straw hat on either side of her cheeks like a schoolgirl's. The smile was enigmatic and made her seem older than she was.

'Are you worried about the Salon, too?' asked Nelly.

'Of course. The judges prefer historical or literary subjects treated naturalistically. I don't paint those, I'm afraid.'

'What sort of things, then?'

Edith Holden shrugged. 'A jug with flowers. A coachman in his white coat. My bathtub. A door open to the garden. Anything, really.'

'Do you sell them?' Nelly liked the sound of the girl's paintings.

'One flower picture last Christmas. What I do for a living is to sew the costumes at the Feu Follet.'

Nelly was enchanted. She and Patrice had been to the Feu Follet, a tacky vaudeville theatre in the Rue des Anges.

'What a lark, working backstage. You must sew wonderfully, I do think you're clever.'

'I don't and I'm not, Miss Briggs. Not a bit. And it isn't a lark, I give you my word. The costumes are horrid. Daffodils bigger than butter tubs sewn all over the costume called Spring, and huge paper chains painted silver for Roman slaves. As for the Spirit of the Eiffel Tower!'

Nelly was more intrigued still.

'Don't you want to *wear* them. I mean, isn't it a chance to be on the stage?'

'I'm too small. The show girls are as tall as poplars. Rather cross poplars. One of them, a giantess with golden hair, nearly pulled all mine out by the roots. She was Neptune and had lost her trident. She said I'd hidden it.'

Nelly whistled.

Edith Holden was a girl of good education who lived in raffish society in the capital of pleasure, yet remained the schoolmaster's daughter from the Scottish Borders. When both her parents died she was only seventeen, and life had stretched out in a vista of threadbare gentility. The prospect of governessing for rude rich women not a tenth as clever or book-learned as she was had daunted Edith. She knew she would be treated worse than a servant.

She wanted to paint and knew she had a certain talent. She came to Paris to nourish it, and found herself a post as governess to a wealthy French family in a large stuffy house near Les Invalides. She had to teach English to the son,

Auguste, twelve years old and too delicate to go to school. Edith and Auguste loathed each other. He was bored, lazy and rude, and after a month of trying to bear him and his monstrously selfish parents, Edith ran away.

Montmartre was the place to be. It was cheap and shabby and paint was in the very air blowing across the hilly streets. It was her spiritual home. It was also filled with vice and degradation but Edith's Scots nature protected her like a cloak. She set off to find a clean lodging, part-time employment and a cheap teacher. She soon found a room in an artists' lodging-house off the Rue Cortot. One evening, sitting in a café working out how long her savings would last, Edith sighed. Looking up, she caught the glance of a young man opposite her. A thin man with steel-rimmed pince-nez and innocent brown eyes. His hair was wispy, his moustache and cravat untidy. She smiled without realising it, and was given a shy smile in return.

Edith was reserved, the stranger timid. But perhaps it was the sigh she'd given, and the sums in columns in her notebook which made them begin to talk. Of painting. He told her, after a while, that he was interested in a movement started by his friends, they called themselves the Nabis. Edith had heard of them. 'They feel, and I agree, that we must not follow the trodden path,' said Edith's companion. 'We must cut our way through the long grass.'

He told her his name was Pierre Bonnard, and Edith said her name. He bowed slightly, although seated. They continued to talk quietly. Edith liked the theories of the Nabis but the young man disagreed with most of them.

'However, they are right to follow their intuitions. And, as Corot has told us, we must never, never lose sight of a first impression.'

'I will remember that,' she said gravely.

When he said goodnight, Edith saw that he'd begun to look nervous, as if fearing she would suggest a further meeting. But she indicated with Scots formality that this was certainly goodbye. He looked relieved.

Edith thought about him just the same, and it was after their talk that she began to take her sketchbook with her everywhere, making quick drawings to capture things that interested her at that moment. That first impression.

She soon made acquaintances in her lodgings, including Réné Filliol, who fell in love with her, bought her violets, shared his supper with her, and, to Edith's relief, found her the work at the Feu Follet. After a good deal of thought, she accepted his offer of love and bed. She liked him but did not love him. Réné exclaimed, as men will do, 'Oh, you will learn to love me! You won't be able to help it.'

Edith did not think so. She was a girl of the times, and already there trembled, like a faint wind which might grow into a storm, an idea of female liberty . . .

As the girls walked together through the sunny woods, one rakish girl in bloomers, one small sedate one in brown cotton buttoned to the neck, Edith said, 'It is a pleasure to meet a new friend. I wonder – could Réné and I come cycling with you and Le P'tit next Sunday? You must tell me, though, if you would rather have Le P'tit to yourself.'

'He isn't a fellow I want to be *alone* with,' said Nelly, amused. 'Of course, you must come with us. Do you fall off all the time, like me?'

CHAPTER FIVE

Spring began to spread across the city and Nelly noticed that the Englishman had not appeared at the Atelier for some weeks. She asked Maître Guelle where Matthew Ayrton had gone. Had he left Paris?

'No. He tells me he is working,' was the reply. 'As if coming here is not work. Do you know how he is occupying his time? As a courier and interpreter. Foreigners are arriving in time for Easter, and Monsieur Ayrton is taking the ignoramuses to the shops or the Folies Bergères. Or to stuff themselves with cake at Fouchet's. If you cross Concorde you will probably see our friend in a carriage with some fat Englishwoman. Oh, I do beg your pardon!'

'A lot of them are fat. But is he coming back to us?'

'One supposes so. When he has earned enough to pay me.'

With sunshine and pale skies, there was tension in the Atelier. Nobody wasted time drawing on the walls. The date was fast approaching when artists must submit some work to the Biennial Salon; the exhibition opened on the first of May. The only way for an artist to show his work to critics, and to have any possible buyers, was to get it accepted at the Salon. Le P'tit told Nelly there wasn't an art lover in Paris who would buy your work unless it had been in the Salon. 'Of course there's the Salon des Refusés, but Parisians only go there to jeer.'

Every student at Guelle's looked worried.

One student called Xavier, who looked as if he never had a square meal, groaned to Nelly, 'Do you know there are *nine thousand* submissions.' They were sitting in the Place Clérissy;

he was sharing her lunch, something he did now and then. Nelly was wondering if she had enough to pay for two cups of coffee.

The following day Le P'tit called for Nelly to inform her that 'of course' they were going to the Tuileries this morning.

'Is it a procession or something?'

'Little Ignorance. We are going to see the Maronnier de Vingtième Mars. I'm shocked that you have not heard of the great tradition.'

He explained that a particular chestnut had been in leaf the day the Emperor entered the Tuileries on his return from Elba. If there were green leaves on the tree on March the 20th, it brought good luck to anybody who visited it. Nelly liked superstitions, picked up pins in the street, chanting the Cockney 'see a pin and pick it up, then today you'll have good luck.' She was always willing to adopt a new one.

They took an omnibus to the Tuileries in spring sunshine. A small crowd had gathered round a venerable chestnut tree and as they approached, Le P'tit gave a whoop of relief. It was covered with bright green, freshly opened leaves. Nelly went up to pat its trunk. Le P'tit stood by religiously. As they turned to go a voice said, 'Why, it's Nelly and Monsieur Tigli. You're paying your respects too.'

It was Matthew Ayrton. He was sitting, his long legs seeming even longer, on a shooting-stick: the very caricature of an eccentric Englishman.

Nelly looked pleased. Le P'tit Charles didn't.

'I've been a stranger lately, I'm afraid,' Matthew said. 'But I hope to be at the studio this afternoon. I'm returning to the fold.'

'Maître *will* be pleased,' said Nelly.

'We have to go, we're late,' said Charles.

When they were out of earshot he said, 'He isn't like us.'

'No,' agreed Nelly, longing to look back.

Matthew had regretted as much as Maître Guelle that he had not been able to paint recently. Like the others, he wanted to take his chance at the Salon, but he was seriously short of money. Nothing had come from Leckford and Matthew guessed why. The family money was controlled by Honoria. I wonder how she manages to send me nothing without lying to Robert, he thought.

To pay rent for his room in a ramshackle old stone house on the Butte, plus use of the stable for storing his canvases, he had cut living expenses to the bone. He ate at the cheapest cafés, had his clothes washed by a young laundress next door. The cobbler who lived in the same house as Matthew – his hammering went on all day – mended his shoes. But it was still impossible to make ends meet, and Matthew saw a post advertised in *Le Figaro*.

'Temporary courier and interpreter. Good English essential. Hôtel d'Angleterre et États-Unis.'

The hotel was unknown to Matthew and he felt dubious when he set off to find it, thinking of the risk of meeting friends. But his luck was in, the place turned out to be dowdy: not at all a hotel for anybody in London Society to patronise. The manager, a Frenchman, hired him at once. He thought the tall shabby man had an air of English elegance.

The work was to last six weeks and Matthew calculated that with care his salary would last as many months. His duties were to accompany foreign visitors, to take them to the Bal Bullier, the Folies (of course), on shopping and sightseeing expeditions, and occasionally to restaurants. He was given a poky bedroom under the roof with the other servants. But everybody was very polite and breakfast was first-class.

He found the work tedious. The foreigners in his care were either speechless or voluble. He was never alone, and the six weeks crawled past. To make things worse, whenever he was in the fashionable parts of Paris, he always expected to see somebody he knew.

He had vanished from England as if he had been drowned: as if the cold sea had closed for ever over his head. All he had left behind was a *poste-restante* address for his bank. He'd also sent it to his brother.

Robert wrote regularly and when Matthew received one of

his letters, it hurt. Robert was no letter-writer, he could not express his feelings but they showed dreadfully. He sent a little news of the estate, a tactful reference to a dinner party. He carefully mentioned their mother, she was well but tired. There were too many visitors at Leckford. She worried about the condition of the family chapel. Robert made a little joke. 'The statue of St Peter is in a bad way. I think the dear old gentleman worries about it himself.'

In every lame sentence, Matthew saw that Robert suffered. And that, like his own pain, the sadness would not go away.

He will get used to guilt in the end, Matthew thought. But he did not know that Robert's debt to him, Robert's burden, was worsened daily by Lady Leckford's love and by the acceptance of friends who delicately avoided any mention of Matthew. All this was torture to Robert's sensitive nature which screamed, when touched, as if it had been flayed.

Matthew wrote in reply, never mentioning anything that could compromise them and never, never saying where he was.

When his work ended at the hotel, the manager cordially invited him to return for a later season; Matthew thanked him without exactly accepting. Privately, he felt he couldn't take one more simpering middle-aged lady to Maxim's. An oddity of the work had been the way it was paid, not by the hotel but by the clients. He received all kinds of money: dollars, Chilean coins, Mexican banknotes, even Papal money. One client had paid in coins from the time when Napoleon was First Consul. Matthew never refused the curious payments: he discovered a coin-dealer opposite the Madeleine.

He felt positively sanguine when he walked home to the Butte from the hotel, back to his own life again. He had no friends, and did not want any. He lived in a poor teeming world where everybody knew everybody. Not Matthew. He exchanged a few words occasionally with the cobbler: Matthew was at home with men who worked with their hands. He joked with the little laundress, who flirted with him when filling his arms with clean linen. He had one hot meal a day, and watched the world go by.

It was not a long journey from the *grands boulevards* to Montmartre. He passed junk shops where artists were sometimes allowed to hang their work for sale. On the pavement among split chairs and battered tin trunks many used canvases were propped: artists bought them to paint over them. Matthew did so because they were cheap, but he always felt it a kind of sin, wondering who had painted the soon-to-be-obliterated vase of roses or the copy of an old woman by Rembrandt.

As he began to climb the hill of the Butte, the side steets plunged downwards, giving unexpected glimpses of the city below. At an open door a girl sat decorating a hat with cock's feathers. Two women in carpet slippers went by, baskets of vegetables on their arms. As he climbed higher, the road narrowed, the wind began to blow. He took a stairway, and higher still was a mound of grass and a windmill which didn't stir: the Bal du Moulin de la Galette. Past ruined gardens and toppling fences he finally turned into the steep Rue Saint-Sauveur and let himself into his studio. The cobbler was having his midday meal. It was very quiet.

Even after six weeks of absence the dust on the windowsills and along the tops of his canvases, on the bottles of turpentine, methylated spirits and oil of lavendar ranged along his battered carpenter's bench, was a pale country dust. He put his hands in his pockets and looked round his kingdom. The usual divan bought from a junk shop. A few more sticks of furniture. A kitchen which was merely a cupboard with a sink. A door leading to the overgrown garden. He opened it. The birds were singing.

Lining up his canvases against the wall he squatted on the floor, trying to decide which to submit to the Salon.

He chose two studies of Nelly Briggs.

They were nudes; in one she was in profile, arms raised, in the other facing outwards straight from the canvas. He looked reflectively at the paintings, thinking they might do. In both

76

he had tried to convey something of his feeling for women, of his own sexual nature. Nelly's skin had no ugly creases, it fitted her body as closely as an animal's coat. She was as naked and lovely as a pearl. He felt he had discovered femininity in painting her, and hoped he hadn't crushed a single petal.

But he could see more work was needed on the profile nude, a single sitting might be enough. He wondered if he could ask her to come and pose for him here . . .

When he went into the Guelle studio that afternoon, the silence that reigned was not the usual one of absorbed work, it seemed filled with misery. Through the cigarette smoke he could sense anxiety, and every man in the room looked tense. Nelly, already posing on the model's stage, was the only peaceful occupant of the whole place. The students' canvases had to be at the Palais de l'Industrie in just three days. When the session ended and everybody left, Matthew hung about. Nelly emerged from the *grand placard* to find he had been waiting for her. She looked flattered.

'I wonder if you'd have tea with me?'

'That sounds just like good old London,' said Nelly, who had thought London anything but good, but was willing to be friends.

'I've discovered an English tea shop near the Opéra,' said Matthew, adding, as if he were coaxing a horse with sugar, 'they have doughnuts.'

They walked down the *boulevard* in relaxed talk. He was attracted again to this girl, as he'd been when they had lunch altogether. She stirred him sexually. He had just spent four hours looking at her naked, and all he'd thought about was the right way to paint the golden pallor of her flesh. It was different now.

The tea shop, called La Théière Anglaise, was determinedly English, with oak panelling and engravings of the Old Queen, but an unmistakably French woman served the doughnuts and strong tea in Wedgwood china. The doughnuts were fresh and oozing with jam.

Nelly was hungry, and pleased by the invitation. She had

had to avoid Patrice as she was leaving, he had arrived on the off-chance and the poor chap, she thought, looked as if she'd stabbed him in the guts.

Her escort on the other side of the table interested her. A gentleman. My first, she thought. She waited to see what he had in mind – hazily imagining a dinner at Maxim's. She did not know what a man like this, with his enigmatic face, would offer a girl for a good time. But there could be no reason for the tea except in the end to get her to bed. And she hadn't made any decision about that.

They talked studio shop, then Matthew put down his cup.

'Nelly. There is something I want to ask you.'

Here we go, she thought.

'Ask away.'

'It is a great favour.'

She looked at him with a charming expression.

'I wondered – well, the fact is, would you consent to model for me? On Sunday? Unless you already have an appointment.'

She burst into a roar of laughter. He was very taken aback.

'Sorry, sorry,' she was still guffawing, her eyes wet, 'but it's just – I mean, of course I'll model for you. Does that mean,' she added, shrewdness coming through the mirth, 'that it's my picture you want to send in?'

'Two of your pictures.'

Nelly, gorged with doughnuts, was told he would pay double her usual rate since 'after all, it is your free day.'

When she went home she was still inwardly laughing. She found Le P'tit sitting on the mounting-block outside her apartment: a favourite roosting place. The sight of his small patient figure gave her a moment of annoyed guilt. He was going to fuss when she said she couldn't go cycling on Sunday. But when she broke the news, he was reasonable. He looked solemn and said he, too, must work. The Englishman was right.

On Sunday afternoon, Nelly left in good time to walk to the Rue Saint-Sauveur. It occurred to her that she did not know anybody who didn't live at the top of a flight of steps, usually more than ninety, or at the summit of a street up which cab-drivers refused to take their horses. When she arrived at the stone house which Matthew had described, the cobbler was making a din and there was a smell of leather. Matthew had been looking out for her. He appeared at once.

'The studio's at the back. Good of you to come.'

She wondered if his studio would be any more comfortable than those of her friends. It turned out not to be. It was almost as bare, and the only difference was that his canvases weren't turned to the wall. They ranged outwards, paintings of waiters and flower-sellers, chalks of a laundress in a white cap, paintings of herself.

'Jiminy. You work hard.'

'We all do, don't we? You too.'

She stood looking at a certain picture, her head on one side.

'That's a house and a half. Is it yours?'

'In a way.'

'Got to get to work, eh?' said Nelly, losing interest in Leckford Court. She unpinned her shawl and hung it on a nail, took off the velvet hat decorated with an ostrich feather she'd found on the floor of the Guelle studio.

'Do you sell a lot?'

She always asked that.

'Not much.'

She gave a laugh like the snort of a pony.

'You're so English, Mister Ayrton. The students moan and groan that the public is a donkey and has no taste. Can I use this?' She pointed at a screen. 'It's handier than the *grand placard*.'

She disappeared behind the screen, draping her clothes on its top. Full grey skirts. Buttoned bodice. Corsets trailing laces. Knickers edged with coarse lace. White stockings. Two frilled black garters. Her clothes, he noticed, were clean. He compared them to dirty underclothes he'd seen in another studio.

She emerged naked as Venus.

'I'm sorry the sun's gone in. I've borrowed this.'

He pulled the small black stove into the centre of the room. Nelly turned her round posterior to the heat. The north light shone in its truth and severity on the girl. She took the pose in the paintings. He began to work. He was more attentive than Maître Guelle, breaking each hour for her to stretch, wrapping her in an old plaid rug. He made coffee. At first he painted in silence but, when the work was going better, they began to talk.

'Le P'tit says there's a way of getting into the Salon on *the* day when the pictures are delivered,' she said. 'You can get past the doorkeepers by helping one of the porters. Some of the frames weigh a ton. You rush up and give a hand. Once you're inside, it's tremendous fun strolling through the rooms looking at what's been hung. He's going to try. Shall you?'

'Perhaps.'

The spring light began to fade, and when it was almost six he threw down his brushes, picked up a rag and began to clean them.

'That's it for today.'

'I don't mind staying.'

'No, no, you've been here for hours. Put on your clothes, that damned stove is going out and we've no more fuel. Let me buy you coffee and a *fine*.'

'I don't drink but coffee would be good. Why don't we have it here? Make some fresh, I mean.'

She wanted to stay awhile. The atmosphere of paint and poverty was familiar, but the man was a mystery. The brother of a lord, a curious thought.

'Might as well save the money. Most cafés charge like shots from a gun.'

'Nelly, you've started translating from French. Of course, let's have our coffee here.'

'Let me make it this time.'

In the kitchen-cupboard she brewed the coffee. While she was waiting for the water to boil, he stood behind her and put his arms round her waist, pulling her back against him. She gave a little scream, removing the saucepan before it boiled over. They stayed a moment or two. He pressed hard against her and she shut her eyes, feeling the tingling beginnings of desire. Feeling, too, that the strong muscular body against hers wanted her. Her heart pounded as he turned her slowly round and began to kiss her. He opened her mouth with his tongue, running his tongue all round the inside of her mouth, he tasted delicious.

She remained in a kind of haze. She could not think. Scarcely knew where she was. All she was conscious of was the stranger holding her and the long, long kiss. The melting dizzyness of desire. She wanted him. Now. Here in the silence of the Paris evening. Not because, as had once been so, she might as well get the sex over and find out about it. Nor because it was pleasant enough and she liked to be kind. But because this time she wanted Matthew. To give her pleasure and take it, too. To own his body just for now. To have him inside her. The future could damned well take care of itself.

He picked her up and carried her over to the divan and Nelly watched him as he knelt and began carefully unfastening all the buttons that five minutes ago she'd done up. He pulled away her clothes, her knickers, peeled off her stockings and then looked hungrily at the body, rich and ripe, which lay waiting for him. She parted her legs and put her arms above her head, staring at him with languor as if they were already mated. It was strange. As he lay down on her and entered her moist body and began to move, he did not seem to be possessing the girl whose opalescent body glimmered on the still-wet canvas on the other side of the room . . .

Matthew was more affected by sex with Nelly than he admitted to himself. It was the first thing which had happened since his exile which literally brought him joy. He was filled with wonder at her passion and simplicity. She made love as if it were the beginning of the world. As for Nelly, she was frightened at what had happened.

She insisted on leaving him before it was light next morning. She wanted to walk home alone. When she left the house and began to descend the hill she thought – nothing has happened, has it? He's not my sort. I suppose that's why I feel funny. He's different. Beautiful, he is. Remembering how she'd felt under him, the thrust of his strong body into her, his weight on her, she did not compare him to any of her other lovers. Poor Patrice's love-making, so silent and energetic, vanished from her mind. It was as if she had never been with him.

She turned a corner into the flower market which was already busy, great baskets filled with lemon-yellow carnations, with expensive roses – too much alike and not nearly as lovely as the Parma violets ladies pinned to their muffs or wore in their belts. Nelly couldn't afford a flower, and envied them like a child at a baker's window.

Going into her poky room in the Rue de la Mire, she thought there was no point in asking herself what she proposed to do about the English gentleman. It had been gorgeous and he'd gone on for ever so long. She supposed he'd want to do it again. She supposed she'd say yes. That was all there was to it.

But she was disturbed. Now and then her stomach dropped as she remembered Matthew. And as she went into her room she was suddenly hit so hard by desire that it was like being kicked by a horse.

Two days went by. There was no sign of Matthew and she decided he must be working at home. She wished every morning that she didn't go to the Atelier in a stupid state of hope, and feel even more stupidly disappointed.

It was a relief to Nelly but not to her friends when the morning came for the pictures to be delivered to the Palais de l'Industrie. No work at the Atelier today. Every student, every painter in the quartier walked to the Salon with his work and then crowded outside watching the other artists delivering theirs.

Outside the great glassed-in building was a festive line of tricolours, a constant stream of vehicles rumbled up and stopped at the entrance. Broughams and growlers, hansoms, even furniture vans containing mighty historical canvases destined for town halls. There were also greengrocers' carts, wheelbarrows brought by young artists whose canvases were wrapped in newspapers, and now and then a porter with a big painting strapped on his broad back. Nelly, Le P'tit, Xavier and the rest gave a cheer when Maître Guelle stepped out of his hansom.

'What have you got there, Maître? One of mine?' shouted somebody. There was applause when a young girl in a cape arrived with a parcel. Girl painters were rare and this one was fair and pretty.

'Want some help? That's a big burden for your little arms,' shouted the same comedian, who liked to get a laugh.

The girl smiled and shook her head, then saw Nelly and waved.

It was Edith Holden.

The fun continued right through the afternoon. Despite his small stature, Le P'tit managed the old ruse and helped with a large canvas, succeeding in getting inside the building. He emerged half-an-hour later to report that there was nothing to worry about, which meant that no other artist had treated his own subjects of Spanish beggars as well or as imaginatively.

Nelly and her friends had ham and bread under the trees at midday, returning for the best part of the event, the moment when six o'clock struck from a nearby church, the whole Palais emptied, and everybody waited for the late arrivals.

'Wait till you see this,' said Le P'tit, when Nelly said her feet hurt.

A moment later, four artists, two young, two middle-aged, arrived with their canvases. But the huge studded doors had clanged shut. The newcomers argued, grew furious, one of them hammered on the doors. The crowds shouted.

'Love locked out.'

'Shame, shame, and such a masterpiece you've got there.'

The artists, either red or pale and all angry, came down the steps. Nelly was filled with sympathy.

'The poor things, how horrible for them.'

'Pouf,' said Le P'tit, tucking her arm into his. 'They get in later. A ten-franc note unlocks every door in Paris. Belle Nelly, if you don't know that by now, you ought to.'

They went to the Boulevard des Italiens to have an expensive coffee at fashionable Tortoni's. Le P'tit had received money from his family in Provence and was flush that week. Nelly had enjoyed herself, but as they sat talking and drinking their coffee, she was quiet. She had not once seen Matthew. Had he already taken his canvases to the Salon early this morning? She wished she didn't keep thinking about him.

The next day was back to normal. The students were on their low stools, Nelly on the model's stage. She looked across the room and felt a sharp stab, almost as if she'd been wounded. Matthew Ayrton was at the back of the Atelier, meticulously placing a canvas on his easel.

Maître Guelle decided on a new pose this morning – Nelly's hand on her hip, the weight on her front leg, she was turning from the shoulders to look at the wall. She obeyed with docility, fixing her eyes just above Matthew's barley-coloured head. When Maître Guelle had first talked to her about modelling for the nude, he had said her face must be without thought.

'You have a personality which is *piquante*. It could distract. You must try, *ma belle*, to look a little blank. Aphrodite should reveal nothing of her soul. Her body is beautiful and that is all.'

Today, without knowing it, Nelly's face was not blank. Maître Guelle did not notice, and nor did the students painting, measuring, smoking, concentrating. But one artist did and the change affected his work.

When the luncheon break was called and the students all surged out of the Atelier. Nelly disappeared into the *grand placard*. She knew who would be waiting when she emerged. He was sitting on a long bench among jars and brushes and rainbow rags. She gave a bright, meaningless grin.

'Maître says you are not posing this afternoon.'

'Disappointed?' said Nelly flippantly. 'I've got to rehearse some new songs at Chez Paul-Marc.'

He ran his hand along the bench, lumpy with long-dried paint, blue and lilac, dark purple, orange, yellow.

'I didn't take the two nudes to the Palais. I think I can do better in the autumn.'

'Oh.'

'I've missed you.'

She stood, startled and still.

'Come home with me. Now.'

'But –'

'Please.'

She was too lost to say a word, but was conscious of the terrible extravagance when he hailed a hansom. It left them at the bottom of the hill. As they climbed upwards, he held her hand. He unlocked the door and they went into the studio. She expected them to fall on the divan. It was why they were here, wasn't it? She wanted him so much that she couldn't bear to look at the tall, thin figure, the haggard, guarded face. But he didn't touch her. He went to the window and opened it, looking out at the bushes and wild tall weeds. There was a wind and the branches streamed. He turned round.

'I must ask you something.'

'You don't need to,' she said, with a faint return to her real self.

His face showed strain. He didn't smile in return.

'I would like you to come and live with me. Could you do such a thing?'

She swallowed.

'I thought we was, I mean we were going to make love.'

'That too. All the time. Until we drop, probably.'

'That sounds nice.'

He stared across at her. The wind went on blowing eastwards and the sun had gone. It looked as if something was pursuing the branches. Destiny, perhaps.

'Nelly, be serious for a moment,' he spoke as if to a child. 'I am asking you to do me the greatest favour, the greatest good I can think of. I'm not asking you just to let me love you now and then, beautiful though that was and will be. I want you here. Part of my life. I want to share it with you and in return to share yours. Don't give me your answer at once. Take time before you reply. You can go now if you wish. Tell me tomorrow or the next day. But don't, I beg, leave me too long in suspense.'

It was a speech which with small alterations could have been made as a proposal to a young girl in the conservatory of some great London house. It was full of Matthew's way of life, his ancestry, his natural tenderness and gallantry. He had never kept a mistress, merely enjoying casual affairs with married women in his own class. This girl was different. She was strong yet vulnerable, brave and kind. She seemed to rule the kingdom of the senses; to be, as no woman he'd known had been, the essence of delight. Even the set of her shoulders, her hair, the small chin and full lower lip, awakened desire.

She was silent for so long that he began to think he must have lost her. She was looking at the floor, making a pattern in the dust with the toe of her boot. Her head was bent and the battered velvet hat showed its stitched brim, the feather which he'd seen her lick to keep it from getting ragged.

When she looked up her eyes swam.

'I don't need five minutes to answer about what you just said. Yes. Yes. Yes.'

CHAPTER SIX

Nelly paid a week's rent, packed her clothes in the Gladstone bag, which still had the yellow label, and moved in with Matthew.

Despite her generous heart, she knew she must get rid of her followers. She met Patrice at a quiet café, not La Vache Enragée. Beaming with pleasure, he was at a table by a glass screen which reflected his dark face and big powerful figure. He stood up as she came towards him, putting out both hands. She couldn't let him go on looking happy and blurted out the news at once.

She had never in her short life hurt anyone deliberately and found it horrible. His brown eyes filled with tears. She could scarcely bear it. And he said a dreadful thing.

'Oh Nelly. Why can't you love me?'

Her meeting with Le P'tit was scarcely much better; the poor little fellow looked like a lost dog, almost frightened, and Nelly was more shocked than she'd been over Patrice because he was strong and Le P'tit wasn't. She said she might come cycling with him sometimes, 'If Matthew doesn't mind.'

Le P'tit, overcome with grief and hatred of the Englishman, made a speech about how losing her would open his veins and bring on a lingering death, holding up his wrist to illustrate the point.

She arrived at the Rue Saint-Sauveur less than her usual self. It occurred to her, approaching the house and hearing the cobbler at work, that she was giving up a part of her life. She'd always been poor. Sometimes hungry. Sometimes, despite her magnificent health, tired and obscurely sad. But she'd been her own master since, at ten years old, tall and strong for her age, she'd stopped the drunken sot who called herself her mother from hitting her. She'd simply pushed her over.

Matthew had left the studio door open and as the gallant figure clutching the Gladstone bag came into the room he strode over, picked her up, bag and all, and gave her the first long, long embrace.

Nelly's arrival in his life was wonderful to Matthew just then. She excited and touched him. He'd never known such a creature and here she was, lying in his arms or singing in the kitchen. She was like a balm. He adored the sex they constantly shared; it grew in joy. He was astonished at his passion for the young Cockney girl, so unlike his mistresses of the past. Those affairs had been followed by satiety, a loss of interest when the woman's secrets were all known. But he never did *not* want Nelly. Mystery was necessary to sex and there was mystery about her. She was open to love and life but she was strange. Her face under his, radiant or swimming, never told him what was in her soul.

'I haven't lived with a man before,' she remarked, clattering back into the house on their first morning, to feed him pieces of a yard-long loaf called a *restaurant*, plus a bowl of coffee. 'I don't count Ma Briggs. When she hove into view, I scarpered.'

'You talk as if she were not your mother at all.'

Apparently this urchin, like himself, had no feeling for her maternal parent.

'Don't expect she is. She called me Briggs and I'm stuck with it but I dunno who I am. Where we lived down Blackfriars, women foster a kid to be useful later on. I was – for a bit.'

Settling into a shared life, they found difficulties. Nelly owned nothing but managed to leave possessions all over the place. Matthew was fiercely tidy. She was chilled by his disapproval when he found the velvet hat on his bench, or she lost one of her boots. They were, respectively, lark and nightingale. She rose with the sun. He lingered in bed, drinking coffee until it grew cold and reading the English newspapers she disliked because they took his attention from her. But he was sexy after breakfast. And again before they left for the Atelier. It was odd to pose nude with her lover at the back of the studio. But she got used to it.

Nelly's singing voice pleased him, and he often went to Chez Paul-Marc to have a *fine* and coffee, and to sit in a corner listening when she sang. It gave him a proprietary pleasure to see the men look up eagerly when she came in, wearing her only good dress and that sunny look. She stood by the piano, exchanged a look with the pianist, and, like a thrush, burst into song. She sang Cockney songs he'd never heard before. 'It's a marvel 'ow 'e does it, but 'e do!' and 'Stop as long as you used to'. Now and then she added something French and rather sad, and the sweet melancholy of her voice moved him. Then back she'd bounce into 'Daisy, Daisy'.

On Mondays when Nelly was free, she and Matthew went to one of the *guingettes*, the pleasure gardens under shady trees where accordions played, *fiacres* clip-clopped by, and girls who had sewed or washed all day long found dancing and romance. She did not need to worry about seeing Le P'tit again. Matthew, it seemed, was not jealous of him. Nelly had said nothing about Patrice and wasn't going to.

'Sure you don't mind me going cycling with Le P'tit?'

'Don't be foolish. Enjoy yourself.'

One morning when she and Matthew walked across the Place Clérissy, they stopped to look at a poster nailed to a tree. It showed a capering girl, all raised skirts and knickers.

'The Bal des Trois Quartiers at the Galette. Hoo-bally-ray,' said Nelly. 'Last year they said the *chahut* was the best of all.'

The *chahut* was a coarse, crazy, earthy dance which Nelly and her friends loved and which ended all the Montmartre festivities. It had begun down the hill in the Elysée-Montmartre but years before had been turned into the Can-can which was now the sensation at the Moulin-Rouge. The swells came from the Faubourg St Honoré to watch it, gaping at La Goulue and Rayon d'Or and the angular explosive dancer called Valentin the Boneless, Goulue's lover. Nelly and her friends disliked the mixture of snobbery and prostitution at the Moulin-Rouge. The Galette was real, and its *chahut* was a dance into which they threw themselves as if into the sea.

'Le P'tit says it's the greatest fun,' said Nelly, still admiring the poster.

'Don't think you can go with him, *ma belle*. You are with me.'

He pinched her. She looked complacent. Her arms were scattered with little bruises.

But in the evening when they were home in the studio, she looked at her dresses hung on the usual string in a corner, and began to swear.

'What's the matter?'

Matthew debated whether to tell her to clean up her language.

'I can't go to the ★ ★ ★ Bal, that's what.'

'Of course you can,' he said absently.

'No I can't because all I've got is this blue silk Miss Fisher left me when she went back to London. Xavier spilled absinthe over the skirt. I scrubbed it with soda. Needn't have bothered.'

He came over to look at the wreck of the dress.

'I was looking forward to going ever so much. Filthy absinthe. It's ★★★ well ruined the silk. Oh Matt, just look.'

'Stop wailing, Nelly. It isn't like you. I know you want to go to the dance so we'll do something about it. Go out and buy some book muslin.'

'*Book muslin.*'

'That's right. Enough to make a dress. You sew, I suppose?'

' 'Course I do, but what's the idea, why that stuff?'

'Don't argue and don't wail. Do as I say and we'll make you a dress that will turn every other woman green with envy. Off you go.'

Incredulous, but responding to Matthew's confident voice, Nelly did as she was bid. In the market she bought many yards of the vaporous webby stuff used for binding books; it was dirt cheap, which was a mercy. Returning home, she was told to cut out a dress. Matthew helped and they knelt on the studio floor arguing. When it was ready Nelly went to a house three doors down the hill to borrow a sewing-machine from a friend, a seamstress called Titine who was as mystified as she was.

'You will look like a nun or a ghost, Nelly. Is that your man's clever idea?'

After hours of machining and swearing, Nelly bore the finished dress home to the studio. He told her to put it on and stood regarding her. The dress fitted perfectly. Ample-skirted, cut low to show her bosom, with extra fullness at the back to exaggerate her bottom and show off her small waist. But it was a phantom dress, the fabric thin enough to make blackcurrant jelly. And, worse still, it was a dull yellowish-white.

'You'll need two petticoats,' said Matthew.

'I got two.'

'Good. Now leave me in peace,' he said, taking the dress and draping it over his arm. 'Oh, if you have a sash, I'll have that as well.'

She fetched her only sash, a poor washed-out thing, and respectfully closed the studio door.

She was due at Chez Paul-Marc to rehearse some new songs. Nelly's memory for the Cockney songs of her childhood was almost inexhaustible. Ragged and dirty, she and her gutter companions had always enjoyed singing, often loudly to annoy passers-by. Now, when she needed a change of repertoire, she hummed a song to Louis Duval the pianist. Louis was elderly and fat and looked like a bloodhound. He concentrated, following the tune, and soon played it perfectly. Today, she'd decided to added 'Where did you get that hat', and 'Pretty Polly Perkins'. She and Louis spent an enjoyable two hours.

It was early evening when she returned to the Rue Saint-Sauveur. She had been thinking about her dress, off and on, ever since she had left Matthew. Usually she was too superstitious to look forward to things in case, she thought, they punched you in the face. But she did feel excited as she pushed open the studio door.

'Not ready!'

Nelly moaned.

'You've been hours.'

'Five minutes. Don't dare peek until then.'

'You're driving me mad.'

She went round to the back of the house and into the garden. There were some wild roses. She liked the buds best. She sniffed one, then came back to the studio door yelping like a dog to be let in.

'Aren't you ready *yet*?'

'Very well. In you come.'

She burst into the room.

Matthew, hands in his pockets, was grinning broadly. Draped across two chairs was the most extraordinary dress Nelly had ever seen. Round its hem, spreading up to mid thigh, the skirts were painted with climbing water-lilies, great flowers with yellow stamens against a background of sapphire blue and emerald green. The flowers bloomed and budded, coming from twining stems, peering from flat or curling leaves. There were water-lilies on the full sleeves and coiled round the bosom of the dress. The sash was banded with stalks and leaves in a long sinuous trail.

'Oh Matthew! Oh Matthew!'

She threw herself into his arms.

'One thing, *ma belle*,' he said, after a while, 'let's hope to God it doesn't rain.'

It was the wildest dance Matthew had been to in his life, crowded with students and laundresses, artists' models and waiters, roughs and scullery maids, the men in rakish caps or battered top-hats, the girls in whatever finery they could make or borrow or maybe steal. They lifted their skirts and whirled and danced on the tables, they jumped down into the waiting arms of their lovers, they ate from each other's plates and drank the Galette's special mulled wine. They frolicked out into the gardens where it was impossible not to fall over embracing couples. The music never stopped, and Nelly, twined in water-lilies, was the very heart of the long, long, noisy night.

She had a second chance to wear the dress for Le Quatorze – the enormous carnival celebrating the Fall of the Bastille. All Paris took to the streets that day, flags hung from every window and lamp-post; the gigantic party went on until the fourteenth was well into the fifteenth and it was dawn. Matthew and Nelly walked for miles. They ate hot pancakes with their fingers, sang, arms linked, with the crowds, and ended up near the Place de la Concorde where fireworks burst in the sky like vast chrysanthemums, to the blissful sighing 'aaah' of the throng.

It was a magical summer. Nelly went out early in the morning, padding down the hill to fetch the bread, climbing again, hearing the talk from door to door and passing the corner where an old flower-seller sat with her basket of moist violets. Nelly knew the laundresses whisking by with their loads of sheets and piles of starched petticoats. She liked the very smell of the day, fres baked bread, and the fragrant cheap violets, still wet, stuc. into the bosom of her dress.

Matthew encouraged her to go cycling with Le P'tit. 'Be nice to the poor little chap. He's vulnerable,' he said, adding – he saw she didn't know the word – 'that means he can be hurt.'

'What about me? Who fell off last Sunday and got her legs skinned, I should like to know? And you remember what Maître Guelle said when he saw the bruise.'

'Until I covered it with wet white.'

'Oh you. You take the credit for everything!'

Matthew now paid for Nelly's bicycling expeditions; Le P'tit accepted this with a frown and a good deal of relief.

By midday, on fine Sundays, he and Nelly were spinning into the greenest part of the Bois. Large tracts of the woodland were quite wild and they saw magpies and jays. Sometimes, riding home in late afternoon, they heard a nightingale.

'Don't know why people make a fuss about that bird,' said Nelly when Le P'tit looked romantic.

He loved nature as well as Nelly and taught her the names of butterflies, the sulphurs and painted ladies and the curiously serrated comma.

One Sunday, as they were riding to a certain reedy pond where Nelly had seen a large basking pike, she caught sight of two figures sitting in the tall grass.

'Why, it's Edith!'

'And René,' added Charles.

The quartet chatted for a while, and then the temptation to talk about painting was too much for the young men who walked round the pond, interrupting each other a good deal. Edith winked at Nelly.

'René loves arguing and I won't. How are you, Nelly? You look very well.'

She thought her changed, but couldn't decide how.

'In *pleine forme*. Lots of news. I'm with somebody now. An Englishman. What down Blackfriars we called a toff.'

'Is it Matthew Ayrton? René said he saw you together.'

'Do you know Matt?' said Nelly, pleased.

'Only about him. He's Viscount Leckford's brother, isn't he? Lord Leckford is in the Society papers now and then. My friend at the kiosk lends me the *Tatler*. I saw a picture of your friend's brother and a huge house.'

Nelly looked at her and suddenly said, 'I believe you know. About the scandal and that.'

'Well . . . I do remember something in the French papers.'

'That's why he came to Paris. To get away from the nasty business,' Nelly said. She was relieved when Edith changed the subject and asked if Mr Ayrton was worried about the possibility of war.

'What does he think about Lord Milner? Many people think he's dangerous.'

'Golly, Edith, who's Lord Thingamebob? You sound as if you understand about it.'

'Everybody should. It is our country that is in trouble.'

But if Edith hoped to stir Nelly's patriotism she failed. Nelly leaned back under the deckled shade of a tree, chewing a piece of grass. Edith persevered. Despite a French lover and the Feu Follet, she was much like her schoolmaster father.

'It is so hard to decide if England is right, Nelly. The Boers long for their independence. And, after all, South Africa is their home and the English –'

'The English,' repeated Réné, as he and Le P'tit joined them. 'The English have built an Empire and want to hang on to it. Even if the countries they stole will soon be rid of them.'

Edith looked surprised and delighted at the attack, and launched into passionate discussion. Nelly admired Edith and was bored. Le P'tit snuggled up, holding her hand and thinking any talk save of art or sex a perfect waste of time. But when they said goodbye, Nelly impulsively invited Edith to tea one day soon at La Théière Anglaise.

Arriving home Nelly sent her hat spinning, roamed round the studio and found one of Matthew's newspapers. She fetched a cushion, lay on her stomach, and painstakingly began to plough through it.

Matthew had been out to buy some colours. He needed a certain alizarin crimson, which Nelly had said looked plain maroon to her. When he returned and saw her on the floor with the paper spread out in front of her, he roared with laughter.

'I've never seen anything so out of character. Come here.'

She sprang up and flew to him like a homing pigeon. She sat on his knee, murmuring.

'Shall we do it before or after supper?'

'Before. I shall enjoy my meal more. What are we having?'

'Sex *à la carte*.'

Before she left for Chez Paul-Marc, she shouted at the door.

'Hey. Don't throw the paper away. I only got to page three.'

During the autumn of 1899 the world's press was filled with reports and comment upon troubled South Africa and Imperial Britain. Both sides declared they wanted the country to be united – but who should be in power? For the Boers, an

Afrikaner South Africa was their fervent but distant hope. For the British, Lord Milner declared, 'It is the British race which built the Empire, and it is the undivided British race which alone can uphold it.'

Both Nelly's friend and Nelly's lover seemed to do nothing but devour newspapers. Edith read *Le Figaro*, like most Parisians. She also borrowed *The Times* from her friend at the kiosk. Matthew extravagantly bought *The Times* which arrived in Paris late the day of its publication (it was proud of its foreign deliveries), or at latest the following morning. Nelly usually collected the newspaper for him, to be rewarded with kisses and exclamations. He never took a kindness for granted.

In Nelly's knocked-about London life she had never had a girl friend, and she and Edith fell into the habit of meeting weekly at La Théière. One afternoon during a golden October she finished her day's work at the Atelier, and Edith her hours of sewing at the Feu Follet. They greeted each other with pleasure.

'My fingers,' said Edith, pouring the tea, 'are like pin-cushions.'

'They don't hurt, do they?'

'No, they just look hideous.'

Nelly made sympathetic mutters, drank the tea and left a milky moustache on her upper lip. When Edith wiped it away she kept her face obediently still, like a child.

'I haven't looked at Matt's beastly newspaper. What's happening *now*?'

'All the other countries are against us. They say our Imperialism is aggressive and greedy. I'm afraid I agree.'

'Aren't you on Old England's side, then?'

'How can one be on the side of a huge bully threatening a little man? How does Mr Ayrton feel about it?'

'I wish you'd call him Matt.'

'I couldn't possibly. He's an Honourable.'

'I'm blowed if I see what difference that makes.'

'Rank doesn't impress you. You're lucky.'

'Matt's a man, isn't he? And he likes you. I say, let's have *gâteau à l'orange*. I did an extra hour at the Atelier and I can splash out with the cash.'

Nelly went to the counter to point out two of the largest slices. Giving to Edith was like giving to Matthew. You couldn't offer them a fifty-centime bunch of violets or make them a bowl of mayonnaise without them thanking you as if you were the angel Gabriel.

Sitting down again, she attacked the cake.

'Now, what were we talking about?' she said.

'Your Honourable Matthew being brother to a Viscount. I'm sure you treat him just the way you treat anyone. The students. Your friends in London.'

'You mean the chaps in the fish market, Edith. You're so polite. Well . . . I don't treat him exactly the same. I try to clean up the swearing. What are you laughing at?'

'You.'

'Oh good. But Matt's a lovely man. He's gentle, do you know what I mean? Can't bear to see a girl cry (not that I ever do). Once we were walking past Les Halles and I was busy hoping I didn't see poor dear Patrice, and suddenly a porter sloshed a girl right across the face. Matt flinched as if *he'd* been hit and then over he went and socked the fellow who went down like an ox. I did laugh.'

'People like Mr Ayrton have rules of behaviour. A man must never hurt a woman, that sort of thing,' said Edith solemnly. 'They all keep the rules in a sort of unspoken law. If anyone breaks them –'

'He has to ★ ★ ★ off to Paris,' said Nelly.

She was not as light-hearted as she seemed. She did not say that Matthew worried her, because she believed if you talked of something you made it worse. She was anxious about him all the time now. She thought of him with pain. As the weeks went by and they grew sexually closer, she wanted more than just to make love until she thought she'd go crazy. She wanted to become Matthew, to breathe his breath, possess his mysterious self. Not only the body, which so pleasured her, but also the soul. He had grace and sexual mastery but now, often, she did not understand him. Not his words but what he was truly saying. She had made a terrible discovery. She was in love. As weak and obsessed as Patrice or Laurent or Le P'tit. She used to scoff at them for being so foolish, glad that she could keep reins on love, enjoy it without a single pang. She had lost that the day she climbed the hill to the Rue Saint-Sauveur. She was at Matt's mercy now. Sometimes after a long throbbing hour of sex, when he had fallen asleep, Nelly leaned on one elbow and looked down at his sleeping face. She listened to his gentle breath. Her breast seemed full of broken glass.

The Indian summer went on, day after misty golden day. One Sunday Matthew said that Le P'tit couldn't have her company, he would take her out on the river. They hired a rowing boat and went down as far as the Île de la Grande Jatte. Matthew rowed well and Nelly trailed her hand in the water as the boat glided in the strong current. They tied up to a willow tree and landed on the island.

It was a grassy, lonely place, just a café, one restaurant and the landing-stage. They walked to a bank sloping down to a pebbled beach, and swam. Matthew had taught her to swim, and she splashed and gambolled, her long hair dripping. As she came bobbing up to catch him in wet arms he said, 'You're like a girl on a fountain. But you should be holding a large spouting fish.'

They dried in the sun, picnicked, and grew lazy during the long day in the open air. The pull back was hard work but Matthew enjoyed it, and to encourage him, Nelly sang. They caught an omnibus for the long ride home to the Butte.

Sitting beside her, Matthew took her hand, and Nelly sat peacefully, filled with happiness and a vague, sleepy state the colour of the sunlight.

Suddenly the hand holding hers tensed.

The omnibus was at a halt and they heard a boy shouting.

A newsboy on a corner was selling papers, calling for custom as he handed them out.

'He's saying "*la guerre*",' said Matthew. 'We must get out.'

'But we're half-an-hour from home,' complained Nelly.

He took no notice and bundled her out of the omnibus, a moment later reading the newspaper with a horrified look.

'War's been declared. They say England is wild with enthusiasm. My God.'

Nelly said nothing. She felt frightened.

A wave of hostility against England swept over Paris, the French receiving news of the war with a jeering '*Enfin*'. When Nelly arrived at Maître Guelle's she was greeted with whistles.

'*La Belle Nelly* is going to sing for the gallant British troops while they murder the Boers. Are you proud of your country now?' said one young man unpleasantly.

Nelly gave as good as she got. Her vocabulary of French obscenities was large and came in handy, and the students hooted with laughter and applauded.

She and Edith were meeting for luncheon in the Place Clérissy and when Nelly came across the square where the fallen chestnut leaves lay like fragile gondolas, her friend was waiting on their usual bench. She didn't smile.

'It's happened, Nelly.'

'But we expected it, didn't we?' said Nelly, who had not. 'And the papers say it won't last long.'

' "A short Colonial adventure",' quoted Edith. 'I don't believe that. I wish I did.'

The wind which blew and shook down more leaves had a cold centre to it. Edith, wrapped in a voluminous blue and brown knitted shawl, looked like a colourful chrysalis. They munched for a while in silence.

'Nelly.'

'Mmm?'

'Have you thought that Mr Ayrton may go to fight for his country?'

'After they threw him out! He never would.'

'*Noblesse oblige*. That sort of thing.'

'Edith, he's a *painter*. He isn't a lord, thank heaven.'

99

The coming of a war on the other side of the world changed Matthew. He wasn't as passionate as he used to be, and he scarcely ever laughed. He brooded. Nelly, adoring and despising, wanted to yell at him to stop. What the ★ ★ ★ was the use of going into a mood and reading those ★ ★ ★ newspapers all the time? He didn't want to talk about it, either. She had to keep her ignorant questions for Edith.

Matthew never said how he felt, but Edith was plainly anti-British. She was in tune with the Liberals, the radicals and the socialists who denounced the war. It didn't surprise her that when the British troops landed in a strange, hot arid land they had never set eyes on before, their campaign did not succeed. After the first two weeks the situation was grave.

'The Boers have been making secret preparations for years. They're born fighters.'

'So we are, for God's sake!'

But Edith said the Boers were on their own terrain, moved as secretly as Red Indians, were stubborn and brave and much, much harder to subdue.

Nelly wanted to argue but she knew only odd facts picked up from Matthew's newspapers and the anti-British gibes of her friends at the Atelier. Edith, unlike herself, was a taker-on of causes. When she wasn't talking earnestly about the Boers and their rights, she launched into other things about which she felt strongly. Women's freedom was uppermost.

'We must stop being dominated by men,' she often said, fixing Nelly with her serious eyes.

Nelly was too fond of her to giggle out loud. Edith had Réné under her thumb, and when had any man dominated Nelly herself? But then Nelly returned to thinking of Matthew; she had room for no other cause but her own.

The weeks went by, there were fogs in London and the newspapers were often late. When they did come the news was never good. Why does he want the beastly things only to read that it's all going badly, she thought, and it puts him off his painting. There was fog in Paris, too. Nelly looking at the Montmartre chimney-pots, saw them slowly disappear, and she could just imagine the pea-souper in the London docks, the stifling filthy air, flares on the street corners. London seemed like a bad dream.

December came. The great Samaritaine and Printemps shop windows were festive with lights – in one of the biggest windows was a life-size statue of Saint Nicholas. He wore cloth of silver and crown, and in front of him wobbled a procession of clockwork angels. Tempting packages, half open, spilled luxurious gifts – hatboxes with magnificent feather-decorated hats, jewel-cases from which pearls cascaded, satin lingerie embroidered with butterflies, cedarwood boxes of cigars, buckled shoes, waxen-faced dolls.

And in all the gaiety, as the Parisians bustled through the bitterly cold streets in their furs or buttoned in long thick capes, the newsboys shouted 'La Semaine Noire'. It was Black Week for Britain.

When Matthew read the paper he threw it on the floor and walked out of the studio.

Nelly, alarmed, picked it up.

'Only a temporary reverse,' declared the newspaper, but even ignorant Nelly understood that it looked as if England could lose. One Boer force had invaded Natal and shut up the British commander in Ladysmith; another had invaded Cape Colony in the west; Lord Methuen had failed in his attack.

'Black Week for the Empire,' said the headlines. 'The gloomiest week in our history. A national fiasco.' Further down the columns it was reported that thousands upon thousands of young men 'are besieging the recruiting depots'. She shivered.

At the Atelier she was greeted with glee.

'Ouf, the poor British Empire. How we weep for her. Now she's getting a taste of her own medicine.'

'The brave Boers are giving her a bloody nose, eh, *Belle Nelly*?'

But their model was beautiful and warm-hearted, they did not tease her for long.

Edith was having a worse time. The cast of the Feu Follet

looked as if they hated her when she went in through the stage door and two of the chorus girls picked a fight with her, or tried to. One scratched her, the other pinched her arm. She showed Nelly a large greenish bruise.

'For Lord's sake, Edith! Pinch her back!'

'Be realistic. Both girls are over six feet tall, I wouldn't stand a chance. How is Mr Ayrton taking it all?'

'He's a misery. I don't know how to cheer him up.'

'It is best not to try.'

Nelly thought the advice ridiculous.

She was relieved when Maître Guelle obtained a commission for Matthew to paint the portrait of a rich patroness of his.

'She lives in Versailles, and her husband wishes the portrait as a gift for their twenty-fifth anniversary,' said Maître Guelle. 'You are the best portrait painter of my acquaintance who will not charge a high fee, Monsieur Ayrton. For myself,' he spread out his hands, 'I can scarcely paint the lady as a member of a seraglio.'

Matthew left the Rue Saint-Sauveur early, and was away all day. When he returned, and before she had to leave for Chez Paul-Marc, Nelly, exuding cheerfulness, waited to hear the news.

'Well? Did you like her?'

'Not much.'

'What sort of a person is she?'

'Stout, fiftyish. Self-satisfied.'

'Why shouldn't she be, she's rich. So what dress are you painting her in?'

'White satin patterned with red flowers. It is her husband's favourite. I asked her to wear all her jewels.'

'Mmm. If she's fat, better without them.'

'Jewels are a symbol, Nelly.'

He did not say that when he painted Nelly he was in sympathy with her, just as when he painted the cobbler. But to paint somebody rich, he would concentrate on the fine texture of her clothes, the sheen of her hair, textures and forms of the tangible world. Not much of the spirit.

'I daresay it's interesting to paint diamonds and pearls,' said Nelly, and they began to talk about painting.

That night he made love to her as if it was the first time.

Saint Nicholas was carried away by the window-dressers, and in his place were put stately waxen ladies in balldresses, and gentlemen standing by long festive tables ranged with bottles of champagne. Balloons and streamers were stretched across the windows, and lettered in gold was: 'NOUVEL AN! NOUVELLE SIÈCLE!'

Imagine, thought Nelly, in three days' time it will be *1900*. She marvelled at the odd idea. Before setting off for work that morning, she decided to run down the hill for Matthew's newspaper. He had already left for Versailles and might return early, the painting was almost finished. It was needed for the couple's wedding anniversary, and he had had to work faster than he preferred. Nelly had noticed that, although Matthew disliked the newspapers, he couldn't stop himself from reading them. When he saw one in the studio his expression sometimes reminded her of her mother's when spying a bottle of brandy. Best let him get it over before I come home, she thought.

It was icy cold and trying to snow, and she borrowed his long knitted muffler, tying it round her head in place of a hat. It smelled of him, and of the bay rum he used. She ran all the way down to the kiosk, the wind blowing grit from under the trees, bought the paper and hurried back up the hill. A strand of hair blew in her eyes and she gave ineffectual dabs to push it away, thinking – I must wash my hair after work. There might be enough water for a bath in front of the stove and I could do his shirts in the water. His collars get so filthy.

The studio felt lonely as she came indoors. It was always like that when he wasn't there. But his paintings were lined up along the walls and when she looked at them it was like hearing his voice.

She stood unconsciously pressing the newspaper against her breast, thinking about the man whose presence, in her body, her soul, was stronger than the smell of the scarf. She stared across the studio at the watercolour of the huge elaborate house. Pinnacled. Set about with trees. My God, she thought for the hundredth time, it's enormous. How can he be happy here after living there? I'll never understand him. I wonder what his Ma is like, he doesn't talk about her. That's because he loves her too much. So we're back not talking of things in case they hurt, eh, Nelly my girl?

She went to the window, squatted on the floor and spread out the paper, turning its pages.

And then she saw Matthew's name.

CHAPTER SEVEN

With the disappearance of Matthew Ayrton, Society settled back with relief. London was at its opulent best during the Season. The idle rich were busy indeed. Invitations and reminders to ensure guests had not forgotten slithered through letter-boxes in Mayfair and Belgravia. During the day, Hyde Park was crowded with horsemen and horsewomen riding thoroughbred hacks. As the evening approached and the golden afternoon light bathed the huge old elms, the last riders trotted home. Broughams and calèches stood waiting at doors, red carpets spread their ribbons across pavements. The big squares were empty except for a few ragged children. Nelly had once thought of joining them, to gawp at jewelled women crossing the carpets to their carriages.

Robert Leckford was seen a great deal in Society during the Season. He was titled, eligible and good-looking. His figure stood, as it were, with a tapestry of glory behind him. He accepted many of the invitations, yet he was never easy, as his brother had been; he hid a nervous shyness. But it did not occur to him to escape the tyranny of social engagements. When his servant helped him to dress, Robert vaguely felt that by going to tonight's ball, dancing with tonight's debutante, he was doing his duty. Atonement by dancing.

What made this first Season without Matthew more of an ordeal than ever was not only what had happened to his brother. More selfishly, more painfully for him, Robert could no longer escape into sex. Something had happened to him the night Gertie Jewell died. His taste for whores died, too. It was as if he'd been possessed by a lustful demon of sexual enjoyment, and the thing came out of his body the moment the girl was killed.

He was sexually empty. He wanted no woman and when he flirted from politeness and saw their shining eyes, he was sorry for the young girls.

He never returned to Madam Ruth's, and never walked down St James's. He forced himself to forget Gertie's sweet vacuous face and lovely willing body. In his thoughts there was a blanked-out part like a minor amnesia. A bruise upon the mind. But his love for his brother and a haunting guilt were not banished and, as time went by, the thought of Matthew hurt more, not less. He had lost him. They could never have a life together again.

The threat of a coming war, which Matthew, Nelly and Edith heard in Paris like distant thunder, was louder and more ominous in England. During the Season, people talked of it too much, and the arguments that resulted were bitter. It was the first time in the Old Queen's long, long reign that opinion had been so violently divided. To the old guard it was a blasphemy that people of the upper class believed England should not fight.

Honoria Leckford's old friend, Jack Ashley, was talking to her about the probable war on a warm evening in late September. They sat on Leckford Court's terrace in the late sunshine, the wall of the old house at their backs radiating a warmth absorbed from the bright day just gone by. Jack Ashley, Robert's godfather and a distant cousin, was nearing seventy, a Général in the Seventh Fusiliers and tough as leather, the epitome of a Victorian soldier. Honoria sometimes wondered if the bluffness and bluntness, the way he stuck out his formidable chin, the diehard opinions, were the least interesting parts of the man. Years ago, so long that it seemed hard to believe it had happened, he'd been in love with her.

'My younger boy –' he began, looking across the lawns.

'Yes, yes, Jack, I am not senile. You are speaking of Guy. What about him?'

'I do beg your pardon, Honoria, it is just that when one

speaks of one's offspring most people don't listen. Guy, now. He's getting himself right and ready. And costing me a king's ransom.'

She raised her grey eyebrows.

'What do you mean? Is he to be married?'

'No, no, my dear. Getting himself ready for the war! Best pigskin luggage from Tom Fry's. You never saw such workmanship. New gun from Purdeys. And so on. It's a lot of money, I have to admit, but the boy must be prepared for the fray, what?'

She was silent for a moment.

'My dear Jack, there may never be a war.'

'My dear Honoria, you already know that there will.'

She wondered whether Jack Ashley's pleasure in what he called a good scrap – on his return from India he had described the North-West Frontier fighting in just those terms – affected his judgement. She changed the subject, and asked his advice about her rambler roses.

The General, who put the same energy into growing flowers that he had used to do in military campaigns, was about to spring up and inspect the flowers on the walls behind them when there was a step on the terrace. The two elderly people turned and saw Robert.

He was in travelling clothes. The greenish colour of the tweed suited his dark looks and his mother, in her surprise at seeing him, had a moment of sheer admiration. He kissed her hand and greeted his godfather.

'I am sure you're both wondering what I am doing here,' he said pleasantly. But his voice was tense. 'I left Locharne yesterday. I've been thinking a great deal over the last few weeks about the trouble in South Africa . . . that sort of thing . . . and I've finally made up my mind. I'm going into your regiment, Sir.'

'*My dear chap!*'

Jack Ashley went the colour of beetroot with pleasure. 'What news! What first-class news, eh, Honoria? That's what I call a decision. Something young fellows of our sort will all

107

be making. Going to the wars, eh? Wish I could join you to take a pot shot or two. Well, well, well.'

Robert accepted the congratulations with a strained smile. He found it nauseating that war should be treated as a sport; his godfather might have been talking of a pheasant shoot. He glanced at his mother. She echoed Ashley's good wishes. But when she poured him some tea, her hand shook.

Two hours later, knowing where he would find her before the dinner gong, Robert made his way through the many interlinked rooms until he reached the Long Gallery. It was one of the house's glories, with an elaborate ceiling of Jacobean plasterwork, windows glowing with the family arms in 18th-century stained glass, the walls crowded with precious books. Honoria walked there every day, pacing up and down and saying her rosary – a small solitary figure in black.

'Mother, forgive me. I am disturbing you.'

'No, no, I've only just begun.' She lifted the ivory beads, her fingers clasping the fourth in a total of fifty-five.

'About my going into the Army.' He fell into step with her. They walked together towards the far windows. 'I hope you don't disapprove of my decision.'

When she looked up at him, her face, lined with wrinkles like crushed tissue paper, was old and set.

'You said you have been reflecting about it. You must follow your conscience, do what you know is your duty.'

The worn-out phrases gave him a spasm of the heart. She meant every word of them and they were threadbare.

Walking beside her, up and down, up and down, he said nothing for a while. The only sound was the swish of her silk dress. Then there was a solemn chime from a grandfather-clock somewhere in the depth of the house. The gallery smelled of beeswax, of ancient furniture, of the dust that lingered in tapestries, of the books, and the pot-pourri in a huge Chinese vase nearby – but that was dusty, too. He was filled with passionate love for the little person beside him, stiff-backed, and frail and almost pitiless. And he loved the house, its silence, its secrets, its grace. He had a tormented longing to tell his mother the truth at last. He loathed his own hypocrisy. He would pour out the story of Gertie, and why he'd never married, and speak of Matthew's courage and his own guilt. And then she would see why, because of all these things, he was taking up the alien disciplines of soldiering.

Honoria stood still and put a hand on his arm. She looked at him, radiant with melting love.

'My dear son. My darling child. I am proud of you.'

Less than three months after Robert took up his commission with the Seventh Fusiliers, war was declared. His regiment sailed for the Cape.

Alone at Leckford – Honoria considered herself alone although there were twenty servants – she began to do war work. People in the county gathered at their different houses eager to do everything they could, they planned parcels for the troops, ways of raising money for the wounded – though they were too sanguine to imagine there would be many of those. Honoria did not join the energetic ladies packing tinned foods. She provided money, and occasionally sat on committees where she was listened to with respect. The county treasured her.

She missed her son every day of her life and wrote to him in South Africa once a week; lover-like she wanted to write every day. He was never out of her thoughts and each morning she went to the family chapel across the courtyard to hear Mass for him. And for her own immortal soul, but that came second. The priest who celebrated daily Mass at Leckford was Father Brendan McKenna, a poor parish priest and the least obsequious man of religion Honoria had met in a long Catholic life. She respected him and he irritated her. His parish was some miles away but he managed to come daily – because Honoria sent the dog-cart for him.

Father McKenna thought it a dreadful waste of his time, to spend it on one old woman and her servants. The gardener tolled the bell, Honoria was already on her knees, and the servants trooped out of the house leaving their work unfinished. One scullery maid confided in the priest that she was told to drop the pail and scrubbing-brush when she heard the bell, and run. Father McKenna was absorbed in the troubles of the poor, and life at Leckford Court shocked him. But he had noticed recently that Lady Leckford was anxious and sad.

The letters Robert sent his mother from the Cape and later from the Front were even scantier than those he used to write to Matthew. But he had not written to his brother since joining the Army. For his own reasons.

He took trouble with his letters to his mother but they still did not contain a shred of his feelings or of himself.

> My dearest Mother,
>
> How are you? I am well but last week had a touch of fever. It is too sad about poor Paxton, did you hear he had his pony shot from under him? He's now a prisoner of war.

One letter she particularly treasured because of a little sentence. 'It was so good of you to send my old window-pane checked waistcoat. The nights are very cold. I do hope you are quite well, and not getting grey with anxiety on my wretched account!'

The exclamation mark was to show it was a sort of joke. But they were words of a son who loved her and she pressed the letter to her heart.

Autumn turned to winter. The last winter of the century. Christmas at Leckford Court was quiet except for a few old friends who called to see her. On 30 December Honoria received a telegram. In Natal, Sir Redvers Buller's forces, attempting to cross the Tugela River in a deep valley to relieve Ladysmith, had been repulsed. Ten guns lost. Nearly a thousand dead or wounded. Leading his men into action Robert had been killed by a Boer sniper.

*　　*　　*

Sitting on the floor in the studio, Nelly read of the 'Gloomiest Time in Our History'. And then she saw a name which leaped out as if it was printed in phosphorescent paint.

TRAGIC DEATH OF VISCOUNT LECKFORD

Killed leading his men in attack across Tugela River.

The paragraph was short. Then there was a last sentence. 'The heir to the title is the Honourable Matthew Ayrton.'

A thrill of fear went through her. Matthew's brother, the young man rushing up the stairs after Gertie Jewell, was dead. Matthew had never even told her his brother had gone to the war. He never spoke about him. Perhaps he didn't know. She thought – what will happen? Oh, what will happen now?

He'll leave me. He'll go back to England. It's over, him and me. What will I do without him? The scent of the scarf round her neck filled her with anguish. She thought, I shan't be able to bear it. I'll die. I'll love him and drop dead. I can't bear it.

Scarcely knowing what she was doing, she began to fold up the newspaper. The familiar front page with columns of announcement was uppermost. Births. Marriages. Deaths. And suddenly she recoiled as if hit a second time on an excruciating bruise. For there in the Personal column was Matthew's name again.

> AYRTON. Would the Honourable Matthew Ayrton or anybody who has knowledge of his whereabouts please get in touch immediately with Messrs Dobie and Dobie, Solicitors, 18, Rue de l'Arcade, Paris.

She looked at it. Paused. And then, with the newspaper folded as small as she could make it, went to her own chest-of-drawers and stuffed it under her clothes. He would never look there. They'll find you in the end, she thought. But not yet. Not quite yet.

When she came home from Maître Guelle's, Matthew was

111

already back and the first thing he asked was if she had bought the newspaper. He did not sound as anxious as usual, and when he came to her, he kissed her.

'Did you manage to go to the kiosk?'

'Of course I did. But the fog's as thick as soup in London, the man said. No papers today. Probably not tomorrow either.'

It was true that London was beginning to be shrouded in fog. That, too, had been in the newspaper. And when Nelly nervously went to the kiosk the following day there were no newspapers from England. She couldn't believe her luck.

'Did you go to the kiosk, Nelly?'

'As per yuge. Still the pea-souper.'

In Paris, it was foggy, too. Foggy and bitterly cold. Matthew, unconsciously relieved from the guilt and anxiety about his country, took Nelly in his arms every night. Woke her in the middle of the night to take her again. For Nelly this possession, this man pressed into her, giving her almost unbearable joy, this man who knew how to make her hover on the verge of her climax yet still not come until he said she must, all the things he did to her, all the things she received and returned, were more poignant and ecstatic than ever before. Four days after she'd learned his brother was dead, the English newspapers were again at the kiosk. Nelly bought *The Times* and stood in the street, trembling while she looked at the front page. There it was. The same advertisement. The same: 'AYRTON. Would the Honourable Matthew . . .'

She threw the paper away.

When they had first begun to live together he had told her that nobody in England knew where he was.

'How do you get letters, then?' Nelly had been curious. She had seen him reading one, although he hadn't spoken of it to her. 'And what about money? Do they send any?'

He was not offended by the vulgarity of the question and said that 'they' did not send him a farthing but he had a very small amount of his own. The only letters he received were from his brother, he'd briefly added, *poste restante*.

112

She always knew when one of those arrived. He was quiet afterwards.

With the thoroughness of a criminal, Nelly decided to call at the post office to collect any letters. She toiled across Paris to the main post office by the Hôtel de Ville, made up a cock and bull story about Matthew being ill and was refused the letters. 'One must have the authority, Mademoiselle, a letter from the gentleman giving the necessary permission. His identity card too.' Nelly saw a packet of letters in the pigeonhole waiting for him. They scared her as much as the advertisement.

She supposed what she was doing was wicked. She didn't care. What was more wicked was to tear them apart. The idea of losing him filled her with terror. Her love-making became so violent that he was excited and mystified.

But she had to tell somebody and there was only one person in the world she could trust. Edith was waiting at the Atelier one evening, muffled in the chrysalis of the coloured shawl. Nelly, thinner than a week ago, broke into a smile of relief.

'You're a sight for sore eyes. I keep thinking of you.'

'That's a nice welcome. I know it's been ages but Réné had a cold and behaved as if it were pneumonia. Men are such babies. He made me brew a tisane with dried nettles and then said his mother always made poultices with boiling water and wet bread,' said Edith, giving a burst of laughter which ran in four notes up the scale like music. Nelly was glad to hear it. Glad that anybody could laugh.

She waited until they were in La Théière, then, unable to eat or drink, burst out with the story. She felt the relief of a Catholic in Confession and waited humbly to hear the penance she wasn't going to obey.

'You'll say I've got to tell him.'

'Of course you can't. You're in love with him.'

'You think me a bitch. A wicked bitch.'

'How could I?'

'They'll find out in the end. Where he is.'

'Maybe not for weeks,' said Edith, looking at her friend's face, 'unless they get the French police to help.'

113

Then Nelly was really scared.

'But wouldn't that take time, too? Oh God. I don't know anything any more.'

Edith pressed her hand. Her passionate partisanship was for Nelly. She had met Matthew Ayrton once or twice and liked him as a pleasant upper-class man with good manners and the usual reserve. He did not attract her. And she thought he did not appreciate the jewel, so shining with life, at times so beautiful, whom he was lucky enough to possess in his bed. And who, poor thing, had *him* in her heart.

'Don't be too upset, Nelly. It's done now and you must stick with it. Even if it is not for very long you will have had a few extra days or weeks, won't you? That's what you did it for. I mean, it's worth it. Isn't that always how it is with love?'

Edith knew about love, she had read poems and great classical romances, she understood its pain and had never been in love. Réné knew, though. He said he'd walk barefoot in the snow across Paris to spend five minutes with her.

Comforted by Edith's acceptance of her crime, Nelly walked back to the Rue Saint-Sauveur. Matthew had gone for a final session at Versailles, and before he left he had said, 'Shall we have *blanquette de veau* to celebrate? I'll buy some wine. I shall get paid today.'

'Will she really be finished?'

'Every last ounce of her. The pearls. The satin dress. The eyes like raisins, and even the rosettes on her shoes. Her feet bulge out a bit.'

'Have you painted that?'

'An indication, anyway. One must be truthful, eh?'

'In painting, yes,' replied Nelly.

With Matthew not home yet, Nelly carried up her basket of shopping: the onions, carrots and veal and branches of bay leaves, and put them on the bench. She felt more cheerful after talking to Edith. It was Monday and she was not singing at Chez Paul-Marc that night. She tied on her apron with a satisfied sigh and, when the doorbell rang, ran laughing to the door, thinking it was Matthew with his arms full of bottles and maybe some flowers.

A dapper, sandy-haired man stood at the door. He wore a frock coat, the lapels faced with satin, his top-hat held in one gloved hand. In the other he had a leather attaché case. Something about him was utterly un-French.

'Is this Mr Matthew Ayrton's residence?' he said in a loud voice and an execrable accent.

'Mr Ayrton lives here,' replied Nelly in English. It was dark outside, and he stepped slightly nearer.

Her heart was pounding.

The man looked surprised at hearing his mother tongue.

'Is he at home, if you please?'

It was clear by his manner, the unmistakable manner she had not met since she left Miss Fisher, that he thought her a servant.

'No, he isn't,' said Nelly, rude from fright, and was about to slam the door in his face when she saw Matthew coming up the road. The stranger must have guessed who it was, for he went straight up to him and said in English that he was a solicitor. As they approached the front door he added he would 'be most grateful for a few minutes of your time.'

Matthew looked angry at the intrusion. Nelly followed both men into the studio.

'Please sit down,' said Matthew icily to the visitor. Nelly, feeling sick, took a chair at a distance.

'I am the bearer of tragic news,' the solicitor said in a colourless voice, addressing Matthew. 'I wish there were some better way of breaking it to you. Your brother is dead. He was killed in South Africa six days ago.'

What happened was very terrible. As Nelly watched, Matthew's whole face blanched, then went almost green. He looked as if he himself were about to die.

After a moment's awful silence he said, 'When exactly did it happen?'

'On December the 30th, my lord.'

For a second, Nelly didn't understand. Then she thought – Christ, he means Matthew.

The man spoke in a reverent voice, which now and then lost its undertaker's tone. He glanced in her direction once, as if to indicate she should leave. He was soapy and she couldn't bear him.

Matthew listened to the bald facts about his brother's death. He hadn't known, he said, that his brother was in the Army. When had he joined? He asked the name of the regiment and Nelly, astounded, thought what the hell does that matter. The solicitor spoke of the Tugela River battle and added that there was a letter from the Viscount's Colonel which had been sent to Leckford Court.

'I must explain that I am one of the younger members of our firm. Mr Dobie, Senior, is anxious to meet you. Most anxious. We represent your own lawyers in London, but we have offices in Paris, my lord. Mr Dobie wonders if you would be good enough to call at our offices just by the Palais de Justice. When it is convenient, of course.'

Matthew nodded. He said nothing for a moment.

'How did you find me, Mr Dobie?'

'It has not been easy, Sir. Not easy at all.'

Dobie's voice grew louder; he no longer behaved as if he were at a funeral. 'Especially when we received no reply to letters sent to the *poste-restante* number which Mr Walter Smythe gave us. There was also the matter of our advertisements. We have been advertising in *The Times* to ascertain your whereabouts. The news of your brother's tragic death, of course, was in the newspapers. You do not take them, apparently, my lord?'

'Of course I do. But the papers have been held up by the London fog.'

Dobie gave an incredulous smile.

'Surely not. The fog lifted some days ago.'

For a moment, a single pause no longer than a heartbeat, Matthew did not understand. He was thinking only of Robert. He would never see that dear face again. The very name, Lord Leckford, was Robert's name, their father's name, not his. He turned to Nelly for the first time as if seeking consolation. She

116

was as crimson as if she had been thrown into scalding water. Her face burned to the roots of her hair.

He stared at her. Then looked away.

He agreed to call the following day at the solicitor's office. He saw him out, waiting as the man walked down the hill, probably to a waiting cab. He returned to the studio.

Nelly hadn't moved, but her blushes were ebbing.

Matthew shut the door carefully and leaned against it, closing his eyes. His face was broken with suffering, she had never seen such a look. She was trembling. At last, as if dragging himself back from somewhere else, he said, 'What did you do?'

'I hid the papers. I hid them. I didn't want you to know!' Then, reverting to her years of poverty, 'Hit me. You want to. Why don't you hit me?'

He looked as if he didn't know her. All he could think was that this creature had concealed Robert's death. How could she have done such a thing? Robert was dead when we made love this morning, last night, all the days just gone. Every time I took her – *she knew*. He gave a shudder and walked out.

He went into the misty road and Nelly ran after him, shouting and weeping and trying to catch hold of his arm. He shook her off so roughly that she stumbled and fell. He did not look round, did not hear her. Almost running he went, high-shouldered and thin and without a coat, down the steep hill away into the wilderness of Paris.

Part II

CHAPTER EIGHT

It was a day for sailing. The wind was brisk but not so strong that it could mischievously blow mainsails into the sea and capsize the smaller craft. It was lively enough to fill spinnakers like snowy balloons, to cover the sky with a few racing clouds, and whip pink into the cheeks of the girls who were gathered like a bunch of flowers on the terrace of the Yacht Club.

Cowes shone in the sunlight and so did the marquee, with the tables set out and looped with trails of smilax. Mourning and half-mourning for the Old Queen was over and Matthew noticed how women now were dressed as if there was a permanent summer. The dark colours (suited to grief and London fog) were gone. Dresses were flimsy and fragile, easily spoiled by a few raindrops, just as shoes were totally unsuited to walking. Women's clothes had become delicate and luxurious. It was very charming, he thought. All soft creams and greens and the pale delicate shades of wild roses.

He had set up his easel as far as possible from the marquee; he would have preferred to paint in the solitude of a private garden, but the view from the Club terraces was superb. And, besides, he was at present escaping from his hostess. Ambrosine Wilton had taken him under her wing two years ago when he returned to England. She liked to keep him there.

At first she had been the only member of Society who had come to Leckford Court to see him, appearing in black for his dead brother, and offering her cheek for a kiss.

'I've decided,' she said, after kindly remarks of sympathy, 'to get you back into everybody's good books. You must leave it to me.'

Ambrosine had known the Leckfords all her life. Matthew rather liked her, she made him laugh. She was a stylish forty-five, worldly, unfaithful to her elderly husband when she had the chance, and hard as a diamond. She greatly respected Honoria and was fond of declaring that Matthew's mother was 'a sort of saint.'

To get Honoria's son (whom the old lady, she knew, quite detested) accepted again in Society was a challenge. Ambrosine was sure she would succeed. She sensed that the rigid rules of the past would soon be as dead as the Old Queen. *Comme il faut* was not the unbreakable law it used to be, and this indefinable change came from the King. For all his majesty, he chose rich, cosmopolitan friends, whose reputations were scarcely white as snow, and he himself had a succession of enchanting mistresses known even to the wronged Queen.

Memories, decided Ambrosine, would be short. Matthew was now a catch and almost too attractive. He attracted *her* and she made this evident in a subtle way. So far, Matthew, who hadn't missed what she had in mind, had avoided becoming what he thought of as a male whore.

This afternoon he was painting a sea and landscape, a change from his usual work with figures. He had begun on the water scattered with yachts, the sky's flotilla of clouds, but had only sketched in the figures grouped on the lawn. He was absorbed in the problem of the sea's varying blues and greens when a voice said, 'I consider that real pretty.'

The accent was American. A girl was looking at him from under the shady brim of a hat garlanded with poppies and wheat. She was very pretty and very confident and, for a moment, something in her smile, vital, sexy, reminded him of the lost Nelly Briggs. This, however, was no London-born urchin but a poised, doubtless wealthy young lady.

'I'm glad you like the painting,' he said dryly. 'But there is something wrong about it.'

She put her head on one side and considered the canvas.

'I don't reckon there's a thing wrong with it.'

'It would be better if I could get rid of that beastly great yacht in the foreground.'

She burst out laughing.

'I can't agree about that since the beastly great yacht belongs to my father.'

She waited for apologies. The fancy politeness of the English tickled her.

'As the yacht belongs to your family, you'll agree on how appallingly large it is.'

'But size is just what we like. Do you sell your paintings, by the way? I might want to buy that one when it's finished. I said to my sister – she's the one in pink – that I'd bet a dollar you're a professional.'

'How does one define a professional, Miss – ?'

'Vandermeyer. Frances. I'm called Fran.'

There was not a simper in her.

'And I can answer that. My papa says you can call yourself a pro if you've made a hundred dollars at whatever you do. Don't matter if it's plumbing or painting. Admit it. You've made more than a hundred.'

'A little more.'

'How English you are. In the States a man would tell. Probably increase the figure a good deal. Are you ashamed of your profession?'

'No. It mystifies me.'

She gave him a laughing look. She really was remarkably pretty, with a shining look of good health and youth as strong as scent. Her eyes were wide apart and blue as chips of sapphire. Her cheekbones high, her chin small and neat. She looked amused, not only by Matthew and the people at the far end of the lawn and her father's imposing yacht moored in the harbour nearby, but by the world and most of all by herself.

'I know who are you,' she remarked. 'I was only funning about you being a pro, though you paint well. You're Viscount Leckford. Ambrosine has told us about you.'

Since it was now out of the question to go on painting,

Matthew began to clean his brushes, stacking them in the wooden travelling-box he used out of doors.

'So we have mutual friends, Miss Vandermeyer.'

'One or two. Which reminds me, Ambrosine and Bernard are dining tonight on the yacht you so dislike, and *you* are supposed to be coming too. Didn't she say?'

'I am sure she did. You must forgive me,' he finally came round to an apology. The truth was he rarely listened to Ambrosine's social chat and simply went where he was taken. Most of her friends were his own, and all were amusing when he was – as now – in a good humour.

'Oh, I daresay you can't count the Americans who want you for dinner, Lord Leckford. And can't sort 'em out either. Well. Tonight it's us,' said the girl. 'And now I must go, for I spy Mother shooting arrows in my direction. She can hit a bullseye at two hundred yards. *Au revoir*.'

That evening in the saloon of the luxurious 1,400-ton *Constance Mary*, the lady after whom the ship was named had dressed for dinner. She shone with a good many diamonds including a brooch she had commanded her maid to sew on to the bosom of her dress for safety. She was now seated upon a divan, looking her two daughters up and down like a judge at a dog show.

'Alice, pull your skirts straight. Frances, button that right-hand glove. I've told you about that slovenly habit before.'

She waited for the girls to do as they were bid.

'I saw you talking to Lord Leckford this afternoon,' she continued, addressing her elder daughter.

'Sure. I liked him.'

'The Leckfords are one of the oldest Catholic families in England. I hope you realise that.'

'He didn't make the sign of the Cross during the conversation,' said Fran.

Her mother shut her eyes and wrinkled her nose in disgust.

'Do not be sacrilegious. I will not have it.'

The usual silence following one of her reprimands ensued. Fran found it hard not to laugh.

The Vandermeyers were a family close-knit by the will of one single member, and that was Constance Mary. She was five years older than Ambrosine and as different from the Englishwoman as chalk from cheese. She hadn't flirted with a man since she had married Lorn Vandermeyer when she was seventeen years old. She was still handsome, without a grey hair on a head dark as a raven. Her parents had been lace-curtain Irish and she had the Irish looks, wide-apart eyes, a broad face and long upper lip, but her nose spoiled the face, it was beaked like a parrot's. Her daughters had inherited the Irish beauty but without the nose. They did not resemble their well-born but rugged-looking father.

Lorn Vandermeyer knew what he was taking on when he married Constance Mary. She blazed with energy, was born to dominate, loved a scrap. 'If I'd been a man I should have been a boxer,' she liked to say, to the horror of Lorn's relatives.

Lorn was tough-looking, he had a rugged Dutch face and a most patrician background. His manner was easy but abrupt, he was wrapped up with his own thoughts and ambitions. He had been born into the real aristocracy of New York, part of what were called 'the old families'. He grew up in a brownstone house near Fifth Avenue which was stuffed with trophies brought back from a Europe his family had often visited and not much admired. The other New York, of blond strong German immigrants, of nervous Russian refugees, the temperamental, handsome and usually poor Irish, the Italian grocers, the clanging cablecars and the noise and mess of Third Avenue – the Vandermeyers were nothing to do with those.

The family were people of leisure. Lorn's father's large-ish income rose and fell with the price of real estate bought by his parents and grandparents. Young Lorn wasn't content with anything so tame. He'd absorbed something from the sparkling air, and shocked his quiet-living parents by investing some money settled on him at twenty-one in a small steel foundry.

Lorn discovered that business excited him. The old families lived in their exclusive world, visited and married each other, talked, not of art or ideas, but of Cousin John and Aunt Agnes. After Lorn began to succeed in a rougher, fiercer world, they talked about him – with disapproval. He was behaving like the new millionaires whom somebody had nicknamed the 'Robber Barons'.

Lorn was disapproved of more when he married Constance Mary, a very young parvenue with flashing eyes and an overdone Catholic piety. The girl was a nobody and they were all set to cold-shoulder her. But the old families with their proud American ancestry and imperturbable social assurance were losing their energy and strength. Already in the 1870s they were beginning to surrender to the new families, who seemed to spring from nowhere.

'Where were the Vanderbilts even five years ago?' wrote a columnist in *Town Topics* in 1877. 'The Astors had just fifteen years the social start. And how many of the swellest of the swell today were anything at all, twenty years ago?'

The New York social world was changing. Until recently birth had been the only entrée. Now wealth opened its high gates, too. And Constance Mary, with the Vandermeyer name and both old and new money, didn't stay outside the gates for five minutes.

Lorn developed a pure American passion for business, and Vandermeyer Steel Incorporated began to rise like the sun and to shine across the United States. Absorbed in the great game, he left the raising of his daughters and the conquest of Society to his wife. She put her assets to good use. She was musical, as many of the Irish were, and she enjoyed the opera. She went to the old Academy of Music at Irving Place, a musical shrine for the old families. But she also went to the new Metropolitan Opera House built by the young millionaires and became friends with many of them. Adaptable, positively splashy, as ambitious in her way as Lorn was in his, Constance Mary became one of the great hostesses, and was high among the magical number known as the 'Four Hundred'.

Fran took it in her stride. The Vandermeyers naturally went to Mrs Astor's ball given in late January, where the hostess, regal in red velvet, kissed them fondly. Supper was served on real gold plates.

As members of the ultra-fashionable young, Fran and Alice were spoiled, written about and, as Fran said 'suffocated with flowers'. The Season in New York began on December the 1st and ended in April, and much of the fun was to be had in a whirl of snow. The sisters went sleigh-riding and skating. The snow lay in a dazzle on the sidewalks or drifted down on to the roofs of the horse-cars. The girls' cheeks glowed like poppies. At the balls, waltzes, quadrilles, square-dances and the cotillion went on until the dancers, breathless, stopped for midnight supper. It was an enchanted life. And in whatever was fashionable and costly, Constance Mary led. She was among the first to build a house in Lenox, Massachusetts, which was soon to rival Newport and Bar Harbour as *the* place to spend the summer. The Vandermeyer house was massive, there was a lake for boating, and elaborate gardens. They spent the summer and the glowing New England autumn there.

This year, however, Constance Mary had ruled that they must all go on a European tour. Lorn, with business connections in most of Europe's capitals, was pleased to agree. The yacht sailed for France. In Paris, the family went to the Opéra, walked under the chestnut trees, and visited Jean Worth, who himself supervised their fittings. In Rome, as leading American Catholics, they had a private audience with the Pope. His Holiness was most gracious, chatting to Lorn, and blessing the bowed heads of the ladies in their black mantillas. They were invited to dine with a Roman Prince. 'Everybody there will be the cream of Roman Society,' Constance Mary told her daughters. 'So I trust you will both do me credit.'

When they arrived at the palace, however, Fran decided that most of the guests were old and ugly into the bargain, including the three cardinals in scarlet to whom there was a good deal of bowing and scraping.

'They were too worldly, if you ask me,' Fran said to her sister, when they returned home. 'Confess. I'd rather have our nice New York Irish parish priests any day. As for that gloomy palazzo . . . well. All I can say is I hope things brighten up in England.'

The family arrived in London for the new King's June coronation but disappointment was in store. The King was taken ill, subsequently he had an operation, and the coronation was postponed. Many of the royal visitors had to leave before the monarch had recovered. It was a great anticlimax and Lorn, bored by royalty, urged his wife to 'forget the whole darned thing.' They would go straight on to Cowes for some sea air.

Constance Mary refused to budge, and the family stayed in London until the August coronation, when the Vandermeyers, leaning from their hotel windows in Piccadilly, waved enthusiastically to a King whose ancestor their own had so determinedly sloughed off.

'Wonderful! Magnificent!' cried Constance Mary.

Fran told Alice later that she didn't agree. 'The King is just a stout elderly gentleman, after all. In fancy dress.'

She never said things like that to her mother, with whom she was always diplomatic – yet there were times when Constance Mary thought she scented opposition. She told herself the idea was preposterous: her daughters obeyed her and so they should. But Fran alarmed Alice once by remarking, 'If it ever comes to a show-down, Sis, don't put your money on Ma winning that boxing match she's always talking about.'

Now, as their mother swept out of the saloon, Fran looked at her sister and made a face.

'If you were a dog, you'd show the whites of your eyes. You always do when Ma sounds off.'

'I can't help it.'

'Darling, I know. But don't let her see. When she picks on me, I'm ready. One look at you and she's marching over you in hobnailed boots.'

'You shouldn't talk that way.'

'For pity's sake! She does walk over you. But if you don't mind, I'd best mind my own affairs and wash my hands of you.'

'Oh, Fran!' exclaimed Alice piteously. 'Don't do that.'

Fran patted her sister's hand. Privately she despaired. You couldn't put gumption into Alice and perhaps if you did it would change her and she wouldn't be the lovable goose she was.

Their mother reappeared, to give the girls her usual evening lecture on behaviour. They'd heard it a dozen times since coming to Europe. They must sit properly. Not sprawl. Their manners were too free and easy. Hadn't they noticed the way English girls were? Reserved.

'You mean prim and prissy.'

'Frances, we are in Europe and not in New York. Your father and I brought you over here for your education. I trust you will both benefit from the trouble and expense of it all.'

She walked over to rearrange a strand of Alice's hair, shoving in a hairpin which practically skewered her scalp. Catching sight of her husband on deck, she swept out again. Fran made a second and more hideous grimace and Alice couldn't help laughing.

'What does she mean, brought us over for our education?' whispered Fran. 'She's on the look-out for husbands in ermine topcoats and coronets with strawberry leaves. What'll she say when we turn 'em down?'

'We might fall in love,' murmured Alice, unfurling a little fan. She was looking downwards, her long eyelashes delicate as the antennae of a butterfly. Fran's love took the form of wanting to give her a good shake.

'I tell you, Sis, I shan't fall in love with an English lord if he's muffled to his nose in ermine.'

The dinner party on the yacht went well. Constance Mary was an excellent hostess, the music was good and the young people danced on a deck strung with Chinese lanterns. Lorn was busy with two German colleagues, he was in excellent

129

humour and danced twice with Alice, while Fran was whirled round by the tall Englishman, Viscount Leckford. She appeared to be enjoying herself.

When the party broke up it was almost two o'clock, the night warm as new milk, the moon an extra lantern in a sky thrown with stars.

Constance Mary was already in bed in their state room when Lorn came into join her. He wore a brocade robe, and went to the chest-of-drawers to arrange his usual line of sovereigns in a neat row. Then bent to brush his hair. Everything about the short, tough-looking man was as clean as a baby, his hair, skin, his rounded fingernails, the very look of him. Constance Mary had found this irresistible when she was seventeen and still took deep satisfaction in it. Leaning against her pillows, she spoke of Lord Leckford. What had Lorn thought of him?

'Not bad-looking in an inbred kind of way.'

'Very much the aristocrat.'

'I thought you Irish Paddies didn't like the English,' said Lorn, to tease.

'His family have been Catholics since before the Reformation!'

'Have they, then?'

Constance Mary disapproved of his tone.

'It is nothing short of a miracle when you remember all the hanging and dragging the faithful to be burned alive. The atrocities of the Reformation,' said Constance Mary, who had been reared on books about priests martyred at Tyburn. 'Makes one shudder to remember.'

'Both sides did a deal of hanging and dragging, Connie.'

'Lorn! The Leckfords kept the Faith!'

'Well, well,' he said, climbing into bed and putting his arm round her shoulders. 'Which of our girls is to be Milady Leckford?'

'Fran, of course. She'll soon be twenty-one,' said Constance Mary who thought Fran was getting elderly.

Matthew had much to think about after the dinner on the

Constance Mary. Nowadays there were always problems, and they distracted him from painting. It was curious to think that two years ago, apart from his anxiety over the South African war, he had had no worries save the desire to paint better.

Lying in bed in Ambrosine's comfortable house within sound of the sea, he put out his candle and lay looking at the moonlight shining through a gap in the curtains. His worries were a thicket of thorns and he pushed his way through them, bleeding, to a place of pleasure. For a long aching time he remembered Nelly in his arms. How he'd wronged her. Taken so much. Given so little. He thought of the nights they had made love so passionately, when they had loved a third, a fourth time. Something in Nelly, some generous, pliant, infinitely sexy quality had excited him as no woman before or since. Her turned-up nose gave her face its impudence, her lower lip was so full that he loved to lick and gently bite it. At times she would set out deliberately to make him want her, kneeling down to kiss him into desire. When he looked down, he saw only the top of her thick curling hair, a wicked halo pressed against him. Sometimes she laughed with pleasure when they made love. All the time she'd been his lover, it seemed to Matthew extraordinary that he had had time to paint at all. When he remembered the studio, he remembered only the sex.

He had walked away from her. Savagely angry, totally incapable of telling her so, cut to the heart by Robert's death, he had walked away.

What had become of her?

She was in another man's bed, of course. As poor and merry, as generous and light-hearted, as passionate and pleasured, in another man's bed.

God, what am I doing, thinking about her?

He pushed her away and turned to face the problems which filled his head, like rocks in a dangerous sea.

When he'd come home to England nearly two years ago there had been worse things than his mother's cruelty and his brother's burdens. Robert's body was not returned to the family, he had been buried 'in the field' as they called it. There was something desolate about that.

Matthew looked older now than in his Nelly Briggs days. His face had always been rather lined, now it was haggard. He had not recovered from the loss of his brother and at times sorrow still came over him in a drenching wave. He knew why Robert had gone to the war, why he had died. In expiation. He had thrown his life away in exchange for Matthew's sacrifice. It was a heroic and unforgivable waste. That was the hardest to bear; Matthew could not forgive him for dying.

The behaviour of his mother had been scarcely less bearable when he arrived at Leckford Court. Honoria refused to see him. She remained in her rooms, emerging only to hear Mass at an unearthly hour altered without any consideration for the priest.

Matthew gave her two days, then marched into her boudoir and ordered Keely, her old maid, to leave.

Honoria looked at him with a face of stone.

'Mother. This must stop.'

'What are you talking about?'

'You hold me responsible for his death.'

'Oh yes,' she said, without a trace of feeling.

'It was Robert's decision to fight for his country. It was nothing to do with me.' He lied from pity.

'He went to exonerate our disgrace.'

Matthew gave something like a groan.

'I will not have another war between us, Mother, I will not have it. Robert is dead, and I have to take on the burden, it certainly is a burden, of the family and this house and the estate. I will not,' he finished violently, 'have your hatred as well.'

He was nearly forty years younger than she, and for all his indolence, he was strong. Going up to her he seized her hands. She was too contemptuous to withdraw them. Her rings, there were six, bit into her fingers.

'You must behave,' he said. 'I know how you feel, how you've always felt. Don't bother to pretend there was ever any maternal affection. Oh yes, I proved by that scandal that I'm

132

the sort of man you thought me,' he went on with some heroism. 'But that's over and done with. I repeat, you must behave. If you do not, I shall find some way to force you to do so. Now this place is mine, it would be easy enough. I could close Leckford. Alter your life. You would very much dislike that. If you agree to speak to me in public, to be civilised, *to behave*, we can remain as related strangers. Is that understood?'

It was the first time since her marriage that anybody had conquered her. Her husband, her elder son, had not dared. She had a sort of unwilling respect for the detested man holding her hands. He released her, and she chafed them, finger by finger, removing her rings.

But she was incapable of admitting that she had lost.

'I will pray for you,' she said.

Matthew raised his eyebrows in an expression of ferocious mockery which she pretended not to see.

His ultimatum bore fruit. She must have seen he held every card in the pack because she did speak to him when necessary. Still cold as charity, she sometimes appeared at breakfast to pour out his coffee which the servant then carried to him at the other end of the table. A few mornings after their argument, she breakfasted with him and when the footman, at Honoria's gesture, was dismissed Matthew wondered curiously what she was about to say.

'I have decided to have a memorial of Robert carved for the chapel. The sculptor is coming to see me today.'

'I am glad.'

She took no notice of that.

'I have chosen Mario Abbatista.'

'The Italian sculptor? He is much admired.'

'Yes.'

'But –' Matthew wondered how on earth to say it. 'Doesn't Abbatista cost a great deal of money?'

'I have no idea.'

During the morning it poured with rain. The park and the gaunt winter trees looked drowned. Walter Smythe, the family lawyer, was due to arrive at eleven. While he waited for him, Matthew roamed round the house. The rain outside beat steadily, indoors it was almost dark, and as he wandered into the Long Gallery and then into one of the drawing-rooms, he noticed something he'd never actively done until now – Leckford's state of decay.

When Smythe arrived, the two men went into the Library. Matthew had not seen him for five years. Then he had been personable and middle-aged with a bright eye. Now he was stout and dusty-looking, his thinning hair like string. He fell rather than sat down in a high-backed chair.

Matthew rang for coffee.

'Tea, if you don't mind, Matthew. Good and strong.'

When the tea served in 18th-century Worcester china arrived, Matthew left his. His years in Paris had made him dislike it.

'I'm glad to see you,' Smythe said. 'We had difficulty in tracing you, and one much dislikes using a detective agency.'

An expression of distaste went across Matthew's face. He said flatly that he'd only learned of Robert's death four days ago. Walter Smythe muttered something about tragedy, waste and loss. The trio of words – tragedy – waste – loss – remained floating somewhere. On an old-fashioned desk nobody used was a photograph of Robert in uniform. Handsome. Immortal.

'I want you to be frank with me,' Matthew said, 'about our family money. I can only imagine our finances are in some sort of mess. I cannot talk of this to Mother. She and I –'

'Of course, of course. Honoria is not the easiest person,' said Walter Smythe, who knew exactly how it was.

'Suddenly everything I gave up, which gave *me* up, has descended on me, Walter. This house. Even the responsibility of my mother. You see, I must know how the family stands.'

Smythe was looking at him oddly and Matthew said, 'You're not listening. You've brought news. Worse news. What could be worse than Bob's death, for God's sake?'

'No, no, it is not worse. Difficult, but not worse. I have something for you.'

He opened his attaché case and passed Matthew a familiar-looking envelope. On its underside was the Leckford coronet.

There was something agonising about seeing Robert's handwriting, and the crest in red sealing-wax. For a moment, Matthew couldn't open it.

'Robert also wrote to me,' Walter Smythe said kindly. 'He said he wanted you to show me your letter. And that it has to be seen, also, by Honoria.'

Matthew tore open the envelope. The letter was dated three months ago before he had sailed for the Cape.

My dear Brother,

I've told Walter to give this to you if I am killed in the war. So if you read this, and I'm inclined to put *when* you do, for I have a feeling I shall never come home, you and I will have said goodbye for the last time.

Matt, I can't leave things as they are. I state here, and Walter and Mother will read these words, that it was not you who was responsible for Gertie's cruel death at Granville House. It was I. I had an association with Gertie for two years. She mattered more to me than I can say. I was furiously jealous when she told me she was going to leave me. I frightened her, and she fell to her death. You happened to be in that place by chance, looking for artist's models. You nobly took the blame. For the sake of the family.

Oh Matthew, it is an inexpressible relief to write this at last. I will say no more, for you *know* how dear you are and have always been to me. God bless and keep you.

Your devoted brother,

Robert

Mother *must* see this. R.

Inside his head, inside his heart, Matthew wept. He thought of his brother when they had been children and had stayed by the sea. Robert, barefoot, could run effortlessly across the shingle as if the soles of his feet were like shoes. They had built elaborate sandcastles inside which Robert made a fire, so that smoke emerged from the wet sand chimney. He remembered their fights and jokes, the way they'd laughed so much it was painful, lying helplessly on Robert's bed. He remembered their schooldays, riding with Robert, drinking with Robert. And always, always, Robert shared. Once as children when they were out visiting, Matthew, who had a cold, lost his handkerchief. Robert tore his own in half.

For a while he sat looking at the letter in silence. In the end he passed it to Walter Smythe, tensed for horrified exclamations.

When Smythe put on his spectacles and read the letter he showed no emotion at all. His face was impassive. Feeling leaves the old, Matthew thought, they've seen too much.

There was a pause.

'Well,' said the lawyer, handing back the letter, 'Of course, I knew all that.'

'*What do you mean!*'

'You don't credit me with much sense, do you? Robert was just the sort to go to those places. I didn't believe that trumped-up tale for an instant, although Society apparently swallowed it hook, line and sinker. They didn't know you both as I do. I saw Robert before he sailed. Poor fellow. Poor fellow. He was suffering.'

Matthew shut his eyes.

'Honoria won't take it well, I fear,' added Smythe in a sombre voice.

'I don't intend her to see it.'

This time Smythe was flabbergasted.

'Not show it to her! My dear boy, my dear Matthew, what can you be saying? Why, Robert expressly left this to prove your innocence. What you did for him was noble. You can't go against his wishes now.'

'I can and I will. I shall tell her nothing and nor must you. Do you suppose,' went on Matthew, with a ghastly smile, 'do you suppose the truth would change her? What did poor Bob imagine would happen when she read this? Did he think, poor old boy, she'd feel differently towards me? Yes, it would have an effect. It would rob her of the son she loves.'

He threw the letter into the fire.

There was a long pause. Walter watched the blackened paper until it disintegrated. Matthew was far away. Robert had won a cap for cricket at school. Red and white, with long silk tassells. He wondered if it was still upstairs in the old toy chest.

When they began to talk again, Walter Smythe was blunt.

'The estate's in a bad way. Very bad. Robert sensed it, but Honoria kept Leckford business from him. He was worried about the house, there's an enormous amount of building work that simply must be done. When he tackled her she was evasive. I'm afraid he thought her mean. The fact of the matter is that the estate can scarcely get enough together to pay the salaries. Honoria seems to think money comes out of the air. She inherited so much, d'you see. Can't accept Aubrey frittered away a fortune. Did she tell you she's employing Mario Abbatista to sculpt a memorial to your brother? I'm sorry to speak of that, Matthew, but Abbatista charges a thousand pounds . . . I'm not saying,' Smythe looked round the room, 'that we'll be in trouble in a few months. You can hang on a while longer, I suppose. You could sell the little Rembrandt. But that would be a drop of water in a lake.'

Matthew also looked round. At the dulled gilt of the elaborate ceiling, the chipped plasterwork, an embroidered curtain which had a long jagged tear. Down at the floor where the parquet, rich as dark syrup, had many missing diamonds.

Walter Smythe regarded the teapot, but calculated the tea must be cold by now.

'I'm afraid there's only one thing to be done, my dear boy. It's quite acceptable nowadays. You'll have to marry American money.'

Matthew actually smiled.

But in the weeks that followed, he kept remembering the idea. He could not pretend it was a new one. Even Matthew until his exile had noticed what was called in the United States, 'the export of our American heiresses.' Enormously rich young girls, the daughters of millionaires who had made their fortunes in the mid to late 1800s, were marrying into English society. They had started to come to Europe as long ago as 1880 and now they had arrived like an invasion. Wealthy Americans had long been fascinated by Europe. They came looking for history, for ancient culture, and for similarities between their own world and Europe's; many of these American princesses had married great titles. May Goelet was the Duchess of Roxburgh, Mary Leiter became wife to the Curzon heir. The glorious Consuelo Vanderbilt was mistress of Blenheim Palace and Duchess of Marlborough. Matthew had met all three girls. They were, in their different ways, ravishing. And they were fresher and freer than young English misses.

The American influence was strong nowadays and, to the surprise of the English, the wealthy Americans brought ideas and standards higher than their own. They were civilised as well as rich; many noble families considered that winning a beautiful spirited girl, and re-establishing the family fortunes, was the most excellent of plans. Of course the Americans had their snobberies, too. Their blood ran to the pulse of democracy. They were proud of their own freedoms. But humans were full of paradoxes, and they were delighted to see a well-dowered daughter become a duchess; titles still possessed a mysterious authority.

Matthew decided he had something to offer. A name over four hundred years old. A house which, in spite of its decaying state, was of exquisite beauty and long history. Thinking about it, he thought he could make some girl happy. But she must be rich.

Faced with the idea of Leckford in danger, he was surprised at how deeply he loved the house. Every brick floor, every uneven gallery, every unexpected stairway or stately corridor, and outside in the park, every huge three-hundred-year-old oak tree.

More than a year had gone by since that conversation with Walter. Matthew spent a London Season, thanks to Ambrosine, pretty much re-established in Society. He had gone to stay in a Scottish castle, and returned to winter at Leckford, with the presence of a cold but reasonable mother. A second Season glittered by. But he had not met an American heiress whose dowry might save his beloved house. Until tonight.

Lying awake after the evening spent on the *Constance Mary* Matthew felt that at last there was a chance of restoring Leckford's fortunes.

Twenty-four hours after the evening on the yacht, Matthew was invited there a second tme. Without Ambrosine and her husband. She was not best pleased.

'You are being pursued. Beware, beware, her flashing eyes, her floating hair.'

'Whose flashing eyes? There are three Vandermeyer women, Ambrosine.'

She looked at him cynically. She was dressed for a Cowes morning and, wearing a fetching version of a sailor suit, knew she looked her best. She tapped him on the cheek.

'The fact of the matter, my dear, is that you wish to be caught.'

Constance Mary Vandermeyer never wasted time, and she was soon welcoming Matthew on board the yacht as if the family had known him all their lives. Saying 'I'll just leave you with the gals,' she would trail away to talk to businessmen, other lords, or both. Matthew was pleased to spend his time with Fran and her younger sister. They were refreshing. Fran took the lead. She suggested the trio should go riding, should be driven out on expeditions to see the islands. When there was a ball, and during the short season at Cowes there were several, Matthew's company was divided fairly; he danced with each sister the same number of times. Ambrosine was catty about that.

'A sort of bigamy. If you must have one of them, take the elder. She's a handful, but she has pluck.'

Matthew was attracted to both girls, in a way.

No normally sexed man could stay unaware of Fran Vandermeyer's challenging appeal, the promise of her melting eyes, the figure more rounded and rich than her sister's. Fran was the dashing one, who made jokes no English miss would dare to (probably wouldn't even know). Fran demanded attention and admiration and treated both as she treated the world. Yet, thought Matthew one night as he went to bed late after a dinner party at which he had sat next to Alice, she had charm, too. In certain lights, the girl was beautiful, her face a perfect oval, her hair glinting with golden lights, her shoulders, in a gown sewn with pearls, the colour of cream. There was something wondering and nervous and appealing in the way she looked at him.

And then uninvited came the ghost of Nelly which he had to push out of his thoughts, slamming a door on her naked beauty. One day that spectre would stop haunting him. Wouldn't it?

Constance Mary allowed Matthew's friendship with her daughters to ripen, like a gardener watching a favoured fruit in his greenhouse. When only a few days of the Cowes visit remained, she spoke to her husband. She was in bed first, as usual, and under a nightcap sewn with rosebuds her face was sharp.

'Lorn.'

'My dear?'

The tone was absent.

'I wish to talk to you. About the girls.'

Rousing himself, he sat on the bed near the hillock made by his wife's feet. She moved.

'Matthew Leckford must propose. There's been enough shilly-shallying.'

Lorn rubbed his chin. His eyes, piercing in matters of business, wore the indulgent look of husband and father.

'How many proposals has Fran received since we came to Europe?'

140

'I've kept you up-to-date. What are we discussing those for?'

'Did she refuse them all? I suppose she did, but who were they from? My memory is hazy on this important matter.'

Constance Mary replied that there had been the Austrian prince without a red cent, two Honourables, and Freddie Feasey.

'Isn't he a hero?' was the sardonic question.

'He fought in India and won the Military Cross and bar. What's that got to do with it?'

'I should have thought Fran would like a hero.'

'Well, she didn't and neither do I. You were too busy and had no need to put up with him. Brave or not he drove me crazy. One of those English nincompoops talking about Fran as "that awfully fine filly." In any case I have,' added Constance, straightening the silk sheet, 'refused all the offers for Fran, and a couple for Alice. I told the girls whom I'd turned down.'

Lorn had a moment of wondering if his daughters had objected. Then he remembered their merry faces. But Connie was getting worse. However, it was no good trying to make her behave unless he took her on as a full-time problem. He couldn't do that and run Vandermeyer Steel as well. To tame Constance Mary would need as much time and energy as the whole States-wide business. Well, thought Lorn, I sign the cheques. They're large enough in all conscience. That's my part of the bargain.

'So Fran is definitely going to be a Viscountess, is she?' he said, smiling.

Lorn breakfasted alone each morning at the American hour of six, working in the tiny shipboard study until ten o'clock when the fashionable world began to stir. Constance Mary liked to breakfast in bed, and she enjoyed her solitude. She worked out invitations and acceptances and future arrangements, marshalled her forces. She sent for Fran when she had finished.

Her daughter, looking like a furled green leaf, came into the cabin with a springing step, pulled up a chair and regarded her mother with confidence. Yes, thought Constance Mary, collecting some invitations together as expertly as a card player and putting them aside, you do me credit.

'Lord Leckford has not yet spoken to me, Frances. I sincerely trust he hasn't made an offer direct to *you*.'

Fran's dimples showed.

'Gracious no, Ma.'

'Mama, please. How many times must I tell you. And why hasn't he done so?' asked Constance Mary, perversely.

'I reckon because I don't want him to. He's a man who understands things without you having to say them.'

Constance Mary could not believe her ears.

'Don't want him to? What do you mean?'

'I mean I don't wish to marry Matthew. Or any other Englishman, come to that. They're not my sort.'

There was a dangerous pause.

'That's what I think, Ma,' added Fran airily.

'I do not ask you to think, Frances. I do the thinking. You will indicate to Lord Leckford that you're willing to accept him.'

Here it is at last, thought Fran. What I've been training for, for years. She looked at her mother for a moment, wondering how this despot would take defeat. It did not occur to Fran for a split-second to ask herself who was going to win. She was twenty years old, had inherited her father's astuteness and her mother's will. Her very youth armed her with power: her veins were full of it. She gave a knowing smile.

'It's no good, Ma. Sorry, but it's no good. I shan't do as you say and you're just going to have to get used to it. No – let me speak. What I'm saying matters to you as well as me. I shall be twenty-one next month, and I can do as I like then. I'm going to marry Teddy Oliver. We fixed it before this European trip. I shall marry him when we go back home.'

Constance Mary went as white as a sheet. She shouted and raved. She called the girl names, listing ingratitude and impertinence as if they were mortal sins. She swore Lorn

142

would cut Frances out of his will, she'd be penniless and an outcast and they would have nothing more to do with her. Her rage continued for just about the time Fran had calculated. She listened unmoved and could have pretty well spoken every word beforehand. She had been in her mother's company, or to be exact had been her mother's creature, for her entire life.

'Ma,' she said when Constance Mary, quite hoarse, ordered her 'to get out of my sight and stay out', 'Ma, it's no good you cutting me off without a cent and all that because Teddy and I guessed you would. You forget that Teddy's filthy rich. What's more, his dad is such a friend of Pa's. And what's more still, the Olivers are mighty important to Vandermeyer Steel Inc. You won't win this one.'

Her mother, glaring, reminded her of a bird of prey.

'Stop wanting to kill me,' said Fran. 'I know you've set your heart on a title in the family. What about trying Sis? She likes Matthew and I'm sure he likes her. And she isn't engaged, is she?'

Early every morning Matthew went riding on the Downs. Ambrosine had provided a reasonable hack; it was good to be in the fresh sea air. And he escaped the elaborate breakfasts. The horse was fresh and glad to be out, too; they quickened to a gallop. Matthew finally reined in where the stretch of green turf overlooked a calm sea. He was walking the horse, the reins looped over his arms, when a voice said, 'Greetings.'

He had not heard hooves on the soft grass and looked up to see the object of his thoughts, Fran Vandermeyer, poised on a bay mare, impeccable as a duchess. Before he could offer her a hand she'd slipped down skilfully.

'I've been following you, Ambrosine told me where you ride. Your movements fascinate your hostess, Matt. Everything you do is her favourite topic. You've made a conquest there.'

'There are other conquests one would welcome more.'

She laughed, showing her dimples.

'Don't be so predictable, Matthew. You don't need to be.

143

However, I can't pretend I haven't noticed that you've got your eye on me, can I?'

'It's more than that.'

He meant it just then.

She gave him a friendly look. She liked the tall haggard man. If it were not for a far tougher and more exciting person back home, somebody who made her bones turn to water, she might have considered this one. But as things were he didn't have a dog's chance.

'Listen. I have something to say, and no, don't take my hand, I wish to swing free. I plan to marry a certain person when we go home in a few months. The sooner the better. I love him dearly. His name is Wendell Oliver. Teddy. I didn't tell my father or Ma when we became engaged, or Alice either. I thought the trip to Europe would be more fun and more peaceful if I saved my bombshell until we got back. As it is . . . well . . . as it is, you hove into view and I know what you're thinking, Matthew, and it won't do.'

'I see.'

'You're doleful. Don't be. You are not in love with me, you just think we'd make a match. We might have done if it weren't for Teddy. My heart is quite quite full of him, you see, there isn't a corner for anybody else. But you are fond of our family, aren't you?'

She didn't say, 'you're fond of our fortune too,' but they both heard it.

'You manage Ma wonderfully, and Dad likes you or would do, if he knew you better. And we're all Catholics which is our great blessing. So . . . why not consider Alice?'

He looked as if his horse or hers had just kicked him. She couldn't help laughing.

'I've taken the wind out of your sails. Alice is a darling, you know, and you might be good for her. You'd be lucky to get such a prize. You haven't considered her, have you? Well, start now. And don't, for pity's sake, ever repeat this, because if she knew my mother would skin me. And as for Alice, she'd die of shame.'

144

He scarcely knew how to be reply. He suddenly hated his own position and the burdens that had weighed on him since Robert's death.

'I wish you wouldn't look so flummoxed. It doesn't suit you,' said Fran. 'We like the easy worldly Viscount. That's the one who intrigues us. Shall we ride? I bet I can beat you. Not a fair race, though. That nag of yours is rather ancient. But who imagined life was fair?'

Matthew's altered course towards Alice was skilfully done. Fran managed to be absent a good deal during the few days the *Constance Mary* remained at Cowes. Matthew and Alice went out driving. He took her to tea with Ambrosine, and to a ball. Alice looked a little strained and shy. The only time she showed much animation was on the subject of her own country. One evening after a dinner party, when she and Matthew were on deck, she burst out, 'English people know nothing about the States! Do you know what Mrs Longstaffe said? She asked me if we had slaves in New York. And how often my parents had escaped being scalped by Red Indians! Oh, I could have – could have –'

'Shaken her until her teeth rattled. I quite agree. I would have helped,' said Matthew. He made her smile, but she was seriously offended.

Constance Mary's Irish rage evaporated over her elder daughter's defiance and she began unwillingly to respect her. She's like me, she thought. She soon became used to the idea of Alice as the Viscountess and almost preferred it. Fran decided not to sound her sister out on the matter. One of Alice's faults was her reserve, another her self-doubt. If I start ranting on about what a good husband he'll make, she'll only get scared. This is something she must make up her own mind about. I did.

In her self-satisfaction and optimism she forgot, for once, that Alice had never made up her mind in her life. Alice certainly liked Matthew and enjoyed being with him. He knew how to give a young girl a happy time, and pleased her by an undemanding, indolent gallantry. But when Constance Mary came into her cabin one night and said Lord Leckford had asked for her hand, Alice was horror-struck.

'*I can't.*'

Her mother's face shut like a trap. Was she to have this all over again? To be defied this time by a silly chit who should be on her knees grateful for a mother looking after her future, and doing her duty as God decreed?

'Alice, I am not going to talk to you if you behave like an idiot. *Can't* marry Lord Leckford? You will do as I and your father tell you. Be grateful you are who you are. Here is a fine man, whose company you enjoy. A great title . . . why, you should be proud. A Catholic who has – has been a defender of the Faith,' went on Constance Mary, quoting something or other.

Her younger daughter sat as helpless as a bird with a snake.

'Learn to behave like an adult,' said Constance and went out, slamming the door.

Fran came in later to find Alice shaking with sobs.

'What's happened? My poor Sis, what's happened?'

'Mother says, she – she says Matthew's asked me to m-marry him.'

'That's good, isn't it?'

Fran was shocked at the sobs.

'I never – never – why, I thought you were the one he wanted,' wept the girl, crying as if her heart would break. 'I can't marry him. I can't.'

Fran reasoned and kissed and chided and embraced. She explained her own engagement, and begged Alice to forgive her for the secrecy. She assured her that Matthew had never been serious over *her*. She did not feel guilty at this, she already half-believed it. But for the first time in her life she could not make head or tail of what was troubling her sister, and why the girl seemed terrified at the idea of marrying such an attractive man. All she knew was that Alice hated the idea. Just hated it.

Fran went to see Constance Mary. Her mother was at her worst.

'Ma, Alice feels –'

Constance Mary looked at her murderously.

'Listen to me. I will not have you coming in here to get me to change my mind. I won't listen to a word of such tosh. Your sister is a fool. Yes, yes, I know all about you marrying the Oliver boy, we'll talk of that later. What I'm saying now is that my decision is made. I have told Lord Leckford she will marry him and that's what she's going to do.'

'But if she doesn't want to, Ma.'

Constance Mary's voice was vicious.

'Tell me,' she said, speaking to an equal, 'do you know, does your father know, do I know, what Alice has ever wanted in her life?'

This time Constance Mary was not to be baulked. She liked Matthew Leckford and he was everything she wanted for a doltish girl who didn't know what was good for her. Fran gave up the struggle. It was on Fran's shoulder that Alice wept, but she never could explain what she had against her suitor. She knew she hadn't a hope of standing against her mother; she had always been frightened of her. Now she was afraid of her sister, too, because Fran thought her so stupid and Fran was so strong.

The pictures her mother, in angry condescension, painted of a huge English house over which Alice would reign, of a life among aristocratic English people, filled the girl with fear and dismay. She wasn't capable of living such a life. Even the New York Season was quite an ordeal, and the idea of meeting all those cold English nobles, of becoming one of them, was infinitely worse. And Matthew was part of it all.

She went to bed early, having sobbed for so long that her eyes were like slits. Mother will be angry again because I look ugly, she thought.

Across the water she heard the wailing of seagulls. Who had said they were the souls of drowned sailors? Alice wrapped herself in a shawl and sat on the bed. Now and then giving a sob, she was writing a last desperate plea. To Fran.

CHAPTER NINE

Somebody once told Matthew that a gentleman was a man who never inflicted pain. The true gentleman avoided whatever might cause the slightest jolt or jar. But he had not merely hurt Nelly Briggs. He had stabbed her to the heart.

When he remembered her, at times with an urgent sexual longing which eventually faded, he knew he had been cruel. He had realised almost from the start of their affair that she'd fallen in love with him. It had showed in her eyes, the way her whole body reacted if he merely touched her arm; it was in her love-making, even in her voice. But Matthew did not think he'd ever actually been in love. He had been excited and attracted by Nelly who was woven into his life then; she had made him intensely happy. But the sadness and need and haunting obsessions of love, he'd never known those for her or any other woman. *She* had felt them. She had been deep in love, passionate, possessive, dangerous emotions to rouse in any woman, and worse he supposed in a girl of the lowest class. He had walked away in anger and grief, leaving her without a sou.

On returning to England he posted her five pounds, folding the money into a piece of his club's writing-paper on which he scrawled, 'For N from M.'

Five English pounds would last her quite a while, and the Rue Saint-Sauveur studio was paid for, a month in advance. There was nothing to reproach himself with. Was there? And besides, she'd go to the next man's bed in a week.

But his judgement of her was wrong. She did no such thing. The shock of losing him left her quite mad with grief. She spent hours lying on their bed surrounded by his shabby clothes. They smelled of Matthew and like a dog she lay on them for comfort. Never for a grief-torn moment did she think he wouldn't come back, that she wouldn't hear his step and look up, waiting to bear his anger and reproaches. It was awful to know how he felt about what she'd done. But he would forgive her because they loved each other. It was frightening to know he must soon return to England. But they would be lovers still.

She would go back, too. Now he was a lord, he would have money. They could find rooms somewhere in London. With her face pressed into his creased jacket she imagined him coming through the door of one of those narrow houses in Seven Dials. She'd be waiting. We'll make love *sometimes*. I'll have him inside me *sometimes*. And I can go to an art school and work as a model and keep myself . . . then back through her wild longings came the remembrance of his stony face and blind eyes, and the way he pushed her from him.

She stayed alone, weeping, falling asleep, eating nothing, saying aloud, 'Oh Matt, where are you? Please come back, oh, please come back.' More than a day had gone by before there was a tap on the door.

Dishevelled and wild, and for a moment imagining it was he, she stumbled across the studio. Edith's small figure, wrapped in the rainbow shawl, stood in the doorway. She looked alarmed.

'He's dead, Matthew's dead, you've come to tell me he fell under a cab –'

'Nelly, dear Nelly, what a dreadful state you're in! Come here. Come to me.'

Edith threw open her arms. They both began to cry; Nelly from dreary grief, Edith from sympathy.

Edith made strong coffee and found some stale bread and jam. She sat on the bed coaxing her friend to eat. Nelly did not need to tell her what had happened. Edith had seen it in the newspaper. She sat holding Nelly's hand, drying her eyes, painfully listening to the broken sobs. And she saw what now divided the distraught girl and the man who was gone – the terrible chasm between passion and ignorance.

Nelly was crazy for her lover, mad with grief for him. But she'd never known the man upon whose discarded clothes she lay trembling. How could Edith persuade her that Matthew was lost? It was like being forced to cut a bullet out of bleeding flesh.

At first Nelly wouldn't believe her, screamed out that Edith was making it worse, why couldn't she go away, Matthew would be here soon – now – this moment. As the terrible hours went by Edith begged her to come back and spend the night with her. Nelly wouldn't stir. So Edith remained, too, leaving the studio only to buy food, and returning to find her friend in an exhausted sleep. Two days later Edith at last made Nelly accept that Matthew was gone and would not come back. She showed her *The Times*, which carried a brief line or two announcing the return of 'the new Viscount Leckford' to England.

Nelly's lover, known as 'cet Anglais' had never been popular at Maître Guelle's. The students resented his reserve and behind his back did grotesque imitations of him. They jeered at the accent they adored in Nelly. What they had disliked most had been that the Englishman had won *La Belle* and taken her into his bed. They were disgusted at their favourite deserting the Parisians for a foreigner. Her own foreignness was not the point.

Picking up the news that 'cet Anglais' had returned to his own country of hypocrites and mint sauce, they were delighted. When Nelly reappeared for work, pale and wan, they crowded round her, kissed her, and declared she was so much better off without him. Somebody spat.

At midday the students dragged her off to La Vache to buy her food she could scarcely eat and absinthe which she never drank. Le P'tit and the big silent overjoyed Patrice reappeared in her life like magic.

Like a drooping flower in fresh water, she revived a little. She had a relapse when, returning to the Rue Saint-Sauveur, where she was staying until the rent ran out, she found all Matthew's paintings had gone. And a receipt from the English solicitor pinned on the door. She cried all the afternoon.

She recovered again, but now her good spirits were by effort of will and did not bubble naturally like water from a spring. She worked extra hours with Maître Guelle, and also agreed to sing on Mondays, when Chez Paul-Marc was closed, at a *café-concert* down the hill, shabbier and noisier than Chez Paul-Marc.

Edith, having tea with her at La Théière, disapproved.

'You ought to have some time off. And it's bad for your voice. Which needs resting, just as you do.'

'I'm strong as a horse.'

'Even horses . . .'

Edith's face was calm in a city of drama and desperation.

'Edith, I've got something to tell you. I'm in the family way.'

Edith started violently. Looking across the table at her friend she saw the curious dimming of her beauty, as if Nelly's young features were out of focus. Why hadn't she noticed it until now?

'Matthew's, of course,' she said.

'I should ✶ ✶ ✶ think so.' Nelly for a moment sounded like herself. 'I haven't looked at a man like that since him. Can't bring myself to. I know poor old Patrice is hoping. No luck for him, though. Anyway, I keep being sick. What a nuisance, eh?'

'I hope to God you are not thinking of getting rid of it. There are some filthy people who –'

'Keep your hair on. I'm *having* it. I want it. Quite surprises me how much I do. I suppose because it's his. Besides, I don't feel too bad. Now you know why I'm posing too long and singing myself hoarse. Any minute and Maître Guelle will take a look at my belly.'

She set down her tea-cup.

'Matthew sent me five pounds. Would you say that's a fair price for having me all those months?'

'He didn't mean it like that.'

'Oh you. You're so fair I don't know why it doesn't kill you. He sent the money as a sop to his conscience. My fingers didn't half itch to tear the note up and send the bits back to Lord Muck as he is now. But I'd missed my first curse when it came. Then the next, so I knew I couldn't afford to throw money in anybody's face.'

Elbows on the table, she outlined her plan. She'd bought a wedding-ring ('chronic, isn't it?') and would be going to Pontoise, where she could get a job in a baker's. Madame Moréas, Paul-Marc's wife, came from Pontoise and said she could arrange it.

'She guessed about me days ago. Eyes like gimlets. Quite kind, though, and says the hospital isn't half bad. So, with the five pounds and what I'm putting by I shall be all right.'

She looked challengingly at Edith.

'What about afterwards? What will you do with him or her?'

'It's sure to be a him.'

Edith said impatiently, 'What will you do as the mother of a baby? You don't seem to have thought beyond Pontoise.'

'Come off it, Edith, that's six whole months away!'

Nelly had never actually chosen any part of her life. What she did was to face the big waves or the calm seas and keep swimming. And when what happened to her was startlingly different, Nelly did not change. Carrying trays in a brothel, dancing the *chahut*, lying in the arms of an English lord, blissful or bereft, she was the same. Ardent and brave and alarmingly philosophical. But Edith thought there were times when you had to take fate by the throat.

'Don't you worry about me, Edith. I'll get some work somehow.'

They said goodbye, kissing in the French way, three kisses. One on each cheek and a third for good measure. Nelly swung off to walk to the café, Edith to her apartment.

As Réné had sadly foreseen, Edith had parted from him. She had explained seriously that she loved him as a friend, but no longer with her body. Proud and angry, refusing her offer of comradeship, he only just stopped himself from clouting the earnest little face. He swore at her, packed and left.

Edith had not seen him since, and although it was rather sad, did not regret it. Since he had gone, she had time to herself. She wanted to think about where her painting was leading her. The things which moved her, the things she needed to express, were close to her own life. The people in a sunny road, the flowers in a vase, a child at a table, a window half-obscured by ivy. She wanted to be in touch with nature and human nature, too. And something hidden. Perhaps its mystery. Perhaps its pain.

After talking to Nelly, Edith worked at her new picture, a scene in the Bois de Boulogne, a sweep of green trees blurred in yellow and green, a dog, a rider. When the light failed, she put her studio into its usual immaculate order, every brush cleaned and arranged in size, the unfinished painting covered with a checked cloth. She had a bath and went into the kitchen to peel some potatoes. She did all this like a woman in a trance . . .

The following morning, spending more than she had budgeted for, she paid for a session at Maître Guelle's, explaining that – if he would forgive her – she just wanted to work for that morning. Maître Guelle liked her and consented. Edith worked in silence, and Nelly stood like a statue, a transparent scarf held in one hand, half-wrapped round one naked leg. She was posing as Salome.

When the four hours were over, Edith waited while the studio emptied as fast as a theatre. In less than five minutes there was nobody left but Edith. Nelly emerged from the *grand placard*, pinning on her hat.

'That's nice. Why did you come?'

'I wanted to be certain of seeing you.'

'I call that handsome. Shall we eat together?'

'I bought the *baguettes* and *Saint-Paul*,' said Edith, indicating her basket.

The two girls, one tall and shapely, the other small and

slight, went out into the square where an intermittent sun turned the ancient buildings into the colour of doves. An artist went by, staggering under a huge canvas. He specialised in scenes of Rome blazing and Etna erupting. Nelly waved at him.

They chose a bench which was the least covered with pigeon droppings, and cut up the cheese, using a studio knife. There was the friendly silence of a picnic.

'I came to see you because I've been thinking,' said Edith at last.

'So I can see. But don't start saying I shouldn't go to Pontoise because I've made up my mind.'

'I wasn't going to. It sounds an excellent idea. Nelly. I want to say something and you are not to interrupt. You know how you chip in. Well, this time don't. About after your baby's born. I think you should both come and live with me.'

Nelly shook her head with such violence that her back hair fell down. Pinning it back, she said loudly.

'Don't be daft. Don't be plain *daft*.'

'What's daft? I might quite like it.'

'No, you wouldn't, you'd hate it and what about Réné?'

'Didn't I tell you? He went last week.'

'Oh, poor Réné, I bet it was your idea –' began Nelly, but it was Edith who chipped in.

'There's no point in talking about that, Nelly. I don't care for him any more. Not as a lover that is, I expect you find it difficult to understand but some women don't need a man all the time.'

'I haven't got one at all.'

'Only because you're expecting. That won't last and – Nelly, do be serious. My idea about you and the baby is good.'

'Daft. A kid squalling. Me crashing about when you want to work. And you're as tidy as a nun. Even Matthew thought I was the messiest creature he'd seen in a month of Sundays. You don't know what you'd be taking on.'

Edith was ready for every objection. The ball of disagreement flew between them. Nelly was a realist. She knew that

Edith was offering her a lifebelt. But she tried not to accept it. Her generosity was stronger than her self-preservation and, besides, life had always given her, among the blows, a caress or two.

Edith knew her friend inside out. She also knew something Nelly couldn't know, which was the idea of having mother and child with her had a strong appeal. She was Scots to the marrow of her bones, Presbyterian Scots. She understood self-denial. She resembled a girl addicted to freezing cold baths in winter, welcoming the moral challenge.

'Listen, and see how sensible this is. I'm at home for hours during the day before I go to the Feu Follet. I can do some of the sewing at home, too. They don't care as long as it's done. Babies sleep in the morning, Madame Gourmelon's does, she puts him in the courtyard and watches him from the window. We can do that. I can paint and still see the baby's all right. You can do your modelling. And in the evening when you sing – I'm sure Monsieur Moréas will have you back – I shall be home. We'll do it in shifts with the baby. I shall *enjoy* helping with him.'

'How do you know it'll be a him?'

When two women with strong if differing characters band together, miracles can be achieved. Nelly and Edith had taken on the almost insurmountable problem of a penniless and pregnant woman with no man to support her. Pregnant artists' models were nothing new in the *quartier*, and nor were the tragedies. Nelly and Edith planned each move. It was Edith's suggestion that Nelly should spend some of the hoarded five pounds to see a good doctor. Edith remembered one from the time she had been a governess.

'Don't forget that wedding-ring.'

'I suppose I must be Madame Briggs.'

'No. Be Madame Ayrton.'

'Why?'

'Because your real name's chalked up outside the café, numbskull.'

'I wish you'd stop being right.'

The doctor examined the new young patient, told her she was in perfect health, that her dates, he was pretty sure, were accurate, and did she wish him to enter her into the (chic) Hôpital de la Sainte-Mère? Nelly, ready for that, said she would be returning home to England.

'There is just one thing I would like to know, Doctor,' said Nelly, looking at the middle-aged man with expressive blue eyes. Like every male in the world he reacted, giving her a smile.

'It's just that, well, it's my first and – and when does it *show*? To my husband, if you see what I mean?'

It was a question the artists' model wanted very badly to know.

The doctor thought his patient charmingly modest and said in paternal tones that he considered with her silhouette her condition would not be apparent for another two months. 'After that there may be a little curve which will naturally increase,' he said. Nelly thanked him. She was mentally calculating that she had eight weeks' more pay.

She returned with the news to Edith. The scent of coffee had begun to make Nelly queasy and she blessed La Théière which hadn't a sniff of it.

'You must give Maître Guelle notice,' said Edith.

'Must I? I thought I'd just vanish.'

'You'll do nothing of the kind. You might need a recommendation later. Give notice tomorrow, and I have thought of the reason you're leaving. You have an aunt and uncle in England. They live in Woking (I'll describe it to you). She had pneumonia and is taking a long time to convalesce.'

'You're a holy liar,' said Nelly with awe.

The *quartier* gave Nelly a wild farewell party. Everybody was crammed into La Vache Enragée, there wasn't a seat to be had and certainly no room for anybody but Nelly's friends. The noise was deafening, the jokes coarse in the extreme. Edith said she would not come, she hadn't the trick of parties.

'You don't know what you'll be missing,' said Nelly.

The party only came to an end when Monsieur and Madame Moréas and Nelly left for Chez Paul-Marc. If it had not been for more of Edith's imaginative falsehoods, the entire *atelier* would have seen *La Belle Nelly* on to the train at the Gare du Nord next day. But the phantom uncle was coming to Paris to collect her, and they were paying a quick visit to Chantilly to see some friends. '*Des gens de bonne famille*,' said Nelly airily.

Whistling at their model moving up in the world, hugging her, and in Patrice's case, his eyes brimming, Nelly left La Vache for the last time. She had a feeling she would never go back.

Nelly was very young, with the broad hips and full figure of a girl of the people. She went to Pontoise and worked well, and when the time came had the baby easily. After the requisite twelve days, she left the hospital with a large healthy baby in her arms. A boy, as she and Edith had predicted. She baptised him a Catholic like his father, called him by Matthew's second name, Thomas, and hung a medal round his creased neck. He was stout and hearty, and, with the shrewdness of a baby who knew how things were, no trouble.

Edith came from Paris on the train once a fortnight, and developed a secret passion and an outward skill with young Tom who was soon giving the girls knowing but impartial smiles. Sometimes when Edith looked at Nelly, she marvelled that her friend had recovered from her lover so completely. The girl seemed to bloom while she watched, her beauty becoming richer. What Edith could not know was that nature had been busy with Nelly, taking from her for the months before the child was born, the weakening grief of love.

After Tom's birth, Nelly was absorbed by the extraordinary, yet everyday, miracle of motherhood. He was a pretty child and she thought him a marvel. The hours when she was working in the baker's shop, and he was in a cot in the kitchen among the baker's tumbling mass of children, Tom was always in her thoughts. Matthew was gone. He had never loved her. She accepted that as women in Blackfriars accepted

157

a blow in the face, with an awful, simple philosophy. When Tom was close in her arms, she had no time to pine.

She stayed in the baker's, handing out fragrant bread in the myriad varieties of provincial France, in batons and circles and figures of eight, dark brown, honey gold or floury and pale like cream. After the baby's birth she soon had to fend off a number of men who came after her, including the future mayor. She was lively and pleasant with them, but extricated herself from their lustful intentions. She concentrated on Tom. He was excellent company.

But eventually Pontoise lost its charm and she began to long for Paris. At the turn of 1901, six whole months since she had left the city, a year since Matthew had gone, Edith came to fetch her. They travelled home by train, alternately passing the bundle in the big white shawl from one to the other, bouncing and rocking him.

'I'm a city girl. I can't pretend I'm not,' said Nelly, with a sigh of satisfaction as they boarded a crowded omnibus for the Butte. She exchanged an insult with a woman who had pushed in front of her.

Nelly's return was not to the same life she had led since her exit from La Vache Enragée. She was a mother, and eighteen years old. These two things, the fact of Tom, and her own insouciant youth, did not strike her when she and Edith came into Edith's apartment. She unpacked her few possessions, every now and then laughing at the handsome child she carried in and out of the studio.

'He's saying, "Where's the bakery? Why can't I smell the fresh bread?" '

Edith made tea and they sat down on the divan, among its handpainted cushions of the kind in almost every studio in Montmartre.

'I must try and get some work right away. Can't go back to Maître Guelle's,' Nelly said.

They had talked about that. Nelly had studied her naked self a good deal with the appraising eye of a girl in the market, assessing its contours. Her body was still beautiful but not as flawless as it used to be. She was not going to risk the raking eyes of old friends.

'I'd best call at other *ateliers*. Or some of the little schools.'

'I know a man who might hire you. But he has very little money. His name's Anselme Rocheville. He paints historical pictures. You'd need to pose in costume.'

'I'd pose standing on my head.'

There was a slight pause. Edith sat watching Nelly who rocked Tom to and fro, humming one of her Cockney songs. Her hair spiralled round her face, she looked peaceful and serene – a Madonna by Raphael.

'We haven't talked about Tom.'

'What do you mean, we talk of nobody else! I don't know how you bear it, with your painting to think about.'

'I like it. Don't be silly. What I mean is – will you tell your friends?'

'Don't see how I can help it.'

'Most of the students have left Guelle's. There's a whole new set. Even Le P'tit has gone home to Aix-en-Provence.'

'Oh ★ ★ ★ . I was fond of Le P'tit.'

'But what about Patrice?'

'Edith. I know what you're thinking and the answer's not a chance. I don't want a lover. All I want is work to keep Tom. And maybe finding a way to improve at whatever I do and earn more. You never know. I've been lucky so far.'

In this mood of optimism she set off the following morning, leaving Tom in his cot in the studio, to call on Anselme Rocheville. The painter had spectacles and a mop of black hair stained here and there with paint. He worked in a dilapidated studio in an alley near the still-unfinished basilica of the Sacré Cœur – Parisians were getting very sarcastic about the church. They said it would never be completed.

Rocheville shook hands with her and showed her his present work, an enormous canvas of Italian figures in what looked like a dungeon or a crypt.

'The Borgias are popular just now.'

159

Nelly asked in a friendly voice which were the Borgias, and he pointed out various figures. One female figure, dominating the foreground, was still a spectral outline.

This turned out, as she guessed, to be herself. She was given a costume far more dusty than anything in Maître Guelle's Grand Placard.

Anselme Rocheville was not a good painter. He worked hard but often lost heart, and despite her magnificent spirits, Nelly in her crowns and velvets found he made her nervous. He was given to fits of gloom, and Nelly's way of catching these was to worry about whether she would be paid.

She did, however, start singing again at Chez Paul-Marc, where Monsieur and Madame Moréas welcomed her back as a long-lost daughter, gave her more songs, but no raise in her salary. Changing patiently from one shabby costume to another, making coffee for Rocheville and privately praying he would sell a painting and hire her for the following week, running to the *café-concert* at night, or rushing up the stairs, two at a time, to release Edith, and snatch up the baby, it was months before Nelly made love again. The baby absorbed her. She laughed over him, cuddled him and slept with his warm little body beside her on the divan. She and Edith knitted his clothes, coaxed him to eat messes of chopped chicken and toasted fragments of *baguette*.

'Know what you are? My blessing,' said Nelly to the chubby-faced child.

Patrice had haunted the road where Edith lived since Nelly first left Paris. He now turned up at Chez Paul-Marc, scarcely ate his meal and applauded, when she made her entrance, as if she were a great star of the Comédie-Française.

He was waiting for her when she came out of the kitchen entrance. His bony Jewish face was solemn. He opened his arms and enveloped her in a suffocating hug, pressing her so hard that she was breathless. She kissed him back.

'Going to walk me home?'

He put her arm under his. He never said he had missed her

and did not ask a single question. Nelly told him. She'd had a baby, she said.

'It can happen,' said Patrice. Something in his face made her press his arm.

'He isn't yours, *mon ami*. I hope,' she added, with devastating politeness, 'you aren't disappointed.'

Silence followed this revelation. They walked down the road for a while. In the distance they heard music coming from La Galette.

'What is he like? Pretty like you?'

'Much prettier. Want to see him?'

'You know I do.'

Patrice became a fourth member of the family, doing errands for Edith, minding Tom if he had spare time and, when allowed to do so, taking Nelly to the circus. Edith treated him like a brother. Nelly smiled welcomes and pushed the baby into his arms. Then, at last, one afternoon when she called in at his studio, she lay again on Patrice's bed and allowed his big hungry body to enter hers.

One night during a late wet spring in 1901 Patrice was attacked by a drunken porter in Les Halles, hit him back, won the fight and lost his employment. The foreman had always disliked Patrice with one of those reasonless dislikes, and got rid of him.

Patrice was shattered – speechlessly shattered – until Edith had one of her inspirations. Why shouldn't he try for work at the enormous new exhibition hall off the Champs Élysées, the Grand Palais? To all their relief, he was taken on as a gilder. He had to spend his days gilding wreaths of laurel leaves, elaborate cornices and mouldings on ceiling and doors in the vast stately rooms. The pay was bad, the new building damp and dusty. Nelly was alarmed when he developed a persistent cough, bought him an old battered flask in the market and filled it with brandy. She made him sandwiches thicker than his fist. He looked at her as if she were an angel.

He still painted his strangely coloured paintings but rarely sold one. When Nelly posed for him she couldn't recognise her own body in the picture. He didn't use delicate brush-strokes, as Edith did, but painted thickly and coarsely in purple, orange, greenish blue. The pictures were disturbing. There was something tragic in them. In a curious way the bodies were more like rocks or trees than human beings.

'Perhaps you're a genius,' Nelly once said.

She knew he suffered over his painting. And part of his unhappiness was not his total lack of success, he was too absorbed to care about that, it was to do with her. Nelly could enter his mind as he entered her body, with tender ease, and she knew he wanted to give her so much. He believed she should have clothes and flowers and happiness. Well, he gives me the last, she thought. And meant it, as long as she kept Matthew out of her memory.

One early evening Nelly left the baby with Edith and called to see Patrice on her way to Chez Paul-Marc. They just had time to make love, and had that moment finished when the doorbell rang. Nelly, mother naked on the tumbled bed, her eyes enormous as they always were after sex, swore.

'Tell them to go away.'

Patrice wrapped a towel round his waist. Without clothes he was magnificent but his arms, she thought, were too long and like a gorilla's. And he wasn't hairy like Matthew.

She lay with the pillows where Patrice had pushed them under her bottom, staring at the ceiling. She heard an unfamiliar masculine voice. A rumbling reply from Patrice. More talk. Finally, the door shut and she sat up expectantly as he shambled back into the room. He held the towel in one hand, and in the other what appeared to be a large sheet of cardboard.

Sitting beside her he showed her – it was a photographed painting. Two lovers in medieval costume locked in an embrace.

In her days at Maître Guelle's Nelly had heard the students deride the new photography. Le P'tit called it 'that mechanical 'thief of nature' and said it would never express the spiritual world of art.

'A photograph!' she exclaimed now with disdain.

'Don't you like photographs? Edgar Dégas painted his portrait of Princess Metternich from a photograph,' muttered Patrice, staring at the lovers.

'Did he? Then there must be something in them,' Nelly was always willing to abandon a prejudice.

'I think this one's by Francesco Hayez,' said Patrice.

'And who's Francesco-un-tel?'

'Italian. Dead twenty years ago. Not much admired by some. Did troubadour paintings.'

She was still puzzled.

'But what did the man bring it to you *for*? And who was he?'

'Never saw him before in my life. He said he saw me at the Grand Palais and asked for my address. He looked . . .'

'Yes?'

'Shifty.'

Nelly waited. The story was unfinished.

'He wants me to copy it.'

'How much?'

'Ten francs a day and I can take a week.'

He did not join in her delighted laugh. He still studied the photograph.

'I agreed. But when I asked about the original he didn't reply. Then I said – what are the right colours? Know what he answered? "Why not make the girl's gown a nice pink".'

He and Nelly gazed at each other.

She knew he'd only agreed to paint the masterpiece from a photograph because of her. He wanted money to buy her things. It gave him no satisfaction to paint pictures of charm or eroticism, to repeat the style of the Impressionists, to follow the fashionable Japanese influence. Patrice painted his own feelings. His pictures were neither real or imagined, they were his reality transfigured by emotion and these, like his thoughts, he turned face to the wall. Except for her own portraits and nudes, he rarely showed his work to Nelly.

When he did they affected her, particularly the self-portraits. The painted face looked out with a sombre expression, dark eyes fixed without the softness which love and sex brought to them. She always kissed him when he showed her a painting, but never said a word. They were bigger than she was.

Abandoning his own painting when he came home from the neck-aching gilding at the Grand Palais, Patrice settled down to copy the Francesco Hayez, using glowing colours he never touched in his own pictures. The girl was in peony-coloured satin, the troubadour in rich brown with pale ermine on the sleeves . . .

Patrice's visitor appeared a week later, nodded approval and paid cash. He then gave Patrice two more photographs. Nelly was present this time, and as intrigued as only the mistress of a very poor artist could be. The man introduced himself as Paul Vézin; he was fattish and dark and looked like a sleek neutered cat. He seemed to carry a good deal of money.

He turned up at Patrice's studio a number of times, bringing more photographs. After the Hayez, Patrice did not recognise any of the paintings, which would have remained mysteries if Nelly hadn't spotted some faint pencilled marks on the back of the mounts. Patrice had very good sight and succeeded in deciphering them. There was a painting by Philipp Otto Runge of two lovers under a gnarled and doubtless symbolic tree, and a Georg Friederich Kersting of a woman at a window. Both were German Romantics. A photograph by somebody called Mulready was a street scene, full of grotesque figures which reminded Nelly of the docks. And a French artist, Théodore Chasseriau, painted a despairing Russian girl in costume, dramatic pose, and inches of snow.

Patrice worked hard. When the visitor reappeared with still more work he again tried to get hints, however slight, on colours. He was given a highly romantic Siegfried and Brunnhilde.

'What about Siegfried's cloak?' he asked politely.

Vézin shrugged.

'As far as colour is concerned, Monsieur, I neither know nor care. Let's say scarlet. And lots of gold. You are experienced with the use of gold at the Palais, are you not? Give the hero a gold helmet and spear.'

Helping Patrice to pack the finished paintings later, Nelly said, 'And I know where these are going. To be sold as originals to foreigners who know no better, poor ignorant beasts.'

Summer had come and on a rainy July night Patrice finally completed his last masterpiece and appeared at the kitchen door of Chez Paul-Marc to collect Nelly. She now had her name chalked even larger on the blackboard outside the café.

'Songs by *La Belle Nelly, Chanteuse Anglaise.*'

But not a centime more pay.

Patrice's face was brighter than usual and so were his eyes.

'He paid for all the rest. Didn't even ask why *Delilah* took extra time. I'm going to buy you something. A dress? Some hats? A lace parasol?'

She clapped her hands.

'Oh, I do love a present. Shall I tell you what I'd like most of all? If you could afford it, that is.'

'I can afford whatever you want,' said Patrice.

'Some singing lessons.'

Edith had put the idea into her head after coming to the café one afternoon with the baby in his pram to hear Nelly rehearse.

'You do sing prettily,' she had said later. 'Your voice is sweet. Husky and sweet, like a wave breaking. But you ought to be trained.'

'What on earth for?'

'One never knows.'

Patrice, who would have paid for his mistress to learn lion-taming, was proud to be what she called '*mon patron*'.

Bundles of francs from the Siegfrieds and troubadours now gave Nelly the chance to go twice a week to a music school near the Jardin des Plantes. The red-brick house was in a quiet respectable street and jangled with noise which could be heard the moment she turned the corner. As she approached, she could make out the cries of the teachers, '*Non, non. Encore, s'il vous plaît!*'

Nelly's singing teacher was a dark handsome Parisian called Matelon. He was always waiting at the piano when she arrived. The room had thin walls, and if voices penetrated he pursed his lips and looked annoyed. The moment Nelly's half-hour was up he more or less marched her to the door.

When she had her first lesson, he asked her to sing an unaccompanied song. She gave him one of her successes, 'Brown boots, I ask yer – brown boots. While all the rest wore decent black and morning suits.'

When she had finished he said, 'You do not know how to breathe. It must come from the stomach. The stomach. Deep, deep. No, that is wrong.' He placed his hands on Nelly's flat stomach and listened like a doctor as she inhaled. 'Now. *Aaaaah.*'

When he sang, his voice was young. A surprise, she thought, he'd never see forty again.

'Are you a professional, Monsieur?'

'I sing at the Opéra.'

'*Tiens.*' She was impressed.

The nationality of his new pupil rather pleased him. He had not been, he said, 'infected by the anti-English feeling'. The Boer War which had so changed Nelly's life was still dragging on, and England was generally loathed these days. But Nelly never read the newspapers and Edith, perhaps deliberately, never spoke of the war. The Parisians Nelly knew talked about painting or sex or money or food.

Monsieur Matelon, however, spoke of a new subject.

'The London theatre, Mademoiselle, is worth your attention. In your great capital there is now flourishing the charming new *comédie-musicale*, so much more entertaining and new than our old-fashioned *opéra bouffe*. You have seen *San Toy*, of course? Oh, but you must arrange to do so!'

Nelly was flattered that he thought she could afford such a thing. She said she really must.

Patrice kept all his francs in his tobacco jar – no Parisian, even the wealthiest, would put their money into banks. The cash in the jar earned from Vézin lasted three months. Then in September he actually sold a picture; a mustard and dark green nude study to a man who owned a small shop selling paintings. His name was Ambroise Vollard and he told Patrice that 'new artists excited him'. Patrice, breaking this news to Nelly, said the gentleman had been serious. He looked serious, too, and a little shattered at what had happened.

With the Vollard money, he could afford a few more weeks for Nelly to go to the school.

Her voice was growing fuller, even Monsieur Moréas noticed it. And Nelly was so grateful to Patrice that her love-making became quite lavish. It might lack passion, but it was seductive, lazy, accepting, sensual. Patrice, who had only to look at her to want her, thought but never said that he would die for her.

One evening, before her final lesson, Nelly was feeling especially happy. She spent a long sunny afternoon in the Jardin du Luxembourg, lying on the grass with Tom. She listened to his voice talking its incomprehensible language, it was just like a pigeon cooing. And he had begun to crawl. She kept putting a brightly coloured ball just out of his reach, and watching his earnest, concentrated progress towards it.

She walked slowly home, pushing the perambulator, and turned up the hill of the Butte. Edith greeted her, looking relaxed. She'd completed all her sewing and had spent an hour at her easel. Nelly set off later for the café in a street still bathed in sunshine.

Chez Paul-Marc was near the Place des Abbesses, and the tables under the trees were crowded. Montmartre looked friendly and festive, she thought. It was home. She went round the back of the café and through the kitchen door. Monsieur and Madame Moréas were sitting at the table. Not bustling about preparing the food, but drinking glasses of port.

'Ah. Nelly. Let me offer you a glass,' said Monsieur Moréas.

'Paul-Marc, you know Nelly does not drink. Give her a *citron-pressé*.'

Nelly exchanged a friendly look with her employer's wife; she liked owing debts of kindness and her stay in Pontoise, the good hospital, the work at the baker's, had all been arranged by the plump little person sipping port. Madame did not catch her eye. Monsieur placed the *citron-pressé* in front of Nelly and resumed his seat. Madame said, 'Nelly. This afternoon we sold the café.'

It was a hideous, a totally unexpected shock. Never, never, had she thought this work was not safe, that her patrons wouldn't go on hiring her, that they even contemplated selling the place. What made it worse was their lack of what in English people would have been a hypocritical concern. They didn't soften the blow. They didn't say they were sorry not to warn her or would miss her. They informed her that the new owner would not be taking her on, he didn't need a singer, and was going to change the café into a '*petit restaurant de bon cuisine*.'

That night, walking home with Patrice, she was near to tears. She hadn't cried once since Matthew deserted her.

The next morning, with a sort of deathly inevitability, Anselme Rocheville told her he couldn't afford her as a model any more. He would work from books in future. He could pay until the end of the week. That was all. In twenty-four hours Nelly lost the whole of her meagre income.

Edith was too imaginative to show that she was as stunned as Nelly herself. Patrice swore he'd spend every spare hour visiting every café on the Butte. Edith wrote out a list of all the artists and schools they knew.

Nelly arrived for her last lesson at the music school without the usual spring to her walk. Beneath a hat sprouting with its ostrich feather, her face, freckled from July sun, was pale. Matelon bade her good morning, fiddled with some sheets of music, and then said abruptly that he had news.

'You're going to sing at the Opéra again,' she said, unpinning her hat and fluffing up her hair with the hatpin.

She thought, perhaps he'll give me some free tickets. Might cheer us up. Might not if the opera's one of those miserable ones.

'It is nothing about myself, Mademoiselle. It is for you.'

Dragging herself out of the swamp of anxiety, she managed a smile. Now he's going to say I can come here for half-price or something. Embarrassing.

'An Englishman I know is in Paris at present,' said Matelon, striking a chord on the piano. 'You remember we spoke of the *comédies-musicales*? He is connected with one. He showed me the score. I spoke of you.'

'*Me?*'

'I told him of your voice. Its quality and so on. Of course it still needs work but perhaps that is not to be at present. It seems he is short of a singer. Would you be interested to perform in a theatre?'

Nelly had the same feeling of incredulity that had come over her on the day when Madam Ruth suggested she should leave England. Collecting her wits she said somewhat wildly that she'd had no experience and was sure Monsieur could not mean it.

He interrupted impatiently.

'I would not suggest it if I weren't serious. Why waste time? Come along, now, there is work to do. The Englishman is due at the end of your lesson.'

Feeling slightly dizzy, Nelly sang. Her heart was thumping when there was a rap at the door. A man came into the room and he and Matelon shook hands.

He was burly, tweedy, and brought a strong scent of cigars with him. He carried a silver-topped cane. He was nearly as large as Patrice but twice as heavy and twice his age. His manner was unlike any Nelly had encountered since Blackfriars: crude.

'I'm told you can sing,' he said, interrupting Matelon's introduction. 'Go ahead, then.'

He sat down.

Matelon played the introduction to a song he had taught her. It was a French song with mockery in its refrain.

'*Ah, que les hommes sont bêtes, qu'ils sont bêtes,*' sang Nelly, with a laugh in her voice.

The man, whose name she'd learned was Grover Jones, sucked the knob of his cane. When she finished singing he stood up.

'You'll do. I'll take you on. You'll have a line or two and a couple of specials. Rehearsals start Monday.'

'Rehearsals of *what*? *Where*?'

'*Cora*. I'll give you details later and we rehearse in London, of course. We'll be going on tour. Thanks, Matelon. See you tonight at Lipps.' His French was awful. 'Don't forget, you're finding me a music copier.'

Nelly was still dumbfounded. Grover Jones turned to her again.

'Thirty shillings a week, pay for your own lunch, shoes and stockings, and fares. That's the way I do business.'

Nelly ran all the way back to the studio, bursting in, breathless. Edith was calmly painting a composition of saucepans, apples and a loaf of bread. The baby was on the floor, banging with some easel pegs and enjoying the din.

Nelly gasped out what had happened.

'Thirty shillings a week is more than I've earned in my life! When you think of it, Edith. And I can't accept.'

She waited for Edith to exclaim about the savage irony of life. Imagine refusing all that money, when next week she wouldn't have a sou.

'I kept thinking when I was running home how I could take the work and still have Tom. Do you remember Yvette at the Feu Follet? She used to bring her baby backstage and the clown kept an eye on him and she heated the baby's food on the gas ring in the Green Room.'

Edith put down her brush and pushed back the easel. It shuddered on the bare boards. The baby continued to thunder with the pegs.

'Did you refuse?'

'I didn't say a word. I was winded. Oh Edith, when you think of thirty shillings a week!'

'You can still accept.'

'So you *do* think I could take Tom? It's a brainwave, isn't it?'

'Nelly, stop talking rubbish. Let me understand this. Is the man casting a new show?'

'Not exactly. I think it was on in London before and he's taking it on tour, getting a new company together to go to America.'

Edith looked at her.

'Of course you can't take Tom to America.'

It was a sort of relief to hear that. Nelly said in a more normal voice, 'Yes, I was being dotty. I'll tell him no.'

'I think perhaps you should tell him yes.'

'*What do you mean?*'

'Patrice was here. He has been to every single *café-concert* on the Butte from the Rue de l'Abbreuvoir right down into Clichy and Rochechouart. Not a hope. All the places have their own singers. And I've racked and racked my brains about a new modelling job, but there are so many new girls and all the artists I know have the ones they like.'

'I'll find something. I've got to.'

Edith came across to her, took her hands and made her sit down on a rickety, paint-splashed chair.

'Nelly. You need that work. This looks like one of your strokes of luck. You've often said they happen and now here's one out of the blue. You've done well so far. You managed in London when it was very rough. You've managed wonderfully in Paris. You even,' added Edith cheerfully, for Nelly looked anguished, 'became the mother of an English lord's son. Well. It looks to me as if another door is opening.'

'I can't leave Tom.'

The words burst out in a dreadful cry. They came from somewhere in Nelly's soul.

Edith's face was full of pain.

'My dear, dear friend. I think you will have to leave him with me.'

171

'I can't. Oh I can't. I'll lose him.'

The tears ran down Nelly's face and she wiped them away with the back of her hand and they poured down still. The baby looked up at her. For one of those mysterious reasons in the infant young, he began to laugh.

CHAPTER TEN

Mr Grover Jones appeared at Chez Paul-Marc on Nelly's last evening, ploughed his way through *choucroute garnie* and listened to Nelly's songs. He then beckoned her to his table.

'Got a contract at this place?'

'No. Anyway the owners are selling.'

'I came in time, then. Be in London by the end of the week.'

She hesitated. He looked her up and down. She wore her only *café-concert* dress, a russet silk which showed her swelling bosom.

'Worried about the fare, are you? You girls are all alike. Never put a farthing away for a rainy day. I'll advance your fare. Don't bother to thank me, it'll be docked off your salary a bit at a time. Got friends and relations in London, I daresay.'

An odd expression was in Nelly's eyes. She thought – well, there's a sot in Blackfriars. And a Madam in a smart *whorehouse*.

'Not a soul, Mr Grover Jones.'

'Then you can put up at the Girls' Friendly. It's along the road from the rehearsal rooms. Clean and cheap. Plenty of the girls go there when they're new to town. And some,' he added reflectively, 'just to save money.'

When Nelly said goodbye to her baby on a late autumn morning at the Gare du Nord, she thought her heart would break. Matthew's leaving had almost broken it, but somehow this pain was worse for now it was *she* who was going away. When she kissed the child's fat cheeks and heard him chuckle, she began to tremble. Edith hugged her, not saying a word.

The Calais express puffed its way out of Paris.

It was the sort of autumn day she used to spend with Matthew rowing to the Ile de la Grande Jatte or with Le P'tit cycling in the Bois. Sometimes with Patrice, just making love. It was blue and golden and misty, and in Normandy great white horses were pulling wagons.

She fiercely refused herself the luxury of tears. I'm on my way to make my fortune, she thought, using the old Cockney phrase. All her possessions – three dresses, four skirts, four blouses, a pair of best corsets, stockings and boots – were stuffed in the Gladstone bag Madam had given her what seemed a century ago. It still had the yellow label.

Thinking about Tom, yearning for the feel of his small body filling her arms, she swore she *would not mope*. She despised people who went about with long faces. Wasn't she going to earn money and send it all back to Edith? Wouldn't she come back from the tour with enough to return to Paris and real life?

The train drew up at last, belching steam, into the glass-covered station at Victoria. She swung down the bag and joined the crowds streaming down the platform. I'll take a look at London, she thought, determined to keep her mind on the present. Looking back hurt so damnably.

She climbed up the stairs to the uncovered upper deck of the omnibus. As it rumbled down the street, Nelly looked and looked. Ragged children caught her eye. They played on the dusty pavements, some with rusty iron tyres, one with a kite made from newspaper. Some at a corner were marking the ground with chalk for hopscotch. It wasn't so long since she'd done that.

How crowded, compressed, loud, pitiless, London was. There were no broad *boulevards* stretching their leafy spaces into the distance, no pavement cafés with tables under the trees, no fountains, no scent of coffee in the air. And how inexpressibly dirty was the city of her birth. Even in the warm evening, there seemed to be a foggy mist. Smuts had already marked her skirt. The dirt was everywhere. On the back of the

174

omnibus seats, on the windowsills of shops, on pavements, and smearing the faces of children in stained greasy caps or torn straw bonnets.

The traffic seemed worse than in Paris — a mass of omnibuses, growlers, hansoms and carts in the narrow streets. The cyclists, unlike Nelly and her friends spinning in the green Bois, were everywhere. Telegraph messengers on bright red cycles flashed by and a woman with a bicycle basket filled with books. While Nelly watched, one cabman had to swerve violently to avoid a red-headed girl cyclist on the wrong side of the road who just missed his horse's head.

As the omnibus went along Piccadilly, Nelly glanced down the sloping elegance of St James's. Five minutes away was a certain alleyway. Madam would be having her brandy and cake just about now . . .

The façade of the Gaiety Theatre in the Strand attracted Nelly, and she decided to get down. Dodging an electric brougham, she went to stare at the theatre. Now I'm going to be a real actress, she thought. Large displays of framed photographs hung outside. They were mostly of girls. Girls ogling above silk parasols. Girls on rose-wreathed swings. Girls with their arms outstretched, their smiles melting. Nelly envied the blank-faced beauties. These were the darlings of London; Nelly knew about Gaiety Girls and their success and their rich lives and their brilliant marriages. A girl like that, thought Nelly, staring at a wasp-waisted charmer with blonde curls, bowling a hoop, doesn't have to leave her baby and go travelling across the world.

The Girls' Friendly Club smelled of disinfectant and hummed like a giant beehive with scores of young women glad of its economical and respectable welcome. Nelly was given the key to a bedroom and a sharp look from a housekeeper like a wardress. Nelly knew the kind. Wearing cotton gloves, they used to cross-question her drunken mother; much sense they got out of her.

The club was noisy and chill and, when she went up to the first-floor landing, she saw a long passage with rows of doors on either side like a barracks. Green linoleum stretched down the corridor, glassy with polish.

When her spirits had been low in Paris, a rarity but just occasionally she had found herself inexplicably sad, Nelly always ran fast as if to chase away the shadow. Now, looking at the lineoleum, she suddenly launched herself into a run. She ran quickly and turned her progress into a slide – faster and faster she sailed down the corridor as if on ice, gaining speed . . . until she collided violently with a girl coming out of a bedroom.

'Sorry!' shouted Nelly, putting out both arms to save herself and the girl. Too late. They both collapsed in a heap.

'Ever so sorry,' repeated Nelly, scrambling to her feet and automatically putting out her hand to help. The girl, in a rose-pink silk, pushed her away furiously.

'What the hell do you think you're doing?'

'No harm done, is there?'

'If you can't behave like a lady – no, that would be too much to expect! – if you don't stop turning this place into a slum I'll report you to Miss Pater. Get out of my way.'

She gave Nelly a second push – Nelly just missed losing her balance again – and swept away.

Dinner at the Club was as bad as English food could be. The boiled beef was stringy, the carrots like bullets, and an awful apple pudding stuck to Nelly's teeth. She ate because she was hungry, marvelling at the disgusting meal. Paris has spoiled me, she thought. This is England and I'd best hold my tongue. There was no sign of the Fury in pink silk who must have gone out for the evening. The girls with whom she gossiped were like the Club's name, friendly. It was not until she was in an unfamiliar bed, with an unfamiliar city outside, that she allowed herself to think.

For a long moment she lay imagining she was at home with Tom. She knew how he would look, the way he slept with his baby mouth slightly open, and, when she bent to pick him up, the smell, a mixture of soft skin and new wool. How she loved him.

Oh well. Better soon. It was what the boy in Blackfriars, her first lover, had said when she squashed her fingers in the door.

'Put them in your mouth. It'll warm them and they won't hurt. Better soon.'

'What you really mean,' Nelly had said, loudly sucking, 'is that with my hand in my mouth I'll stop bawling.'

The first rehearsal of the *Cora* tour was for nine the next morning; but Edith had told Nelly that all theatre people had a mania about punctuality. They were worse than Maître Guelle, Paul-Marc or even her singing teacher. 'Don't you ever be late,' Edith had counselled. Nelly, bathed and dressed, with clean corsets, knickers with pink ribbon, two clean petticoats and her blue cotton which showed off her breasts and twenty-inch waist, energetically polished her boots with newspaper.

The man at the door of the Arlington Rehearsal Rooms had a bent cigarette in his mouth, and didn't wait for her to say who she was.

'Cast of *Cora*? You're the early bird. Mr Grover Jones, he's here. Room Four with the piano.'

Nelly found her way up some stairs to a room with '4 painted on it. A man's voice was singing.

> Side by side with a four-in-hand
> I can hear all the talk so grand –
> If their blood is a brilliant blue
> Why, so's their language too.

Then the refrain,

> Oh, I love Society, Real Society, Real Society,
> I'd ride on horses with fine long tails
> If my Papa was the Prince of Wales –

She opened the door. Grover Jones continued to sing and play to the end of the song, nodding towards her. She went over to the piano and stood listening. The tune was catchy. When he finished, she applauded. He shut the piano lid with a slam and turned round on the stool. He looked even larger than she remembered. His face was fleshy, his black moustache did not hide his thick mouth.

'Know the song?' he asked. 'Have you seen *The Runaway Girl*?'

'No to both, Mr Grover Jones. It hasn't come to Paris.'

'Ah yes. Paris. How long were you there?'

She was not in the least shy. She had a kind of camaraderie, optimistic, wary. Her figure was sexy, and he recalled that she could sing. He'd arrived at the Arlington this morning in a bad mood and had been singing and playing to get rid of it. He'd been musical as a young man and still liked to hear his own pleasant voice. The trouble, as usual, was a row with Violet who'd refused to come back to his lodgings last night and had slapped his face. Violet was given to scenes and sometimes his fingers itched to put her across his knee and give her a damned good hiding. But it was Violet who had *him* at her mercy. He found it a welcome change, just now, to be alone with this fresh-looking girl. He stood up and came near to her.

'Your first morning in the theatre, Nelly. Have I got the name right?'

'That's me.'

How far is he going to go? Some of the others will be here in a minute, she thought. But Grover Jones knew they would not. He had changed the rehearsal time by half-an-hour. He spoke with the purr of a big cat.

'You'll need some help at the start of your career, you know. I want you to feel you can get anything you want from me.'

He put his arm round her shoulder, and with his other hand cupped her breast.

Nelly backed away. That excited him and he came closer, putting up both hands to undo the top buttons of her dress. For what to him was a delicious pause, she stood with her breasts slightly thrust forward as he continued to unbutton, revealing the full white throat and white flesh. The ripe bosoms were still hidden by a camisole. She had raised her hands as if to make it easy for him. He was breathing faster. Nelly was smiling. She remained a moment longer to be sure she had what she was searching for. Then, in a deft movement, she pulled out her longest hatpin and stuck it in his arm.

He gave a shout of pain.

'Did I hurt you?' she asked.

He drew back, swearing like a navvy, while she refastened her buttons and repinned her hat. Tugging at his sleeve he saw with fury that blood had begun to flow.

'You bitch, you've pierced an artery, I'll have to go to Charing Cross Hospital – I think I'm going to faint –'

'Let's have a look.' She took his arm. 'Pooh, a scratch. Only needs a hanky. I've seen hatpin wounds ten times worse, the boys in the Atelier were covered with them. What a fuss you're making.'

'You're a filthy bitch,' repeated Grover Jones, still swaying in pain and fury, yet ludicrously allowing her to bind his arm with his own handkerchief. 'I'll get even with you.'

'You shouldn't have tried to do what you did. I never said you could, did I? We can still be friends,' said Nelly, knotting the bandage and thinking she'd been very stupid.

Just then the door slammed open.

The scene was a tableau. Grover Jones, his face twisted in exaggerated pain, holding out his bared arm while Nelly as a latter-day Florence Nightingale finished bandaging and assured him he'd 'stop bleeding in a jiff'. The girl in the doorway stood looking at them. It was the same girl Nelly had knocked over last night.

'Oh, I do apologise,' she said in a loud voice, 'I apologise for interrupting. You must forgive me!'

She came straight over to Grover Jones, looking as if she wanted to hit him. She behaved as if Nelly were not there.

'He hurt his arm,' muttered Nelly, trying to roll down the sleeve.

179

Grover Jones gestured her away.

'That will be all,' he said, as if she were a housemaid.

Nelly felt in need of food after the first morning's rehearsal. She had not been asked to sing a number by herself, which would have been interesting, but to sing with the chorus. Their voices were, to be kind, extremely shrill. The ordeal had been dancing – she was in a row of girls who were practised dancers. The old days of the reckless *chahut* were gone; this kind of dancing needed timing and concentration. She was tensed for Grover Jones to shout out that she was no good, and better pack her bags. But it did not happen.

Walking down Drury Lane, still nervous, she sighed for a *boulevard* café. Where were the marble-topped tables and drooping palms, the great looking-glasses reflecting men reading *Le Figaro* and girls writing letters? Lads hurried by on their way to dingy offices, they carried piles of plates under tin covers for the clerks who had their meals sent in. A beer boy darted past with ten cans of beer strung along a pole. Everybody, she thought, is eating and drinking except me. Passing a public house called The Top and Whip, Nelly's professional eye noted how clumsily painted the sign was. She decided the place would have to do.

It was smoky and crowded. She bought a slice of pie and a token glass of stout which she certainly was not going to drink, but public houses disliked teetotal customers. She pushed her way into a corner. Outside the smeared window London was as grey as a dustbin. Somebody came through the crowd.

'May I join you?'

It was one of the actors who had been at rehearal.

'Do.'

He placed a glass of sherry, bread and cheese and a jar of pickled onions in front of him.

'I keep telling Bessy not to give me those,' he said, indicating the onions, 'but she knows I love 'em. If I as much as sniff at one, Violet will scream blue murder.'

'Violet Lane, you mean?'

'There isn't another.'

Nelly had learned from a girl at rehearsal the name of the young woman Nelly had knocked over. 'She's our star, you know.' The star was fair-haired and had, thought Nelly fairmindedly, a very pretty face when she condescended to smile.

'You're Claude Stanway,' she said. 'You play opposite her.'

'Right first time. And you're new.'

'Nelly Briggs. Mr Grover Jones found me in Paris.'

'Did he, though?'

'Through my teacher at the singing academy.'

'You don't have to look so holy, Miss Nelly Briggs. It doesn't suit you. Besides, Grover Jones wouldn't dare pick up a girl for himself in Paris or anywhere else. Even a stunner like you. Violet would flay him alive.'

'Perhaps she's going to,' thought Nelly.

Claude Stanway was a thin graceful young man, his movements as loose as a puppet's. His blond hair was parted in the middle, he had a pale face and slightly protuberant blue eyes. The eyeglass on a black ribbon he used mainly to wave about or play with. He sipped his sherry.

'Was it my fancy or did the shrinking Violet give you a nasty look when we broke just now?'

'You didn't imagine it, I'm afraid.'

'Know her before, did you?'

'Never set eyes on her until last night. Somebody in the company told me she's the star of *Cora*.'

'She is. She has a voice and dances like a leaf. Audiences love her. *We* don't, though. Forgive my French but young Violet can be a cow.'

Nelly laughed. She described the collision last night and the hatpin this morning, telling the tale rather well. She was surprised that he didn't even smile.

'Violet is someone it's better not to offend, I'm sorry to say – if you don't want life made into a misery. She has Grover Jones squashed under her thumb like a beetle.'

During their lunch, his conversation was as filled with shop as the students' used to be. He was kind, and she saw he was attracted to her.

'One thing I haven't asked,' he said, as they were walking back down Drury Lane, 'how do you feel about Grover Jones? Do you want to fight for him, I mean? That might make a difference. You look sparky enough to win.'

'Fight for him! I wouldn't touch him with a bargepole. Honestly, Mr Stanway, there's no reason on earth why Violet Lane should take against me.'

Claude Stanway looked dubious.

And Nelly was wrong. Violet Lane already detested her.

It was possible to declare war without uttering a word, and Violet did exactly that before the day was out. The campaign continued during every day of the rehearsals. If Nelly stood among the girls, Violet managed to join them so that she could push Nelly out of the way. Coming up behind her, she stood on the hem of Nelly's skirt: it was sheer luck that Nelly didn't step forward and have her only practice skirt torn off. Wherever Nelly was, there was Violet ready to elbow, edge or shove. Nelly was seasoned by her dockside youth, but she knew she daren't fight back this time. It needed hardihood not to be affected by such venom.

Her new friend Claude Stanway became anxious about her. During their now daily luncheons at The Top and Whip he asked, 'You did sign a contract, didn't you?'

'Oh yes. My teacher witnessed it.'

'For the whole American tour?'

'That's right. Mr Grover Jones said we might be away six months or even longer.'

'What did your family say about that, Nell?' He knew nothing about her. All they shared were jokes and shop.

'Bless you, I have no family,' said Nelly, seeing in her mind Tom's beaming face.

'Little Orphan Nelly Briggs.'

'That's about the size of it.'

She remembered the woman who'd called herself her

mother. Ought I to cross the Bridge and find out if she's dead? Not sure I will.

Sharing a new and jangling life with the other girls at the Friendly, tall chorus beauties like poppies in the Nôtre-Dame flower market, learning to dance, to be an actress, and having two numbers of her own to sing – she enjoyed those – Nelly would have been reasonably happy, in spite of pangs over her little son, if it were not for Violet Lane and Grover Jones. In his way, he was as bad as Violet. Nelly had seen men behave badly when sexually rejected; in the past she had usually managed to alter their spite by her own warmth. Not now. Grover Jones never said a kind thing about her work. All she was given was sarcasm. Once he went too far.

It happened when Nelly had finished rehearsing one of her songs.

'I presume, Miss Briggs, you're too ignorant to know that we *smile* when we sing in the theatre. If one can call what we've just heard singing.'

Violet looked bland; but there was a sound, soft but quite distinct, a disapproving intake of breath. It came from the other twenty people, young men and girls, who'd been listening to Nelly sing. Grover Jones heard it. He asked her to sing the number again.

> Oh, it's go-go-going down the river,
> It's coo-coo-cool when the sun goes down,

carolled Nelly.

'Much better.' It sounded as if the words had been forced out of him.

Claude liked to walk Nelly home after rehearsal. Arms linked they walked close, deep in talk which was carried on without a pause. She turned to him for advice.

'About Violet Lane, Claude, I feel a bit helpless. Why does she bother to hate me? Her being beautiful and a success and all that. An upper-crust girl like her, too. I knew someone who spoke like her –'

'Your lover in Paris?'

She looked at him under her eyelashes.

'I never said.'

'You don't have to. It's written all over you. Makes you alluring, you know. A man likes a girl with a past. And you're wrong about Violet, she's no more upper-crust than I am.'

'What rot, Claude!'

He was making one of his jokes. The essence of Claude's comedy was the silly ass, the aristocratic personality. He had a charming, affected voice, screwed his eyeglass into his rather large eye with just the right air, wore a vacuous amiable look. His very jokes were based on Society, the Season, earls and girls. Claude was straight from the top drawer. Making mock of it pleased those who belonged, and those who didn't. Nelly had learned what an established success he was, with his attractive looks, his singing voice, his loose-limbed dancing. Critics called him 'our most elegant, tailored comedian.'

'I'm glad to see you don't believe me,' Claude said.

'Of course I don't. The upper classes never talk about *being*. They just are.'

He looked at her curiously. He was sure she had been mistress of some aristocrat or other. What fool had left this lovely, ardent girl?

'Nell, you're making a mistake about me and about Violet as well. Actors act, haven't you noticed? My Mum and Dad have a vegetable shop in Sutton. I've always had a good ear and I picked up my accent from a schoolmaster at the Board School. Poor blighter had come down in the world. Then I used to go to the theatre in the pit nearly every night when I could beg the money from my parents; I used to watch the rich chaps in the stalls. That gave me the idea of Claude Stanway. My real name's Charlie Sly. Violet's just the same. *Her* name's Aggie Dunkley, and her mother still calls her Ag. It makes her so mad. Ag's father works in the East India Dock Road.'

She was amazed. And amused.

'You're just like a lord to me, Claude Charlie Sly Stanway.'
'So I should be. That's the beauty of the thing.'

The work was hard. She had to practise her dancing, her singing, learn to fence for balance and posture, be at the rehearsal rooms, with a break, for ten hours a day. She was tired when she returned to the Girls' Friendly. Yet every night before falling asleep there was time for heartache. Edith wrote with news of the baby. Patrice sent a scrawl. Both letters made her want to cry but she wouldn't let herself, tears were a luxury. And since the two days in Montmartre waiting for Matthew, she had been afraid of tears.

When she woke it was to new work, new techniques to be learned and remembered. Claude was never far away, ready to encourage if the chance came. She guessed he fended off Violet's worse assaults – Violet clearly liked him. Nelly had never needed a champion, and it touched her that he thought she did.

He was different from the other men who had taken a place in her life. He wasn't a lover. He was friendly and funny, gifted and kind. She sensed that beneath the charm he was ambitious, quite hard, practical. Their friendship was comforting. Patrice wrote again, such a pathetic letter, short and ill-written. Nelly felt guilty about Patrice, so mute, so powerful and so locked in. She had never known how he felt about her, had only sensed it in his intense sex and glimpsed it in his dark eyes.

Sometimes when Claude was needed for an extra rehearsal, or was meeting some of his many theatre friends in the West End, Nelly liked to walk down Shaftesbury Avenue or the Strand to look at the theatres. Now that she herself was in a real musical comedy, her favourite was the Gaiety. She enjoyed the performance pictures hanging outside, and if she was there just before eight, she watched the arrival of the audience – rich-looking men and women who might one day, she thought optimistically, be coming to see *her*.

One warm evening, she walked from the Arlington Rehearsal Rooms down to the Strand and arrived just in time to see the procession of hansoms and four-wheelers lining up in front of the Gaiety. She watched the well-dressed parade for a moment or two, and was about to turn away when she heard a voice. It wasn't the shout from the street-corner, ' 'Orrible Murder, Read All About It!' – the same shout she'd heard every night as a child, as if the hoarse yells described the same victim having his throat cut nightly. This voice was low, lazy, drawling – and so familiar that she felt she was going to faint.

She spun round.

Alighting from a hansom, the first in a line arriving outside the theatre, was Matthew. He wore a perfectly fitting tail coat, a white tie, a white carnation in his buttonhole. There was sleekness and idleness in every line of him – he was the epitome of wealth. But the haggard smile was the same, and the way he bent to speak to the girl on his arm. Nelly saw a glimmer of white satin . . . the couple began to walk towards the theatre. Matthew looked round, vaguely.

He saw Nelly.

For a frozen moment, they stared at each other.

Nelly was the first to recover. With a look of fixed mockery, she turned her back on him. And walked away.

She walked back to her lodgings, scarcely knowing where she was. How painful, in a dreadful way how funny it had been, to see that stranger wearing a white carnation, and remember that he'd made love to her until they had both groaned out loud. Tom's father. Her lover. The master of her body and her heart. She knew every bit of him still, knew him naked and roused, asleep and lost to her, enigmatic, sad, teasing or happy. And there he had stood, looking at her without a word, real, alive, and indifferent. As if she was nothing.

At that moment when Nelly had seen him, she'd felt a sensation which whirled her back to childhood. She had been standing with her nose against a window of a shop filled with food. Aching with hunger.

I suppose he left a scar on me, she thought, as she went through the doors of the Girls' Friendly Club.

Thank the Lord it doesn't show.

CHAPTER ELEVEN

Matthew had been affected more strongly by seeing Nelly Briggs for a fleeting second than he could have expected. Unlike his morbid imaginings – probably they had been vanity – she wasn't wasted and thin with consumptive spots on her cheeks. Nor did she look, God forbid, as if she were now a prostitute. She was thriving and comely and bursting with her particular vitality. Standing there in a preposterous hat, she'd looked so richly sexed. That thought of his shocked him.

For weeks now he had been spending all his time and thought on his courtship of Alice Vandermeyer. He was unused to shy young virgins. His mistresses in society, in the past and recently, were always married women. His one venture into low life, Nelly, had been a sexual law to herself.

He enjoyed talking to young girls of his own class, it was amusing to make them laugh. His painter's eye took in their flawless skin and silky hair and the exquisite softness of youth. Now for the first time he was in the constant company of a little thing of eighteen years old without a word to say for herself. It took determination not to be bored.

His senses told him she was pretty, with a slender graceful figure, full breasts, a complexion like a rose. He would like to paint her. Her slightly frizzy pale brown hair was lifted in the fashionable line above her forehead, piled up on her well-shaped head. Her mother dressed her in superb clothes, cascading with Brussels lace or stiff with embroidery. His favourite was an evening gown sewn with pearl dragonflies. Alice was elegant, wealthy, reserved and appallingly young.

When he'd proposed to her on their last night at Cowes, she

had blanched. They had been standing on board the *Constance Mary*, looking at the calm sea.

'Alice. May I call you that?'

One had to say such things; in his mind he had called her Alice from the start.

She bent her head. He saw she was nervous.

'Alice. Do you care for me at all? Because,' his voice grew deeper, 'I care so very much for you. So much that I beg you to share my life. My dear girl. Marry me.'

She said something he could not catch, and turning dark eyes towards him, he saw they were filled with tears. He took her in his arms and kissed her for the first time. She did not return the kiss, but let his mouth press hers and that was all.

He had been canny enough to consult Constance Mary before making the proposal, and after the news she positively blazed with satisfaction.

'Such a blessing you are a Catholic,' she said, allowing him to kiss her cheek and reminding him of her daughter, 'and that you come from a family who has kept the Faith. Alice told me that one of your ancestors was executed at Tyburn.'

'Alice seems interested in the odd slice of history.'

'My dear Matthew, I myself dote on history. I want to know everything about your family, just every little thing. Surely there is a saint among the Leckfords of the past? Well, now, when shall we come to visit you at Leckford Court? I declare, it must be soon. My husband is set upon taking us back home in October.'

In the slow and elaborate and lumbering way of the rich, the Vandermeyers left their yacht to be anchored off Southampton. Alice and Fran said goodbye to Matthew for the short interval before they should meet in Dorset. Fran pressed his arm. But he thought her blue eyes clouded. It can't be anything to do with her sister, he thought, that young woman is far too much of an egotist.

Ambrosine Wilton was too worldly to show that she had lost a potential lover when she heard of the engagement. Privately, she thought Alice Vandermeyer a wishy-washy creature, not a patch on the high-stepping sister. She couldn't imagine why Matt had chosen the younger girl. However, the great thing was to keep him as a friend and get invited to Leckford Court after all the American money had made it more comfortable.

It was late September, soft and tawny, and Leckford Court was looking its ancient best. There were clumps of pink and bronze chrysanthemums in the brick-walled garden, and Michaelmas daisies, and the lawns had been cut. Matthew arrived late one night, slept well, and when he had dressed and breakfasted sent a message to inquire if he could see his mother. He'd already glimpsed the small black-clad figure walking to the chapel.

Honoria's maid, as old but far kinder than her mistress, came in search of him. He was in the study, thanking the gods each time he looked at another bill that he no longer needed to flinch when he opened them.

'Her ladyship,' said Keely, in her soft Dorset voice, 'is in the Yellow Drawing-room.'

Matthew found his mother by the open french windows in a high-backed chair which made her seem very small. The chair had been made for Matthew's great-grandfather, a giant whose portrait stared down from a far wall. Honoria was watching a speckled thrush balancing on the terrace balustrade, picking at some grapes the gardener had forgotten to cut.

'When did you return from Cowes?' She did not look at him.

'Last night, Mother, and Ambrosine and Bernard send their affectionate respects.'

'Thank you.'

She continued to study the thrush. Hearing a noise in the garden it flew, scolding, away.

'Mother, there is something I must tell you. I am to be married.'

She did turn then.

'Indeed.'

Having sworn to himself that he wouldn't, Matthew couldn't stop a sarcastic laugh.

'Her name is Alice Vandermeyer, her father is what they call a "magnate" in steel in the United States. He and Mrs Vandermeyer and my betrothed and her elder sister Frances are coming to Leckford Court at the end of this week. They are most anxious to meet you and see Leckford, since it is to be Alice's home. By the way, the family is Catholic.'

For a moment he thought – surely this time she'll be human. Just this once. He looked at her more earnestly than usual, sitting in his familiar pose, which once upon a time Nelly had loved, leaning forward with his arms on his knees. He was handsome. Worn and handsome. Returning his look, she thought – how it is possible to bear this man? Worse, to have *borne* him. She could not abide him. Unspeakable depravities seemed to her innocent, ignorant mind to hang about him. He brought sin into the room.

'Very well. I will receive them,' she managed, astounded by her own generosity.

To his wife's disbelief, Lorn Vandermeyer received the news of Alice's engagement with an outburst of fury. He had known of his wife's plans and tacitly approved of them. Suddenly he changed direction. This was due to an American friend's report on the state of the Leckford finances. He hadn't realised, being too absorbed in his business affairs, just how far the courtship had gone and when faced with its conclusion was very angry indeed.

The family were staying for a day or two at the Royal Walsingham Hotel in Piccadilly. Fortunately, they were dining in their suite, for after the waiters had gone Lorn yelled at the top of his voice. His daughters were thunderstruck.

'*I will not have it*. I will not have one of my girls marrying some broken-down Englishman without my going into the whole thing first. What do we know of this man except that he hasn't a cent? Connie, be quiet and listen to me for a change.'

Constance Mary blushed scarlet and ordered the girls out of the room.

Alice ran down the passage to her bedroom and slammed

the door, but Fran followed. She found her sister crouched on a chair.

'Saints alive, you're trembling like a horse. Calm down, Sis, I beg. Dad's bark is worse than his bite and do you imagine Ma will let him rave on for long? It must be years since he raised his voice to her.'

Alice shivered.

'P-perhaps Father is right, perhaps I shouldn't . . .'

'Marry him? You don't want to, do you.'

Alice wiped her eyes like a desolate child. Fran groaned.

'Oh Sis. Oh Sis. If you don't want to get married to him, here's your chance. Go and side with Dad.'

But Alice began to weep. Fran tried to reason, to pet, to comfort and advise, but she was wasting her time. She was up against Alice's fear of their mother and not even one of those angels with flaming swords they'd seen on every ceiling in Florence could do anything about that.

Fran guessed right about their parents; the row was not mentioned the next day. Lorn was out seeing some business colleagues in the City.

'Your father,' said Constance Mary, 'can manage to come to Leckford Court with us. Matthew will be so pleased.'

When she was certain Fran wasn't going to try and change the inevitable, Alice asked her sister why their father had suddenly taken against her fiancé.

'Money, darling, what do you suppose? He's discovered how much Matthew hasn't got and how much, yards and yards of it, will be needed to pour into some British bank before you waltz up the aisle. There'll be a rich old settlement on you. More than on me.'

Alice's eyes widened.

'But yours should be bigger, you're the elder.'

Fran gave her a suffocating hug.

'The trouble with you is that you're a saint. We can only hope you won't stay that way.'

Waiting for the arrival of the girl who was to be his wife,

Matthew was restless. He walked round the park, sat on the rim of a stone basin wishing the fountain (broken twenty years ago) was working. The autumn sun warmed him, and he looked at the great Jacobean house, which soaked up the sunshine into the reddish-pinkish bricks. Dear place. Ancient place. Beloved and filled with history, birth and death, sorrow and joy. He thought of his ancient Faith kept since Henry VIII had deserted it for a girl's sexy eyes. He remembered the hideous punishments that Protestants, then Catholics in their turn, had inflicted on each other in the name of God. People in England did not seem to mind so much now if you were a Catholic, prejudice was beginning to die out; the Norfolks, too, had weathered the storms.

In his present mood, all tangled up with the past, he remembered the moment when Robert's young prostitute, poor, beautiful creature, had fallen to her death. I suppose it was Leckford that made me take the blame that night. And Leckford forced Bob to let me.

Sitting looking towards the peaceful house and the slow onset of the autumn, he had a wave of revulsion at what he was doing. I can't fool myself, I don't love Alice Vandermeyer and I'm marrying her for her money. What sort of future is that for her? He only thought her mildly attractive, her timidity irked him. It occurred to him that his marriage, on a smaller scale, resembled royalty's. He'd chosen his bride to save the family and duty would consist of coupling with a frightened virgin and making her pregnant. That was needed too. Alice and he were symbols, in a way.

And then he remembered Nelly Briggs. And wished and wished to God she was in his arms, and it was raining on the Butte outside, and they could stay in bed all day long.

The Vandermeyers arrived in a new and handsome motor, a Panhard, which Lorn had hired in London. It was not only business interests which drew Lorn to the new motor cars. Speed and engineering stirred his nature. The Panhard, high-built and taking four passengers comfortably, shone with brass and sherry-brown coachwork. The three ladies were swathed in veils, and there was a flutter among the staff when the vehicle drew up.

If the butler and footmen were not prepared for the Panhard, Lorn was staggered at Leckford Court. As he drove round a corner of the drive he saw a Jacobean mansion, pinnacled, gabled, an ancient and fanciful palace. He'd seen grand houses before. He hadn't been about to buy one.

Matthew, in the garden, came hurrying to welcome them. There was much handing out of ladies, kissing Constance Mary's hand and his betrothed's cheek through her motoring veil.

'Hey, what about me?' said Fran.

In the Yellow Drawing-room they were presented to Honoria and tea was served. Conversation was mainly between the two ladies; Fran had been told to stay quiet and it was never necessary to say such a thing to Alice. Lorn rarely took much part in female conversation.

Honoria looked with observant eyes at the American women who had invaded her home. She thought the girls handsome and the elder one flashy. She disliked the clothes of all three. Honoria had not been to London for thirty years, her friends were neither fashionable nor young, and even the young generation of her son's friends were not as elegant as the Vandermeyers in their Paris clothes. Pale colours were disgraceful so soon after mourning for the Old Queen, she thought. And her visitors fidgeted and sat so badly. Honoria had been taught by her governess half a century ago that ladies sat upright; their backs should not touch the backs of the chairs. They must 'leave room for the cat.' Ladies never lolled. These Americans did.

'And how was your journey, Mr Vandermeyer?' inquired Honoria when she considered she had listened sufficiently to his wife's commonplaces.

'Pretty satisfactory, Ma'am. But the Panhard developed a slight cough at one time and I thought we were precious near breaking down. I misjudged her, however. The company's a good one. French, you know. Panhard and Levassor, they won the Trophy a couple've years ago.'

'How interesting,' said Honoria.

Constance Mary thought Lorn sounded rather American.

He was feeling aggressively American, and showed it when he and Constance Mary changed for dinner in the bedroom called the Queen's Suite. 'The Queen,' said Constance Mary glibly, 'was Charlotte of Mecklenburg.'

'I don't give a damn about queens or kings either. This marriage won't do.'

Constance Mary, fastening a pearl bracelet, pursed her lips. They had argued this out in London and settled it.

Her husband walked over to her, hands in his pockets, light-footed. Short as he was, he looked formidable. It was the face of a well-bred man who knew how to make his millions.

'Have you looked round this place? Have you? Did you look at that ceiling in the Long Gallery.'

'It's Jacobean plasterwork.'

'For the last time, Connie, I don't want to hear another word of what you've just picked up. I have no doubt the place is old and would be valuable if it hadn't been left to rack and ruin. That panelling they showed us, why, it's split so wide I could get a hand through the gap. The carpet in the drawing-room is badly darned, and will you look at that four-poster! I wouldn't expect my chauffeur to sleep in it. I'll lay twenty to one it's riddled with worm and about to fall to bits. While you and the girls were in the garden with Matthew,' he added, prowling about a room as faded and once lovely as dead roses, 'his mother took me to the family chapel. My God,' he went on, and was not joking, 'if I couldn't do more to praise my Maker – it hasn't seen a lick of paint since before I was born. I told you in London I wouldn't have this marriage and you talked me round. Now I see just how right I was. I won't have my little girl marrying a pauper. Nor will I spill my family's and my own dollars into a bucket as full of holes as a colander. You can tell Alice. Or I will.'

194

Constance Mary hid her rage and frustration. When Lorn was like this, only a fool would go into the open to fight.

'It will break Alice's heart,' was all she said.

'That girl's heart is a pat of butter. She'll find some nice American boy back home. Which is what Fran's already done. She's the smart one.'

Fran, in a smaller room nearby, had guessed her father's feelings. On the way upstairs, she had stolen a look at him. She now hurried through her dressing, hindered more than helped by a young maid who spoke with such a broad Dorset accent that Fran couldn't understand one word in six. Fran did her own hair, fastened most of her own hooks and eyes, stabbed her feet into satin shoes and almost raced down the main staircase. She was praying to Saint Expédit, a Roman centurion saint whose acquaintance she had made in Paris.

He must have been listening. Matthew was alone in what the family called the saloon, a room which was the set-piece for a good many family portraits. Leckfords looked down at her, their hands on the heads of enormous dogs or sword-hilts. The room had dark red velvet walls and dark furniture. Like an expensive funeral parlour, thought Fran.

Glancing up, Matthew saw a figure in cream-coloured satin. She swept in, closing the double doors.

'I need to talk with you.'

'I am always at your service.'

'I daresay. But there's nothing you can do for me, Matt. There does happen to be something I can do for you. My Pa wants to stop this marriage. No,' lifting her gloved hand, 'don't interrupt. Listen and use your brains, you'll need 'em if you truly want my sister. Pa doesn't like all this –' with a gesture at the room. 'I know Pa. He's sharp and now he's seen Leckford he knows you're marrying Alice for her money. Don't think I disapprove of you. Only fools say money doesn't matter. But Pa *adores* Alice. He thinks Leckford's falling to bits – I'm sorry, Matt,' Matthew had winced, 'but I'm the gal with a needle probing for the splinter. I have to hurt if I'm to do any good. Now,' she added, and looked at him piercingly, 'what's the verdict? Leave your home and the cash out of it for the present. The point is, do you love my sister?'

Matthew was gripped with strong dismay. He was genuinely shaken by Fran's sharp talk, and part of his emotion was the thought of losing the gentle girl upstairs. He felt possessive, tender, desiring, and baulked.

'I love her very much,' he said at last.

Fran stared at him.

'Then you'll get her,' she said.

The passengers on the transatlantic liners who stood on deck to watch England fade into the early winter mists experienced mixed emotions. Sometimes they were as filled with grief as emigrants in the past had been. Sometimes they were glad to see the last of Europe. With his family safe on board and the task of visiting the Old World thankfully accomplished, Lorn stood on deck watching the coastline disappear. His face was thoughtful. Nothing was simple when you brought, beg his pardon, a Viscount in the baggage. Constance Mary had won, and Lorn had agreed to a more-than-handsome settlement.

'Pouring it down the drain,' he said.

'You're so lavish,' answered Constance Mary, who knew he could afford double. 'You have the real golden touch.'

Matthew Leckford, thought Lorn, seemed pleased, but who could tell what Englishmen were thinking behind those masks they wore? Connie was quite above herself at the idea of Alice as a Viscountess with a Jacobean mansion thrown in.

There is an old tag about ships passing in the night. They can also follow, one after the other, in the same direction. Two ships left Southampton within twenty-four hours. In the first was Matthew, travelling towards a resplendent marriage. In the second was Nelly Briggs. Scarcely a day of the ocean lay between the vessels ploughing into the early winter gales, making their steady progress towards a great strange country which neither Matthew nor Nelly had ever seen.

Grover Jones had arranged to use the ship's smaller ballroom during the day for rehearsals. While the first-class passengers walked round the deck, played quoits or flirted in the elaborate lounges, the cast of *Cora* danced to the thump of a piano. The passengers were amused at having a crowd of real actors and actresses on board. At luncheon and dinner, they looked across at the vivacious group with tolerant eyes.

The *Cora* company had brought their own pianist, Tommy Wright, a mosquito of a man who smoked too much, drank a bit and worshipped chorus girls. He was perfectly content to play for hours, cigarette between his lips and eyes screwed up to avoid the smoke. He played with a light touch and gave real feeling to the sentimental songs.

Claude told Nelly how much he was looking forward to seeing America again.

'It's the country of tomorrow, Nell. You've got to be there in the race, and you've got to be first. No room for slackers in the US of A.'

'Who's slacking?' said Nelly, rubbing her ankle, which had just been hacked by Violet Lane.

On their second morning at sea, when the company assembled in the ballroom Violet had arrived. She was dressed in a white serge sailor suit and was hanging on Grover Jones's arms with more than usual affection. The chorus sat down on the row of gilded chairs. Claude sat next to Nelly and whispered under his breath, 'I heard a rumour. She wants one of your songs.'

Nelly gave a slight start. Violet was now whispering to Grover Jones and patting his lapels. She looked enchanting. There was something silky about her, about her skin, her clouded blonde hair, she even gave the impression of invisible silk underclothes.

'She can't. I've got my contract,' whispered Nelly.

'Don't be too sure.'

Nothing happened during rehearsal or for the rest of the day, and Nelly had stopped worrying as she dressed for dinner. She decided on her new bronze silk, bought in London from a dressmaker selling off last season's models

197

cheaply. While she fastened her thick hair with tortoiseshell combs there was a knock on the cabin door. Mr Grover Jones, said the steward, wished to see her in his state room.

Mr Grover Jones's state room, in the Venetian style and most elaborate, was four times larger than anything Nelly had expected. There was a heavy swell and the room slowly heaved up and down, making the papers and whisky decanter on the desk slip and slide. Grover Jones just caught the decanter in time.

'Sit down.' His back was still turned.

'How does he know it's me,' she thought, obeying.

He swivelled round.

'I've been having one or two thoughts about the show, Miss Briggs. I've decided the "coo-coo-cool" song must be Miss Lane's. It's right for her voice. And it brings her onstage earlier in the act. Understood?'

He waved in dismissal – a habit of his.

Nelly didn't move.

'But my contract said I am to sing two songs.'

He scowled. He'd been nagged interminably by Violet about this girl. Had sworn he would do as Violet wished. Before sex with Violet he would promise anything. He was gazing at the cause of a lot of upsetting nights and he felt worn out.

'Are you arguing with me?'

'How can I? You're the chief. But you said in Paris I was to have two songs and you put it in black and white. I suppose you think Violet –'

'*Miss Lane.*'

'I suppose you think Miss Lane sings "coo-coo-cool" better. But I did sign.'

It was a hopeless attempt. He finished his whisky and poured himself another. This nobody, sexy though she looked, spelled trouble. He had picked her up out of nowhere, glad to find a kid with a voice. Voices, unlike faces and figures, were a problem. Most pretty women opened their mouths and sounded like cats on the roof. All he had done

198

with this one was to fumble a bit and Violet had driven him crazy ever since.

'Get out,' he said.

Nelly stood up and did as she was told.

'You'll have to put up with it,' Claude comforted her later. 'Violet always wins.'

The voyage was almost over and Nelly was sorry. Despite Violet, despite losing her song, she had enjoyed being at sea. The change of scene had done her good, and here in a little world travelling across an enormous ocean she was too young and too busy to pine for her baby. She could bear to think about him now, and feel she'd done the right thing. He was safe. He might not have been if she'd faced poverty on the Butte.

On their final night, Claude persuaded her to stay up so that she could be ready for her first sight of New York:

'I just can't wait to see your eyes pop.'

It was scarcely daylight when the ship slowly, slowly, sailed towards the land. Then . . .

'There!' cried Claude.

She had never seen so majestic a sight. The enormous buildings rising out of the mist . . . it was wonderful, unbelievable . . .

After the excitement of landing and the sound of American voices all around, as strange to Nelly as French had once been, she was sure they would be staying in one of the skyscrapers. But she, Claude, and a dozen other members of the company were deposited at a small and unpretentious hotel, the Carisbrook, on Fifty-Sixth Street. There wasn't a single cloud floating past Nelly's second-floor bedroom window.

'Cheer up,' said Claude. 'At least GJ and Violet aren't here. They're at the Waldorf Astoria spending our profits in advance.'

Cora was to run for a month in New York. Grover Jones had negotiated that with difficulty, before the long tour began. There was just the possibility that if the show was liked when it opened in New York, it might return for a short spell, provided Grover Jones could find a theatre which was dark at that time.

Advance bookings were good and the company sanguine. New York bewitched Nelly. Claude said she went around with her mouth hanging open. He was pleased at her pleasure.

'Can't you *feel* the difference between our old country and their new one? Over here they don't even judge you for what you are. It's what you're going to be that counts.'

Nelly threw herself into rehearsals, working hard, supported by the thought that when she had earned enough she could be with Tom again. She stayed as happy as she could be. Claude, warmed by her pleasure in New York, took her out and about. She found the city exhilarating. They went to Fifth Avenue which he told her was the richest street on earth, filled with more wonderful treasures, even, than the Rue de la Paix. It was odd how various avenues were quite close, yet the people who walked along them appeared totally different. The actors Nelly saw on Broadway were like another race when compared to the working people hurrying long Sixth Avenue. Fifth Avenue was filled with people as elegant and rich-looking as any in the most fashionable streets in Paris. Yet a few blocks away were the huge solemn houses of New York's millionaires, with scarcely a soul in sight. Beyond, again, Madison Avenue was noisy with tramcars. Every avenue in New York seemed to belong to a different world from its neighbours.

The famous American hospitality was evident from the time the company arrived; they were overwhelmed with invitations. Grover Jones was not best pleased and at a rehearsal when they had been two days in New York, shouted at them.

'Your dancing's ragged and your singing is a disgrace. For the next three days nobody is to go out anywhere. I want energy and I want concentration. When you finish work, you go straight back to your hotels to rest. I won't have faces worn out with lack of sleep and breath smelling of alcohol.'

Violet, centre stage, gave a pained frown at his coarseness. But, of course, the embargo did not apply to her. During the three days of enforced Lent for the cast, she and Grover were entertained to dinner by a millionaire in Lafayette Place. She described the entertainment later to a circle of admiring actors, including Alfie Goschawk, a walk-on with whom Nelly noticed Violet often gossiped and laughed. Nelly had heard rumours about those two but kept them to herself. Violet disliked her enough without open war.

'The house was straight out of the *Arabian Nights*!' cried Violet to her admirers. Her special touch with men was a girlish wonder. 'The marble steps led up to a place as big as a cathedral. I wish you'd all seen it. The Beauty Roses on the tables were taller than me. And the food! Shrewsbury oysters and something called canvas-backed duck.'

Murmurs of admiring incomprehension.

'Grover let me have a teensy glass of hock. Wasn't I naughty when you poor things can only drink lemonade.'

Claude had advised Nelly to keep out of the leading actress's way as much as possible and Nelly agreed. The only time she was within range was when she and Violet played a scene together, followed by Nelly's only remaining song.

Claude had grown fond of Nelly, and continued to worry about her. She now only had her one song, and even that had had a verse lopped off. He saw the steady erosion of Nelly's chances and recognised Violet's skill. When she disliked somebody, Violet turned into a rival-eating shark. Yet there were times when he, like Grover Jones, found her irresistible. She had a habit of patting his arm and cooing like a dove.

'Darling Claude. You're so funny, I worship your jokes. Clever Claude, that's what I shall call you.'

Instinctive about women, he knew she didn't imagine that Nelly would replace her in Grover Jones's bed. Her feeling about Nelly was plain fear. She was afraid of Nelly's heart-catching voice, her glowing looks. Nelly was five years younger than Violet, and every day of those years was a century to a woman who hated the calendar and the clock. Under Violet's silken self-assurance were shaking nerves.

Now and then, Claude debated whether to put in a word for Nelly. Wiser not, he thought.

Before the dress rehearsal Violet pulled off a coup. Standing onstage in red satin and feathers she suddenly gave a scream.

'What's this colour called? Bull's Blood Red. It's disgusting. The costume makes me feel sick and that's just how I look. Who brings money into the box office I'd like to know? That girl Briggs wears white in my scene. I must wear white. Put her in brown or dark blue.'

Nelly was given new costumes which extinguished her as if she'd been pushed under a candle-snuffer.

She and Claude sat in the dressing-room after the cast had gone home. Claude sent out for some whisky; he'd forgotten Nelly did not drink.

'What am I to do?' she moaned for the tenth time, surveying the two dreary costumes, one of smudged blue, the other of yellowish brown.

Claude picked up the brown dress. The silly-ass expression was gone.

'Can you sew, Nell?'

She was pierced by a flash of memory just as if something had hit her. Suddenly, she was back in the studio, wailing that she had no dress for the Bal des Trois Quartiers. She heard Matthew's voice. Remembered the painted book muslin. Unconsciously, she put her arms across her stomach. She ached.

'I said, can you sew, darling?'

'Yes.'

'Then just get sewing,' he said.

He and Nelly took the costumes back to the hotel in a brougham. During the night they picked the clothes to pieces, and Claude, fortified by the whisky, helped her to spread out the fragments and attack them with her nail scissors. They cut down the bosom of both dresses. Claude, after an indecent joke or two, persuaded her to rip the lace off her knickers. They shortened both gowns, nipped in the waist, and when she walked up and down the bedroom, she showed a titillating glimpse of ankle, a valley between her breasts, a flick of lace.

Looking at her two transformed dresses as dawn began to pale across the city, Nelly was jubilant. Ignorantly, she imagined that she'd won.

On the night of the opening, it was raining. It came down in torrents, turning the streets into seas of mud, thudding on the carriages and on the new motors driving up to the theatre. The wind battered at ladies as they climbed out, ballooning the waterproofs over their satin dresses – they fled to the foyer like refugees.

Nelly had never before experienced the tensions of an opening night. When her dresser helped her into the transformed costume which she and Claude had worked on in her hotel bedroom, she shivered as if she had a fever. A sleek blond head looked round the door. Claude walked in, put his arms round her and kissed her ear, under the sardonic eye of the coloured American dresser. Limeys, she thought, they tiptoe about like girls. Don't they know how to kiss?

'Chin up,' said Claude. 'You're lovely and sweet and comical, and they'll agree with me.'

Nelly clung to him.

The overture struck up. The show began on its dancing way. The innocent tale was just right for a pouring wet New York night. There was approval in the air; for the cast, the music, most of all for Violet who began to wear the look of an actress who knows she is being loved.

It was not until the last act that Nelly and she had their short scene together, followed by Nelly's song.

'Come along, little cousin,' cried Violet, putting her hand on Nelly's shoulder. But not in the usual casual way. This time she dug her nails through the thin fabric. Terror at seeing the blurred faces of hundreds of people on the other side of the footsteps stopped Nelly from giving a scream. Violet's nails dug deeper. Nelly, managing a sort of trilling laugh, spoke her lines and moved forward to sing.

Then it happened. Right through the song which was Nelly's only chance in the show, Violet was busy. Instead of staying still, wearing an expression of cousinly affection, Violet was occupied with her large picture hat. She took it off with a sweep. She waved it to and fro, making its long ribbons fly. She fanned herself, and got a laugh when the brim tickled her nose. She removed a big daisy from its brim and tried it critically on the skirt of her dress. The hat became a third actor on the stage, there wasn't a member of the audience whose eyes were not fixed on it . . .

When the curtain fell at last, and the applause was over, and the bouquets heaped at Violet's feet and filling her arms had been carried away, Nelly changed out of costume and left the theatre. There was to be a big first-night party; she wouldn't go near it. I won't give her the chance to say a bloody word to me, the clever cow. Her nails went right through my dress.

Going to her room in the quiet hotel, Nelly undressed and lay listening to the rain. Violet's hatred scared her. Suppose Grover Jones gives me the sack, what will become of Tom and me? Children turn us into cowards, I was never afraid until now. Oh, why am I here so far from Paris, with that woman who loathes me and no man to love, she thought. Her aching memories did not go towards Matthew, the scar had begun to heal. She thought of Patrice.

There was a tap at the door, which opened and the slight figure of Claude was outlined in the gaslight of the corridor. He came in softly, carrying two bottles of champagne, winked, and put them down. He locked the door. Then sitting on the bed, gave her a passionate kiss. Miserable, bereft, her head full of sexual memories, she opened her lips and kissed and kissed him. When they separated, his eyes were heavy.

'I want to make love to you, Nell.'

'I haven't said you can't.'

When their passion was spent and they were worn out with loving, he lay gently embracing her. Then gave a violent start.

'Good God, *what's that?*'

A great black and greenish bruise had spread across her shoulder, its centre jagged with a scab of dried blood.

'It's Violet's mark from this evening during our scene. Don't worry, I've given it a wash.'

Claude couldn't speak.

Next morning, the reviews for *Cora* were excellent, the critics received the light-hearted piece with praise. Violet's success was unanimous.

'Her sweetness reaches the heart,' said the *Tribune*.

'What a charmer,' said the *News*. 'You'll fall in love with her the moment you see her. Mr Grover Jones is taking the lovely Miss Lane in *Cora* on a tour of the States. His plan is too modest. *Cora* must come back to us.'

During the morning, while Grover Jones and Violet and the rest of the actors in their different hotels were enjoying and discussing the notices, Nelly had a large solitary breakfast. Claude's love-making had done her good. She'd never allowed people to knock her about, had given as good as she got in the dockside streets, and once when her so-called mother had smacked her face, Nelly had socked her. Crawling to your enemies never kept you safe, she thought. If Violet wants to be rid of me, she'll do it anyway.

Outside, the sun had come out and the pavements had begun to steam.

Nelly knew Violet had the habit of being early at the theatre before a show. She rested in her dressing-room, and took hours to dress. 'She grooms herself as if she were her own racehorse,' Claude once said.

Arriving an hour-and-a-half before the overture, Nelly slipped up the stair to Violet's dressing-room. She didn't knock. She marched straight in.

Violet, wearing a long gown the colour of her name, was dozing. Opening her eyes, she looked at Nelly in disbelief.

'Get out, you.'

'Not a chance.'

'I said get out. Or I'll ring and have you thrown out.'

'You can't. The bell's here.'

Nelly put her hand over it.

Violet's face without paint was slightly lined and colourless,

Nelly noticed with interest. The actress stared at her. It was a technique which like a snake's terrified her opponents.

'I just popped in to warn you,' said Nelly, 'that if you wave that hat about, or if you lay a finger on me again, I shall pick you up and throw you into the orchestra pit. I'm strong, you know. I could do it.'

Silence.

'Don't pretend you don't understand what I'm talking about. And don't pull that face, there's nobody here but me. You did this.'

Unbuttoning her dress, Nelly revealed the bruise and the dried blood.

'And it still * * * well hurts.'

It was comfortable to revert to the fish market. In one of those uncanny flashes when a person unwittingly betrays his or her thoughts, Nelly saw the bruised flesh gave Violet pleasure.

'Yes,' said Nelly, buttoning up the dress. 'I shall pitch you right into the pit, Violet. Grover Jones will then get rid of me, but it'll have been worth it. What a fool you'd look, wouldn't you. On your arse among the violins. So. Keep that hat still and leave me alone. Understood?'

Violet arranged a pillow under neck.

'One can see you come from the gutter.'

'That's right. It's in the gutter you learn tricks like this,' said Nelly, pointing at her shoulder. 'And how to use this,' raising a clenched fist. 'You and I are the same sort. We understand each other.'

She went out. For the rest of the New York run, Violet kept still while Nelly sang. And kept her nails to herself.

Nelly did not tell Claude about the interview. He liked a pleasant life and although he was critical of Boofles, as Grover Jones was said to call Violet, he quite liked her. He preferred not to take sides. But it was with Nelly that he fell a little, not completely, in love.

The New York interlude was soon over and it was time for the long tour. The cast were in good spirits as they crowded into the train which would take them, scenery, costumes, props and all, to their first stop, Boston. A mild winter had been forecast, all the auguries for the tour were good.

The rain had stopped, and when the journey began sunlight poured through the train windows. The carriages were soon tropically hot. They'd be smoked like kippers, Nelly said, if it were not for the Venetian blinds. Actors and actresses lay relaxing in a striped shadow.

Now and again during the first day's journey, Nelly glanced up to see Violet's large eyes fixed, not on her, but on Claude. He woke up after a while, yawning.

'Where are we?'

'Is there a place called Providence?'

'That's right. We'll be there after dinner.'

'Claude.'

'Mmm?'

'Why does Violet keep looking at you like that?'

'Like what?'

'Like she's plotting something.'

'Nell, you mustn't be twitchy about Boofles. She probably thinks I need a haircut.'

But Nelly was right. Before dinner, while the train hurried towards Boston and a delicious meal was about to be served, and pink lights gave romance to the scene, Violet shimmered into the dining-car in *eau-de-nil* silk, came across to Claude and – ignoring Nelly – asked him to sit at her table.

'Grover has to look after the Countess,' said Violet, using the company's nickname for the elderly actress who played her mother in the show. At a far table down the car, Grover was doing his duty by the lady, kittenish and sixty-five. He'd ordered himself a large whisky.

Always the gentleman, Claude excused himself to Nelly and sat with Violet. During her solitary meal (for all the rest of the company were more or less teamed into couples), Nelly heard Violet's determined-to-be-noticed laugh.

Claude apologised later. 'I've known Boofles for years. You understand, don't you?'

Nelly said she did. She was aware that this new lover was no Patrice, mute and faithful as some huge and loving dog. No Matthew, whom she had never lost to another woman, but to a meaningless thing named Honour. Her lovers up until now had been what the word described – lovers. But Claude was sexual company, it was not the same thing. She liked him, and admired his clever silly stage personality, perfect timing, loose-limbed dancing, sweet-toned singing voice. She did not fool herself that he was strong. But good Yankee dollars were going to Edith for Tom. And Claude made love, and made her laugh. It was enough. Wasn't it?

The tour ran into difficulties from the start. Grover Jones was a seasoned campaigner, but he had only organised short American tours in the past, and his calculations and arrangements were based entirely on money: a great deal of money. He had not considered that his actors would have to journey for thousands of miles into the rapidly advancing winter. The tour went from Boston to Baltimore, then up to Chicago, down the great map of the States to St Louis, on to Cincinnati, to Indianapolis, and finally to Detroit before returning to New York. He had a cast of fifty actors, tons of scenery and costumes. He had to hire special trains many of which would arrive in strange towns in the middle of the night. He hadn't grasped – what Englishman did? – the size of the country, the length of the journeys, even what could happen to mounds of luggage on the American railways.

On their very first night in Boston, the company slept through a blizzard, and woke to find a city transformed. Snow two feet deep. The place was already a painting from *Grimm's Fairy Tales*. Turrets of pure white shone under an icy sky, omnibuses, grocers' carts and wagons were now all sleighs.

'This would ruin business in London,' said Claude, as he and Nelly waded through the snow on their way to the theatre.

But the Boston audiences came in droves, and large after-the-show parties were given to the company during the run. Bitterly cold and still snowing, the Boston winter indoors was delightful, graced with large fires and warmer welcomes.

'How friendly Americans are,' said Nelly, when she and Claude were being driven back to their hotel in a real sleigh. 'The women actually like each other. In Paris I only had one woman friend.'

'Do I hear a note of criticism for good old Europe?'

Claude was feeling sexy, and kissed her neck.

'There's no class and that stuff over here either,' said Nelly, bending her head to give him more neck to embrace. 'I love America.'

The weather did not return her affection. When the Boston run ended, the heavy snow still fell. The next stop was Baltimore, the train was delayed and they had to wait for hours on the icy platform. The baggage train, six huge cars, was to be transported by boat, the raft and train being attached to a tugboat. The train was then run on to a floating track to be reconnected at Jersey City. Grover Jones was worried and disagreeable, his actors almost frozen, but at last the train arrived. They streamed into the tropically hot railway car for supper of oyster pie.

Journeys grew harder. Snow thicker. One train that they were due to take was literally blown up on the track; it ran into an enormous drift and fireman and stoker were killed. Grover Jones had chosen the worst winter in ten years for his tour. In Chicago the city was snowbound, the rivers closed, Lake Michigan was solid ice for twenty miles from the shore. The actors muffled themselves in furs.

Nelly and Claude liked Chicago, which sparkled with new buildings. The city had been twice burned down, twice built up, and they thought the new architecture glorious. The marble-fronted buildings along Michigan Avenue were, Claude said, 'just like Regency Brighton but better.' He shouted with derision when Nelly confessed she had never been to Brighton in her life.

The tour had a strange quality, a dream which turned sometimes into a nightmare, a journey of mystery and fear, sudden joys, sudden dangers. They boarded train after train, crossed vast frozen landscapes, faced hardships, and won crowns of success. They were freezing cold, or wrapped in warmth and praise. In St Louis the people were walking across the frozen Mississippi River. After the first performance the company was given an enormous dinner, with *CORA* framed in real flowers, and a speech from the Governor about 'our English cousins'. The tour continued. They saw frozen rivers beginning to break up, great fragments of ice rushed by, and the terrible sight of a flooded city where thousands had been made homeless. They escaped a riot. Claude was astounded next morning to read newspapers supporting the rioters.

'They tell the truth in this country. Why don't we?'

Nelly did not reply. Lies, she thought, could be as necessary as bread.

During all the trials, exhausted, excited, scattered with snow, pelted with flowers, Violet was too occupied, too gracious with admiring strangers, too complacent with admiring notices, to bother again with a vulgar nobody she'd kept from any kind of success.

At last, in a blessed spring that covered Central Park in tender green, in balmy air which brought the New York girls out in pale modish colours, the company returned. Grover Jones's negotiations had succeeded, and the show would run for four weeks at the Daniels Theatre, which had no new opening booked for two months. After their four-week run, the *Cora* company would sail home.

The New York press welcomed *Cora*'s return. 'Every man who hasn't bought his wife and self two tickets to see these English folk at the Daniels must hie there,' wrote the *Tribune*. 'Touring our country has added a certain something. Now they have English polish and American sparkle. Go see!'

With the end of the run in sight, the company talked of nothing but plans. A few of the prettiest chorus girls had been hired for a new Broadway musical comedy – they were staying on. Aggie, a lissom blonde, was marrying a New York businessman. Some of the actors had already arranged for new work in London. Claude and Nelly walked in the park one sunny morning, and stood by a lake feathery with ducks.

'Odd to think, a couple of weeks ago we were in a country nearly dead under the snow,' said Claude, looking up at a tall building white in the sun. 'I feel good today. I just signed my contract for *Kitty*. I like things settled. Of course, you haven't seen the script yet, have you?'

'Not yet.'

'You should do, Nell. There's just your part in the show. I'm surprised GJ hasn't told you. Up to his eyes, of course. Tell you what, you'd better see him about it.'

'I suppose I should.'

'Don't look like that. Boofles is all smiles nowadays and *Kitty*'s tailor-made for her. She's over all that nonsense about you. Why not talk to Grover Jones right away? Strike while the iron's hot, don't you know!'

He bundled her into a brougham, and waved his cane, mouthing, 'Good luck.'

On her journey to the Daniels Theatre, Nelly sat thinking how much she envied Claude. Envied her chorus girl friends. Envied everybody who knew where the next pay cheque was coming from. Yesterday she had received a letter from Edith who had written cheerfully, but said that her work at the Feu Follet had been halved. 'They're economising on the costumes! And I'm afraid I haven't sold one of my poor paintings. What a blessing, dear, that you're earning good wages and little Tom has everything he needs. I enclose a photograph I had taken for you. The photographer is a friend, and didn't charge me!!'

Nelly had slept with the picture under her pillow. The small boy was eight whole months older than when she had left Paris. Why, he would soon be two. He was the same but so grown, so changed, staring sternly out at her from under a little cap.

Grover Jones was in an untidy backstage office at the theatre, alone, smoking a cigar and deep in his accounts. He looked up and saw Nelly coming into the room. The sun was on her lemon-coloured taffeta threaded with green ribbons. She wore a rakish hat, and pushed up her veil.

'Miss Briggs?'

She apologised for disturbing him. He gracelessly agreed that he was very busy. He didn't ask her to sit down, but Nelly did so anyway.

'Mr Grover Jones, I wonder if you would consider me for the part of the maid in *Kitty*,' she said. Claude had told her the part she should have, and the scenes in which she would appear.

He drew on his cigar and said nothing.

Nelly persevered.

'I feel you aren't displeased with me. I'm working at my voice and when I get back to London I'll have some lessons to make it stronger. And then, my dancing . . .'

He interrupted with a sigh. He looked quite human, no longer the glowering lump of a man who seemed to dislike her as much as Violet did.

'I'm afraid that is not possible. I have already cast the maid.'

Nelly felt a knife wound of disappointment. She swallowed.

'Perhaps in the chorus –'

He shook his head. Then, still in the unfamiliar voice, 'Miss Briggs, I can't employ you for *Kitty*. Not to put too fine a point on it, I can't employ you at all.'

She felt as if he had knocked her down.

'Because of Violet,' she managed in a choked voice.

He ground the cigar out in an ash-tray. The air smelled bitter.

'I won't fool you. We both know that's the reason. Miss Lane don't like you. She never has.' He had forgotten about making a grab at Nelly months ago.

'Actresses are temperamental folk, you must know that. Miss Lane is a gifted actress and much loved, and the plain fact is that she is not happy playing with you. There's something in your two personalities that don't match. Who can say why?' said Grover Jones, exchanging with her a philosophical look about the mysteries of acting. 'There it is. I'm sorry. You're right, the maid would have been just your

212

part, and the character has some pretty songs. But I have cast another actress. Very experienced, and Violet, Miss Lane, has played with her before. So. I wish you luck.'

Leaning across the desk, he shook her hand.

Claude had already heard the news by the time Nelly saw him that evening in the wings. He kissed her.

'I'm taking you to Delmonico's. A real smart twenty-dollar meal. We'll talk.'

What about? thought Nelly. Hearing her music cue, she fixed on a brilliant smile and joined the girls tripping on stage.

The restaurant was crowded with New York's élite but Claude was given a good table. With an actress's sense of occasion, Nelly wore her favourite dress embroidered with sequin butterflies. She'd bought it cheaply during the tour. She had tucked two white roses which Claude had given her into her bosom, and wore, with the silks and flowers, the bright radiance of desperation.

Food was respectfully placed before them in the manner used by waiters when both food and customers were rich.

Claude talked. Had Nelly heard the gossip about Violet and Alfie Goschawk? Worse, about Violet and the railway king? Grover Jones had been purple with rage. Did she know the railway johnny was giving a party for the last night?

Nelly smiled and said little.

'You're wondering how the hell to get through this meal, aren't you? I'm only babbling because I hoped it would make you eat a little. Apparently not. You have decided to starve to death.'

'It was kind of you to ask me to this lovely place. I'm no company tonight.'

'It's never kind to want to be with you, Nell, it's selfish. But that look doesn't suit you. I have a surprise. Take the rabbit out of the topper, what? Have you considered,' he screwed in his eyeglass, 'becoming a straight actress?'

'I don't understand.'

'Tush, Nell. A straight actress. No singin'. No dancin'. A

Mrs Pat. A Connie Collier. An Ellen Terry. That sort of gal.'

'Oh. You mean real acting.'

He couldn't help laughing.

'And what, pray, do I do onstage every night? What do you do?'

'Sing one sing and try to dance as best I can.'

'If there's one thing I abhor, it's false modesty. You are good. Audiences like you. You are worth watching. Did it never enter that beautiful thick head that Boofles is only too aware of how good you could actually be?'

'Don't be *stupid*. It was because of Grover Jones.'

'Ancient history, and you're wrong. Violet was jealous of your talent. And the way you look, of course.'

Nelly shook her head impatiently. She did not believe him. As for real theatre, the idea was just crazy. She was still arguing, and getting irritable through anxiety, when a man came up to the table.

'Mr Seidl,' said Claude, springing up, 'Do join us.'

'Coffee and brandy would be welcome,' said the newcomer, giving Nelly a searching look. When Claude introduced him, he gripped Nelly's hand in his large strong one. He was burly and powerful-looking, his round head covered with short, crinkled black hair. His face was fattish, his eyes small and twinkling. She remembered now that she had seen his name on playbills: he was a producer.

'Well, Miss Briggs,' he said in a businesslike manner. 'I have seen your nice little performance in *Cora*. But I hear you are leaving Grover Jones when he sails home. Claude is a great gossip, and tells me you won't be too sorry.'

He swirled the brandy round the glass, glanced from Claude to Nelly and said confidentially, 'I told this young man that I wished to explain my predicament to you yourself, Miss Briggs. He and I were talking it over this afternoon, and your name came up.'

Nelly didn't understand a word. He explained that he had begun to rehearse a new play by a young American dramatist,

214

William Gorman. Did she know his work? Up-and-coming. The play was called *The Truth Game* and had a part for 'an English lass'. He had always disliked American actors playing English rôles, and vice versa.

'However good the ear, they don't really get their tongues round the accents, Miss Briggs. I like reality in my make-believe. The English actress who has been rehearsing the part is Ida Greene.'

'Dear Ida. A clever actress,' Claude interrupted.

'Certainly, but not clever enough to avoid bronchitis.'

'Surely she'll be better in time,' said Nelly.

Seidl looked amused.

'I see what Claude means about you, Miss Briggs. Certainly Ida will be better in time. But not in my time, you see. There isn't a chance of her playing in *The Truth Game*. It's her own fault. She will wear such thin clothes. It's a marvel she isn't twanging a harp. Well, then . . . I've been wondering about you.'

Nelly's eyes grew enormous.

'Me?'

'Exactly so. Shall we say ten o'clock tomorrow at the theatre?'

The following day he spent four hours with Nelly at his theatre. He made her read lines, enter, exit, walk, stand up and sit down. She had to run across the stage with outstretched arms. She had to laugh. He did not ask her to cry. Halfway through the ordeal, he gave her hot coffee and talked about the difference between musical and straight theatre.

'Music supports the actor. It keeps him buoyant. With words alone, it must all be here,' he said, pressing his hand against her forehead.

Nelly stood listening with rapt attention, staring at the floor. She was wearing a hat decorated with a blue feathered bird and, while he talked, Leon Seidl stroked the bird over and over again. It was like being hypnotised.

Finally, he gave her some lines to speak to a young actor

who was waiting in the wings. Then she had to put her arms round his neck.

The young man smiled at her. Nelly said her lines, and threw his arms round him. They kissed, drew apart, smiled, kissed again.

When the embrace ended, Seidl said, 'You're hired.'

CHAPTER TWELVE

The switch from one song and some dancing in the chorus of a musical comedy to a real part in a real play happened too fast for Nelly to lose her nerve. Leon Seidl had seen in *Cora* that she had the mysterious quality of stage presence. It was something one player possessed but another, as gifted, did not, and Leon had never understood it.

But Nelly had a thousand things to learn when she started in what Americans called the 'legitimate' theatre. She did miss the music at first. She missed its support and had never realised how much she'd used it to keep afloat. She missed the very atmosphere of musical comedy. Violet Lane had been a threatening presence, it was true, but there had been the frivolity and merriment of the girls. Their faces broke into sunny smiles when they heard the music cues. They danced onstage like the arrival of lovely weather. And there had been the pleasure of Claude's dancing. And his friendship.

She had never used her brains at work until now. She returned at night dog-tired to the tiny apartment in Greenwich Village which Leon Seidl had found for her. To act, to *be*, was so difficult. She grew slowly. She had voice problems until she learned how to place the voice without straining her throat. In *Cora* the cast had simply bellowed their lines. In the new play, the actors appeared to speak in a relaxed, natural way yet they could be heard at the back of the gallery. She worked all day and often half the night. She learned exercises, she learned to move, to relax, to tense, to stand immobile.

'Now you do *that* well,' said her teacher, a wizened ex-ballet

217

dancer, Hungarian and a despot, when he had told her to freeze into stillness.

'I was an artists' model once.'

'So. So. Then you must know that the back is the source of strength,' he said, and gave her a positively staggering blow.

Cripes, thought Nelly, watching the leading actors at rehearsal, they make it look so easy. At night she rehearsed in front of a looking-glass, repeating her speeches over and over. She finished with a fierce, 'You're lousy.'

'Nelly,' said Leon Seidl, on the day of the dress rehearsal. 'There is something I must tell you.'

Pale with tiredness, she was sitting cross-legged at a corner of the stage.

'Don't be anxious. I just want you to remember that in acting the doing is four-fifths of everything. You'll discover later what it *is*. See what I mean?'

'No, Mr Seidl.'

'You will. Get on and do it. That's all.'

Nelly's part in *The Truth Game* was not long but it was one which actors would call showy. The character she played, an English girl, had only two scenes. But they were essential to the story, showed the reactions of the four principal characters, and needed a sense of comedy.

Had she thought she was nervous when *Cora* opened? On the first night of *The Truth Game*, when she was making up in her dressing-room, her hand shook so much that she dabbed the powder puff into her mouth.

Her entrance was not until after the first half-hour of the play. Nelly, in white silk blouse and trim dark skirt, stood in the wings waiting for her cue. Russell Thompson, the leading actor, also made his entrance at the same time. He was attractive, rather short, with slanting eyes and a wide expressive mouth. As he took his place by her, he squeezed her hand – and felt it trembling.

He bent and whispered to her, '*Enjoy yourself, Nelly*. If *you* do, the audience will.'

The play ended, the curtain fell, flew up again, the audience loudly applauded. After the first bows, Nelly and the other minor players left the stage, and she stood watching the main actors taking their curtains. Suddenly, she heard her name, 'Nelly Briggs! Nelly Briggs!'

The audience was calling for her. Russell Thompson came running offstage, grabbed her hand and pulled her into the patch of brilliant light. As Nelly curtseyed, the applause seemed to drench her all over. It was like a wonderful, a vast Chez Paul-Marc.

Within a few days of signing her contract with Leon Seidl, Nelly had written to Paris, sending Edith more money than she'd ever sent before. The girls exchanged excited letters. Finally, Nelly booked two berths on the *Kaiser Wilhelm*, which proudly claimed to be the 'largest and fastest ship in the world'. The berths were expensive and she had to borrow an advance from Leon Seidl.

'Edith,' she explained, 'is my great, great friend.' And the child was a young tragically orphaned cousin. Seidl, with Jewish warmth for family feeling, approved.

'Poor little kid. No parents, eh? Yes, bring 'em both over for a while. As long as they don't stop you working hard.'

'I'd never do that, Mr Seidl.'

'You might. I reckon your heart rules your head.'

'Oh no. I'm hard as iron.'

He said he was glad to hear it.

She scarcely matched that description when she went to meet Edith and Tom off the boat. It was due to dock at half-past eight on a misty winter morning. Clouds floated across the tops of the skyscrapers. Nelly joined the crowds along the quay, pulling her coat round her, and telling herself that she was only shivering from cold.

A flat stretch of water lay between ship and shore. Nelly looked across, and thought – he's there, and he isn't going to know me. Months had gone by since she'd parted from him at the Gare du Nord, a baby with a round face, slate-blue eyes and an upper lip like Matthew's. His pudgy hands had creases, his nose was an absurd blob. That baby must have vanished by now.

All the time she had been in America she had never lost the feel and look of Matthew's son. But the memory was static. The stiff little photographs and pencil sketches had been Edith's way of getting Nelly used to the changes time had wrought on her baby. But Nelly only remembered him as he was *then*. He'd known her then. And had been hers. She had given away all those months of his life for the best of reasons, which had hurt like hell and still did: to keep a vow that he would never be poor, dirty and foresaken, always be safe and loved.

The ship began to move very slowly towards the quay. At last the great snaking ropes were made fast, gangways like high bridges fixed from ship to quayside. And in an interval like a journey through pain she waited until she saw Edith's neat figure. And a little person whom Edith was holding by the hand . . .

When, blushing with excitement, she threw herself down on her knees to kiss him the child did not recognise her. He backed away, clinging to Edith's skirts.

'That's Tante Nelly, you silly boy,' said Edith in a cooing voice, picked him up and firmly dumped him in Nelly's arms. The little boy looked up at her, wonderingly. Edith knew he'd noticed Nelly was crying.

It took Nelly days to get used to her son and to accept that she was a stranger to him. A stranger who soon won shy smiles, but an unknown lady just the same. The baby was gone for ever, and in its kissable place was a small person with a vocabulary, Edith had counted, of a dozen words. He had serious eyes with long eyelashes, was good-looking and shy and climbed a good deal on to Edith's lap. The girls showed him picture books. He identified in French a dog, a rabbit and a cow. When Nelly bought him some coloured bricks he went crimson with pleasure, and spent an hour banging them together. She remembered the easel pegs.

Edith and Tom shared the Greenwich apartment with Nelly, and every morning she heard Tom laughing in Edith's room. One afternoon it was arranged for Edith to smuggle him into the theatre during a matinée. They sat in a box. Edith had the child on her knee. Staring at the brightly lit stage, his eyes were like saucers until his mother entered. Suddenly, he said in a ringing voice, '*Nelly!*'

Time went fast. Their return passage was booked; only a few days remained. One morning Edith came into her bedroom with Nelly's breakfast tray and sat on the bed.

'I've been thinking about something. I'm sure you have, too. About Tom knowing you are his mother.'

'Edith. I do long for him to know.'

'Of course you do.'

'But you think,' said Nelly, reading her friend's face, 'I shouldn't tell him when he's older.'

'I think that you can't.'

'You mean because he'd hate me.'

'What stupid things you say sometimes. How could he hate you? He will always love you.'

'It's you he loves.'

'Yes, he does. Because he is so little and I am the one who looks after him at present. But when he is with you all the time he'll love you with his whole heart . . . he won't be able to help it. You still can't tell him, Nelly. He'll go to school. Grow up. You can't put that burden on him. People are cruel. Even when they don't mean to be.'

Nelly looked at her, and gave a long shuddering sigh.

There was a pause.

'Keep him with you,' Edith said suddenly.

'I – I can't.'

'Why not?'

'It would be cruel.'

'If you mean cruel to me, that's twaddle. You want him. He's yours.'

'But you're his real mother now. You're everything to him. It's like the story in the Bible about two women and the baby,' said Nelly, incoherently recalling a sermon she had once heard.

'The judgement of Solomon? So which of us wants to saw Tom in half?' said Edith dryly.

Fate intervened, in the thick-set figure of Leon Seidl. Instinctive about his actresses, he came into her dressing-room after a performance.

'When is your friend taking the lad back to Paris?'

'Edith is sailing next week. I thought,' said Nelly, taking it at a run, 'I thought I might try to get a nurse and keep the boy with me.'

Leon tugged a piece of his short hair.

'Well, now. I'm not sure that's such a good idea.'

She realised at that moment that he knew. The story she and Edith had concocted first in Paris, now in New York, had not deceived him. Perhaps people in the theatre who lived by their imaginations were the ones you couldn't lie to. Leon hadn't believed those cousins in London, conveniently dead with typhoid, the small orphaned child whom Edith had taken over as guardian and godmother, and Nelly's second cousinship to him. How admiring American friends who were not in the theatre had been, on hearing the tale. Leon had listened without comment.

He did not spell anything out now either. It did not concern him.

'I've fixed up a nice tour for when the show eventually closes. Of course, dates can never be firm, but Boston and Washington very much want us. It will be a high-class tour. Nothing like that nightmare you had to suffer with Grover Jones – I'm afraid there were a lot of jokes about *that*! Well, Nelly. I have a feeling you shouldn't be distracted right now. You're at the start of a new career and you need to concentrate. Now and later. Nose to the grindstone. You just pack the youngster back to Paris with that swell Edith.'

It was months before Nelly saw them again. The run ended, it had been a great success, there was a short tour, and then a new play, *A Runaway Wife*, went into rehearsal. Nelly had a considerably larger and more important rôle, again as an English girl. Leon actually had the part rewritten for her. This time she did not need to borrow any money when she wrote and begged Edith to bring Tom to New York for a second visit.

When they arrived, Nelly found seeing Tom upset her more than the first time. He seemed to be growing and changing while she watched, looking at her with Matthew's eyes. She felt she couldn't bear to lose him – ever again. Leon was hospitable to the visitors, bought Tom expensive toys and didn't inquire when they were going back to Paris.

It was bitterly cold, snow was whirling, stopping, whirling again. With Tom muffled like an eskimo, Edith took him out to Central Park when Nelly was at rehearsal. They built a snowman. Then he trotted ahead, sliding experimentally on the frozen pathway.

'Look out or you'll fall!' called Edith. But too late. He came down with a bump, and wept loud indignant tears.

A girl nearby burst out laughing, picked him up, kissed him and brought the desolate bundle over to Edith. Tom was mopped and comforted. He then walked between them and they swung him, now and then, like a shopping-basket.

The stranger was a pleasant, direct young girl whose name was Kirstin, she was half-Danish. She told Edith she wanted to look after 'a little fellow just like this one. I am good with children. And they with me. I am,' said Kirstin gravely, 'very attentive.'

A week later Nelly had met the girl's parents, Kirstin had spent a day with Tom and Edith, and the thing was arranged. Tom liked her. But, as Edith said, what man of two or seventy-two can resist a pretty woman giving him hours of her devoted time?

'Oh Edith. It is all too good to last,' said Nelly.

Edith replied that she supposed nothing, good or bad, lasted for ever. But Kirstin might until Tom went to school.

The two girls were sitting in Nelly's cramped room in

Greenwich Village on a Sunday morning. Tom was out in the park again with Kirstin. Nelly was sitting on the floor. She looked up at her friend.

'I wish I didn't so dreadfully want him back. And that –'

'That you weren't in my debt? Is that it? But you aren't, Nelly.'

'I have taken so much from you.'

'How can you say that? Did you take my time? Looking after him never wasted a minute. Liberty? I was never freer. Other friends? I was never lonely. He has been my blessing. Now he'll be yours.'

Kirstin stayed at home with Tom when Nelly went to the docks to see Edith on board. Her friend was wearing a thick new cape and her sketchbooks were strapped together with a big handsome new folding easel. In her buttonhole was a tinsel flower Tom had given her.

The girls embraced in the old way – three kisses in the French fashion. And it was only when Nelly held her at arm's length and looked at her that she saw how Edith suffered.

Money and the beginnings of fame, those gods with claws, were kind to Nelly. She was still the same girl as at La Vache Enragée, she still 'lent' money to people in trouble and to others whose troubles were invented. What had begun to change out of all recognition was her life.

Not so for Edith who returned to the same Montmartre studio, working the same long hours until the enemy of painters, fading daylight, came stealing up on her.

When she was home again in Paris she missed Tom at first for every waking moment. She dreamed of him like a lover, and sometimes woke crying. But there was work. Her weary task at the Feu Follet was reduced, but still paid her rent and slender meals. For all the rest of her waking hours, she painted.

Young painters in the new century were finding many odd and unexpected problems. Painters were no longer required to imitate nature, to use her literal forms and colours. They could reshape forms, heighten or change colours, add and subtract what they wished. Such freedom, hacking down the laws of the past, was full of danger and Edith knew it. She painted subjects of complete simplicity. A tree in flower, a girl in a café, a dusty road on the Butte, the outlines of the still unfinished Basilica of Sacré Cœur, a table with a loaf, fruit and a jug arranged for a meal. Her touch and colour grew more sure. But she was much alone and without the child in the centre of her life, she became curiously unanchored. Her Scots reserve kept her from making another of those passionate Montmartre friendships which turned so quickly into sex. Since Réné had angrily left her, she'd had no other lover. She was slowly healing from a different kind of love. Anyway, painting was a lover; often a cruel one.

Walking along the walled, tree-shaded Rue des Saules one summer morning, she saw Patrice. He was carrying two canvases, and staring at the ground, so absorbed in thought that she didn't like to speak to him. Just as he passed, he looked up.

'Edith!'

They hugged as only friends did in France.

How long since they had seen each other! They fell into step, with Edith talking and Patrice listening and smiling and not saying a word. She spoke of Nelly and Tom in America. He did not smile then. When they said goodbye she felt daring enough to ask, 'How is your painting?'

'I don't know, Edith. It seems we're all only beginning. Do you feel so?'

'Oh yes. Yes.'

After that they met now and then. One evening, he called at her studio bringing, of all things, three cauliflowers which he carefully placed on the bench.

'You could paint them. Or eat them,' he said. Then, 'I've been thinking,' he said. That amused her, since he did nothing else. 'Go and see Monsieur Vollard.'

'The dealer? But – '

225

'He buys pictures from people like us. Even when nobody else will. He believes we can do it.'

'Has he –'

'Yes. He put me under contract,' said Patrice, almost helplessly. When she saw him to the door he gave her one of his throttling hugs.

'Did you know I am married? She is a good girl. Comes from Crèvecœur. Good to paint, too. A fine model. Monsieur Vollard thinks so.'

He stood brooding over the cauliflowers.

'And Nelly is in America?'

'She is doing well.'

'Naturally. Naturally.'

'Perhaps you will see her again one day.'

'I see her all the time. Monsieur Vollard wants my nudes of her.'

The silence that followed was so long that Edith supposed the conversation was over.

'He can't have them,' said Patrice. And gave his heart-breaking smile.

The next morning Edith rolled half-a-dozen canvases into her only silk scarf, and set off for the gallery. All young artists knew about Ambroise Vollard. After ten years in Paris his name carried weight. He had been Cézanne's clever champion, arranging two exhibitions for him. Artists now clustered round the man, who was both shrewd dealer and powerful patron. I will be right out of my depth, thought Edith as she walked through the summer streets. She knew none of the burning new talents. By chance, she had once talked to Pierre Bonnard who had made it plain he didn't make friends in cafés with stray young female painters. Quite right too, thought Edith.

Telling herself in Scots not to be a 'wee timorous beastie', she pushed open the door of the gallery. The place was small and wonderfully untidy. It was cluttered with rolled canvases on dusty shelves, portfolios of drawings, large faded books, framed pictures propped against chair legs, two brimming paper baskets, and a large iron safe. The bearded owner in a frock coat that had seen better days was at a table, head in his hands. He appeared to be dozing.

'Monsieur Vollard?'

He turned and looked at her with eyes so sharp and so deep they were like weapons.

Edith left the gallery an hour later with the silk scarf tied round her shoulders. And empty hands.

During the two years in which Nelly's star rose in New York, Edith was able to give up the Feu Follet, and simply paint. Like Patrice, she was put under contract by Ambroise Vollard. She no longer needed to do long sums to see if she could afford a new canvas. Vollard bought her paintings; now and again he sold one.

It was never easy to buy a picture from him, Edith noticed. Once she happened to be in his gallery when a prosperous-looking lady in furs came in. She looked about, and returned to study for a second time one of Edith's street scenes which was propped against the wall. She then made an offer for it. The price was just about what Vollard had set on the painting, and Edith, hastily turning her back to stare at some drawings, listened eagerly.

To her horror, Vollard said after a pause, 'I'll think it over.'

A longer pause.

He then named a price ten times more than the figure he had scribbled on the back of the painting.

Edith could have wept.

But the lady laughed, told Vollard he was 'a perfect monster', and bought it.

On the whole, Vollard paid Edith adequately but never generously. What was generous was his interest; he knew how to bind an artist to him hand and foot. She was inspirited and encouraged by the sword-sharp look of his eyes. When he stayed awake, that was. She was not the only painter to be discomfited when, during a conversation, he went straight off to sleep.

Part III

CHAPTER THIRTEEN

'I wonder if perhaps I might stay in Leckford this year?' said Alice on a spring evening before the start of the London Season.

She and Matthew were alone in the Yellow Drawing-room. Honoria was in the chapel, there were no guests, and Matthew himself would be out tonight. Alice knew why.

She had matured a little since her marriage, but not very much. She was still the quiet girl whose light had been dimmed by a brilliant sister. But she was very splendid in her Worth gowns and her figure was rather fuller. She had a little air of authority which amused Matthew. What did not amuse him was the expression in her eyes.

He knew that *she* knew, by instinct, of his present affair, the second since their marriage. But he had no intention of allowing his wife to dodge her duty.

She bent over some embroidery and he wondered as he often did where the devil all that sewing landed up.

'Alice, is there – well – is there a particular reason why you don't want to come to London? Have you seen Doctor Atkinson?'

'No. Why should I? I am perfectly well.'

They both knew what he had meant.

'Surely it would be possible for me to miss a Season now and then. I – one – is expected to do so much. Be seen about so often. And there are so many rules. Englishwomen do seem hedged about with them and I still find them very –'

She was too polite to finish the sentence.

'The rules are only to protect you, my dear girl.'

Matthew spoke with his usual grace, but they had had this conversation before.

It was a paradox that, once banished, he now kept Society's rules so dutifully. He rode with her in Hyde Park, visited their countless friends, went to Court, to receptions and dinners and balls, and for long dazzling country weekends where peaches ripened on old brick walls and the air smelled of syringa. Alice was always beside him; his consort. The girl he had married as an offering to Leckford. He no longer thought it a sin to have sacrificed her on so questionable an altar.

'I am sorry,' he said, 'but of course we will have to go. Perhaps you'll see more of Mrs Keppel this Season. She is so charming, and has many American friends.'

He stood up, asking her permission to leave.

She watched him go. She put down her petit-point, its dull seventeenth-century colours and grotesque flowers sickened her. She looked out of the window at a mass of red tulips. Another kind of woman, living here with a handsome titled husband, money, would be happy. It is my fault I can't love him, she thought. It's true that Mother forced me to marry him but I should be able to bear it by now. And I can't.

She had known almost nothing about sex before she married and had tried to ask her mother 'What is going to happen?' Constance Mary had looked at her in disgust.

'You've seen paintings and statues. You know perfectly well that men are made differently from women. Don't ask such questions. You are not as stupid as you look.'

Later, finding her in her bedroom, Fran had guessed. Girls didn't look like that on the evening before their wedding except for the obvious reason.

'Ma didn't tell you.'

'What do you mean?' Alice flinched.

'What you're in for tomorrow night. Typical of Ma. I've often thought I ought to tell you, and now seems to be the right time, doesn't it?'

But Alice put her hands over her ears.

Why did I do that, she wondered later. What an idiot I was.

But it had been because she was afraid. Her sister had looked at her with pity, and left her.

The New York wedding was large and fashionable and the bride, like all brides, beautiful and bashful. After the reception the Viscount and his lady had driven to Lenox to stay in the Vandermeyer house for a week's honeymoon before returning to Europe.

Alice's old nurse, Mary Murphy, now promoted to personal maid, was to come on the honeymoon and to accompany her to the new English life. Mary was sixtyish, stout, loyal and holy, as staunch an Irish Catholic as any woman in New York, who larded her conversation with invocations to saints and angels.

On the wedding night, coming into her young mistress's bedroom, Mary helped her to undress, slipping over her head the new white satin nightdress decorated with lace. Neither bride nor nurse spoke. Mary Murphy brushed and plaited her hair, said 'God bless you,' and left her.

Alice climbed into bed.

Matthew came out of his dressing-room a few minutes later, an ominous stranger in a dark gold and brown brocade robe. He turned out the gas lamps until there remained only the tall candle by the bedside. Sitting down by her, he took her hand and kissed it. It was very cold.

'Dear, dear girl. You must not be frightened of me.'

'I'm not.'

'We love each other. Everything we are going to do is right. The way it should and must be. You've heard of the right true end of love, my darling.'

She didn't answer and Matthew had a pang of pity for the young creature lying, virginal and untouched. He had never taken a virgin before and he was moved and concerned for her. He took off his gown and got into bed and at once could feel how she trembled. Suddenly, he forgot pity and felt only the excitement of conquest surging through him. Putting out his hand he pulled up the heavy satin of her nightdress, stroking her flat stomach. He caressed her hips, slipped his hand under her to cup the rounded bottom, then stroked the maidenhair and plunged his fingers into the soft flesh which in a moment he would thrust into with the weapon of himself. She made no sound as he climbed on to her, opening her legs with his own, pressing into her, quite slowly, then more strongly. As he penetrated deeply she gave a gasp of pain.

'My little virgin,' he said, thrusting hard, and the very words excited him, and he remained, thrusting on and on and getting a strange pleasure from the quivering body under his. When he reached his climax, he gave a low ecstatic groan and rolled off her.

He slept at once, separated, but grasping her hand.

Alice did not sleep. So this was the secret of sex which she had only dimly guessed; its power made her tremble still. She had never imagined that that part of a man could be so hard and inexorable, could take away the self which had belonged until now only to her. She was his possession. The mysterious fleshly act would turn her into a mother soon; the seeds Matthew had forced, groaning, into her would burgeon in the body which at present she felt she simply didn't own. Do women really enjoy it? How can they? Perhaps they pretend, she thought. And tears came into her eyes, lying awake through the long night of her lost virginity.

The first desperation left her, she grew used to Matthew's demands, but she never knew a climax or realised women had such a thing. He never spoke of it and, unenlightened, she believed that women simply lay supine while men took their pleasure. He wanted her often. And, when he took her while the candle was still burning, making her sit above him so that he could thrust upwards and watch himself going into her, she never lost a feeling of the deepest shame.

Matthew enjoyed his love-making but thought his little bride too innocent and too nervous. He was convinced all that would be better in time. He was in a mood to enjoy. His brief sojourn in America interested him. The women were as lovely as in his own country; they wore as many diamonds and even, on grand occasions, tiaras. But he was conscious of the democracy round him. Who would these shining creatures actually curtsey *to*? The idea of their curtseying at all was impossible. Americans believed in themselves, believed that everybody was as good as everybody else. There was no precedence, no ladder made with the knotted hands of time. If you had initiative, you climbed up to the top. These people were strong and, for all their faults, their democracy made his own seem a false word for privilege.

But he did not for a moment wish to remain in Alice's country, and during the journey home talked to her tenderly about the new life she was about to enter.

'But I have been in English society, Matthew. We were there for three months. Longer even.'

'You were a foreigner then. The rules did not apply.'

'Oh, you mean making one's début and so on. It's the same in New York when a girl enters Society. Thirty years ago, you know, girls in New York were just given a small family dinner when they came out. Archibald Gracie King changed all that when he gave his daughter a coming-out ball at Delmonico's. Now it's all the fashion. Fran and I both had our parties there . . . it was quite an ordeal, really.'

Early on in her marriage, she had liked to tell him things. Matthew said gently.

'I'm sure. But our rules are scarcely the same. There are a good many rules for English ladies.'

'Not married ladies.'

'Those too. Let me see. What shall we start with? Well, you mustn't walk alone in London, y'know.'

She was amazed.

'But I can shop by myself in Bond Street.'

'I'm sorry. No. You must take a companion.'

Her American blood quite boiled at anything so outlandish and Matthew saw her face. He took her hand.

'Wait, Alice. What I am saying will help. Please understand that. You will have to remember that it is not done for a lady to travel in a hansom alone. Just as it would be considered fast to dance more than twice with the same person at a ball. That is important.'

235

'Oh Matthew, you must be funning!' she exclaimed, blushing with annoyance.

He said patiently that she would understand the rules after a while because they were common sense. If a lady danced three or four times with the same man, the wrong construction would be put on that. It might be believed that there was something too close in the acquaintanceship.

'As if *you* could do anything so impossible,' he added.

During the voyage, Alice kept thinking of how Fran would laugh. It seemed that visiting Americans, much fêted, had no true conception of what went on in Society. Alice was shy and had been forced into her marriage but she was not a fool. Listening to him, she saw her husband was as serious as the worst snob who knew *Debrett* by heart.

'You will learn it all easily. You're so quick, Alice.'

'And your relatives. I must meet them of course.'

'There are rather a lot, cousins, second cousins. You'll be able to read them all up in *Burke*. Some are very boring, we only need to see them once a year at Leckford.'

'For dinner?'

'For a month.'

He warned her that on her arrival at Leckford Court there would be a 'sort of shindig' of welcome. Alice imagined a few of his friends. She did not expect to be met at the station by a carriage with four horses and two outriders, the whole equipage decorated with ropes of flowers. It was July and there must have been thousands of marguerites, their round white faces and yellow hearts plaited and bunched and looped and tied, and pushed into the horses' browbands.

A triumphal arch, more marguerites, was strung across the Leckford drive. As they drove to the house the entire village school was waiting to greet them, the children waving Union Jacks and the women curtseying like so many respectful, bobbing corks. Where, thought Alice, were all those Britons who never, never would be slaves?

During the first months of her marriage she learned in a hard school. She must visit county neighbours or tenants and the visit should never be less than half-an-hour, 'but preferably forty minutes'. She had to have ready a supply of small-talk and local news. Nobody seemed to Alice to say what they really thought. Not to her anyway.

Her American love of comfort rebelled at the total lack of bathrooms. Leckford did not have a single one and she had to bath in a zinc tub in front of the fire, hot and cold water, towels, mats, sponges, all carried in by long-suffering Mary Murphy who invariably remarked, 'All the English are mad.'

'I know, Mary, but don't let's show them we think so.'

'Holy Mother of God, Miss Alice, I can't hide my feelings even if you can.'

Elderly Mary was unpopular with every member of the Leckford staff. Her stout figure in long starched aprons, her strong face with grey plaits, were regarded coldly by butler, housekeeper and all the servants except the youngest. Mary Murphy grew more American with every day that passed.

There were compensations in Alice's new life. At first. Her father's prediction that his good American dollars would pour into a bucket full of holes did not prove true. In the first year of her marriage, Alice put all her energy and imagination into Leckford Court. She rebuilt, repaired, redecorated and, slowly, the lovely place became the masterpiece it used to be. Alice had flair. She went to Sotheby's, to Spinks to choose more silver, to a City warehouse for Oriental silks. The fascinating task was finished at last. And it was then that Alice had nothing to do but be Lady Leckford.

She grew quieter. Matthew guessed she was not happy. What the hell can I do about it, he thought. I treat her well enough. If I have an affair, I'm discreet. I'm certainly kind to her. I simply don't understand what she's thinking.

The London Season held its pitiless reign from April until the end of July, followed by Cowes and then Scotland (Alice did manage to avoid Scotland). The exhausting opulence cost a small fortune, but Alice had that and Matthew helped to spend it. She learned like an actress to play the part. She grew up fast. She had so many acquaintances that her scarlet leather address-book ran into two volumes. She did not have a single close friend.

When Alice was engaged, Fran had discussed the fearful prospect of old Lady Leckford living in the house.

'You poor thing. She chills the marrow of my bones. Why don't you get Matthew to pack her off into a Dower House? That's what they do in novels.'

'Leckford hasn't got a Dower House.'

'Mmm. I can see you can't suddenly build one. Too crude,' said Fran, shooing Mary Murphy out of the bedroom and beginning to brush Alice's long hair.

'Six, seven, eight . . . what pretty hair you have. I like it better than mine. Well, I can't see how you're going to cope with the old witch, beg her pardon, Viscountess.'

'She's very holy.'

'So she can spend her time on her knees, is that the solution?' said Fran, roaring with laughter.

Fran's jokes turned out true. Old Lady Leckford did spend a great deal of time in prayer in the chapel which Alice had restored to its former glory.

Like her father, she had been dismayed by the condition of the chapel, and had also thought there were more monuments to the family than to the Almighty. Near the altar was the statue of Robert Leckford. It was in white marble, a beautiful youth in uniform his eyes looking heavenwards, his rifle clasped in his hands. On rainy days or at twilight, it looked exactly like an apparition. Robert's mother knelt at the front of the chapel on the right, just by the statue. She kept a blue oil lamp burning in front of it, as she kept a red one burning in front of the tabernacle where the Blessed Sacrament was.

'Matthew, is the statue like your brother?' Alice asked.

'Not really. It's Robert, but not Robert. And I never saw him look upwards in his life.'

'Not at the sky?'

'Literal girl. I mean he wasn't religious. If he'd seen that statue he'd have had a fit. Let's talk about something else. Who is dining tonight?'

238

Matthew seldom spoke about Robert and Alice could scarcely ask the mother who mourned him still. In Alice's mind Robert remained a marble spectre.

Old Lady Leckford in her cold way was quite kind to Alice. They had their religion in common but they were not friends. But who, thought Alice, could be friends with her? Only Father McKenna occasionally made the old lady smile. Alice wondered if her mother-in-law would change when – if – there was a baby.

The Vandermeyers arrived in London to see their younger daughter in the spring of 1903. They stayed in a fashionable hotel which Lorn disliked, not an electric light in the place and Piccadilly more often than not drenched in rain.

Alice had not seen her parents since her marriage and when she first kissed them, she cried. Fran was not with them. She was expecting her first child soon.

'She positively shouted when the doctor said she couldn't come,' said Constance Mary. 'She was being ridiculous. Her husband indulges her so. A man should not give his wife her own way all the time.'

Lorn was inevitably called away to the telephone just then, his business colleagues were legion. Constance Mary looked pleased to be alone with her daughter. She went over to her and took her by the shoulders, giving her an observant look.

'Well, Alice?'

'Very well, thank you, Mother.'

'Of course you are. What I am saying is are you like Fran? Expecting? You certainly should be by now.'

'Not yet, I'm afraid.'

Constance Mary raised her eyebrows and returned to her chair. Alice stood by the curtained window, looking out at the rain. Then she, too, sat down. Her mother thought her too self-possessed.

'I take it Matthew is all that a husband should be? In that way, I mean.'

'Of course.'

'There is no "of course" about a man's marital duties. Is he – ah – regular?'

Good God, thought Alice, am I expected to give her the dates and times when Matthew decides to do it. It's often enough. I wish I wanted it as he does. I wish I wanted *him*.

'Yes, Mother, he is. I simply have not conceived a child yet and I know he longs for one as much as I do.'

'One will come in God's good time.'

Constance Mary decided her daughter was receiving enough sex, and that Alice would become pregnant eventually. She had a sort of pity for any woman who didn't fall, as she phrased it, right away. She'd conceived Fran on her honeymoon and her own problem with a far-too-rampant Lorn had been not getting pregnant year after year. For Catholics this meant self-denial which they hadn't enjoyed at all. Constance Mary had borne four children, two unfortunately stillborn. If she and Lorne hadn't restrained themselves, she would doubtless have been mother to ten. She halted her sexual musings to look at Alice again.

Her daughter sat straight-backed, very unlike Fran who, big with child, sprawled all over the place. Alice's rich dark gown swept the ground, to reveal the toe of an impeccable bronze shoe. She wore old-fashioned diamonds and a brooch in the shape of a coronet outlined in emeralds. I don't know my child any more, thought Constance. I wanted her to be one of those titled people and that's what's happened.

Her parents' visit upset Alice for all her hard-earned guard. She'd forgotten the frankness and sturdiness of her own people, their vigour and flexibility, so unlike the tradition and formality in England. She had forgotten how natural and down-to-earth they were. *They* called all their servants by name, and some of them were their friends.

But Alice's life was full, and homesickness receded. She still hoped desperately for a child. She began to wonder if love-making meant anything to Matthew at all. He never used endearments when he spoke to her, never touched her hand when they walked in the garden or put his arm round her waist if they were alone in a room. He only touched her by taking her. Naked beneath him, a conquered city with gates broken and forced wide, she could not respond. When he possessed her she submitted. Thinking it would make a child.

On the evening Matthew told her she must go to London for the Season as usual, a letter was brought to Alice after he had left. She read it in her bedroom and it made her cry.

Unknown to her husband, recently she had gone to London for a charity committee and had taken the opportunity to consult a Harley Street specialist. He asked her to see a second doctor, and now sent her both opinions. The doctors were convinced she could not have a baby.

Alice sat looking at the letter as if it were a death sentence. Matthew did not love her. He had never made her the wife of his heart. He had married her to Leckford Court and to the men who doffed their caps to the family who had been there for nearly five hundred years. He had wedded her to the arrogant portraits, the names in the chapel; he had made her the wife of that white marble brother.

Without children, what was left? The ritual. The crowds of frivolous, patronising foreigners among whom she lived. The English rain.

She felt slightly ill and when she was dressing for dinner, Mary Murphy took one look at her and reverted to her own Irish childhood.

'Glory to God what is it yer doing and not in yer bed this instance?'

Alice protested. Mary took no notice but folded down the bedcovers.

Mary Murphy sat dozing in one of the footmen's chairs in the hall when Matthew returned at midnight. He looked startled when he saw her.

'She's in bed with a temperature of 102 and best you take yourself into your dressing-room. Your lordship doesn't want to be ill, too, and she's a throat that's a burning fiery furnace.'

When Matthew left for London a few days later he was all concern. Alice was still ill, and he begged her not to come to town until she was strong enough. She nodded dumbly, her face flushed, her eyes heavy. It hurt her to talk.

As he turned to go, he used the fashionable phrase which all the gentlemen used at the time, 'Take great care of yourself.'

Alice did not recover quickly. Her throat was so swollen she could only drink lukewarm soup or eat jellies. She burned with fever, and Mary Murphy put cold compresses on her aching head. When the high temperature finally subsided, she looked frail. Mary Murphy took her temperature, and, looking at her throat, did not say that it was hell-fire surely. But she made her charge stay in bed another three days.

Alice didn't mind. She read a little, slept a lot, wrote to her parents and woke to hear birds singing in the lilac trees. She felt weak and sad.

On her first day up she went to pay her respects to Honoria. The old lady was in one of Leckford's towers, sewing for the poor. For an old woman who had never done a hand's turn in her life, she sewed well. She nodded at Alice and told her to keep out of draughts. But made it clear by her manner that she preferred to be alone.

Alice went down the staircase to the Yellow Drawing-room. A fire flickered in the huge fireplace. She sat down and sighed. She had youth's expectation that good health must return with a rush. She leaned back and looked into the fire.

John, Mary Murphy's only friend among the footmen, young and red-headed, came in with a salver.

'A visitor, my lady.'

It will be somebody for my mother-in-law, thought Alice indifferently, picking up the card.

'Vance Weston.'

Below it was an address in Philadelphia.

Telling John to show the visitor in, Alice had a flutter of pleasure. A friend of the family's, perhaps of Fran's? She felt curious when the doors opened and John, half chanting as if intoning a psalm, announced, 'Mr Vance Weston.'

The man who entered was short and thick-set, in his late thirties perhaps. Older than Matthew. His face was chiselled, full of harsh lines, a strong square jaw, a thin straight mouth and eyes which were bright and almost black. His brown hair was parted in the middle. He was clean-shaven. Everything about him, even his way of moving, was American. Except that he did not seem friendly.

'I hope you will excuse this uninvited call, Lady Leckford. But I am in the district, and was informed when I made inquiries that you were not yet in London.'

'You are a friend of my sister's?' said Alice pleasantly. She thought his manner dour.

'No, Ma'am. I have not the pleasure.'

'My father and mother, then?'

'Unfortunately not.'

She asked him to sit down; she felt unwillingly amused. Who was this man who stormed the distinguished portals of a house that people only entered with a sort of class pass-port?

'I have no claim to know you, Lady Leckford. But I am in anxious quest of any friend of my sister Margaret. I believe she came to a winter ball you gave in this house. It would do me a service if you could tell me who brought her here.'

Oh would it, thought Alice. You may be a fellow countryman but your manners leave much to be desired.

'Surely your sister herself will tell you that, Mr Weston.'

'She is back in the States.'

'I see,' said Alice, who didn't. 'Well. I will think about it. I could look through my lists, I suppose. In the meantime may I offer you tea? People in England quite enjoy it.' It was a small joke, she felt at home with him because he was American.

He said she was very kind. Alice couldn't imagine he had come to drink English tea. He wanted something, and was clearly staying because of that. When tea arrived, he made a certain effort at conversation. The footman offered the visitor sandwiches, muffins, seedcake. He accepted a muffin but did not eat it. The conversation was stilted, and Vance Weston only looked at ease when the doors were pushed open by Matthew's red setter, Lola. She came up waving a feathery tail

243

and almost bowing with pleasure. Lola had no discrimination and was as sentimentally affectionate with a stranger as with her master.

While he caressed the dog, Alice glanced at him. How harsh-looking he was. Even his voice, despite its familiar accent, was grating. Why was he here? And what on earth did he want with his sister's friends? He did not look a man who went eagerly searching for his own friends, let alone other people's.

'You are in England for some time, Mr Weston?'

'I hope not, Ma'am.'

Alice couldn't help smiling.

'If I can manage to locate Margaret's acquaintances, I have business with them. Then I must return home. I wonder if you recall my sister coming here?'

'She has the same name as you? Miss Margaret Weston?'

'Yes. She is unmarried.'

She repeated the name in her mind, and unexpectedly a picture came to her of a dark girl with a thin glowing face.

'Why, yes, I believe I do remember her. She is like you.'

'Except that she is beautiful and I am ugly,' he said impatiently. 'Who was she with?'

Alice was suddenly annoyed by his tone, which was positively accusing. She had lived for three interminable years with people who used courtesy as a way of keeping people at a distance, looking at them, so to speak, through barbed wire. Nothing like that was necessary now. She felt an unfamiliar relish in speaking out.

'Come, Mr Weston. We are both Americans and can look on this room at present as American soil. Like an Embassy. Shall we say what we think? You arrive here out of the blue and I am willing to receive you. You ask if I remember your sister. You then *demand* to know who brought her to Leckford. The answer is I don't know. There were two hundred people for the winter ball and many of the guests brought their own guests with them. Why is it so important? I

244

can go through my lists, as I told you, but that takes time. And I consider I should know why you wish to put me to the trouble.'

He looked at her with a certain respect.

'You are in the right. An explanation is needed. I came to England to fetch Margaret. She knew when I was arriving, I had written in advance. But when I came to London, she had taken ship for home. It is a long journey, you'll admit, to make and be informed by a stranger that my sister had left the country, and not left *me* a word. Not an apology or explanation. Nothing. Her chaperone during her stay over here, the Honourable Mrs Bannister, was also absent. She had left for India.'

'Mr Weston –'

'Wait awhile, Ma'am. I'm not quite through. I beg your pardon for being long-winded. I have now received a letter from my parents and Margaret is back home.'

'That's good, surely.'

'It is not. Something happened to her in England. My parents are convinced of it, but she refuses to say. I mean to find out what it was.'

He set his lips, looking almost angry. Yet in his face she still saw a likeness to the girl at the winter ball. A girl wearing a crown of gardenias, her thin face brilliant with laughter. In her mind's eye Alice saw whom she had danced with. Matthew's cousin Harry Grafton.

Vance Weston had been watching her. He must have read her face.

'I believe you've remembered something.'

On her guard, Alice said that yes, she'd already told him she remembered his sister. But as to who had been with her, she would have to look through her invitation lists. He said nothing for a moment. Then, 'Are you quite sure that's all you can do for me?'

Her slight feeling of kinship for the man evaporated. This was altogether too much. She had no intention of sitting in Matthew's house, which had ceased to be temporarily a piece of American soil, and give an uninvited stranger information about the Leckford family.

'I am quite sure. If you'll give me your address I will send you an answer, supposing I find one. But it will take time.'

He stood up and bowed stiffly.

'You want me to go. Very well. But you know more than you're saying. I was crazy to think you're still an American.'

Alice blushed angrily but he gave her no chance to reply, he walked straight out and a few moments later the shabby station brougham was receding up the drive.

The visit upset her. She should have helped him. She'd taken a false upper-class attitude from alarm, sensing something dangerous about Vance Weston. Nobody outside the charmed circle told tales. And Harry Grafton was a bad lot.

Scandal. She recoiled at the thought of it. She had grown up protected by parents, religion, her position as a Vandermeyer. Before Matthew and she had married, he'd told her briefly about something shameful that had happened in his past. A girl's accidental death in a house of sin. Alice was afraid of such things, and had tried to forget it. But here now was a fellow countryman needing help because of another Leckford.

How do I know what Harry Grafton has done? she thought.

The cold April afternoon dragged by. At half-past six she went into the entrance hall to find out if John was still on duty. He was sitting in the hall waiting for non-existent visitors. He sprang up like a jack-in-the-box.

'My lady?'

He looked at her with devotion. The young staff at Leckford adored her. The old ones did not.

'The gentleman who called this afternoon. Did you give me his card? I don't seem able to find it.'

'You looked at it, my lady, but left it on the salver. It's here.'

Delighted to do the least thing for her, he fetched it. Under the Philadelphian address, in ink, was 'The Leckford Arms, Taviton.'

* * *

'Neither my husband nor I like him. And his reputation with – with women is not good.'

London, thought Vance Weston, looking through the smutty windows of the train, was filthy. The buildings which backed on to the railway were dark with soot, there was a sordid damp blackness in the prospect, and when the train finally halted and he alighted on to the platform, a glutinous sticky feel seemed in the very air. The people were frowsty, the glass-roofed station appeared to be in a permanent pea-souper.

It was a relief to be set down at the hotel in Clarges Street, to enter a warm red-carpeted kingdom and be taken up to a bedroom whose lofty satin-draped windows shut out the London night.

He had much to think about.

He had never needed many hours of sleep, and, until nearly three in the morning, he lay in bed in the quiet featureless room, staring at a fire he had ordered to be lit, until it slowly died away into embers. He supposed Harry Grafton held the key to the mystery. This unknown man, some sort of aristocrat, had been close to Margaret. He must see him. Would the man tell him anything? If he did, the story would be dishonourable. What then?

Vance had been moved by Lady Leckford driving all the way to find him at the inn. A kind, intuitive, beautiful young woman. She must have felt for his family, strangers though they were. And he respected her for not telling him at once what she knew, but taking time to consider it. When she had eventually told him, he had seen in her face that she was wondering what she had actually done.

He was not sure, either. He thought of the 'new' sister described by his parents, angry and strident. Then he began to reflect over young Lady Leckford, an American girl with none of the daring and informality of their own country, a shy, shining girl. He had wanted to stay with her, to listen to her rather flat little voice, take her hand, and study the flawless oval of a face which seemed obscurely sad. It was ironic, he thought, that he should be so captivated by a married woman. How old was she? Nineteen? He finally blew out his candle and fell asleep.

Alice Leckford had not given him Harry Grafton's address and Vance had certainly not asked for it. When he breakfasted downstairs in a well-appointed dining-room, he sent for Burke's *Peerage*. He had already found his way through the enormous volume to discover the Leckford's address. The book rather amused him. 'Lineage . . . Charles Fitzalan, illegitimate son of King Charles II . . . Arms, a man's skull encircled with branches of palm . . . two pellets each charged with a martlet.' What did it all mean? I'm a foreigner all right, he thought, turning the pages.

Ah. Here they were. The Leckfords, their coat of arms: 'A Wyvern, wings expanded . . .' It looks like a dragon to me. The relatives? Well down the column was the name he was looking for. Harold Cosby Graeme Grafton, Born 1873, Address: Alton House, Piccadilly, W1.

He poured himself another cup of strong coffee and took out his watch. It was scarcely nine o'clock. What did Englishmen of the 'leisured class' do early in the morning? Ride? Take their breakfast in bed and spend hours getting dressed, like Beau Brummell? I must risk it, thought Vance. If he isn't there I shall go on trying until he is.

Alton House was an eighteenth-century series of buildings off Piccadilly, with a glass-covered passage running between them. A flunkey in blue and gold, wearing a cocked hat, guarded the entrance. Keeping off chaps like me, thought Vance, guessing that his own appearance and a sovereign would open Sesame. He was right. The man touched his hat and Vance walked past the gate and down the passage, looking to left and right. There were lines of black-painted doors, each leading to a separate set of rooms, and very intimate and quiet they were. The number he was seeking was almost at the end of the passage – 38.

He rang the bell.

The door was opened by a tall, round-backed servant with a

yellowish face and a pinched nose which could only just bear the smell of humanity.

'Sir?'

'Mr Grafton at home?' said Vance and hearing a voice from the inner room, pushed by and marched straight into what looked like a bedroom.

A handsome tousled young man, with a thin moustache above a smiling mouth, was seated in a dishevelled bed tying the belt of a brocade robe. Seeing Vance, he laughed.

'Gentle heaven, who have we here? It's all right, Wilkins, don't stand there fluffed up like an old hen. Off with you. I shall deal with my unexpected visitor.'

He gave a ghost of a salute in Vance's direction and remained seated.

Vance was unaffected by the *sang-froid*, the humour and the male beauty of the man he had come to find. He shut the door in the servant's face. Harry Grafton lit a cigarette and leaned back against his pillows.

'Well?'

Vance remained standing. He saw just then everything that had happened to Margaret. Saw a man women could not resist. An alluring, brilliant, sardonic, handsome man who hunted women as he probably hunted animals, and conquered them as he shot and killed some panting, shivering deer. Vance knew what Harry Grafton had done to his sister.

'And whom – have I the honour?' inquired Harry Grafton, through a veil of cigarette smoke.

'My name is Weston.'

'Ah.'

Harry Grafton's eyes did not drop.

'I am Margaret's brother.'

'Yes, yes, you have a look of her. How is the dear girl?'

'That's what I'm here for. To ask the same question.'

'My dear Mr Weston, alas, I cannot tell you. Have you not seen her? I heard somewhere that she was gone back to Philadelphia.'

'She has.'

251

Harry drew on his cigarette and shrugged.

'I'm afraid, then, I don't understand. How may I be of service?'

'*Christ!*' Vance's voice was muffled with fury, 'I didn't know what had happened to her, why she'd gone back home distraught, yes, distraught, out of herself, near mad from what my family tells me, until I saw you. What did you do to her, mmm? What did you do? You seduced her.'

He took a step forward and Grafton stood up, tall and slightly delicate and for a split second at a loss. Returning to irony, he said, 'She's very lovely, your sister. But very wild, y'know. Liberated. American, and so forth.'

And then Vance hit him. He punched the well-bred face, aiming for the jaw, but the blow glanced upwards and met the cheekbone with violent force. As Harry Grafton tottered Vance hit him again, this time meeting the jaw with all his strength. Grafton fell unconscious, his mouth pouring with blood.

'Bastard. Bastard. I wish I could kill you.'

Shoving the servant aside, Vance rushed out, slamming the door as if he wanted to break it to pieces.

CHAPTER FOURTEEN

Alice was well enough to leave for London at the end of a rainy week. On the morning of her departure, old Lady Leckford took breakfast with her as a kind of compliment. To break the rather absurd silence during the meal, Alice said pleasantly, 'I do hope Matthew and I can come back to Leckford for a day or two before the tulips are quite over. They're especially good this spring.'

'I daresay,' said Honoria.

Alice thought her mother-in-law looked whiter than usual. Small and crushable like a dried leaf. She wore exquisite lace on the top of her grey head and not a jewel except her thick wedding-ring. It was extraordinary to remember that she was Matthew's mother, and had once lain with a baby in her arms. Alice felt a surge of pity.

The old woman said after a long pause, 'I have something to say, Alice. It is this. I wish to take the opportunity, since you will be away a good deal, of saying I am grateful for what you have done.'

She saw that the girl didn't understand and added, with impatience, 'To the chapel, of course. When the work on the sanctuary is finished it will be as it was when I came to Leckford before my betrothal. It will be *beautiful*.' She spoke with more energy than Alice had ever heard her use, 'I have to thank you. And I do.'

Alice murmured that the colours of the chapel had been chosen by Matthew. His mother gestured as if brushing away a bluebottle. She told the butler to pour her more tea. She never said please to servants, and when Alice did, looked particularly cold.

Travelling to London on the train with Mary Murphy, Alice was quiet. Ahead was the hideous prospect of telling Matthew what she'd learned from the doctor's letter. I am barren, she thought. Dry and parched, a desert. It's a kind of curse visited upon some women. Upon me.

Alice, Mary Murphy and a mountain of boxes finally arrived at the Belgrave Square house. Mary disliked the London Season as much as her mistress, and muttered crossly that Alice must go up to her room to change.

'Have to get you up like a doll, I suppose, so's you can tire yourself out chat-chat-chatting. You look wore out.'

'You don't look too good yourself, Mary.'

After she had helped Alice to change into an elaborately embroidered tea-gown, Mary limped away complaining about her rheumatism. She appeared again to say his lordship was out and nobody was calling for tea, 'praise be to God.'

Alice trailed down to the drawing-room alone. A fire flickered, but there was sunshine out of doors. The room was broad and long, running the full length of the house, with windows at each end. In the front across the circular courtyard was the prospect of Belgrave Square, empty at this time of day except for a single hansom ambling by. At the back was the typical London garden, its walls of blackened bricks disguised by creepers, and beds of late daffodils.

She sat down. A wave of intense almost physical home-sickness swept over her. How she longed for the sound of American voices, Fran's cheerful shout from the top of the stair, the slam of doors, her father's sudden laugh. Longed to look out of the window and see the New York skyline. She was imprisoned in this alien place where tonight, tomorrow and every day she was forced to meet people who didn't give a straw for her. This one a distant relative. That one a duchess. She must listen to people paying her what they imagined was a compliment. 'Why, nobody would take you for an American.'

She did not belong. She was repelled by the English polish

and brutality, the smiling unbreakable confidence, the cruel practical jokes which made them howl with laughter. She dreaded the weekends. The houses were wonderful, but the people moving through them were the same reserved, empty and – to her American heart – cold men and women. There had been luxury at home, too, and good manners and breeding. But it had been fun.

Wandering listlessly to the window, she looked out into the square. The clouds were melting away and patches of blue appearing. A thin shaft of sunlight shone down on the kind of new glittering motor car that would please her father. Yellow and black like a wasp, its brass winking, it came slowly nearer. To her surprise, it turned through the open gates of the house and stopped at the entrance. Vance Weston climbed out. Alice backed away. She had wanted to hear an American voice. It seemed she had conjured one.

When he was shown in, they were both ill at ease. She found herself asking inane questions. How long was he in London? Where was he staying? He answered politely and then, before she could think of another, said, 'I came to tell you that I located your cousin, Ma'am.'

'Oh.'

'I want to say – to explain – curse it, there's no way round this. The moment I set eyes on the man I knew what had happened to Margaret. When I said her name I could *see*. It was written all over him. I beg your pardon if I offend you, Lady Leckford, but he fairly made me sick. I knew.'

'What did you know?' she asked faintly.

'What he'd done. He didn't even try to hide it. He laughed.'

'Mr Weston – I am deeply, deeply sorry.'

Her eyes filled for a girl she had never met. She hated Harry Grafton and would never speak to him again.

Vance Weston said in a low voice.

'I have something to confess. I hit him. I am not asking you to forgive me. I'd do it again. They don't have duels any more over here, do they? I always thought the idea despicable. But. But I knocked him unconscious.'

Alice was speechless.

'Don't look so shocked, Ma'am. If you hit the jaw strongly it often happens. At school I was out like a light on one occasion. And staggering as if I were drunk for at least ten minutes afterwards.'

He was silent for a moment, then went on, 'I suppose I've settled things as best I can. I confess I am still not satisfied. But I must go home very soon. I am anxious to know how my sister is faring.'

Then, looking at her, 'I'm afraid I did you a great wrong. Making *you* tell me who he was. I should have discovered that in some other way.'

'You didn't make me, Mr Weston. It was my own decision.'

The chairs they sat in were placed quite close, he leaned forward before she realised what was going to happen. And kissed her.

There was a strange silence, like a spell. The faint voice in Alice's mind which told her that this was terribly wrong was drowned in a torrent of feeling. Oh, she'd wanted this. Just this. The feel of the man's mouth on hers, his lips half open so that she opened her own, his tongue faintly brushing the underside of her mouth, his hands gripping hers, the long, tender, sexy silence . . .

When she made a small movement of withdrawal, he let her go.

They stared at each other.

On a sunny cool morning Matthew was out in Rotten Row before any other riders. The yawning park-keeper opened the gates for the solitary horseman mounted on a tall chestnut mare. Clapping his heels against his horse's sides, Matthew tried to ride away his thoughts.

Last night Alice had come into his dressing-room very late after they returned from a ball. She had asked him to unfasten her pearls. It was like her to refuse to allow Mary Murphy to wait up. When he released the heavy tiered necklace, she took it from him and stood with it in her hands.

'Matthew.'

'My love?'

She grimaced. She had never told him how much she disliked the meaningless endearment.

'I have something to tell you. I went to see two doctors. Specialists in Harley Street recommended by Doctor Atkinson. They have written to tell me they believe I can never have a child.'

Matthew's nature, the deep wells that make the self, his breeding and beliefs, controlled him just then. He was all tender concern. He was almost too calm, and Alice, looking at him fixedly, agreed with the empty things he said in comfort. Without showing emotion either, she offered her cheek for a goodnight kiss.

Alone in his dressing-room he stayed awake until dawn.

He had been certain Alice would give him children. His cousins, other relatives and friends of his own age had nurseries-full. He made love to Alice often and enjoyed it well enough. The physical presence of a pretty woman in his bed was sufficient to stir him. But his real desire was not for her pale unresponsive body; he believed that from his loins those wanted ones would come.

He had left the house early and gone to the park in the hope of riding away his useless, harrowing regrets.

The tan scattered from the horse's hooves, the early sun shone on glossy flanks the colour of last autumn's chestnuts. To increase his pace, he squeezed his legs inwards, calves pressing against the horse's sides. The pace increased. He was riding into a new and empty life. What was left to Alice and to him? Her money, yes. They were still rich, and money had rained over the thirsty house, the unkempt parkland, the chapel where his mother prayed. Leckford Court was lovely again. For what? He hadn't known until it was denied him how deeply he longed for a son. He had grown up not caring about the responsibilities of birth. His grandparents, his beloved elder brother had done that.

Now Leckford weighed down on him like a curse, no longer

the treasure to give his children. When he died, it would go to Harry Grafton.

Since the night that Alice had told Matthew she could never have a child, they hadn't spoken of it again. Nor had they made love. Twice Matthew had knocked at her door late after they returned from a party, and on both occasions she had said she was tired, so, 'would he forgive her?' Matthew accepted the refusals as if all he'd intended was a friendly talk.

The third time, coming home from a ball in hot midnight air – it was tropical in London that summer – Alice had wandered out into the garden, ghostly with white roses. He followed, and almost took her in his arms. She looked vulnerable, weighed down in her satin finery and diamond circlet. Why did he see her as a captive? But when he made to embrace her, Alice gave a gentle murmur and slipped away into the dark as if to put distance between them.

He did not resent the rejections. It was his duty to go to bed with her now and then, but was relieved when she refused him. She was frigid. He wondered if that sexual submission without pleasure explained her barren state.

Alice herself, outwardly calm and quiet, was very nervous. The fear that her husband would claim her physically was never far from her mind. Sometimes she dreamed he was thrusting into her, and woke as from a nightmare.

Walking uninvited into her life at present was Vance Weston who had not yet returned to Philadelphia and whom she seemed to see almost every day, usually at a distance. It gave her a *frisson* to listen to the latest Society gossip which was centred on Harry Grafton.

'He's taken up boxing,' Ambrosine told her, laughing. 'He goes to that place off Bond Street, my dear, where Byron used to box. Isn't it just like him? And have you *seen* his poor face? It's slightly better now but when he called last week it was black and blue. Harry just laughed about it. Such courage.'

Alice did wonder why Vance was still in London. In the week following the evening when he had kissed her, she saw him at least half-a-dozen times. As a wealthy presentable American, he was invited out and about to the same places she and Matthew visited, and on Sunday morning she saw him in Hyde Park.

It was 'Church Parade', as people called it when Society gathered to walk in the park after church in the morning. Seeing Vance coming towards them, Alice felt slightly ill. Raising his hat, he bowed and passed by.

'Who was that?' Matthew asked, when they were out of earshot.

'An American friend of my family. I don't think you know him.'

The next afternoon, Alice had to go to an 'At Home' in one of the big houses in Park Lane. The french windows of the sunny drawing-room were open on to the garden, the place was thronged with visitors. An enormous looking-glass on a far wall reflected women in all the fashionable colours, like a bunch of sweet peas. And standing by the window listening to a vivacious young girl was Vance. He saw Alice at once, excused himself to his companion, and made his way to her. Alice's formidable hostess, a Mrs Arnott, also came up.

'Lady Leckford. So kind of you to come. Now here is somebody from your native land. May I present Mr Vance Weston –'

'We have already met, Mrs Arnott,' Alice replied. Vance gave her a formal bow.

'Oh, you know each other. Charming,' said Mrs Arnott and left them. Privately she decided Weston was too attractive to be wasted on that difficult American woman Matthew Leckford had married. She would whip him away soon.

'Shall we take a turn in the garden, Lady Leckford?' said Vance. They walked out into the dusty sunlight. In one corner was a merciful pool of shade from an old laburnum tree hung with curled pods that had been yellow blossom a few weeks ago.

When they were alone he said in a low voice, 'I must see you. When? Where?'

'If you're staying in London, of course we will meet.'

'I don't mean in this monkey show. Do you imagine I'd remain five minutes in London if it were not for you? I must see you.'

She began to tremble slightly.

'We mustn't. We can't.'

They had walked to the furthest end of the garden, and were standing in the shade. In the distance through the windows the voices rose and fell, rose and fell. Alice looked at a rose bush. A single flower shone, its dark velvet petals unfurled.

'Alice. I call you that in my thoughts. I must return to Philadelphia next week. Come to the country with me tomorrow.'

'How can I?'

'My God,' he said in a low voice. 'If you want something, you find how to get it. It's the easiest thing in the world.'

'Not – not for me.'

'So you don't want to.'

'I do. I do.'

He said nothing for a moment. He shut his eyes and gave something like a shudder.

'I will drive you to the country tomorrow. You can say we are visiting friends. The Bambergs.'

'Are they in England?'

'Some of them are. The family is enormous. You are perfectly safe.'

He did not sound kind.

'I will call for you at eleven.'

Then, in a different voice, 'I agree, the dances here are like ours. But I consider our music rather better.'

Mrs Arnott was advancing on them with a determined step and a smile to match.

Alice's nervous anticipation of telling Matthew some rigmarole about her parents' friends the Bambergs was not needed. Matthew was out riding and had not returned when she left the house. Vance's yellow and black motor drew up as the clocks all over the house, French clocks, grandfather-clocks, chimed eleven. His punctuality gave Alice a feeling of home. Both her parents treated punctuality as a kind of religion; her father had once said, 'Alice, you are late,' when she had kept him waiting for two minutes.

This morning she had dressed plainly, waited upon by a Mary Murphy disgracefully pleased that she was going out with an American.

When Vance was shown in, he said, looking at her grey silk, 'You will need a cloak.'

'But surely –'

'You haven't motored for a while, have you? The de Dietrich is mighty comfortable, but you will find a lot of dust. And you need a thicker veil.'

With Alice in a voluminous cloak, her gauzy hat tied down with bands of tulle, Vance drove her out of London. The motor was indeed comfortable, with rounded padded seats and a black hood. Alice had not travelled in a motor car since her father had been in London. She enjoyed the swiftness, despite the dust. Soon they had left the carriage-filled streets behind and were in the country. The roads were tunnels of green, and they passed a river which seemed to be hurrying as fast as they were. Every mile took her further away. She felt happy. Her companion was silent.

'Shall we stop for a while?' he asked, finally slowing down. 'Perhaps for a glass of lemonade?'

He turned the car into a narrow road which crossed the river by a lichened bridge. A barge went by, it was painted with flowers and its deck was hung with washing. The man at the helm gave them a salute. The barge slowly disappeared, drawn by a great patient grey horse, the towrope glistening with drops of water.

Vance stopped the car at an inn dozing in the sun.

'Lemonade?'

'It sounds perfect.'

She slowly unfastened the veil, and rolled it up to her forehead. Vance leaned forward and kissed her. She had tried to keep physical thoughts of him at bay. To let herself simply be happy which, heaven knew, was rare. But when he kissed her she knew she had wanted it ever since their last embrace. He kissed her deliberately, slowly, opening his mouth, then opening hers with his tongue, moving it as if to explore her whole self. The seat behind her burned in the sunlight, she lay taking and answering the embrace, hungry, sad.

When he stopped she looked dazed.

'Lemonade. As cold as possible,' he said, climbing from the car and holding out his hands.

A stout man with ginger hair, his rolled-up sleeves revealing arms covered with freckles, brought the lemonade and placed it on a rickety table. The grass, coarse and cropped, lapped round a single ancient apple tree propped up like an old man on crutches. Down the bank the river chuckled by, the surface strewn with white down from the discarded buds of a row of poplars. Near the banks was a mass of kingcups.

'You're very quiet,' he said, putting down his glass.

'I was thinking that I have no idea where we are.'

'That's because you're a Dorset girl and we're in leafy Buckinghamshire. Like it?'

'Oh yes.'

They were silent in a friendly way. She could almost persuade herself that being in the company of this intense man was an innocent summer idyll. They were playing truant, driving out to get away from what he had called the monkey show. But her body knew differently. Why did I come with him, she thought, and was horrified by the answer that her senses gave her. She thought – everything I want is wrong.

'You said you were going back to the States soon.'

'On the 5th. Nine days from now. My passage is booked on the *Oceanic White Star*.'

'My parents took the same ship,' she said. She paused and then said, 'Has anything more happened about your sister?'

'If you mean, have I seen your husband's cousin again, the answer is yes. Two blows, Alice, have not paid that score. I called last night. Unfortunately, he had friends with him.' He smiled sourly. 'This morning I heard he had left London. Not saying where. To put as many miles between us as he can, no doubt. I'm not saying he's afraid. It's the knowledge, mine, he's running from. And the possibility of some kind of scandal. When he learns I've gone home, he'll appear again.'

He stopped talking for a moment or two and then said, 'In our country, as you must know, we sometimes demand a life for a life.'

'You can't mean that. It's terrible! You sound as if you wished you'd killed him.'

'I do.'

'Then you'd be a murderer.'

'And what's Cousin Harry? What did he do to Margaret? You'll say she is not dead. But her heart is. She's changed permanently, I guess. My parents have written to me again. She's developed a crazy hatred of men, they said. Poor girl. Poor girl.'

'Vance, I know – how you feel, how your family feels. It's dreadful. But murder is a mortal sin. Stop thinking of it. Please. Please.'

He shook his head like a swimmer made deaf by water in his ears.

'I'll try. You can help me.'

They left the inn and the river and drove down more green lanes, finally stopping at an ancient stone hotel set back from the road in a courtyard filled with beds of lupins. The place was far enough from London not to be visited by the fashionable. When they went into the dining-room, nobody noticed them.

She never remembered afterwards what they had talked about or what they had eaten. At the end of the meal they went out again into the sun. The afternoon was a dream of summer. A faint warm wind blew, and they wandered down a lane high with meadowsweet and the lilac-topped grasses which had flowered after the rains. She took off her hat and the breezes blew her hair into little spirals round her face.

'You're very beautiful. Have I told you so before?'

'You haven't, and I'm not.'

'We'll argue about that one day.'

They went into a meadow, shutting a gate behind them. It was a vast hedged field sloping upwards and flattening out at the top where a single oak tree stood. It blazed with buttercups which bent under her long skirts as she walked. As they went across the field, he took her hand.

They sat down under the oak tree in a dappled shade. Somewhere in a nearby wood a cuckoo was calling. 'Cuck-oo. Cuck-oo.' The whole of the soft dreamy afternoon seemed to be in that song.

'Alice.'

Putting his arms round her while he kissed her, he made her lie down. Around them were the miles of lonely country. They lay knowing of nothing but each other. He pressed her against the ground and covered her. For a while she did not resist, returning the kisses with a racing heart, feeling only his mouth, his beautiful self, holding the only man she'd ever wanted, whose weight on her seemed right, as if she'd been born to lie under him. He pressed his hands between the top of her legs, and then pulled up her skirts to explore the place of love. Somehow she gasped out, 'No.'

He stopped, replaced her skirts and raised himself on his elbow.

'Are you afraid?'

'Yes. No. It's wrong.'

'Are you saying I must not?'

Still underneath him, she felt his body hard against her own.

'I've never – never done anything except with my husband.'

He did not answer. He put his hand down the bosom of her dress and stroked one of her nipples. She had never felt that sensation, Matthew had never touched her like that; it reached right down to the rest of her and made the wanting worse.

'You don't love him, do you?' He still stroked the nipple, putting it between his fingers.

'I mustn't say – I –'

'You never loved him. You don't now. I knew it when I kissed you the first time. You need love. You must have it. You were made for it. For it. For me. Alice, you must learn what it is really like.'

They drove back to London in silence. Now and then he glanced at her with concern. Once she sighed. He took her hand in his left hand and pressed it.

When they turned into the open gates of the house in Belgrave Square it was after six o'clock. He said, before the footman had a chance to open the car door, 'I shall see you tonight. At Devonshire House?'

'Oh no – I –'

'I beg you to be there. At least I can dance with you. That will last us until tomorrow.'

She gave him a look of uncertainty and he saw with pain that there was shame in her innocent face. He wanted her all over again, and as her figure vanished into the great grey house he felt he had lost her.

A sense of flatness and boredom had come over Matthew one evening in that magnificent spring. He paid some calls, took tea with Ambrosine, and listened with his usual grace to a good deal of her female chatter. Later he went to his club and sat for a while, hoping to enjoy its silence. But even here the place seemed inconveniently full of his friends.

Deciding to walk home to Belgrave Square in the last of the sunshine he sauntered down King Street. It was almost deserted as he approached the elegant façade of the St James's Theatre, glancing indifferently at the gold-framed photographs of the actors in that night's play.

The piece was called *A Girl from Nowhere*, and a much-admired actor, Digby Lockton, gazed magnificently out at passers-by. Matthew knew how much every woman in London admired him. In the frame next to Digby Lockton was the large photograph of a girl. She was leaning forward in a fashionable, enticing attitude, bust thrust forward, bottom stuck out, giving her the S-shaped appearance of a swan. She looked over her shoulder with an impudent smile.

It was Nelly Briggs.

Wonder, incredulity, a sort of mirth went through Matthew. Idiot that he was, how could he have imagined *Nelly Briggs was dead*? Dying of heartache because he'd deserted her? Coming to London that time in search of work and returning to Paris to catch consumption and expire, a latter-day Mimi in a Montmartre garret? He hadn't used his brains about Nelly. She was a cork and when you pushed it under water it sprang straight up into the air.

Looking at her photograph, he supposed she must now be famous. At the head of the posters were the names 'Digby Lockton and Nelly Briggs' in large letters above the play's title. Other players were listed below.

The red-carpeted foyer was empty. On the walls, among more photographs, one of a magnificent Lilian Braithwaite, another of a romantic George Alexander, there was a painting of Nelly. Matthew looked at it with contempt. Nelly should know better than that; the painter had made her look as if she were on the lid of a chocolate box.

He bought a ticket for the evening performance. 'Not many left, Sir, you're in luck,' said the man in the box office.

When he returned home, Matthew wrote letters of apology to the two friends whose houses he was due to visit tonight. He also scribbled a word to Alice, regretting he could not accompany her. As usual, he gave no explanation.

Cousin Harry may be at both affairs. I know he'll be delighted to look after you,' he wrote.

The St James's Theatre was already buzzing with people when he arrived, but although he saw one or two acquaintances, it was a relief that there were no close friends standing about in the foyer. When the curtain eventually rose and the play started, Matthew did not pay attention. The usual servant was speaking the usual stuff to a companion, establishing the plot. He waited for the moment for which, it seemed, he had waited for more than four years.

There was a scatter of applause.

He could scarcely believe it was Nelly on the stage. The shabby girl who had sprawled on his bed, the opalescent nude who shone in the paintings he always avoided looking at. She seemed to wear a kind of aura. It moved when she did, hovered over her when she was still. Strong as fierce sunlight, it was totally invisible. She was full of an extraordinary vitality. She was a wild, indiscreet, passionate creature who was sparkling and tender. You felt she could be hurt, but her courage would come to the rescue. She was funny. She was rueful. And, the same words came into his mind, so richly sexed. She was the girl every man wanted, and every woman wanted to be.

He could scarcely get through the intervals when he went out into King Street. Members of the audience were pacing up and down in the cool evening air. He heard Nelly's name half-a-dozen times.

The play ended in storms of applause. Standing with the rest of the cast, she made deep graceful curtseys, chestnut head meekly bent. But the audience would not let her go until Digby Lockton took her by the hand, brought her to the footlights and left her to take a bow alone. Then the audience's applause drenched her with love. Again and again, she gave her deep curtsey.

Collecting his opera cloak and hat, Matthew found his way to a narrow brick-walled passage on the left of the theatre where a sign said, 'Stage Door'.

An elderly man with the face of a knight in a William Morris engraving mildly inquired what he could do for him.

'Miss Briggs?'

The stage doorkeeper liked the look of the visitor and said she could be found on the first floor. Door Number One.

Matthew had never been backstage in his life. The stone stairway was like one in a prison, the corridor a forbidding green. The actress who had played Nelly's younger sister dashed past him in what looked like a petticoat, a door flew open and a man shouted, 'Flossie! I die for you, come into my arms, you glorious thing.'

With a burst of laughter, she vanished through the door which slammed behind her.

On a door with the figure 'One' painted on it was a card on which was printed: 'Miss Nelly Briggs'.

He knocked. A voice which made his stomach turn over called, 'Come in, whoever you are.'

After the gloomy gaslight of the corridor, the room dazzled. There was an overpowering scent of flowers, from baskets and bowls on tables and shelves, even on the floor. Roses and lilies, violets and carnations. On a divan by the wall a middle-aged man sat smoking a cigar. He looked through the smoke at Matthew. Sitting at a dressing table, wearing a silk wrap and thick layers of stage make-up, half her luxuriant hair down, the other half still pinned with a diamond aigrette – was Nelly.

She looked at him and grinned.

'So you're here, then,' she said, without a trace of surprise. She held out her hand.

As much at a loss as a self-possessed man could be, he kissed it.

'I wondered when the farthing would drop,' Nelly said.

'Leon,' she addressed the man on the divan, 'this is a friend from centuries ago. Viscount Leckford. Matt, this is Leon Seidl and he's a friend too. Very much so. He produced our play as I expect you saw on the programme.'

Matthew and Leon Seidl shook hands and Matthew paid them both the necessary compliments. Actress and producer accepted these smilingly, but had heard them all before. In a short while the older man said he must be going. He'd see Nelly in an hour?

'Don't be late for supper, otherwise you won't have time to eat it,' he said, in a voice coloured with American tones. 'What you need is your beauty sleep and plenty of it.'

'Don't nag. I'll be there,' Nelly replied.

When the door closed, there was a pause. She unpinned the rest of her hair, which poured down her back in a shining

268

mass. She began to wipe off her make-up. With her face smeared with grease, she turned round.

'You're still nice and thin,' she remarked.

'Did you imagine I'd get fat?'

'One never knows. People eat such a lot. Courses and courses. Last night I was dining with a judge and there were twelve. Courses I mean. I felt I might die, but how to avoid them without hurting him? I thought of a way.'

'And what was that?'

He felt a poignant joy in the changed and unchanged Nelly.

'The orchestra was playing a tune I like, so I jumped up and said I'd sing. People seemed pleased, which was nice. I hopped over to the piano and sang one of my favourites. "*Ah, que les hommes sont bêtes.*" Do you know it? Then I did an encore. Then I walked to the other end of the table and gave them some Offenbach. I managed to avoid two courses. I had to be firm with the judge later, he's the kind who thinks food represents making love. Oh Matt!' she said, and laughed, 'Why don't you say something instead of letting me chat? You always did. Such a mistake.'

Before he could answer, a woman of about sixty came in without knocking, tut-tutted at Nelly and told her to get a move on. She pushed her behind a gilt screen in the corner.

'Ruby's bustling me because she's afraid of Leon,' called Nelly, now invisible. 'She's a bully, aren't you, darling?'

Mutters from Ruby.

'Don't go, Matt. Ruby always tries to freeze out my admirers,' was Nelly's shout.

Matthew raised his voice and said that of course he would stay if she could spare the time, and the invisible dresser replied that Nelly Briggs always spared the time for gentlemen or hard-luck stories.

In a few minutes – Matthew was accustomed to women spending hours when they dressed – a transformed Nelly appeared. She wore dark blue velvet pinched into a tiny waist. The low neckline was edged with white ermine, and round her neck was a pearl dog-collar even higher than the one she had worn onstage. The only thing not completed was her hair; it still hung girlishly over her shoulders.

Ruby, no respecter of persons, pushed her again, this time to sit down on the chair facing the dressing-table. She proceeded to comb and pin and arrange Nelly's hair, fastening a diamond star in her curls.

'There now. You'll do. Don't forget your gloves,' said Ruby, throwing them on to the table. Nelly put up her arms, kissed the elderly woman smackingly on the cheek and was rewarded with, 'You're the limit.'

Ruby marched out.

Matthew sat looking at Nelly. She looked back.

'I do think it's nice, seeing you again. I thought you must have got stuffy. Lords do.'

'And you know a lot of those now?'

'Dozens. The stage has got respectable. Hadn't you noticed?'

'I don't think I know any theatre people. Or didn't until tonight. Well, Nelly. I am glad you think I am the same. I can't say the same about you.'

'Aren't I? B – bother,' said Nelly, using the old trick of swallowing a swear word. She began to button the long white gloves. They reached to her armpits and there were many buttons. Matthew had watched the same fiddling operation performed many times by his wife. The comparison between the two young women came forcibly to him.

'Girls always like to hear from men that they haven't changed by an eyelash,' Nelly said, smoothing the fine kid. 'What that means is that they still look young.'

'How old are you, pray?'

'Your lordship, I am nearly twenty-four. But that isn't what counts. You can live years in six months, and no time at all in six years. It depends what happens to you.'

She looked as if she were laughing at him.

He felt at a loss. He had been wrong to say, to think, that she was the same – she was utterly changed from his impulsive guttersnipe mistress. She had retained her beauty, her impudence, her trick of not being able to resist flirting, even with a man who had mistreated her. But she was as self-possessed as a queen.

She looked vaguely at a table where among gardenias and roses a bottle of champagne stood in a silver bucket of ice. Might she offer him a drink, she asked. Matthew thanked her and refused, adding, could he open the bottle for her?

'Oh, I still don't drink. The children of drunkards never do.'

She stood up with a practised sweep of heavy skirts and held out her hand. It was his exit line but he wouldn't take it. He couldn't drag himself away from this girl now divided from him by God knew what adventures.

Expecting a rebuff, he put his arms round her. For a moment he thought the lovely woman would be angered at his touching her. But then. Then as if she couldn't stop herself, she leaned against him, returning the kiss and when he opened his eyes she was looking at him.

She merely smiled.

Nelly arrived home from supper with Leon Seidl to find that Edith was still up. She was sitting in Nelly's peacock-blue drawing-room, shoes off, deep in a French novel. Nelly kicked off her own shoes.

'Bet you a guinea you can't guess who was in my dressing-room after the performance.'

'I can't imagine.'

'Go on, Edith. Try.'

'I don't see why I should since you're dying to tell.'

'True,' Nelly said. 'Well. The gentleman who made his appearance was . . . Matt.'

Edith started.

'*Lord Leckford*! What on earth was he doing there? And how dare he?'

'Edith, you are superb. He dared, as you put it, from plain vulgar curiosity. I knew he'd come sometime or other. He looks just the same. Isn't it peculiar, when you think he is my Tom's Dad.'

Edith was still alarmed.

'Did you actually receive him?'

'Edith, you don't "receive" people in the theatre. They just turn up. Leon was there, but he left and met me later. Matt's very sweet, you know . . .'

Edith took this in.

'Was it a shock when you saw him?'

'It was interesting.'

'You won't see him again, though,' said Edith, knowing the answer.

'Don't see how I can help it.'

There was a considerable pause.

'And what about Tom?' asked Edith at last, playing with the locket on her bracelet, shaped like a heart.

'What about him?'

'If you are going to see Lord Leckford, it will be your duty to tell him, I suppose.'

'Oh will it? Well I shan't. Just because Matt may appear now and then doesn't mean he is going to know a thing. Not a blind thing. He's nothing to do with Tom. He just happened to make me pregnant.'

'You cared for him.'

'Yes. I did. Horribly much. And he sent me five pounds. Don't imagine I bear him any malice. When I saw him this evening I remembered how endearing he can be. But he isn't a bit important.'

Nelly had been half-expecting to see Matthew ever since she returned to England when there had been a good deal about her in the illustrated papers, and again when *A Girl from Nowhere* opened. Matthew, it seemed, was no theatre-goer.

After years of American success, it had been Leon who had finally persuaded her to come to London. In his efficient way he found her a play which suited her, and a charming house in St John's Wood, 'just right for you, Tom and Kirstin,' he announced firmly. Nelly had havered for a long time about leaving the States, but Leon wanted English audiences to see her. And when she arrived in London she settled with what Seidl thought of as his star's blessed adaptability.

Nelly was very anxious for Edith to come and stay. Her friend had been elusive since the long-ago visit to New York when she had given up the care of Tom. She wrote regularly – Edith was a gifted letter-writer – but she always explained that it wasn't possible to come over for a visit. Monsieur Vollard was making urgent requests for more work. She was so sorry . . .

But things had now changed. Tom and Kirstin were clearly happy in their new home and the play established for its London run. Nelly wrote demanding the presence of her friend. 'The Channel,' she scrawled, 'is *not* the Atlantic.'

Edith's long affectionate reply was still a 'No' with many excuses. Reading the letter, Nelly was greatly disappointed at being robbed of the presence of her 'one friend'.

Leon listened in sardonic silence, finally remarking that he was also a friend, and so, if she gave them the chance, were half the people in London.

'I don't mean that. I miss her.'

Leon soon became bored with his complaining leading lady and put his mind to the problem. He came up with an idea.

'What do you want with that damned great conservatory at the back of the house? And hasn't it occurred to you that it faces north.'

He and Nelly had a good deal of amusement having it turned into a studio which opened on to the garden. After which Nelly sent one of her long expensive telegrams.

Edith arrived one evening when Nelly was still at the theatre. The rôles were reversed – it was she, not Nelly, who dreaded seeing the little boy again. Hearing the cab, Kirstin came to the door with him.

He stood in the porch, dressed in a sailor suit, and when Edith ran towards him, looked at her in wonder. On seeing the woman who had once been his whole life, a feeling of awe came over him – he looked vulnerable. Edith threw herself on her knees.

'Oh Tom! Do you still speak French?'

'A bit. Danish and American better, though.'

Edith disapproved with her whole Scots nature of Nelly's largesse in creating the studio, but she couldn't resist beginning to paint there. In the year that followed she came to stay twice. To her delight, she also took Tom back to Paris for a month when Kirstin went home to New York to see her family. Tom began to speak French again. On one of her London visits, Edith went to the newly-opened Chelsea Art School and met one of its principals, an attractive Irishman with a quick-fire way of talking and, to Edith, a positively overwhelming friendliness. His name, he said, was William Orpen. Was she a painter, too? Of course she was! Living in Paris, eh? Where could be better! He took her out to supper and talked of 'our English contemporaries'. He made her laugh.

She enjoyed her visits to London, in limited doses. There was Nelly's lively company, the theatre, her friend's many acquaintances, the stage and its glamour. But it was none of that which brought her across the Channel. It was Tom. His weight when he sat on her lap grew heavier. His weight on her heart heavier still. Nobody, she thought, should feel like this about anybody.

The two girls never talked about the past. It was months before Edith eventually said, 'Did I tell you I saw Patrice again?'

Nelly jumped. '*Patrice*! When? Where?'

'In the Rue des Saules.'

'With canvases under his arm?'

'Of course.'

Nelly waited for more.

'It was Patrice who sent me to Monsieur Vollard. I have a lot to thank him for. But I haven't seen him again. You know how it is with Patrice.'

'Yes. Yes. Oh, I wish I'd been with you. Is he the same? He must be. He couldn't change.'

'No, he couldn't. Hasn't. Except that he is married.'

Edith did not realise her voice was severe. Now and then she did not approve of Nelly's attitude to men.

'Is he?' cried Nelly. 'What's she like? Do tell!'

'I didn't meet her.'

'How tiresome you are, Edith. Go to his studio when he gets back, do! Has he moved?'

'He said not.'

'That's like him. So you must call round and meet her. I can see in your face that you won't. Haven't you any natural curiosity, Edith Holden?'

'Aren't you going to ask about his work?' said Edith.

'Why should I? His paintings will be the same only more so. Perhaps,' added Nelly, who had said the same things years before, 'he's a genius.'

'I have heard that Monsieur Vollard thinks so.'

They were silent for a while. The night was quiet as a church. The lights from the drawing-room flooded out on to the sleeping garden. Patrice's lumbering figure walked in both their thoughts, and in Nelly's he took her in his arms.

'If you see him again,' she said at last, 'give him my love.'

'No, Nelly.'

Edith was due back in Paris a few days after Nelly met Matthew again, and for once Nelly was rather pleased when she drove to Victoria Station and kissed her friend a temporary goodbye. She had only just escaped, she thought, a lecture from Edith about Matthew Leckford. I don't see why I can't enjoy seeing him now and then, thought Nelly, as she returned home. Everything is different now. And so are we.

To Matthew this was astoundingly true as far as his ex-mistress was concerned. He saw how much time had divided her from him. Her life as a successful actress was very splendid. She went to magnificent parties after the play, met Cabinet ministers, aristocrats, painters and scientists. It was sheer chance that she did not meet Matthew many times at these occasions. There were Gala Nights when the King and Queen commanded a performance for visiting foreign royalty, and the audience wore Court dress. Nelly sometimes looked from the state towards an auditorium glittering with jewels, a dress circle transformed into a bower of flowers.

She had more invitations than she could possibly accept and when she went out she invariably met famous people. Puccini who spoke only Italian and had, thought Nelly, the most beautiful eyes she'd ever seen. W. S. Gilbert, white-haired and amusing, and Max Beerbohm, who stared dreamily at her as if at a vision. Theatre people were her friends, Herbert Tree and his stately wife, the glorious Ellen Terry, George Alexander and the melting Lillie Langtry. At one party George Bernard Shaw had greeted her by raising his diabolic eyebrows and saying, 'Ah, here's the Girl from Nowhere who's arrived somewhere!' to the sycophantic laughter of a circle of friends.

The starry life did not exactly suit her. She was naturally sociable, but meeting people meant, in a way, a second performance. She was rather ashamed of fleeing home to Tom and Kirstin, and going to bed with hot milk and honey.

When she started to meet Matthew again he found it difficult to grasp just how much she was in demand. During their first encounters they came up against the changes in each other, as a carpenter meets knots in wood. But their sexual attraction vibrated, and in Matthew's case it became an obsession. He courted her. Sued for her. Called at the theatre to see her. And used his knowledge of her susceptible heart. In the end he won her back into his arms.

He fell into the habit of calling to collect her at the St James's Theatre after the performance and taking her back to her house in St John's Wood. Tom and Kirstin, about whom he knew nothing, were in the country just then. Nelly enjoyed the quiet drive, his familiar and unfamiliar company. She liked to make him laugh.

'Did you go to the Vine House reception after all?' he asked.

It had been a very grand occasion at which the King and Queen were to be present.

'Leon teased me into it. He said it might be useful,' said Nelly.

'Was it rather boring?' inquired Matthew. The horse was trotting through the deserted midnight streets. He looked lazily at her.

'I wouldn't exactly say that.'

'Did you look magnificent?'

'Oh Matt. I was in full fig and I borrowed a tiara from Props. People like your friends must all have known it was a fake, but who cared? I took that bouquet of gardenias you sent me.'

'I can imagine. You looked delicious. What then?'

'Well. Lord and Lady Laurie said good evening to me and I drifted off to talk to some people I'd met before. But what do you think? Nobody came over to say he was taking me into dinner.'

'That's impossible.'

'Wait till you hear. The King and Queen finally made an entrance (it was an entrance, not just a walk-on) and we all bowed and curtseyed and they went round shaking hands. I thought His Majesty looked at me rather thoughtfully,' Nelly giggled. 'And then, as usual, they all trooped into the dining-room. And I was on my ownsome.'

Matthew could scarcely believe his ears at such a social gaffe.

'What did you do?'

'At first I thought I'd slip off and get a cab. Then I thought how Leon would jeer, and besides, surely there must be one empty seat at the table. So I sort of glided into the dining-room which, as you know, is *huge*. There they all were eating their soup. Quick off the mark, weren't they? And I looked down the table surrounded by footmen and – not an empty chair. It was funny, Matt! Standing there in my prop tiara and nowhere to sit down. The fish came heaving into view then. Excellent salmon (I know a good one when I see one). So I grabbed hold of one of the silver platters, I thought I might as well. I mean, I wasn't doing anything very useful. And then – ' she paused, her face alive with mirth, 'The King saw me.'

'*What happened*?'

'Oh, the look! He was spiflicated! He stared and stared at me clutching the fish. Then he spoke to poor Lord Laurie who went the colour of a beetroot. Somehow the salmon was removed, and I was wedged in between two people who'd been getting on fine until I came along to be gooseberry.'

'But why – '

'It all came out later. They'd forgotten the do-dah about who was supposed to take me in. I danced with the King by the by.'

'And what did you think of him? I don't need to guess what he thought of you.'

'He makes good jokes and smells of delicious eau-de-cologne. But he's too fat for me.'

Matthew enjoyed Nelly's stories. But he noticed that despite them, she was enigmatic about much of her life. She owned a pretty house set in a garden of cherry trees, to which they drove after the play; he was never invited there during the day.

They would sit in the drawing-room with its shaded lights and Matthew listened to Nelly's talk and watched her beautiful face both familiar and strange. He was filled with desire. Why did she continue to see him if they weren't going to make love? Now and then she sat on the floor beside him, leaning against his knees, and he looked down at the gleaming luxuriant hair. He never said he wanted her. She knew it. Of course she did.

One evening when they crept quietly into the drawing-room, before she could light the lamps he laced his arms round her waist and gave her a violent kiss. When the embrace ended he said in a low voice, 'God, Nelly – I must have you again. I must. Don't you – won't you –'

She drew away from him and looked at him – for the first time since he'd seen her again – with an expression he remembered; melting, heavy, swimming, almost moist. Leaning forward, he licked her full underlip.

That night they went up the stairs together for the first time to a big shadowy bedroom. They undressed in silence and when they joined – at last – they made love as if it were Paris again. He took her fiercely, almost wildly, and for so long that any other woman would have been exhausted. But he missed the old simple Nelly of the Butte.

'You never made a scene when I came to see you in your dressing-room last month,' he said one hot June night when they were lying in bed.

Nelly, naked as Venus, long chestnut hair sprayed over the pillow, said idly, 'I never make scenes.'

'I was cruel to you. I left you flat.'

'As a pancake. How hairy you are. What's the word? Hirsute.'

'How many hairless men are you comparing me with?'

'That would be telling.'

She tickled his nose with a lock of hair.

'Aren't you happy with me?'

'You're the most exciting woman I've ever –'

' * * * in your life,' said Nelly. 'Shall we have scrambled eggs? I'm starving.'

'You can't mean you're going to cook?'

'Wait and see.'

She was very soon back with a tray, and sat in bed eating with relish.

'I don't remember sex making you hungry in Montmartre,' he said, after a while. He wanted her. He had her. Their ingenuity in sex, their passion, their climaxes, the ease of knowing each other's body, 'the shape of your arms and heart,' Nelly quoted from a play, all she gave him ought to make him deeply content. It did not.

'Matt,' said Nelly, finishing off her scrambled eggs, 'I believe you've got something on your mind. Spit it out.'

'I'm not sure I should tell you.'

'I knew there was something. Go on. Tell. There's a

strength, you know, in the friend who wants nothing from you.'

When she carelessly betrayed the distance between the girl he had condescended to make his mistress, and this rich, richly endowed actress, Nelly got on his nerves. He resented the four years she had lived without him and what those years had taught her. Sometimes he resented her talent, her vitality, the casual fashion in which she had her own way.

He said pettishly, 'I imagined there was something *you* wanted from *me*.'

'Oh, that,' said Nelly, with a familiar nod at Matthew's male nakedness. 'Of course. The oftener the better. But the rest, Matt, I don't want or need. Come on. Tell a fellow what's making you miserable.'

He felt ashamed, then, of his ungenerous thoughts and told her, quite simply, that Alice could never have a child. It was a great grief to him.

Nelly looked at him for a moment in silence.

'Poor Alice.'

'Yes. But what's so tragic is for the family. We need an heir.'

'I suppose so. But it's worse for her. Much worse. Is she the sort who wants babies?'

'I think she does.'

'You don't sound very sure.'

'I don't believe I know her particularly well. She's a funny little thing. Reserved.'

'Like you.'

'Surely not.'

'Surely not,' mimicked Nelly. 'You're so upper class. I often think you must have given Claude Stanway lessons, he does sound like you onstage. Only more so. Matt, I am very, very sorry about what you told me – for your wife more than you. You'll need to be good to each other.'

'You sound like a Salvation Army lassie.'

'So I do,' said Nelly.

He returned to Belgrave Square when the dawn was paling

the dark, turning trees from black to green. Nelly would sleep until midday.

He was tired from sex, but still disturbed, half from the dissatisfaction which Nelly's company gave him – her freedom was curiously hard to bear – half from the knowledge that he had not behaved well to Alice. He was indifferent, cold even. He had to admit she did not look unhappy; on the contrary he'd noticed she was looking quite radiant. She has become used to the idea already. Women are harder than we are, he thought.

The house was awake; there was a bustle, footsteps, and a footman was whistling off-key. He stopped when he saw Matthew.

'Beg pardon, my lord.'

'Get me some coffee, Hooper. And find out if the post has come.'

The coffee, hot and black, arrived carried by the butler, a venerable old man who had been in the family for forty years, had weathered the scandal of the prostitute's death and the tragedy of another death, the young Viscount's, whom he had loved devotedly. He arrived with a salver-full of letters, bowed and left the room.

Matthew was glad to be by himself. He'd slept little, was tired and drained and looked it. He flipped through his post. Thick creamy envelopes with crests or coronets on the back; invitations, short letters from friends suggesting meetings or thanking him for last week's party. The last letter in the pile was typewritten. Presumably a bill. When he opened it he was surprised at the heading, Monckton and Miles, Solicitors, Paternoster Row.

> We have to inform you that Mr Lewis Shipton of Vancouver is arriving in London this week. We represent Mr Shipton who has a claim upon your lordship.
>
> Our client has already produced, before a lawyer in Canada, his parents' marriage certificate. This

shows that his father was the Honourable Guy
Ayrton, heir to the Viscountcy. He married Clara
Shipton of Whale Creek. At present Mr Shipton
uses his mother's maiden name. His claim is that his
father was rightful heir, and therefore the title
naturally devolves upon himself.

'A meeting would be necessary,' the letter continued,
'between the solicitors "of both parties".'

Matthew read the letter with an expression of stunned
astonishment. He read it again. It had a grotesque ring of
possibility. It was true that his and Robert's father, Aubrey
Ayrton, hadn't been the heir. There had been an older brother
Guy, tragically drowned at sea when only twenty years old. In
the 1840s it was still fashionable to send young men on a sort of
Grand Tour. Guy, with an older companion, a friend of his
father's, had travelled as far as India, gone to Ceylon, visited
Shanghai, and taken a ship to Hawaii, planning from there to
go to Canada before returning home. The ship had foundered
in a storm off Vancouver Island in a place noted for
shipwrecks. Aubrey in due course inherited the title.

Was it actually possible that Guy had not died then after all?
If so, *why* had he never come home? What had he been doing
skulking on the other side of the world? And why had this
man suddenly decided to return and claim his rights?

'I don't believe a word of it,' said Matthew aloud.

Soon afterwards he went riding in Rotten Row. But as he
rode, saluted by young equestrians already out in the bright
morning air, the letter lay in his breast pocket. Seeping its
contents into him like a poison.

CHAPTER FIFTEEN

Walking through the Temple on his way to Walter Smythe's chambers, it occurred to Matthew that fate was in the mood to make a bitter joke at his expense. He had positively resented having the responsibility of Leckford on his shoulders. Now it was in danger of being snatched away.

Climbing a stair in a building so old that the past seemed to press in on him, he arrived at the chambers and was shown into the lawyer's office.

'Good to see you,' said the old man. 'Sit down, my dear Matthew. How are you? How is your wife? It is far too long since I had the pleasure of seeing her.'

Matthew felt the need of energy and aggression, and noticed uneasily that the lawyer appeared tired.

'And is Honoria in good health?' he inquired. Matthew cut him short.

'Walter, I have received this.'

Smythe took the letter and leaned back in a chair which creaked under his weight. While he was reading his face lost its age and geniality. He looked hard as iron. Matthew watched him with a sort of ghastly curiosity, thinking – is this how a prisoner feels waiting for the verdict?

'Well, Matthew,' said Smythe at last. 'This is not nice. Not nice at all. It will upset Honoria. Of course she knew Guy Ayrton, the families grew up together, did they not?'

'I have no idea. My mother never speaks of the past.'

'I think,' said Smythe, 'she should not be informed about this matter for a while. Will you leave it in my hands?'

'I would be very grateful.'

Smythe brooded.

'We will have the necessary inquiries set in train at once. The claim is outrageous. As if your uncle would keep his existence secret while living on – where was it?'

'Vancouver Island.'

'Exactly so. Had he survived the shipwreck he would have returned to England within weeks. Why remain incognito in Canada? This is a trumped-up story by a criminal, and a pretty barefaced one, I give him that. I beg you not to be concerned. The only reason I suggest you keep it from your mother is that she is somewhat elderly,' said Walter, five years her senior, 'and the old are easily fussed.'

He walked with Matthew to the head of the stairs, shook hands and repeated, 'A trumped-up story. We must put a stop to it.'

Matthew did not feel comforted. Smythe had spoken with too much vehemence.

He walked slowly back through the Temple and down the Strand, so wrapped in thought that he did not see Nelly, whose laughing face under a great ribboned hat was leaning out of a hansom; she was waving wildly.

Matthew went home, trying to tell himself that it was absurd to be upset by a pack of disgraceful lies. But the prospect of an evening filled with friends, the need of a mask, was more than he could stomach. He spent the afternoon in an empty parlour on the first floor where he kept his until now discarded paints and canvases. What he produced after four hours was worse than not having tried to paint. He scrubbed it out with turpentine.

A Girl from Nowhere had already played out its first act when he drove to the theatre, paid for the only vacant box (which had a bad view of the stage), and sat down. He waited for the moment when the interval was over and Nelly made her entrance. Ah. There she was. She held the audience, she held him, in the palm of her hand.

Tonight he felt he couldn't go to her dressing-room. Leon Seidl was always there, and always gave him the same speculative stare in which there was no male jealousy. There were usually young men, too, some of whom he knew, paying court to Nelly. Actors and actresses called in, full of compliments. He wanted her alone. And not for sex.

Going round to the stage door, he scribbled a message on the back of his card.

'May I call at your house later? I'd very much like to see you. If you are busy, I will come at whatever late hour you name.'

The old doorkeeper sent a boy up with the message.

'You'll get your answer right away, Sir. Nelly's punctilious.' He retired into his cubbyhole with a smile like a blessing.

Matthew waited, now and then forced to squeeze back against the wall (the passage was narrow) as men and women went by in loud laughing talk. Matthew did not relish Nelly Briggs's world. The callboy in plum-coloured uniform with brass buttons returned briskly.

'Message for you, Mister. Wants a reply, Nelly says.'

On the back of the card, in her childlike writing, she had scrawled, 'Not in S.J. Wood, people staying. Want to take me to supper? Romano's in ten minutes? N.'

'Tell Miss Briggs I will wait with pleasure.'

'Righty-ho.'

Matthew and Nelly had never appeared in public before. They came into the elaborate restaurant, pink-shaded, leafy with groups of palms and filled with music and talk. She wore pale heliotrops, Queen Alexandra's favourite colour, with a train which could have done with a couple of train-bearers. Another of her pearl chokers – this one had eighteen rows and clasp of amethysts – showed off her graceful neck. Her rounded arms were hidden in the long white kid gloves which were *de rigueur* in the evening, and over her wrists were a number of diamond bracelets.

They were shown to a secluded table.

'You order, Matt. Actors are always as hungry as wolves.'

While he chose the meal he wished that she were not so – what? So herself. So full of vitality which seemed to vent itself on him. He was anxious and sad, and when the waiter returned with champagne and he drank a little he thought, how dare I dump my miseries in this lovely creature's lap? Why should she care? She seemed, she was, almost alarmingly happy.

'What's the matter? Alice again?'

It came as a shock to hear her use the name.

'Something almost worse.'

'My poor man. What?'

And then he knew why he had come.

Nelly listened large-eyed to the story, forgetting, for a while at least, to eat.

'A swindler. On a pretty bold scale. Golly.'

'The lawyer thinks he is, too. I'm not sure.'

'Matt, you can't believe that rot! Your father's own brother, secretly married in Canada and staying there without a word to his family. There must be evidence that the ship went down. The poor lad was drowned. You know he was.'

'That's the point, Nelly. I don't know.'

She was concerned, impulsively indignant with him, comforting, above all she was strong. She became a little angry at the idea of treating the claim seriously. She made him laugh. By the end of the meal she had consoled him – in a way. But she would not let him take her to St. John's Wood. She stood, one foot on the hansom step, 'Come and see me at home soon. But send word first. I don't want you driving all the way to find me out. Goodnight, Matt.'

She just stopped herself from using Claude's catchphrase, that worse things happen at sea.

Society could not believe its eyes when the story of Lewis Shipton appeared in the newspapers, accompanied by the picture of a man in a high-buttoned suit and cap, standing outside the Houses of Parliament.

'Here on English soil at last,' he was reported as saying, 'to take my rightful place in the House of Lords.'

'Not the Leckfords again!' people exclaimed, putting down *The Times*. But it was different now and the ranks closed safely

286

round Matthew. The thing was a fabricated story against 'one of us', and so beneath contempt. Matthew and Alice were surrounded by friends who were rather too loyal and rather too interested.

Matthew told Alice about the case only just in time, the day before it appeared in the press. He found her alone in her boudoir before she left for a round of calls. He said, 'There is something you must know,' and put a copy of the letter – sent at his request by Walter Smythe – in front of her. When she had read it, he said, 'It is rather upsetting. But *c'est la vie* . . .' With his wife Matthew was drawn to clichés.

'Have you shown this to your mother?'

'I'm going to Leckford this afternoon.'

'Break it gently,' she said. A stab of shameful joy went through her, knowing he was leaving London.

But when he had gone she sat trying to grasp what he'd shown her. Suppose by outlandish chance the claim was true. Matthew could lose everything. Poor Honoria would no longer pray by the white marble image, everything, everything would be lost. She couldn't imagine the effect of such a disaster on Matthew and his mother. The whole basis of their lives, the way they saw themselves, was epitomised in their name. Leckford. Leckford Court. Its coat of arms. Its pride. Itself. She did not once think about her own position, she was only desperately concerned for them.

And then her thoughts in selfish passion forgot them and flew towards Vance.

She had seen him yesterday. She had been at Hurlingham, at a crowded roses-and-strawberries afternoon, and as she left the family carriage she had scarcely taken a step when he came across the lawn to her. They walked away together.

'I thought you'd never come.'

'I am quite early,' she said, inclining her head to a gentleman going by. More people passed, Alice bowed and smiled. Reaching a far stretch of the lawns at a distance from the polo field, she turned and looked at him.

'My dear girl. You are ill!'

'No. It's only – can we sit down?'

He led her to some chairs under the trees. Somebody else went by, raising his hat. Vance did the same having no idea who it was and wishing him to the devil.

'Alice. I'm sailing at the end of this week.'

She nodded but said nothing. She felt if he did not touch her she would faint, and if he did she would die.

'We must be together again.'

'We can't,' she said, so indistinctly that he had to lean forward to hear.

'I tell you we must. Invent another story. These people do it all the time. Do you *want* to be with me?'

She lifted her head, and what he saw satisfied him.

'I'll call as I did last time. Tomorrow at eleven in the motor. Give me your hand.'

'Why?' she asked stupidly.

He pressed it to his lips. Looking at his head bent over her hand, she was shaken by something violent, desolate.

'Oh, what's happening to us?' she said.

'They call it love,' said Vance and grimaced.

She told herself while Mary Murphy helped her to dress that everything she was doing was wrong. She must never hold him in her arms again. Wanting him could never do her good. She thought her body passionate and wild, cheating and hot, her thoughts were those of a lecher and what she wanted was wrong. And yet. She remembered him in the buttercup field, and how he had been when their love-making was over, so tender and beautiful and full of love. She was in a little boat made of paper, sweeping towards a gigantic waterfall. I shall be dashed to pieces, she thought. So be it.

Vance drove her on a warm afternoon into another part of the English countryside. He had the American trick of knowing what was worth seeing or visiting. He took her to the upper reaches of the Thames, by a lock where the lock-keeper had planted flowers like a band of embroidery. They lunched from cold food he had brought in a hamper.

Afterwards they walked under the willows. Dragonflies darted by, and across the river were swans, motionless on the motionless water. Alice thought – oh, when we are going to make love.

They sat down on the grass under a low-hanging willow. She took off her hat.

'I shan't make love to you yet,' he suddenly said.

She went crimson.

'My little love. You're not used to talking about sex, are you? And you never enjoyed it till now. Don't look away. Wasn't I the first to make you come? Yes, I know I was, I just want to say it and look at you . . .'

Then he said in a changed voice, 'We must talk.'

There is nothing to talk about, she thought. Except parting. And how to bear it, I suppose.

'Alice, answer me something. Do you swear you'll answer truthfully?'

'Of course. Of course.'

'You are not going to like the question.'

He looked at her and said, 'You have told me nothing about your marriage. Did you love Matthew Leckford? Do you love him now?'

'How could I! How can I!'

'They tell me he's a fascinating kind of chap. I reckon a woman would find it easy to love a man like that.'

'I never did.' She did not realise what she'd said.

'So you married him for that blamed title, is that it?'

'It wasn't like that,' she replied miserably.

'How then?'

'I – yes, it was because he was a Viscount, at least that's what Mother wanted, she likes me being in the English aristocracy. First she wanted it for Fran. Then Fran said No –'

'*So why did you?*'

He glanced accusingly at her. She was afraid of him.

'Because of Mother. I begged her. I tried to get out of it, I did, I did! Fran tried for me, too. I told Mother I didn't want to marry him, Fran quarrelled with her about it, but you can't win with Mother. At least I never could. Fran knew a way for herself, just as my father does. But not me. Oh Vance, forgive me.' She started to cry. She waited for him to call her a coward and a fool, and said sobbing, 'You despise me.'

He started forward, taking her hands from her tearful face, pressing them, putting them against his open mouth.

'Dear love, dear love. I only wanted the truth. I felt the moment we met that you were one of our American girls pushed into a grand European marriage. I felt it strongly. Then – then I began to love you and I thought maybe you did love Leckford in some way and that I'd die if it were so. But we made love, and when I was inside you I was certain you didn't love him. Come to me. Be with me. Come here.'

The story of the Canadian claimant became a daily favourite in the newspapers; Lewis Shipton gave interviews whenever he was asked. One or two of his quips were much quoted. Journalists began to call him 'the possible Viscount Leckford'.

Alice met the ordeal with courage, perhaps inherited from some brave Irish ancestor who had fought against Cromwell's generals. Adversity brought out a woman Matthew might have loved. As the Season drew to its close it was Alice who faced the glittering interest of friends, and who was cool and at times humorous about Shipton.

Matthew did not visit her room again. She was blessedly alone at night. She never looked ahead to her own and her husband's future. All she thought about during the long tranced hours was Vance.

She knew their love was over. She must accept that, and concentrate on Matthew's trouble. But although her common sense told her Vance was lost, that she'd never lie with him again, passion did not believe it. He wasn't a Matthew, easy and graceful, who would never be enslaved, Alice thought, by any woman. Vance was a fierce determined man. He wanted her and in a way was at her mercy, the mercy of his hard desire. When they had made love by the river and the climax came, the second in her life, he remained with his body in hers and looked down at her drowned face and said, 'I *will* have you. For ever. I swear it.'

It was impossible. She was a Catholic as Matthew was, there couldn't be such a thing as divorce.

She decided to leave London a few days before the Season officially ended, it had been such a crowded and exhausted one. She looked tired and Matthew was concerned.

'I'm glad you're leaving town,' he said. 'You need a rest. You've been,' he added with admiration, 'such a soldier.'

Alice smiled as she poured his breakfast coffee. He thought, she has many burdens. The threat of this Canadian business hanging over us. The terrible blow of not being able to have a child. The fact in the past that I philandered. That sex gave her no pleasure. And the new presence in my life, although I'm sure she hasn't guessed it, of Nelly. He had always had a compassion for women except once. He found himself wishing he could have loved this dignified little creature whose body was all he knew of her. What more was there to know? It isn't her fault, poor child, that she's cold, he thought. And lately her courage had deeply impressed him.

'Have you seen this?'

He passed her *The Times*, where there was a short piece under the heading 'Curious Tricks of Heredity'. Below, placed together and resembling Tweedledum and Tweedledee, were the pictures of two men. One was Matthew taken at Ascot, negligent in pale grey, his topper pushed slightly back. The other was of a man as tall, with the same thick moustache, the same hair, the same morning dress, even the same stance. Alice studied the pictures, then looked up.

'You aren't beginning to believe it, are you? Likenesses mean nothing. Many people are total strangers and resemble each other. Perhaps that creature has seen you, and deliberately bought those clothes and changed his hair. Anything's possible with a criminal.'

'Alice. You are so good. You have such faith.'

He spoke with far more emotion than on the night she had

told him she couldn't have a child. 'But I went to the Temple yesterday. Smythe has received Shipton's birth certificate. There it is, in black and white.'

'And a place called Whale Creek is a long way off.' She looked at the pictures again and returned them to him.

'What happens next?'

'It goes to court. And will take a long time and a great deal of money.'

He means my money, she thought indifferently.

'Then things will be cleared up and he'll be sent to prison.'

Matthew leaned forward as if to take her hands. She put them in her lap.

Old Mary Murphy left for Leckford Court a day in advance, declaring she wasn't having Limey maids fixing up Alice's rooms. 'And don't I know how you like things, having cared for you since I taught you your first Hail Marys.'

The afternoon train rattled into a country where the hay had been cut and lay in curved swathes waiting for the haymakers to turn it into stooks. Elms stood like giants, surrounded by circles of shadow. It had been a hot, hot summer.

Alice watched the panorama, wondering what lay ahead. Matthew had seen his mother who had taken it, he said, 'calmly. As usual.' Alice didn't know what he meant and did not like to ask. When he spoke of Honoria he always looked blank-faced. She knew mother and son disliked each other.

The train hissed to a stop at the lonely station bright with marigolds. Alice's favourite footman, red-headed John, was waiting on the platform to accompany her to the open barouche. It was a vehicle which Alice had reinstated at Leckford, a graceful open shell mostly used for park driving. Barouches were fashionable but they needed pairs of high-quality horses, and in the past the Leckfords had not been able to afford such a luxury. Until Alice arrived in the family, the Leckfords had used a Victoria with a single horse. Now John pulled down the little step for Alice to climb in. He fumbled with it, seeming nervous.

The perfectly matched pair, the colour of cream, began to move down the dusty road towards the village. Alice suddenly heard a beautiful noise – a peal of bells. It fell like water tumbling down a steep flight of steps, starting high, then falling down lower and lower, right down to the bottom, then magically starting at the top again. The bells sounded the very crown of joy. She leaned forward and unceremoniously tapped John's back with her parasol.

The barouche stopped and John jumped down.

'My lady?'

'Is there a wedding of one of the tenants? If so, why was I not told?'

The young man blushed as only red-headed people can.

'It isn't nothing, my lady.'

'Come along, John. What do you mean? Why are they ringing the bells? Are they rehearsing at the church? If so, for what?'

His face still burned and she said kindly, 'Whatever the reason is, I have to know.'

'It's – it's the gentleman from Canada.'

She positively started.

'*What?*'

'Come to the village yesterday, he did. Staying at the Arms and turned up hisself at the house this morning, bold as brass. He saw the Dowager.'

'And the bells?' was all Alice said.

'In the village they been saying – ' the young man's voice trailed to a stop. It was never openly admitted that the Big House hobnobbed with the village. Alice waited for more, and he said, 'We heard as the bells is being rung for welcome, like. The long-lost heir . . . sorry, my lady.'

'I see.'

How the bells pealed.

'We thought you'd prefer not to drive past the church. There's a crowd there. William's taking you by the crossroad and through –'

'The back gates!' exclaimed Alice, sounding very aristocratic indeed. 'He will do no such thing. Tell him to drive past the church as usual.'

John climbed back onto the box and said a word to the coachman, whose back was eloquent. The barouche moved on.

The small Saxon church looked as if its walls would crack with the glorious waterfall of noise. There was a group of people in the churchyard, only some of whom Alice recognised. The rest, she thought, look cityfied. Just before the barouche went by, the crowd gave a ragged cheer and she saw they were gathered round a well-dressed man in grey. For one unbelievable moment she thought it was Matthew.

William whipped the horses, the people stared, but then the tall man apparently said something, and there was a shout of, 'God Bless Lord Leckford. Back at last!' and 'Welcome home, Sir, welcome home!'

Alice's face was set as she swept into Leckford Court's entrance. The old butler came forward.

'Where is Lady Leckford, Hopkins?'

'In the Yellow Drawing-room, my lady.' His voice sounded uneasy. Everybody's affected by it, thought Alice. Have they started thinking it's true?

She walked through the chain of rooms, and almost ran into the drawing-room. Honoria was sitting by the window. Alice went over and sat facing her on the window-seat, impatiently unfastening her hat and stabbing the long pins into the tulle.

Honoria looked smaller than Alice remembered. She was like old dry paper. Her rosary was in her fingers and, seeing the shrunken figure, Alice spoke with all her kindness.

'You saw that man this morning. I hope he didn't upset you.'

'He did not.'

'But wouldn't it have been better to refuse to see him?'

'Refuse? It was necessary. You heard the bells, of course.'

Alice gave a disapproving 'tut-tt'.

'Disgraceful,' she exclaimed. 'We will speak to the rector. Why, that Canadian fellow –'

'Fellow?' interrupted Honoria, with a flicker of energy despite her ashen face. 'He is not a "fellow" my child, he is the heir. Something we must accustom ourselves to accept. He was quite considerate about my leaving here. Had the courtesy to suggest building a Dower House. So that I might walk to the chapel.'

'*Lady Leckford.*'

'Don't say I am mistaken, Alice, or have been duped. I spent two hours with Mr Shipton, or Lord Leckford as we will soon call him. He talked a good deal. Of course he speaks in the Canadian way, but he will lose that over the years. He told me everything. He was "raised", I think that is the word, by his mother, wife to my brother-in-law, Guy, whom I scarcely recall. It is all very long ago. Mr Shipton grew up with strong traditions of the family, and he knows Leckford as if he had lived here all his life. He recited every painting in the gallery to me. Not only those which are well-known, but the little Honthurst, and the unfinished design by William Kent of a fountain. He even knew about my aunt's watercolour of the cats playing in my family's garden. It was very moving,' she finished in a thin voice.

Alice was appalled. Selfishly wrapped in her own passion, loyally defending a husband she did not love, she had never for a second believed this could happen. That Matthew could lose. That his birthright would be stolen from him. How could he bear to become a nobody, usurped, an object of pity in his own world? And this house into which her father had poured his money as if turning on a gigantic tap, was this also to be lost? She imagined her father's indignation, her mother's fury when the precious title was removed. Her thoughts whirled.

Honoria peered at her, and remarked with less than her usual indifference, 'I daresay it is a shock. You're a good child. It is a blow for you.'

'Oh, so much worse for Matthew!'

'He never cared for the family.'

'*That is not true!*'

'My poor child, you know nothing about it. How could you,

being an American? You know less after years of marriage than Mr Shipton showed in the first five minutes in this room. My second son has no feeling for his name, for his father, for Leckford Court or for myself. He never cared for his brother who was the pride, the true Leckford who comes once in a hundred years. If Robert were alive, what grief he would suffer. Your husband will accept it well enough. Mark my words.'

Alice was shocked to the depths of her soul. Why, Honoria almost hated her own son. She had never shown it openly until now when everything could be lost.

In a voice which became weak when relentless feeling had gone, Honoria asked Alice to ring for tea. The footman brought it and left them. She unsteadily lifted the enormous silver teapot, and then offered Alice a plate of the biscuits always served for Honoria. They were hard and dry. The old woman drank her tea thirstily.

'Before you married, your husband in duty bound must have told you of the shame attached to his name.'

'Yes.'

'It was sorrow at the disgrace which sent my elder son to die.'

Alice said nothing. It sounded like a far-fetched lie to her. Why should Robert Leckford, whom she still thought of as a ghostly statue, go to the war because Matthew was in some messy scandal? It did not make sense. Men went to war from love of country, she supposed. Or because all their friends did so. Perhaps there was a patriotic feeling in the air, in people's blood at the time. What you didn't do was risk your life because your brother was mixed up in the death of a prostitute. People believe what they want to believe, thought Alice. Honoria had canonised her elder son.

'You wonder why I speak of that,' said Honoria after a pause. 'I will tell you. I believe and so will you when you have prayed about it that this is heaven's judgement. Matthew stained our name. He committed a terrible sin and some creature,' she continued, with distaste, 'died because of it.

And again because of it his brother took up his country's cause. He died a hero. In reparation. Matthew had no right, no right at all, to come here in his brother's place. It will be taken from him. Yes. It is a judgement.'

She shut her eyes and rearranged the rosary round her wrist. Alice left the room.

When she had gone, Honoria stopped her prayers and sat thinking about the man who had been here a few hours ago. Hopkins, the butler from her girlhood, had drawn himself up when Honoria said, 'Show Mr Shipton in.'

'I am sure your ladyship does not mean that.'

Honoria, freezingly, repeated the order. She knew the old man spoke from loyalty, but were we to have some kind of French Revolution?

The visitor was tall, stouter than Matthew, and somewhat older. His clothes might have been taken from their boxes that morning. With an accent which made Alice's sound positively English, he said he was 'proud to meet your ladyship,' seized her hand and pumped it up and down. Then he sat down without being asked.

'I feel very emotional, Ma'am. To be in Leckford Court at last. How often I have visited this place in my mind. My astral body, you might say, has been here since I was a little lad.'

It was not an auspicious beginning. Honoria, wondering what on earth or in Heaven an astral body could be, offered him a glass of Madeira. He drank it fast, and she offered him another. He appeared to need it. His manner was gross, his voice loud, but she saw that he was nervous and liked him for it. She was always at ease when in the ascendancy, and it was a paradox that this man, this threat to her whole life, should make her behave so pleasantly.

'Well, Mr Shipton. So you are come to steal away my family's birthright.'

'No, no!' He was sweating. 'Not to steal, never to steal. To claim, I'm afraid, my lady. My dear father –'

He had to stop to pull himself together.

Still victor in this curious contest, Honoria encouraged him to speak about his father. She was filled with a burning curiosity. She had few emotions nowadays, save when praying for Robert, and this surge of feeling was like strong drink. She listened, fascinated. His father had died, God bless him, said Lewis Shipton making the sign of the Cross, when he had been 'a shaver, scarcely so high.' Shipton remembered him as 'noble, Ma'am, just noble.' The phrase used to describe the young man she had known all those years ago struck her. It suited Guy Ayrton.

'You have a portrait of him by George Frederick Watts in the gallery. With that tapestry,' pointing to the wall hanging, 'as the background.'

As a single piece of information it was unimpressive. Watts's work was well enough known. But sipping a third glass of Madeira, and losing some of his nervous strain, Shipton became easier, and louder, as he began to talk about Leckford. It was astounding. He spoke, not of obvious features in the house, but of small things. A pagoda cabinet of Chinese lacquer which one of the Leckfords had brought back from Germany in 1748, 'with flowers and birds. Pink flowers and white ivory birds.' He described the needlework of a bedhanging in her own room, the Grinling Gibbons carving on a fireplace, 'with bars of music carved so clear you can play from them. And my dear father once did!'

He described paintings, glass, silver, rare books, a doll's house 'in the attic in my father's day,' and a certain stuffed white ermine 'which snarls at you to the life. Its teeth are razor-sharp.'

And then, having rambled on with his audience pale as a wax image, he spoke of his claim.

'You'll say, why didn't my dear father come home when *his* father died, when he became rightful heir, if not earlier after the shipwreck? Ma'am, it was my mother who stopped him. He fell in love with her when he landed in a row-boat at Whale Creek. Love at first sight. She was an all-Canadian girl, God bless her, and they married when she was almost a child. Later she couldn't face the honour and the glory of it all. And he loved her, Ma'am. It was a picture to see them together. He stayed for her sake. Immortal love, that's what it was. When they both died, well, I felt it in my heart that it was time. I left Whale Creek. I scraped the fare together somehow. Borrowed a bit. I travelled steerage on a merchantman and was sick as a hog, begging your pardon. But I sure knew I couldn't stake my claim in England if it was not in person. How could I trust the mail? Suppose my mother's marriage lines and my birth certificate had been lost?'

'You could have sent copies.'

'Sure thing. But would they be believed? No, for such a great purpose, such a *quest* I call it, I had to come myself. I see you understand.'

She was silent for a while. Then, 'Are you a Catholic, Mr Shipton?'

'A Catholic, Ma'am! What else can a Leckford be but a member of the True Faith? I was baptised at St Paul's – it's just a small place, but I love it. I always feel it's holy just being inside its walls. I practice my religion regularly, as I guess you must do. My mother used to say, "Lewis, it's my belief you're more Catholic than the Pope." '

'In which case,' said Honoria very dryly, 'I fail to see why you visited the village church. And had the bells rung.'

He carefully put down his glass and leaned forward. He wore an expression of gravity.

'You heard that I called there, Ma'am. It was in no disrespect for our Faith, although the church, of course, is Protestant now. I knew that the Leckford tombs were there and wanted to see them. My poor mother showed me a picture in one of the family books my father had in his valise when he was rescued. Wet with seawater it was. When I saw the tombs, I won't deny it, they went to my heart.'

He banged his chest with a clenched fist.

He remained a long time, speaking of her own future, of a new Dower House (he appeared to know about such things). He was sincere and respectful and continued to sweat. She was exhausted, but sorry when he rose to go.

He stood at the door, with Hopkins hovering like a malevolent spirit, and said loudly, 'All I can say, my lady, is *thanks*.'

Matthew stayed in London not, as he'd told Alice, to see out the end of the Season but to see Nelly. Talk of the 'Canadian Claimant' at his club, among his friends, the name appearing in the newspapers, sickened him. Even Alice's steady faith had told on his nerves and after she left for the country he was glad. He wanted Nelly. Her realism. Her warmth. Perhaps her love. He did not feel he had that.

He hadn't managed to see her for days. *A Girl from Nowhere* had finally closed. It had run for almost a year, and Leon Seidl decided it was time for a change. Nelly was busy with plans, all of which were Seidl's. Matthew resented the energetic American with whom she shared a life he knew little about.

She had told him not to come to her house without arranging it with her first. She might not be there. But he wanted badly to see her and quailed at a casual call to the theatre during the play's last week. He disliked Leon Seidl's thoughtful glance, sensing more in it than mere idle interest.

He was about to leave for St John's Wood on the off-chance of seeing Nelly when he was called to the telephone. It was Alice and he was alarmed, thinking his mother must be ill.

'She is quite well, Matthew. That is not why I wanted to speak to you.'

She told him about Shipton coming to the house.

He was furiously angry.

'You mean that man had the gall –'

'Oh yes,' she interrupted. 'He has a deal of that. Hopkins told me he was with your mother nearly two hours. He knows everything about Leckford.'

'Things read in guidebooks.'

'No, it wasn't that way at all. He knew things ordinary people couldn't know. Yards of them.'

'My mother is old. Easy to confuse.'

Oh is she, thought Alice.

'If he turns up again, you will refuse to admit him.'

'Of course. But *she* won't.'

'Tell Hopkins the door must be slammed in his face.'

'Does that mean,' said Alice's small even voice, 'that he has something we are afraid of? However, let's not argue. I will see he doesn't come again. Did I tell you the villagers cheered and shouted "God bless Lord Leckford"?'

'No. You didn't tell me that.'

He took a brougham to St John's Wood. Park Lane at this time of early evening was deserted except for one or two cabs moving in a leisurely way under the trees. The day had been hot and the blinds, lowered eyelids, covered the windows. Behind them, he thought, were secrets. Mine have never been discreetly hidden, but always on public show. They were when I left for Paris. They are now.

It was nearly seven years since he had fled in disgrace from his own country, and he often literally forgot he had gone for Robert's sake, putting on his brother's guilt like a dirty coat. He now half-believed what his mother wholly believed.

Nelly's house, set back along a road more lonely and empty than Mayfair, had a tree-shaded garden. He'd never been there in daylight, and he went through the gate, noticing the pleasant lawns and blue flowers. This was her home, existing, established. It seemed to distance her more.

Going up to the porch, he rang the bell.

There was no sound of approaching footsteps through the closed door. Nothing but a countryfied silence. He pressed the bell for a longer time.

He heard it jangling somewhere inside the house. But no servant appeared. There was no sign of life at all. Cursing under his breath in disappointment, he emerged and stood looking at the closed face of the house. There was a light trotting sound. A voice said, 'Hello.'

A small boy was standing in a patch of sunlight. He was sturdy and fair, with a round face and blue eyes. He was holding a hoop.

'Hello,' said Matthew. 'Who are you?'

'Well, I'm Tom, of course. What's your name?'

'Matthew Leckford.

'In Paris, you'd be Mathieu. They have different ways of saying names, you know. They call me "Tomà", it is funny.'

A woman's voice called, 'Tom! Tom!'

'Tante is calling,' said the child. 'I have to go. We're in the garden having raspberries. Will you come?'

He put out the hand not holding the hoop and took Matthew's. The gesture gave the big man a curious feeling; he did not understand children and usually treated them with a facetious boisterousness which over-excited them. He had never met so polite and commanding a child.

'Do you know Tante Edith and Tante Nelly?' said his young host. 'There they are.'

Two women were sitting on the grass under a tree, both dressed in white. Nelly sprang up and ran towards him. She said with a very actressy smile.

'What are *you* doing here?' And while Matthew clumsily explained he had called by chance, Nelly said over her shoulder, 'Edith. Come and meet an old friend.'

The small boy lost interest, and went off to bowl his hoop along a paved path. Edith Holden came over to them. Matthew was surprised, for Nelly never mentioned her old friend from Paris. As they shook hands, he thought Edith much changed. She was no longer the girl with the blonde wavy hair hanging down her back. She was plumper and more sedate, her white linen dress suited her rosy face. A fringed scarf hand-painted with roses was tied like a gypsy's round her shoulders.

She said a few smiling words to him to bridge the distance from Paris until now. But she was cool. Nelly continued to give occasional blazing smiles.

Finally, Edith said, 'It's after six, Nelly. Shall I put Tom to bed, as Kirstin won't be back yet? Otherwise he's sure to interrupt. If you aren't careful,' she said to Matthew, dryly, 'he will give you the name of every plant in the herbacious border. He has a passion for lists.'

302

'I used to be the same,' said Matthew. 'Lists of birds. Trees. Even lists of all the people who died in *Hamlet*, I remember.'

After Edith and the child had disappeared into the house, he remarked, 'I had no idea you and she were still friends.'

'Oh, for ever. I persuade her to come and stay sometimes.'

She looked at him and added, 'You're in a fidget. Is it the Canadian again?'

'You hear people talking about it, I suppose.'

'Of course I don't. They may discuss earls and girls at the Gaiety and Daly's, *they* keep marrying each other. Our gossip is different. Just to do with work. Leon has got an idea I should play Viola in *Twelfth Night* next spring. I've told him no until I am blue in the face.'

'He could be right, Viola's a captivating creature.'

'Don't you start. You're not here to talk theatre. What's been happening?'

'Did you see this?'

He took out the picture of himself set beside Lewis Shipton. Nelly spread the newspaper on her lap. He waited for her to say what thousands of people must have said by now.

She was silent. Finally, he exclaimed, 'Well?'

'Well, what?'

'The likeness is uncanny, isn't it?' His voice was savage.

'Is that what you think? How very odd. He doesn't look like you one bit. Look at the shape of his eyes and yours. And there's a bump on the bridge of your nose, see? His is sort of squashed. And then his hair grows quite differently. You're both completely different and that's all there is to it.'

He was taken aback.

'May I keep this paper? You don't want it, do you?'

'I brought it to show you. But why do you wish to keep it,' he said in a changed voice, 'when you think that man and I are so dissimilar?'

'For Edith. Faces interest her.'

She put the paper into the pocket of her dress and leaned back against the trunk of the tree.

'Is that why you came, dear friend? Or is there more? I

303

don't need to go for a little. Tell me what else bothers you. It'll make you feel better.'

He kissed her hand casually, in a way she remembered.

'Nelly. I meant to ask you just now. Who is that child? Is he Edith's by any chance. The idea did occur to me.'

She burst out laughing.

'Of course he isn't. His parents are dead, poor things, and he is living with me now. I thought I might adopt him legally. I can afford to. One of the pleasures of money. What do you think of him?'

'Good-looking.'

'Yes. And rather clever, which is a surprise. If you talk down to Tom, he looks at you with pity. Edith says he's too quick and will need a governess when his Danish nurse finally leaves. She says his little brain is hungry, and actresses and painters won't feed it enough.'

'He seems attached to Edith.'

'Well . . . she knew him in Paris.'

She gave him the actressy smile again. He could not guess that when he'd come into the garden and she had seen father and son together for the first time, she had thought her heart would split.

They fell silent. She thought he looked tense, and prompted, 'You still haven't said why you're here. Not just to show me those stupid pictures, surely? Where have you got to in the case, Matt? Are your lawyers coping?'

'The man has produced evidence. His birth certificate. Parents' marriage lines. If they're genuine, I am finished.'

'But you won't be broke, Matt. Not like in Paris! Isn't your Alice dripping in dollars?'

'I wish you wouldn't call her my Alice.'

'I don't see why not since that's what she is. I pity your Alice. Don't look nasty, you can scarcely be finished, as you call it, when you're married to the daughter of a Yankee millionaire.'

'You don't understand. I thought you might.'

'Understand what? Tell me.'

304

Her voice, her warmth, the dark blue eyes fixed on him, gave him a kind of liberty. He felt free of his class. Of dignity and reserve. He told her how from the moment he'd heard he might lose, he felt he could not bear it. The whole history of his family would be blotted out for him.

'All this man is after is our property. What can he know of tradition? He's a nobody from thousands of miles away. I feel dishonoured. I never did till now.'

'Worse than the scandal at Madam Ruth's?'

'Good God, Nelly. That was nothing compared to this.'

She studied his face. He was digging at the grass with his nails, she saw him in profile.

She looked at the little gold watch which hung round her neck on a chain.

'I have to go. I wish I didn't. Poor Matt. I am so very sorry you're unhappy.'

He glanced up and nodded, as if in thanks. The automatic movement, empty, polite, emphasised the great space of their separated lives.

She went into the house and when he followed her through open french windows, she had already darted upstairs, calling out to Tom. Edith appeared, to say goodbye to Matthew. Nelly reappeared, a primrose silk cape flying, and came running down again, giving impartial smiles to friend and lover. Outside there was a waiting growler. She did not offer Matthew a lift. He did not suggest coming with her, but stood watching the carriage drive away.

Nelly sat back in the carriage and shut her eyes. So Matthew had seen his son at last, she thought, why does it hurt so? Nothing had changed. But the sight of the tall man hand in hand with the confident little boy had been beautiful and curiously sad. Matthew filled her with passionate pity as well as desire. She was always trying not to think about him. He was not for her and she – most definitely – was not for him. Now he was suffering. Self-indulgent, tolerant, quixotic in throwing away his own good name, cruel in throwing *her* away because of it . . .

What an extraordinary thing it was, that pride in family. She thought of those people, their laws, their diamonds, their snobberies, their arrogance, their often iron faces to the poor. He used to say he disliked his own class but he was one of them. And he was right. She didn't understand.

Part IV

CHAPTER SIXTEEN

Vance Weston travelled home on the *Oceanic White Star*, much praised as a fast ship, but the crossing was very rough and took nearly nine days. He grew more and more impatient. Before sailing, he had received letters from his parents saying that Margaret had recovered her health but was an espoused member of what his father called 'all that crazy stuff of Women's Suffrage. She's out at meetings, makes speeches (Heaven preserve us!) and we don't consider she'll ever marry. What man would want a termagant? How our girl has changed.'

Vance's conscience about his family was easier now. He had the satisfying memory of punching Harry Grafton. He didn't feel there was much more he could do for his poor sister.

Docking at last in New York he went to the Waldorf Astoria to dine early and alone. He then made some inquiries, and set off in the evening and the city rain under an umbrella.

He walked to sort out his thoughts. In his work as a lawyer he liked to estimate an opponent's defence, make a plan of action. He was clever at probing for a weakness, piercing the joints between what appeared to be solid armour. He couldn't do this now. The Vandermeyers' armour, so to speak, was invulnerable. They were Catholics and Alice was a married woman.

Arriving at Fifty-Seventh Street, he walked some distance before locating the house, a majestic mansion of cream-coloured stone decorated with balustrades. A number of similar houses built on the same stately lines had risen here in the last twenty-five years. Before that the area had been a shanty town.

He rang the bell, presented his card, and was left by the manservant in a lofty old-fashioned hall. Twin portraits of a man and a woman hung over the marble fireplace. They must have been painted seventy or eighty years ago. He was studying these, thinking both faces looked somewhat too complacent, when he heard a sound. Turning round he saw a pretty woman framed in the archway.

'Mr Vance Weston,' she said, reading the card aloud. 'Now I'll bet a dollar you are a friend of my Sis.'

'You must be Miss Frances.'

'Right and wrong. I'm no longer Miss, alas. I'm Mrs Wendell Oliver. Mrs sounds so elderly, don't it? How do you do? Come along in and tell me about my Sis. It's so long since I've seen her. You're here to call on the parents, I guess. Sorry to disappoint you, my mother has dragged my poor father, screaming for mercy, to the opera. I'm just visiting. Come along in. My, you're wet.'

She led the way into a warm opulent room and sat him imperiously by the fire. Could she offer him a glass of champagne? They sipped for a moment or two. Then Fran put her feet on a tabouret and looked expectant.

He thought Alice's sister beautiful but too knowing, with her clever smile and saucer-like blue eyes. He compared her to Alice with that *frisson* of surprise at meeting somebody who faintly resembled her yet was so totally different. Before he could speak, Fran, who positively bloomed when with good-looking men, said, 'I am here in New York doing some shopping. It is my fate to live in Pittsburgh and I get homesick for New York. I'm a trial to my poor husband. I tear myself away from him and my child, because of my hunger for a new frock . . . now, why are you in the city, Mr Weston? Your card says you're from Philadelphia.'

'I am here for a day or two, Mrs Oliver.'

Fran threw her eyes up to heaven at her own name.

'Tell me, are you a great friend of my Sis? And Matt

Leckford's as well, though that needn't follow. Sis must have been overjoyed to meet a compatriot. She writes that there are a parcel of American girls, all of whom seem to be duchesses, but not so many of our men.'

'No. Not many.'

'I talk too much. What news of Alice?'

'She is well. We met during the London Season. She has gone back to Leckford Court now.'

'No doubt,' said Fran, dryly.

Vance had scarcely paid attention to the young woman's chatter although charmed by the soft tones of her voice. He had been taking her measure. He knew Alice loved her. And he needed an ally. He looked about for a way to tell her something of what was in his mind.

They seemed, thought Fran, to be getting nowhere. She had taken one of her fancies to the stranger, liked both his sharply modelled face which resembled a Red Indian carving, and his manner which was a mixture of gravity and an occasional unexpected smile. How dark his eyes were. Like currants in a bun.

She suddenly said, 'Why are you here really?'

'To have the pleasure of –'

'No, Mr Weston, that's flim-flam. Is Alice really all right? Is Matthew? What has been the matter?'

'I scarcely know Viscount Leckford.'

'And so?'

She looked at him and said slowly, 'I guess you are in love with her.'

'Yes.'

She gave a long 'Aaaa,' and unconsciously folded her arms across her breast as if she were cold.

'I'm glad you didn't say "I'm afraid so." Most men would in the circumstances.'

'There are no circumstances. I love her. I want her to obtain a divorce and become my wife.'

'Goodness,' she said without mockery.

She began to twist her rings.

'What does Alice say?'

'I think you can guess.'

'Perhaps. I imagine she's fallen in love, too. Poor Sis. Poor girl.'

Her face had changed, she looked serious and sad.

'It's impossible, Mr Weston. We're Catholics.'

'I know that only too well.'

'There's no way round. Alice is pious as you must surely know. Her faith is stronger than mine. But even if it was me – why, a Catholic can't do such a thing.'

There was a pause.

'Is she very unhappy?'

She looked unconsciously at a wall on the right and Vance saw, for the first time, a portrait of Alice, her lap full of roses.

'You mustn't think Lord Leckford is cruel to her. I shouldn't think he's capable of it. Unless you count coldness as cruelty.'

'I think I'm sorry for Matt, too. But children. She'll have children and love them much more than I do mine. I'm quite fond, you know, but she's a born mother. Forgive me, but children will solve everything for her.'

He hesitated. He thought of Alice in his arms, when she had cried and said she could have no children. He'd adored her more because of her sorrow.

'The doctors say she cannot have any,' he said.

Fran's eyes grew larger. She sighed, saying it was tragic and Alice must come home for a while. A girl needed her own folk at a time like this.

'I agree. She should come over, but not for that reason. You said just now that Catholics can't contemplate divorce. There is one solution.'

'To leave him? Be with you? Impossible.'

'No. The marriage must be annulled.'

'*What*?'

'Pronounced null and void. Rome could grant the decree. You must know about that, surely.'

'But only for marriages which aren't consummated, you can't be saying –'

'Unfortunately I can't. Of course it was. Forgive this indelicate conversation, but you are Alice's sister. I've no doubt he did his duty as a husband. The worse for her when all she did was submit. And then find she could never have a child. That won't be our plea, Mrs Oliver.'

'For heaven's sake call me Fran! What are you saying? That there's another way. Yes, I remember a case, weren't they called Avery? I read about it in the *Catholic Herald*. The man married, but beforehand made the reservation that if the marriage failed, he'd get a divorce. That made it no sacrament, because he hadn't intended it to be until death parted them. There were witnesses.'

'Those are always needed. Lord Leckford, however, made no such reservation. He wanted to marry her and he needed her money.'

'I'm sure he was fond of her,' said Fran. She no longer thought this man attractive. He brought an icy breath into the hot room.

'Mrs Oliver. Fran. Alice did not willingly go into her marriage. Did she?'

'I – I don't understand.'

'I think you do. Your mother wanted *you* to be his wife. You refused.'

Fran put her hands up to her face.

'Yes. She did – did try to get me to be the one.'

'Then it was Alice's turn. What happened?'

'Oh, it was so miserable! I hate to remember it. I thought maybe now things were all right between them.'

'What happened?' he said again.

'She couldn't stand up to Mother – Alice never could.'

'So it is your opinion that she was forced.'

He sounded like a lawyer just then.

For the next three days, like conspirators hatching a plot, they met. They decided that he should not yet be presented to her

313

parents. When they talked, Vance found that beneath her frivolity she was shrewd and strong. They must both, she said, 'hope for the best and prepare for the worst.'

Dining alone, lying wakeful to the sound of New York way down below in midnight streets, Vance's thoughts rushed across the huge wastes of the sea to Alice. He thought with remorse how she had avoided his eyes when they drove home after they had first made love. She believed they had committed a sin. Yet at their next encounter she had welcomed him into her body as passionately as before. He loved her so. She had been cruelly thrust into matrimony, and *he* would never make her do anything. She must always come to him of her own free will.

In the letters which arrived weekly at Leckford, he never wrote a word of love.

Fran's plan was ingenious. She wrote to her sister, to say it was high time that Alice came home on a visit.

'My letter,' said Fran to Vance, 'was a little masterpiece. I pointed out that Baby Gil is her godson and she's never clapped eyes on him. That's to make her feel guilty. And I added, naughty of me, that Pa is not too well. The truth is he has a filthy cold but Sis will think I mean worse things. That will do the trick, see if it doesn't.'

It was Fran's last day in New York, and they lunched at the Waldorf Astoria, listening to the music. Fran said comfortably, 'Tell me what you've been doing this morning. Before that, I mean to boast. I spent an hour reading a chapter on Canon Law in my father's positively priestly library. Do be impressed.'

'Indeed I am.'

'Good. And you?'

'I went to see Monsignor Vicelli.'

'That old show-off.'

'Isn't he? But I like him. And he's clever.'

'You only like him *because* he's clever, and what's more you don't think he's any smarter than you.'

He gave a brief, allowable smile.

'He is an intellectual. That isn't the same thing. He was very much part of the Avery annulment five years ago and is rather proud of it. He calls it "my coup". Anny Avery remarried and has three children. Monsignor baptised them all. Every child they produce is a compliment to his skill in advocacy.'

He was very dry.

'And you listened, and then suddenly pounced.'

'Fran, I never pounce. I sometimes move quite fast, but only when the time is right. He agreed that there would be grounds for an annulment if one party was compelled into the marriage. As you said, if the girl is unwilling it is not a sacrament. In the far-off past there were many such marriages. He pointed out, as he put it, that "we are no longer in the age of tyranny".'

'Oh. Aren't we.'

'The subject certainly fascinates him,' Vance went on. 'He lent me a book on it. The person requesting the annulment, by the way, must appear in front of the Holy Roman Rota.'

'For crying out loud, what's that?'

'A panel of six or seven priests.'

'Not at the Vatican?'

Fran was horrified.

'No, no, at Archbishop's House in the street behind the Cathedral.'

Fran helped herself to a piece of Turkish delight and appeared to need it.

'My Sis is going to die of fright,' she said.

Alice, hungrily reading the short letters from Vance, living at Leckford and every day wondering when Matthew was going to appear with worse news about the case, received a letter in Fran's handwriting. As her sister was a bad and infrequent correspondent, she opened it nervously.

The letter was not long and although Alice could not know, had taken Fran a good deal of trouble. Its appeal was straightforward.

I do think, Sis, you should come over soon. Now, in fact. Surely Matthew can spare you now the London Season caboodle is over, isn't it? The parents talk of you so pathetically, at least Pa does, and I know Ma misses you. *She* wants to go to Europe again, but at present he can't or won't. And you know she'll never travel on her own!!

The exclamation marks were to remind Alice that their mother was loud in pity for women who travelled with their men. Widows and single women were not the point. A husband was a necessity, and a rich one proved one's success.

Fran might be a poor letter-writer but she knew her sister like the back of her hand. She wrote that their father was 'tuckered out at present', and that seeing Alice would do him good and be just what he needed. The chord reverberated. Alice's thoughts flew in alarm to her family. Fran was withholding something. Their father was ill. She must go to him.

Matthew had still not arrived in Leckford. He stayed in unfashionable London, seeing his lawyer. But his visits to the Temple were not the reason he lingered, he wanted to see Nelly as much as possible.

Alice telephoned him early one evening; he nerved himself to hear her ask when he was coming down to Leckford.

But she said nothing about his absence. She told him she had received a letter from her sister.

'My father is sick, Matthew. She doesn't say much but I can read between the lines. I am sorry. But I really think I should go to New York.'

'Of course you must. You're worried,' he said, jolted out of his own egotism. 'When will you sail? Whitfield can make the reservations.'

Whitfield was the agent, whom Alice often thought wouldn't have lasted as an employee of her father's for a day. A shocking snob and incompetent into the bargain. She was faintly amused that Matthew thought her incapable of making her own arrangements.

'I've been in touch with the shipping company. Mary Murphy and I are sailing on the *Oceanic White Star*, it's the most comfortable, my father always says. But I must come to London first – things to be collected. Shall you come down to Leckford yet? Or shall we meet in town?'

She did not add, 'then we can say goodbye.'

He said of course he would go with her to Southampton.

'That's kind, Matthew. But, well, I think I'd prefer just to travel down alone with Mary,' said Alice. Surprising both of them.

When she rang off, he remained for a while, sitting very still. Alice's picture was near the telephone. The photographer, who had admired the young peeress, had taken a picture which showed the line of her cheek, the graceful circle of her hair. She was looking down, her head slightly bent.

So Alice does not care for me any more, he thought. Has she ever done? He felt the chill of losing something he hadn't particularly valued. Then what he *did* value came back painfully into his mind.

He had just seen Walter Smythe. The lawyer had not only been studying all the available evidence, but also the news items about what was called 'The Leckford Affair'.

'I'm afraid public opinion is strongly on Shipton's side.'

'Walter, that can't be true.'

'My dear Matthew, you must be aware by now that there's a distinct anti-aristocrat bias among ordinary people.'

'I have noticed no such thing.'

Walter Smythe was patient.

'Then you haven't grasped how strong his position is. Of course the evidence must be proved, which takes time. What I'm speaking about is feeling. The old romantic notion of the long-lost heir, the drowned lord and so on. People look on Shipton as a kind of symbol of themselves. He's the humble man, the little man, whom fate robbed of his rights. And who is up against the Establishment. It's becoming almost a political issue, let alone a religious one.'

'Shipton himself is a Catholic,' said Matthew coldly.

'So he says. So he says. He speaks about the Church of England with considerable tact, I notice. He's not a fool. One has the impression that the public think if they must have an English Viscount worshipping Popery, they'd far prefer a simple chap as broad-minded as themselves.'

'I thought lawyers were supposed to encourage their clients. Not spend their time taking the other side.'

'How can I encourage you if I don't take cognisance of what is in the opposition's locker? Shipton is getting very confident and we need to know why. Look at the fact that he visited your mother. I took the liberty of going to see her earlier this week. She worries me. She is too impressed with the man, calls his knowledge of the family "uncanny". She actually referred to him, if you please, as Lord Leckford. She says he has the names of your forebears – or his as he claims – at his finger-ends.'

'Anybody can memorise *Burke* and *Debrett*.'

'True. We must just work as hard as we can. We must not underestimate his effect on the public. And every scrap of evidence will be put through a hair sieve. We are at long last in touch with the Canadian lawyers. Conducting a case across the Atlantic is not exactly on the eagle's wing.'

Matthew accepted Alice's coming departure for New York without a protest. Not so her mother-in-law. Alice found her in a small room called the Latin Cabinet, a repository for past Leckford collections of all kinds of things. Roman coins. A bust or two. A female skeleton suspended on wires. A glass-topped recessed table filled with miniatures and tiresomely covered with a velvet cloth to stop them from fading. All over the walls were rows of Italian majolica plates which Alice disliked, and dominating the small room was a painting of *Susannah and the Elders*, in which the girl and the three spying men were all naked. Had it not been a supposed Titian, the picture would have been banished to the attics long ago.

Alice never understood why Honoria liked to sit in the stuffy, cluttered room.

Coming into the room, Alice sat down and told Lady Leckford about her sister's letter, then mentioned her father's illness and finally arrived, as it were, on the *Oceanic White Star*.

'May I understand this. You propose to go away.'

'Yes. I have explained –'

'That your father is indisposed. He is not young. That is to be expected.'

'The more reason for me to see him.'

'And how long, pray, do you plan to stay?'

'Lady Leckford, I shall remain until I am satisfied that he is quite better.'

'Perhaps he will not get better.'

Alice began to tremble.

'If what you say is true, which God forbid, my place is at home.'

'Home?' echoed the old woman and gave a sort of laugh.

Alice's anger flared up. Then as suddenly died like the flare and ash of burnt paper. Her adversary was old. Frail and cold. You could crush her between forefinger and thumb. She was at the end of her life. She mourned her lost son, moaning like an animal for her dead cub, but Honoria's grief was soundless and therefore worse.

'I'm sorry you disapprove of my going to the States, Lady Leckford. I've spoken to Matthew on the telephone. He understands how I feel.'

Honoria ignored that.

'And supposing the new Lord Leckford comes here while you are absent?'

'The new – why, that's impossible! Matthew said the case isn't anywhere ready to come into the courts. I'll be back long before then, I do assure you.'

On her last morning at Leckford Court she went out into the autumnal garden, thinking about the journey. She was excited at the idea of returning home but more anxious than ever since Honoria's cruel words. She was walking along the terrace when she saw Father McKenna leaving the house.

Alice liked the priest, as Irish as his name, round-shouldered, dark, with a certain Celtic melancholy and an enchanting voice. His church was in a distant village and was poor, roofed with corrugated iron. But he was dignified and when he smiled, humorous. Old Lady Leckford treated him with reverence for his cloth and contempt at its threadbare condition; he never seemed to notice either of those things.

He was walking with purposeful strides towards the waiting dog-cart. Alice began to hurry towards him, and the sight of a Viscountess picking up her skirts and running made him chuckle.

'That's nice of your ladyship.'

'Oh Father, I wish you wouldn't call me that.'

'What else would I be calling you since it's what you are?'

'In New York our parish priest calls my sister and me "daughter".'

'If your lady mother-in-law heard me saying any such thing, she'd be like a birch broom in a fit.'

'Then don't say it when she's around.'

They walked across the courtyard to the dog-cart. It was a worn-out vehicle of the kind found in coach houses in all country houses, used to collect luggage from the station and occasionally for a day's shooting. The dogs were put under the back seats, there were ventilation slats for them.

It was like Honoria to send the priest home in the shabby contraption, thought Alice with a pang as he clambered up. How strong the poor could be.

'Father.'

'Daughter?'

'I am sailing for New York tomorrow. To visit with my family. My father is not well. Say a prayer for him, would you? And perhaps for me, since I shall not see you for quite a while.'

'I shall miss you at daily Mass.'

He looked piercingly at the young face, and thought it was not as transparent as it used to be.

'And you'll be missed in every room in the house,' he said, gesturing at the enormous building as if it were a cottage. 'You've brought youth and a blessing here.'

'Oh,' she said as if he hurt her.

Belgrave Square looked dreary, the street dusty in the dry autumn weather, when Alice and Mary Murphy arrived. It was nearly dusk and Mary grumblingly went down to the servants' hall to make the staff run about after her. Alice noticed that the house had fallen into the hush of a place unused and, except for servants left behind and not caring for it, deserted. Poor house, she thought, I was never happy here. It gave her a *frisson* to remember that she must return next spring, to begin the London fandango all over again. Once she had seen a donkey on a Dorset farm, whose task, humble creature, was to churn the butter. Round and round it went, patiently pulling a sort of wooden arm, moving with a terrible meek acceptance. The worn circular path it trod was called 'the donkey round'.

Mary Murphy returned with two maids in tow. Footmen dragged trunks into the room and the maids knelt down as if in prayer, with much folding and rustling of tissue paper.

'Off with you, Miss Alice, and leave us in peace,' said Mary Murphy, shooing Alice out to the amazement of the two maids who exchanged looks.

Going downstairs, Alice found herself wishing she were already on board ship. She rather dreaded seeing Matthew this evening. She seemed to have little to say to him nowadays, and she kept thinking of that duty her body rebelled against. He won't want to make love to me because I am going away, will he? Her thoughts fluttered like caged birds against bars.

As she came into the hall, the front-door bell pealed. Young John, who had come to Belgrave Square with them, went to open the door. Alice heard a woman's voice, far clearer and more ringing than voices usually were.

'Is Lord Leckford at home?'

'I am afraid not, Madam. Who shall I say called?'

'Who is it, John?' said Alice, going forward, glad of any distraction and wondering who could still be in town.

'Good evening,' said the stranger. She peered unceremoniously over John's shoulder and waved. 'I'm Nelly Briggs.'

'Show her in, please, John. Why, Miss Briggs, of course I recognise you.'

Nelly swept in, a vision in green silk, looking at Matthew's wife with a friendly grin.

'Didn't you sing at the concert for the Dreadnought Fund? I remember how lovely your voice was. It was so good of you to spare your time,' Alice said.

'I'm always glad to do things for charity.' Nelly had had no idea that Alice had been at the concert. She was busy cursing herself for the impulse which had brought her here from Sussex. She'd never been to Matthew's house before and had only come round because she was certain his wife was in the country. She'd thought it rather a lark to appear unexpectedly, tit for tat after his own visit to her.

Looking at Alice she thought, why the girl's really pretty. Such a dainty little thing. I wonder why he doesn't fancy her and I'm sure he doesn't. Sex is a mystery and no mistake.

They stood talking for a moment or two under a chandelier which sent down a curiously unflattering and indecisive light. And then, as Nelly gave a sudden smile, almost a laugh, for no reason on earth but an instinct sensitive as the antennae of a moth, Alice knew who had come into the house. This vibrant woman was her husband's mistress, the one she had half-seen in his eyes, half-discerned in his imagination. She thought – how dare I judge? I am as bad. I have been unfaithful. Her conscience told her so, but she still couldn't bring herself down to the same level.

Nelly's instincts were at work, too. She was an actress, tuned to a fine pitch of feeling and she knew the second that Matthew's wife guessed the truth.

'I'm sorry to turn up out of the blue,' she said. 'It was just a notion. Could you tell him I called?'

Alice did not answer. A maid came down, her arms full of boxes, and put them in the hall. As she hurried back upstairs, two footmen followed with a trunk. Soon there was a positive mound of luggage.

'Will he be back later?' asked Nelly, as more maids and more boxes appeared. 'Perhaps you'd just mention I was here.'

'I don't think I will, Miss Briggs.'

Ah, thought Nelly.

She respected Alice's right to turn into a block of ice, but to pretend would have been better. It would have kept Alice's pride. And her own, now she came to think about it. She remained looking at Alice in a friendly way which betrayed nothing. Before she could stop herself, Alice said abruptly, 'I am returning to America.'

'Then you will see him to say goodbye,' Nelly said with her charming naturalness and poise. She was giving Alice a second chance to behave well.

'Miss Briggs. You are not here, I suppose, to discuss my private business. My husband is in London. I am sure, if you put your mind to it, you will very easily discover where to find him. But not here.'

She left the hall, closing a door behind her.

Nelly remained, calmly standing under the chandelier's gloomy light, her silks shimmering like a dragonfly. John reappeared, and respectfully showed her out.

To Alice's eyes New York was a familiar stranger whom she knew and did not know. There were new buildings everywhere, an air of brisk activity as strong as the wind blowing down the avenues. Fran was at the docks to meet her, rushing up to hug her until Alice was breathless. She, too, was familiar and strange.

'Oh, don't tell me, I've gained pounds since Baby was born,' cried Fran, catching her sister's eye. 'And you're as thin as a beanpole. It just isn't fair.'

Fran kissed her again and bundled her into a carriage.

323

'Both parents are home, Father keeping warm and cosy because this wind is so treacherous, and Mother, I fear, entertaining crowds all over the house. Sis, you look chilled.' She tucked Alice into a wrap she had brought over her arm.

'I'm fine, Fran. England's often cold, too. But how is Father? Don't keep it from me. Is he any better at all?'

'He still has a chest cold,' said Fran, 'and a positively deafening cough. Mother can't bear it and when he starts she rings for hot blackcurrant juice – for herself! But he is rather pulled down. You'll be his tonic.'

Alice looked relieved; it was clear she had no suspicion of being manipulated. All the better, thought Fran. Things have to be fixed sometimes. If I hadn't done so, I'd never have nabbed Teddy.

'It is strange to see home again,' Alice said, as they drew up at the familiar flight of steps, new-washed and white in the chill sunlight.

'More strange you haven't come before.'

Fran paid the driver, giving him a tip no gentlemen would have considered. The driver, Italian and emotional, said so. Fran looked bland and rustled up the steps after her sister.

Constance was presiding over a very large charity tea, on the day her young daughter returned after two long years. The drawing-room was overflowing with ladies, and with more gentlemen than would attend such a gathering in London. The sisters had to weave their way through a room close-packed with tea-tables, parlourmaids with silver trays, small dogs, sweeping skirts, and cries of welcome.

They eventually reached their mother.

Constance Mary allowed Alice to kiss her, looked her over, decided she was too thin, and told her to find some tea. Fran steered her sister back, negotiating trolleys and friends, to the open doors.

'We'll just slip away. Ma won't notice and Pa is upstairs. Besides, I must talk to you. What I have to say is going to need your nerve, so tighten your corsets.'

Fran's flippancy was as new to Alice as her home was. She

felt bothered until she went into her father's study. He was sitting by a large fire. Tables, desk, chairs, even the floor, as well as the lap of his secretary Peter Stringer, were covered with sheaf upon sheaf of papers. It was so like Lorn to be engulfed with work, and so essentially Lorn to throw the papers in his hand right across the desk when he saw her. He sprang up, opening his arms.

Alice ran into them.

Fran looked on with the approval of an audience at a well-played scene.

Father and daughter hugged and kissed, murmuring how long it had been and a score of other foolish things. When they drew apart, Alice's eyes swam with tears. Fran then announced that she was going to help Alice unpack, and anyway their father wanted to finish all that work. 'And you know you have to get forty winks before dinner. Ma threatens twenty guests.'

Lorn agreed, returning to the papers. Peter Stringer, who had a secret passion for Fran, gave her a languishing look, which she returned with a wink.

In Alice's old room, Mary Murphy had begun unstrapping valises. Fran went over to pat her broad, bent shoulders.

'You can just stop. You know you want your tea and I want Sis to myself. Go and bore them in the kitchen about how awful England was.'

'You're worse than ever, Miss Fran.'

'You're not so dusty yourself, Mary Murphy.'

The room was full of welcoming flowers. Alice pushed her face into a big vase of white carnations. Fran threw herself down on Alice's bed, kicking off her shoes.

'Aren't you dying of curiosity to know what I am going to say?'

Alice sat down beside her. Fran lay, showing lace petticoats and white stockings and somewhat resembling one of Louis XIV's mistresses.

'You're having another baby,' Alice said. The words hurt.

'I certainly am not. Baby Gil's enough for the present, thanks very much. Teddy and I want to wait three years before starting all that again. We aren't here to talk about me, you will be surprised to hear. I know I am a selfish pig but for once I am being wonderfully *un*selfish. Beavering away on your behalf. I've been seeing – can you guess? Mr Vance Weston.'

Alice stared.

'Yes, Sis. I commend your taste.'

Still unnerved, Alice began to say something about his being a friend she had met in London.

'Oh do stop!' exclaimed Fran. 'Jeepers, girl, I can see where you've been living for Heaven knows how long. You don't have to tell polite lies to me. I'm Fran, remember? The sister of your bosom. And you needn't look like a dying duck in a thunderstorm either. I know you and Vance went to bed together. And no, he didn't tell me, he's much too honourable. I knew by his eyes. And his manner when he talked about you. By everything. You're in love with each other and that's just fine because I never saw two people more suited . . .'

Alice had recovered. She said slowly, 'All you say is true.'

'Of course it is, and if you start saying you've committed a sin, I shall shake you. The sin was you being dragged screaming to the Cathedral to be turned into Matt Leckford's wife.'

'I am his wife just the same.'

The atmosphere was calm.

'Vance told me the English docs say you can't have a baby.'

'Yes.'

Fran rubbed her short straight nose.

'I suppose it didn't occur to you that it's a jolly good thing?'

'What are you talking about?' Alice said wearily. 'I think we should stop. I am glad you met Vance but this conversation only upsets me and makes things worse.'

'Moses, you do sound English. Look, I told you, I've been seeing him but I haven't introduced him to the parents. He and I have a scheme. Wait for it! We both think it's possible

326

you could get your marriage annulled.'

For a moment Fran felt quite sorry for her sister, who looked like a boxer staggering from a punch on the head. Then Alice said desperately, 'Oh I wish you wouldn't. I wish you and Vance had never met! He never told me he'd come here, he never did and I hate this, I hate it . . .'

Her eyes brimmed and Fran sprang up, falling on her knees beside her, putting her arms round her waist and holding her tightly.

'Darling Sis, darling Alice, you're such a fool! So good and silly and I so love you! Don't you realise Ma is the one who did it? Forced you into marriage? You never wanted it, but she'd always frightened you. And I've got your letters saying so. Couldn't they be grounds to set you free and – and don't you realise you might be able to marry Vance *in church*?'

At the end of the conversation, which left Alice's thoughts in turmoil, Fran said Vance had not yet gone back to Philadelphia but had stayed to see her.

'I feel like the Nurse in *Romeo and Juliet*, except there's no priest to give you some ghoulish drug to fool Ma and make you look dead. I must say, though,' added Fran, regarding her with detachment, 'you don't exactly look the liveliest gal in town right now.'

'It's all too much.'

Fran's sisterly sympathy had quite vanished.

'Come on. *Un peu de courage.*'

She had arranged for Vance to meet Alice at the new Stamford Hotel, which she described as 'absolutely huge and crowded to the gunwales. So many rooms one gets lost and you won't see a soul you know. Vance will be by the fountain in the first drawing-room.'

Taking a cab the following morning, Alice looked out at a city which seemed to be changing before her eyes. She was going to see him. Talk to him. Wasn't it enough? Of course it wasn't. A crumb to the starving.

She went through the swing doors of the elaborate new building and hesitated, looking about. There seemed to be hundreds of people, arriving or leaving, meeting or parting. She wondered where the first drawing-room could be. But even while she stood there, Vance appeared. He came hurrying towards her, to grasp her hands and look, first into her eyes, then at her mouth. No embrace could have been more passionate.

'Oh Vance. Don't.'

'Very well. But go on knowing I want to. Come, sit down. You're as white as a sheet.'

'That's what Fran keeps saying. So unflattering.'

They sat among a forest of palms.

Fran had been right, the place was so busy that they could have been in deserted country. Nobody took the slightest notice of them. Ladies in magnificent hats sailed by. Businessmen shook each other's hands, and young girls kissed and giggled. There was a low hum of voices.

Vance had ordered hot chocolate, and when it came he said she must drink it. 'One more sip. And another. Good.'

'You sound like Mary Murphy after I had measles.'

He hoped he did not show that her appearance shocked him. He had first met this girl at Leckford Court when she'd been – in a way – serene. Guarded and polite, perhaps not happy and slightly frail, but she hadn't looked like this. As if a breath of wind from the Hudson could strike her down. What have I done to her, he thought. And Holy God, what am I intending to do?'

'You're not to be upset by what Fran told you, Alice. It isn't as bad as you think. In fact, not bad at all. And when it's over with, you'll be free. Hang on to that.'

'Vance. It can't happen.'

A chill went through him.

'What do you mean?'

'I have something to tell you. I couldn't say it to Fran, you must have seen how she is. Like Mother. Strong. Only my mother gets angry and Fran just laughs.'

What the hell is coming, he thought. I know she loves me. I can feel it. See it. She wants me as much as I want her, and she never cared for that stick of a husband. What can keep us apart?

'The – the thing you and Fran thought of is impossible, Vance.'

'Of course it isn't. It's *right*. And your church will agree.'

'I am not saying they wouldn't. But I can't ask for it. It's Matthew. I couldn't do such a thing to him.'

He looked at her in silence, realising that he had been crazy to have hoped and planned. He'd left out of his sanguine thoughts and certainties the very nature of the woman sitting opposite him. And the paradox was that he wouldn't love her so deeply if she wasn't that way. Fran would nail her demands to the church door. But Fran would no more have been married against her will than she'd jump off the Empire State building.

He said nothing, and Alice continued.

'I know very well he doesn't love me. I am sure he never did. He married Father's dollars, I suppose. But now he is in such dreadful trouble and may lose his name, his home, why, the very reason for his life. And though he doesn't care if I am there or not, how could I strike at him with more legal horrors? I couldn't be so cruel.'

'Alice.'

'Oh, Vance, don't force me!'

He started forward.

'Don't look like that. I'll never ask you to do anything you don't want. I swear it before God.'

CHAPTER SEVENTEEN

When *A Girl from Nowhere* closed, Nelly was casual about telling Matthew that she was going to Brighton for a holiday. At first she decided she might mention it. Then she thought not. Matthew, lover or no lover, did not belong in her life which was filled with the challenges of acting, the close comradeship of theatre friends, Claude Stanway – they didn't make love these days but he was a dear friend – and Leon's watchful company. Matthew was an alien now. When she thought of him, she sometimes felt a weakness, a longing. But. There were too many buts.

She spent a happy month at the Albion Hotel in Brighton with Kirstin and Tom. Leon took a chaste single room of immense size and came down for weekends. Other theatre folk arrived off the swift trains from London, and groups of vivacious theatre people walked along the broad promenades, and amused themselves on the Palace Pier. Tom and Kirstin spent all day on the beach and swam in the chill September sea. They were sunburned.

Refreshed from her holiday, Nelly returned to London, to busy preparations for the Irish tour. She had thought a good deal about Matthew while she had been away and had wanted to telephone him, but for once her heart had ruled her head. If he knew where she was, he'd want to come to Brighton. That would not have worked. But she wanted to see him before leaving England. I'm bothered if I'm going to turn up at the gloomy great house again, thought Nelly. She guessed he was still in London and telephoned the Belgrave Square house, deliberately not giving her name but using her *Girl from*

Nowhere voice to a sniffy-sounding footman. A friend, she said, who wished to surprise him. She could imagine the footman's face when giving the message.

When Matthew came to the telephone she said, 'It's me.'

'*You.*'

'The bad penny. Miss me?'

'Not for a moment.'

'Oh didn't you? I'm off to the Emerald Isle and I keep tripping over trunks. I wondered if we could meet?'

'When? Where?'

She rubbed her nose with the palm of her hand, a habit when in thought. She'd sworn to herself not to repeat the occasion when Matthew had met Tom. But St John's Wood at night was very quiet, Tom would be fast asleep and Kirstin slept like a log. She had brought Matthew there many times in the summer.

'Come here. But not until eleven.'

It was nearly two in the morning, they had made love, and he was lying with his face in her hair; it smelled of jasmine.

'Nelly. Nelly.'

'Yes,' she said, tweaking his ear. 'You said that.'

'I want you.'

'Not again just yet. Have a heart.'

'I didn't mean – I do mean – '

She laughed. She liked putting him out of countenance. I suppose I shouldn't have brought you here, she thought, looking at the familiar lines of his thin body, the haggard and alluring face. You make me half remember. Leon would say you are bad for me.

'I mean I want you for always. For good. In my life.'

She turned, raising her eyebrows as if waiting to hear what was coming next. Her face was quizzical.

'I think we're quite nice as we are,' she said.

'But – '

'But what exactly did that mean, Matt.'

'What I said. What I mean. I want you for always.'

'And what about your Alice?'

'She's in America and plans to stay there for a while. She has been missing her family very much. But even when she gets back we can be together. We must be. You know we must.'

There was a noticeable silence.

He sat up and looked down at her. He couldn't guess what she was thinking. Her face, still somehow showing the sex which had only just ended, was enigmatic. He thought, I don't know this woman.

'My marriage is not a success,' he said, touching her thick hair.

She still said nothing.

He cradled her in his arms and began to talk in a low tender voice, saying how happy they were together, how he needed her – and didn't she need him? – how happy they had been in Paris, surely she still remembered? She lay and smiled and listened, and when he took her again he was more violent because he felt she was eluding him.

She said he must leave at dawn. Wrapped in a cloak the colour of the sea, she went down barefoot to watch him go.

Leon Seidl came to Dublin to see the play safely into its first weeks before travelling back to London. But after a couple of months he was back in Ireland again, officially to take a second look at the show and gauge how the Irish audiences were liking it. Actually, he wanted to see Nelly.

'I thought you might be getting up to mischief,' he remarked during supper at her old and comfortable hotel. It was after midnight and they were the only two people still in the dining room.

'Don't see how I can get up to anything with Kirstin and Tom about.'

'One might imagine,' he said dryly, 'you were the boy's mother, the way you have him with you.'

'Oh, I'm a most devoted Auntie,' said Nelly, who knew very well that Leon knew.

332

They talked about the play, they talked about Claude Stanway whom Leon wanted to persuade into straight theatre, just as he had done with Nelly. They talked of Leon's plans, always interesting, sometimes complicated. He stirred his coffee.

'I have something to ask you.'

'I know.'

'Are you sure we're thinking of the same thing?'

'Quite sure.'

'So you agree it's time we made love, you and I?'

'That's what I guessed you'd say.'

'A cautious reply. I never think of you as cautious, Nelly.'

She said, sighing and grinning, 'Nor do I usually, dear Leon.'

'But it must have occurred to you what a pair we'd make. We'd be formidable. We might even marry. I would make a devoted husband, and you are a sprightly bed companion.'

'How can you possible know that?'

'The look in your eye, my girl. And that bottom lip.'

She laughed and pressed his hand and said could she have some time to think it over.

'As long as you like,' said Leon, looking her up and down and wishing she were not so voluptuous. He wanted to thrust his fingers into her thick hair, himself into her soft self. Why on earth did she need time to think about it? She moved in a cloud of men who buzzed like flies round jam. He knew she didn't favour one more than another, except Claude Stanway, who had been her lover in America before Leon had met her. That romance, if one could call it such a thing, was over long ago. And Seidl was too potent to feel the comedian a serious rival. Of course there was that Viscount hanging about. But titles were two a penny to Nelly Briggs.

Nelly was rather surprised at herself for refusing Leon. She was very fond of him, comfortable with him. She liked his physical strength, his round head with its short crinkled hair, the brightness of his shrewd eyes, the way he laughed. He was attractive. The trouble was still Matthew. He seemed to have

333

the power to make her heart hurt, to grip not only her senses but also her imagination. And while he was somewhere in the present she did not want another lover. Perhaps he's not in the present any more, she thought.

The Irish run went well, and Leon and Nelly made money. He stayed on. They were invited to exquisite decaying country houses, ate lobster, were nearly drowned on a fishing expedition, and Kirstin and Tom learned the Irish jig. Kirstin was also taught to ride by an Irish jockey who wanted to marry her.

'I tell him "No, No, No," ' Kirstin said later.

Returning to London, starting to rehearse her first Shakespeare – Leon had won the struggle and somehow persuaded her to appear in *Twelfth Night* – Nelly sent Edith one of her telegrams.

'Need two panels for the dining-room. Need original Edith Holdens for the panels. Good price and don't tell Vollard. Need Edith a lot. Nelly and Tom.'

The weather was bitterly cold, the Channel misty and made melancholy by the hoarse siren of the ship which sounded, thought Edith, like a bellowing bull.

Nelly was waiting at Victoria Station where the mist had now turned into a thin black fog. Dressed in crimson and furs, she was the only bright figure on the platform.

'Give us a kiss. Oh, I *am* glad to see you!'

During the first evening Nelly was in the mood for gossip and jokes and questions about Paris, but Edith thought her less than her sunny self. She wondered if she was imagining it.

But she was right, for Nelly had begun to feel uneasy since she came back from Ireland. Away in another country so like yet unlike her own, busy every night with the play which she still enjoyed, and amused by unfamiliar surroundings, she'd been content. In a way. She loved the Irish and they returned her love. But for a particular reason she had determined to keep Matthew out of her thoughts, and when he wrote to her at the theatre, she'd put both letters into the fire. She hadn't done such a thing since poor Laurent's epistles used to flip every morning through Miss Fisher's letterbox. Womanlike, the moment the letters had begun to burn, Nelly wondered what had been in them. But it had been too late to find out.

Now the Irish interlude was over, and ahead was the prospect of playing Shakespeare for the first time. She asked herself how she could have agreed to do such a mad thing. The answer, of course, was Leon. He had been the man who'd made her take her first leap across the chasm from *Cora*'s smiles and songs into straight theatre. Now he was at it again. With a mixture of steely determination and sympathy, he was coaxing her for a higher jump still.

Nelly had the lightest of touches in her playing until now. She knew what came true for her when she was onstage, was at home in her *Girl from Nowhere* rôles. Shakespeare was another story.

'You'll learn different skills,' Leon said. 'You've only acted in naturalistic pieces. With Shakespeare there are –' he paused and gestured, 'such exquisite differences. Don't come to the read-through with a fixed idea. The words will change it. And remember. You will be able to use everything that has happened to you.'

But although she trusted Leon she was very nervous. And the more she read *Twelfth Night*, the more unsettled she became.

Edith spent the morning after her arrival in making preliminary sketches for the panels. Nelly had to go out for a costume fitting, and Edith had lunch with Tom and Kirstin.

'We had tea with Tom's new friend yesterday,' Kirstin said. 'She lives down the road in the big white house. Her name is Elsie.'

'Did you enjoy it, Tom?' asked Edith.

He looked at her with Matthew's expression, humorous, pensive.

'Yes I did. Except, you see, Tante, Vicky had made an enormous gooseberry tart for us specially. And me and Kirstin had to eat some. Oh, how our eyes *poured*.'

As Edith was going back to the studio she heard the piano. She found Nelly in the drawing-room looking dispirited.

'Good. Come and cheer me up, Edith. Do!'

Edith sat down. She noticed a copy of *Twelfth Night* on the top of the piano.

'I'm interrupting. I thought when I heard you playing – '

'I did it to stop myself working. Edith, it's so difficult. I'll fall flat on my face as Viola, I feel it in my bones. I don't even understand her.'

'But you understand about love.'

'Who doesn't?'

'Most of us. Isn't Viola wildly in love? And unhappy?'

'Yes.'

Nelly began to play a somewhat mournful waltz.

'Acting's always been a mystery to me,' said Edith, 'but don't actors use what's happened to them?'

Nelly went on playing the little waltz.

'That's what Leon says. I suppose *you* mean about Matt and me. That first time.'

'I suppose I do.'

Nelly continued to play. For a moment her face had a desolate look. Then it disappeared.

'What have you been doing all morning in the studio? Do tell.'

'Sketching ideas. I thought I'd do scenes from the Butte . . . unless you don't fancy the idea.'

'Oh, I do. Where on the Butte?'

'The Café des Violettes at the bottom of the hill. The arbour in summer, leafy, and a waiter or two. The gas lamps. A dog. A girl in a straw hat.'

'Me?'

'Maybe.'

'It sounds perfect.'

'I don't know about that. You must wait until they're done.'

'You old Scot, you're so cautious. I know they'll be gorgeous. They'll make me feel better.'

'Not yet they won't. What shall we do with you in the meantime?'

'Edith, I don't know. What do *you* do when paintings don't come right?'

'Stop for a bit. Read the newspapers.'

'You don't change. You and your blessed papers. I've never liked them and I still don't. I suppose you've already waded through today's *Morning Post*.'

'Yes, during breakfast.'

'I challenge you,' Nelly said, playing a major chord, 'to tell me a single thing that *I'd* find interesting. You're intrigued with politics and things. You know I'm not. Well? One thing I might want to read?'

Edith reflected.

'Something about that Canadian who is claiming your friend's title.'

'Damn. Is he in the news again? What's happened?'

'He was at the opera and when he left he was practically mobbed by a cheering crowd.'

'Double damn.'

'I agree. It said the case will be in the courts quite soon.'

'Poor Matt. Imagine if he loses,' said Nelly. Her face was shadowed and Edith felt guilty at her own pathetic attempt to cheer her up. She'd made her worse. She said hastily, 'There's another item which is more on the bright side. Somebody you used to know is in London at present. Remember your erstwhile enemy Violet Lane? She's opening in a new show in Daly's.'

'*What*? Where's the paper? Show me!'

Nelly's reaction astounded Edith, who fetched the *Morning Post* and opened it at the theatre pages. 'I only mentioned it idly, I can't imagine,' she continued, 'you care whether she's in London or Timbuktu.'

Nelly was not listening. She was reading the news item.

'How extraordinary. How really amazing. Do you know, Edith, I've been wondering how the ★ ★ ★, sorry, how the ★ ★ ★. Oh, sorry, I wish I could clean up my bleeding language.'

'Start again.'

'I've been wondering how to find Violet. She vanished off the face of the earth.'

Edith was still astonished.

'Surely you don't want to revive that old war? You're a star now, do have some sense. Anyway Violet Lane didn't vanish, she toured Australia.'

'Australia, eh?' muttered Nelly.

She sat for a moment in a trance, then sprang up, opened the door – she detested the bells in the rooms and never used them – and shouted.

'Hey! Gladys!'

'Upstairs, Miss Nelly.'

'Then come down, I need you. No, Edith, I can't tell you what I'm up to, you'll have to possess your soul in patience. Ah, Gladys,' as a fair-haired, pink-faced maid hurried into the room, 'get my hat and cloak, there's a dear. And I need a hansom right away. And gracious, I haven't a farthing. Edith, can you lend me a sovereign? Two would be even better.'

Nelly constantly ran out of money which she gave to crossing-sweepers, beggars, and any deserving or undeserving person lucky enough to cross her path. Gladys the maid, Edith the friend, exchanged looks.

When the hansom arrived, Nelly ran out, told the driver to hurry and as usual offered him double fare.

She sat leaning forward and mentally urging on horse and driver. As they left Marylebone and proceeded down Gower Street, she pulled out her purse, a little embroidered thing Edith had given her before she first went to America, now much worn and mended. At the back was an old photograph of Tom, and a tear-streaked now illegible letter from Patrice. There was also a fragment of newspaper which had begun to turn yellow. She unfolded it on her knee. Two men looked out of the faded pictures. Matthew. And the man who'd been cheered last night at the opera.

When the hansom stopped at the pillared entrance to Somerset House, she hopped out like a girl of fifteen, and asked the driver to wait. She did not notice the looks of disapproval from passers-by at the sight of a young and pretty woman who travelled alone in a hansom. She hurried into the building and was directed up to the first floor to a dark room filled with shelves packed with enormous, leather-backed books.

Nelly had never been to Somerset House before in her life. The sight of all the bound volumes filled with the births and deaths of the past momentarily fascinated her. But Edith's old nickname for her, *'Mademoiselle plat du jour'* was still true. She went along the shelves until she came to the date and initials which she roughly guessed she needed.

She pulled out two of the heavy books and propped them open on a polished counter. It took her only quarter of an hour to find what she was looking for. The quiet room was filled with quiet people searching for Heaven knew what answers in the past. The silence was disturbed only by the noise of a thick page turning. Suddenly, it was broken by a loud chuckling laugh. Every eye in the room turned in disapproval to stare. Nelly put her hand across her mouth.

'Sorry,' she said to nobody in particular.

In agony at the effort of keeping a straight face, she went down the spiral stair and out to the waiting hansom.

Daly's had the look of a playhouse gone dark. There were no tempting playbills and no framed photographs of enticing girls in frills. The swing doors were locked, the foyer plunged into gloom. Cranbourn Street was foggy, the fog had become thicker, and the gaslights shone throught it in yellow circles. Nelly asked her long-suffering driver to wait, and went down the alley at the side of the theatre to the stage door.

'Evening, Miss Briggs,' said a battered-looking man from his cubbyhole; he knew every actor in London.

'Good evening, Herbert. Is Miss Lane about by any lucky chance? I'd like to surprise her.'

'They just broke from rehearsal. Twenty minutes before they start up again. Try her dressing-room.'

'Number One?'

'Right first time, Miss Briggs.'

Nelly put down one of her sovereigns. Now there, thought Herbert with perfect inaccuracy, goes a lady.

She went up the dark staircase, halting at a half-landing, and opened the door marked 'One'. The room was empty. A long sable coat and a muff pinned with dying violets were on a divan, and a music score, dog-eared from use, was on the dressing-table. The gas fire spluttered, but the room was bitterly cold from weeks of vacancy. Nelly pulled her cloak round her and sat down to watch the door as intently as a dog.

A voice called from somewhere outside. A voice prettier in singing than in speech, clear but with unexpected hesitations. The door opened. Violet Lane, dressed in dark grey velvet, came into the room. She was about to lift her script and throw it angrily on to the floor when she saw Nelly.

She stared.

'And who may *you* be?'

'Come on, Violet. You know me perfectly well.'

Violet recovered, gave a laugh and shut and door. She walked across the room as gracefully as if she were onstage.

'Why, if it isn't the great Nelly Briggs. You've managed to come up in the world, I must say.'

She sat down at the dressing-table and turned a face, pale and large-eyed and far from pleasant, towards Nelly.

'What can you be doing here? Want something, I suppose. A part for a friend. Not a chance.'

'I wouldn't be fool enough to think I'd get the smell of an oil rag from you, Violet. I don't want anything. Come to do you a favour, actually.'

Violet laughed again. Her eyes were like pebbles.

Nelly came across to her and put the newspaper cutting on the dressing-table, smoothing it out. She pointed at the Canadian Claimant.

'Who's that?'

Violet glanced at it and gave a martyred sigh.

'What's this all about? Are you mad or something? Those

are the two men scrapping over who's going to be Lord Tomnoddy, of course. Any fool knows that. Even the Aussies were talking about it and hoping the Colonial would win. He probably will. Grover says he has a good case.'

'So Grover's still about, is he?' said Nelly. 'He wouldn't be, though, if he'd rumbled you and Alfie Goschawk.'

She admired Violet just then. The actress didn't bat an eyelid. She looked impatient, annoyed, and bored.

'You definitely *are* mad.'

'And you don't know Alfie. And we're going round the houses all over again, are we? What am I talking about and so on. Violet, it won't wash. You and I know each other very well. We were enemies when I was a kid first treading the boards. You couldn't abide me. There's no reason why you should, one can't like everybody. But let's get to the nub of the thing. Alfie Goschawk was a walk-on in *Cora*, of course, and you fancied him. You and he went to bed. I happen to know because Sal Burgess caught you at it once in Alfie's cabin, and you bribed her to keep her mouth shut. She told me one night when she was drunk. Your precious Grover Jones didn't find out, which was fortunate for you both because he'd have skinned you alive and probably half-killed Alfie. I know a violent man when I see one.

'So. Now we get to the interesting bit. That man in the picture is no more Canadian than I am. It's Alfie. I thought it was like him when I first saw the photograph, and this morning when I heard you were in town again, I decided to ask you. You were his bit of stuff, after all. Then I had an idea. I went and looked Alfie up in Somerset House. And what do you suppose I found? Dear Alfie's the son of a man who was butler at Leckford Court. So Alfie grew up in the servants' quarters and must know just about everything about that family and that house. Claude always said Alfie had talent. I suppose he went off to Canada sometime, ended up in the backwoods, and then had a brainwave. One of your shows went to Canada, didn't it? I daresay you helped him.'

Violet smoothed her velvet skirts.

341

'I don't know what you are talking about.'

'Oh, spare us all that. Just go and warn him to withdraw the case. And to get back to Canada pronto. And you'd better move fast.'

'Suppose I refuse?' said Violet. It was the first crack in her façade.

'Somehow I don't think you will.'

Violet was silent. Then, 'And what does that mean?'

'Come on, Violet, polish your brains. If you get Alfie to withdraw, the case will die the death, there'll be a big sigh of relief from the nobs, and he can scuttle off free as a bird. If you don't,' Nelly continued, fixing her with blue eyes, 'I shall give the story to the *Daily Mail* and the *Post*, together with Alfie's birth certificate. I'll identify Alfie myself. What's more fun, I'll tell about your affair, and Grover Jones will like that, won't he? I must say, in all truth, it was a clever idea. Was it yours or his or both?'

'It was nothing to do with me – I *told* Alfie. But you wouldn't –'

'Are you quite sure?'

For a glorious second, Nelly dared Violet to hit her. Violet was very angry, and looked as if she was going to do it. Since she'd been poor and anxious and eighteen years old, Nelly had longed for the excuse to give that face a hard ringing blow. It wasn't to be. Violet, suddenly looking her age, went to the door and threw it open.

'Get out of my sight, you cow.'

'There's a ladylike way of saying yes,' said Nelly sweetly.

That's the second battle with her I've won, she thought, returning to the cab. I enjoyed it more than when I said I'd chuck her into the pit. Well. What next?

She knew Matthew was in London – there had been a message at St John's Wood to which she hadn't replied. Guessing where he would be, she gave the driver the address of his club in Pall Mall. When she arrived at the eighteenth-century building she was greeted with reverence by the Head

Porter, who gave her a chair under a portrait of Gladstone. The lady, he thought, is a stunner. But what was extraordinary about her was a certain look he had once seen on the face of a jockey who had won on a hundred to one outsider.

'The Viscount will be with you immediately, Madam.'

A moment later there was Matthew, coming down the staircase two at a time.

'Nelly. How good of you.'

He spoke in a low voice, with a sort of intense controlled formality.

'I need to talk to you. Is there somewhere?'

She glanced inquiringly towards a red-carpeted corridor which had never known woman.

'Come into the room we reserve for ladies.'

'Golly. Is there one?'

The lofty room was hung with more paintings of politicians, who seemed to look down at Nelly with surprise. She sank down on to a very hard sofa.

'I have something to tell you, Matt. Here goes. I can prove Lewis Shipton is a fake.'

'*What?*'

Nelly burst out with the story. Months ago when Matthew showed her the picture of himself and Shipton, Nelly had had the feeling that she recognised the Canadian. She had taken the newspaper cutting with her to Ireland, and glanced at it now and again, trying to remember. Then one evening when she and Leon were talking about her days in *Cora*, the thought suddenly came to her. An actor in the company called Goschawk – he was the one. But lots of people reminded one of actors, and she put the idea out of her mind. Goschawk had been a minor player who had left the cast at the same time she had done. But that morning Edith told her that Violet Lane was back in London.

'I thought, why, *she'll* know something about Alfie. They had an affair, and you know how woman always seem to be fascinated by what happens to the men they've been to bed with,' Nelly said in ringing tones. A man sitting in a far corner with an elderly lady looked aghast. Matthew was too interested in what Nelly was saying to notice.

'I decided to see her and face her with my idea. Then – oh Matt! – I had an inspiration. I went to Somerset House and looked Alfie up and *what do you think*? Years ago his father was butler in your house.'

'Goschawk – I think I remember.'

'Isn't it too beautiful? I went straight to Daly's and bearded Violet in her den.'

With an actor's perfect memory, Nelly repeated the interview word for word, only stopping to laugh. The gentlemen and lady in the corner hurried out, but neither Nelly nor Matthew saw them go. Matthew did not smile once when Nelly's laugh bubbled through the conversation. He looked as if he were suffering from shock.

'You're knocked out,' she said, when the story ended. 'You understand I needed some proof, don't you? Just saying a chap looks like somebody is no good. I wanted Violet. And didn't she just walk into my trap. I pretended to know for certain and she believed it. Violet's a cool one. Maybe she's been planning to go off with Alfie when the case succeeded. I expect,' added Nelly with relish, 'the evidence was all faked. You can buy marriage lines or a birth certificate in some places at the right price. I've known it done down Blackfriars.'

Matthew at last had collected his scattered wits. He asked if she would come to Walter Smythe's chambers. They arranged to meet the next morning.

'*How can I thank you?*'

'Violet's face did that.'

She leaned towards him, still with the radiance of the jockey who has won an unbelievable race.

'Oh Matt. Isn't it funny?'

CHAPTER EIGHTEEN

Alice had intended to stay with her family only a few weeks, but somehow she couldn't bring herself to return to England. Matthew wrote, encouraging her to stay longer, and so she did. Vance was not in New York, his work took him home to Philadelphia, but he was back again within the month, and she lived from one meeting to the next. Whenever she spoke to her sister about taking ship, Fran persuaded her to stay 'just a little longer'.

Fran herself was much in evidence; her husband had recently decided to move the family — wife, baby, nurse and staff — to New York. Edward Oliver was the son of a railroad magnate, his future was rich and assured, but he was as ambitious as Lorn had been. Fran admired him for it. Teddy Oliver broke the news that a move from Pittsburg would be necesary, at least for a time. He'd begun to interest himself in Wall Street. Fran was more delighted at the news of the move than she thought it wise to show. A New Yorker to her fingertips, she thought no other city held a candle to her own. And she also wanted to keep her hands on her sister's romance. She loved and pitied Alice. Sometimes when she was with Alice and Vance and saw in their eyes the terrible fever of frustrated passion, she was fascinated and appalled.

Keeping his vow, Vance never again tried to persuade Alice to ask for an annulment. But inaction gnawed at him. If she was in prison, so was he.

One morning after he'd spent a weekend in New York, he was packing at his hotel and feeling more desolate about his life than usual when the telephone rang. Fran's voice with its curious burden of laughter came over the line.

'Have you seen this morning's *Times*?'

'I'm just leaving. There's an important meeting I must attend back home.'

'No meeting in the world is as im ortant right now as *The Times*. Or the *Sun* or *Herald*, come to that. You haven't seen the papers?'

'I get them in the dining-room.'

How tiresome Fran was, he wished she would ring off.

'Going down to breakfast now?'

'As a matter of fact, yes.'

'My, what wouldn't I give to see your face in five minutes' time.'

In the dining-room Vance ordered breakfast and impatiently picked up the *New York Sun*.

Canadian Claimant Disappears

From London, England.

Reports are coming in of a dramatic turn in events – the disappearance of Lewis Shipton, called the 'Canadian Claiment' because he has claimed the Viscountcy of the Leckford family, historic English landowners.

Shipton asserted that his father was the rightful heir, reputedly lost in shipwreck off Vancouver Island in 1845 but actually saved from the disaster, subsequently marrying a Canadian.

Police have received evidence that the claim was based on forged identity papers, and warrant is out for Shipton's arrest. No trace of missing man yet discovered. There are strong rumors he left Britain weeks ago under yet another name.

Alice and Fran were at the hotel an hour later. Vance had all the newspapers. The story was headlined, and in the *Herald* a

346

leader commented: 'How eager the British public have been to welcome the "little man" and to see a new lord who actually sprang from the people. It shows us folk on the other side of the Atlantic that our British cousins are beginning to think twice about doffing their caps to what they call "lineage".'

Fran was excited; the long months had been a trial to her as well as to the lovers. She was a girl who couldn't imagine not winning. But Alice looked serious, and more than usually white in the face.

She sighed.

'So it's over at last. It has been so dreadful for Matthew. How relieved he will be.'

'What about us? Sis, do stop being so holy, it's more than a body can bear. Let's get to the point. Now you can't refuse to see Monsignor Vicelli, can you?'

Vance said nothing. He was wishing she hadn't moved so fast.

'No,' Alice said, and looked at Vance. 'I won't refuse.'

'Then we will break the news to the parents,' said Fran in a businesslike voice. Really, she thought, seeing the two staring at each other, the way they go on in public is indecent.

'I think perhaps I should be there to make our case stronger,' Vance said.

Alice gave a slight smile.

'What you really mean is that it will make *me* stronger. No. I shall do it alone.'

A pause.

'Very well. If you insist,' he said.

'Oh no, Alice,' said Fran, 'I shall be there whether you like it or not. Aren't I the key witness? Nothing is going to keep me away, so don't bother to try.'

Constance Mary had been spending the cold and rainy spring taking her younger daughter about a good deal. Having a Viscountess as one's child, on the other side of the Atlantic was a somewhat ephemeral advantage. But now Alice was here, quietly dignified, wearing her expensive Paris frocks, and with coronets embroidered on every blessed thing, even underclothes and handkerchiefs. Alice was a trump card.

At present Constance Mary was in competition with three well-born ladies of old New York in the organisation of a big charity bazaar. She sensed that she was being outclassed until Alice appeared on the scene. Lorn never helped in such battles, and Fran was just another wealthy young wife without a claim to fame. Fran seemed to be far too often in her parents' house in Constance Mary's opinion. One would think she had never married at all.

Coming into her mother's boudoir at six on the evening that the Leckford news was out, Fran found Constance Mary lying down after a day of committees.

'You see about the Canadian Claimant, Ma? It's all off bar the shouting.'

'I never thought it was anything to be worried about,' Constance Mary remarked. She had indeed never taken it seriously and Alice had been glad not to talk about it.

Constance Mary wore a wrap embroidered with vividly coloured parrots. Looking down at her mother's deep-set eyes and aquiline nose, Fran thought the wrap a remarkable mistake. But she had larger issues on her mind.

'Do you want something, Frances?' Constance Mary asked without a welcome.

Fran, dressed for dinner, looked her loveliest and strongest. She sat on the bed.

'You're resting,' she said, stating the obvious. 'And Pa says you're both home tonight.'

'We were supposed to be dining with the Shelbournes. But he wishes to remain home. I can't think why.'

'You should be flattered that he likes your company.'

The Lord preserve us, she's come in here to annoy me, thought Constance Mary, and debated whether to produce a headache.

'Alice and I want to talk to you and Pa. Something important.'

'And what may that be?'

Fran patted the place where her mother's knees were covered with the eiderdown.

'That'd be telling. Remember what old Cook used to say when we asked what pudding it was going to be. Wait and See Pudding.'

When she had gone, Constance Mary, by now thoroughly annoyed, reflected that Fran had become impossible to manage since she had been married. Teddy Oliver had simply ruined her.

Fran then called in on her sister; she found Mary Murphy brushing Alice's long hair.

'Love,' announced Fran, 'will conquer all.'

Mary Murphy tut-tutted. Fran and Alice had told her the momentous news an hour ago and the old woman had taken it with seventy-year-old calm. What Mother Church decided would be right. And wasn't it gospel that her poor little charge had – well – hadn't been happy married to Lord Leckford? As for the wedding night, it didn't bear remembering. Indecent, it had been, like a lamb to the slaughter, thought virginal old Mary.

When Alice and Fran went down the staircase to the dining-room, Fran gave her a friendly if painful pinch. Alice did not mind. She had been for a rainy walk with Vance this afternoon, and he'd told her that what lay ahead was like a steeplechase. There would be a number of fences, they would look alarmingly high, but she'd go over each one of them like a bird. Her horse was called Resolution.

During dinner Lorn glanced benevolently from one girl to the other. The meal was one of his favourites. Virginia ham, scrambled eggs, broiled fish, creamed chicken as a side dish, and for dessert some light-as-air waffles, a silver jug of maple syrup and a lemon jelly.

'I must say it's good to see you both at home. The family sitting round the table again, eh, Mother?'

Constance Mary frowned at the maternal name but agreed. Criticising both daughters most of the time, she was pleased with them. She had produced good-lookers and seen them make excellent marriages, in Alice's case a brilliant one. She still took pleasure in the Leckford name and history, and the thought of that great old house with its magnificent past (and repairs by Lorn's money). She had thought talk of the Canadian claimant so much nonsense. The Leckfords were unassailable. She was American to her boots, took her freedoms for granted. And was bewitched by values repellent to American hearts. She was full of contradictions. But Alice should have a child; why wasn't she pregnant yet?

After supper the quartet went up to the drawing-room to sit by the fire. Lorn lit a cigar and Fran knelt down to push a tabouret under his feet; Alice fetched his silver ash-tray. He looked at the fair and darker gold heads bent over, ministering to him.

'God bless you, children. And what's this important matter your mother tells me you wish to discuss. Money, I guess?'

'Oh no, Pa,' they chorused.

He chuckled.

'What, then?'

Constance Mary leaned back, resenting her daughters getting all the attention. Fran sank down on the fireside rug.

'Alice, will you speak first? Or shall I?'

'I will. Father. Mother. This will upset you, but you must bear it because I promise you it is right. The right thing to do.'

'The only thing to do,' from Fran.

Alice had also sunk to the floor, her skirts a circle round her. She looked delicate and intense and her father thought, 'What the deuce is up?'

'I am going to ask the Church for an annulment of my marriage'

There was a silence like thunder.

At last Constance Mary gasped out, 'You're going to do what?'

Lorn said nothing. The cigar burned in his hand.

Alice had meant to rehearse the speech and say it over to Vance, but she'd forgotten. Now the words flooded out by themselves.

'I know you will both think it dreadful and I am sorry, oh, I am so sorry. But the truth is I never wanted to marry Matthew. I told you so, Mother. I begged, but you wouldn't listen. I know you had the first idea it could be Fran, but then Fran said about Teddy and you decided it might as well be me. Yes, I know –' raising one diamond-heavy hand and for the first time in her life stopping Constance Mary from speaking, 'I know you thought it for the best. The Leckfords are a famous Catholic family and Matthew is a good man. He is. But I just didn't care for him. Didn't love him. And hated the idea of being in English Society, it was everything I disliked and didn't understand. I didn't want to be with Matthew or in his world. Oh, I didn't want them! You forced me into marriage, Mother. It was my fault for not standing up to you. How feeble it sounds. How feeble I sound. I was afraid of you.'

Constance Mary was as white as a sheet.

'You're making all this up.'

Lorn was still silent – cursing himself for not having seen that Alice, poor wretch, had been unhappy during the engagement.

'She isn't making it up, Ma,' Fran said. 'She loathed the idea and told you so. Perhaps you forget. Perhaps you thought it girlish hysteria, and beneath it she didn't mean it. The truth is that she did. Alice has a case. To get an annulment.'

Suddenly fierce, Constance Mary said, 'And why does she want this terrible thing?'

Fran saw she had guessed.

'Because she has fallen in love. That's right, isn't it, Alice?'

'Yes.'

Her parents looked at Alice.

'It's a miracle she didn't fall ages ago,' said Fran, determined to keep the ascendancy. 'She's so pretty and good, and Ma, don't call her names or me either. She wants a real life. Away from that aristocratic stuff. Away from Matt Leckford who cares for her as little as she does for him. They don't love each other. Alice is not happy. And it is not her fault.'

'Yes it is. I should never have consented,' Alice said.

At that moment she believed it.

Lorn spoke for the first time.

'Do you wish to marry another man, my daughter?'

'Oh. I do.'

He drew at his cigar. The long head of ash fell to the floor.

Constance Mary had been growing more frightened and angry every moment and exclaimed, her voice trembling, 'What am I going to look like in this unspeakable business? Do you imagine I'll consent to give evidence against myself? My God, am I expected to go up in front of a parcel of priests, I won't if you drag me –'

'*Connie*,' said Lorn. He knew her nature and couldn't stand for it to show.

She collapsed, biting her thumbnail. There was a silence. Everybody waited for everybody else. Alice pulled off the thick gold wedding band. Put it on again. Off. On. She laid it in the palm of her hand and Fran could see the date and initials engraved inside the gold circle.

'You won't have to go to Archbishop's House, Mother,' said Fran. 'I've found out about the whole dog and pony show. Sorry, Sis, but that's how it sounds. Alice has to go. Letters will be sent to Matt, of course. And we have to have evidence.'

'Evidence?' said Lorn sharply. He was now alarmed for his wife.

'Alice wrote to me. Both letters say the same thing, about her not wanting to marry Matt,' said Fran, with more tact than was usual to her. 'And the other witness is Mary Murphy – and the wedding night.'

'Great heavens,' cried Constance Mary. She looked as if she was going to faint. 'You've worked it all out.'

'Oh yes, Ma. We have.'

In the last few months Vance had seemed to spend his time in trains. To Philadelphia. Back to New York, then home to

Philadelphia again. He had accustomed himself to a new and strident sister, but life with the family was much changed. There was no youthful fun now, no boys coming around to visit. The only people who came to see Margaret were quiet polite women burdened with papers. Vance had lost the sister who had shared his childhood. It was sad. But he had done all he could. Now his thoughts and concern were centred upon Alice.

She had borne well the ordeal with her parents. Constance Mary had not. She'd produced a real migraine, been violently sick and retired to bed prostrate. She did not get up for the rest of the week. Lorn had never seen his commanding consort struck down before, and the sight upset him. He went to call on Monsignor Vicelli one afternoon and on his return came into the bedroom where Constance was lying with a wet towel on her head. Now and again she spoke in a moaning voice to her long-suffering maid.

Lorn dismissed the maid and sat down, taking his wife's limp hand. He knew she was bored and desperate. Days had gone by and she would clutch at any straw to return to normal. He loved her devotedly and proceeded to throw her a thick rope which he and the Church had woven together.

'Connie. There is something you should know. Monsignor Vicelli tells me the Church dislikes publicity about annulments. He says there is no reason at all for more than a brief announcement after it has been granted.'

'The terrible rumours . . . after the Avery case . . .'

'Benjamin Avery was shameless in telling his friends the details. His unfortunate wife was deeply grieved by the way he behaved. No, Connie, this time it will all be kept very quiet. A short, dignified announcement.'

'There'll be gossip . . .'

'If we say nothing it will simply drop out of sight. See if I am not right. Come along, now. I want to see your dear face at the dinner table tonight.'

Looking fatigued but nearly back to her old self, Constance Mary was up and dressed an hour later.

* * *

353

Vance drove Alice to Archbishop's house one bitter cold morning. Mary Murphy had dressed her charge in the most sober clothes, a dark rich brown. Although it was almost March it was snowing and Mary refused to let her leave her furs behind.

'Are you wanting us to go to your funeral instead of Nuptial Mass?' She wrapped her in her sable coat.

Mary was needed as a witness, having unsuitably declared she would stand by Miss Alice at the mouth of Hell. But Archbishop's House had told her she would be called later in the day. When she saw Alice to the cab, Mary Murphy went to her room and changed into best black, fastening on her chain and all four of her holy medals.

Vance and Alice travelled through streets which were growing whiter by the minute. She was still doubtful about the furs.

'Do you think I look flighty?'

He kissed her through her veil.

'Priests don't dislike luxury. It's my belief they rather enjoy the sight of it. And you'll do better if you are warm. Remember to take your time when you answer the questions. I will be at the hotel waiting for you to telephone me.'

'Will they say if – if I am refused?'

'They won't say a thing either way. But you'll know. And you're going to win.'

He saw her to the door of the tall ugly brick house which backed on to the Cathedral. The snow was getting thicker and when the heavy doors were opened by a young priest, Alice – accustomed to the steam heat of her parents' house – was struck by the chill.

The priest took her down a passage to the library which reminded her of the convent library when she had been at school. Shelf upon shelf of dark volumes, and on their spines the names she had known since girlhood. Saint Thomas Aquinas. Aloysius Gonzaga. Saint Catherine of Siena. Thomas à Kempis. The weight of her religion was heavy on her. She sat down, asking herself all over again if what she was about to say was the truth.

Yes, it was. The sad truth. In love for the first time, brave for the first time, she looked back at her own folly with a desolate heart. How could she have been so craven? She remembered her fear of her mother; it had been physical, striking through her, through her clothes, her being, making her weak. Sometimes when Constance Mary spoke to her she had sweated. She remembered her wedding night and the loss of virginity without love. The life she had lived. Its aridity. Its chill. She thought about Matthew. What had been in his thoughts and his heart? He had never once revealed them. And then she remembered without meaning to do so the radiant woman who had come to the Belgrave Square house one autumn evening . . .

The door opened and a priest came into the room. He was fiftyish, short, with grey hair cut in the way of the tonsured monks in medieval paintings. He had a ruddy face sparkling with life.

'Well, Lady Leckford, here we are. I should have met you sooner, but I've been away, and I know the Monsignor has been looking after you. I am Dominic Dogherty. Your advocate.'

He shook her hand firmly.

'Nervous,' he said, ushering her out of the library into another, icier corridor. 'Good. Good. Over-confidence is a mistake with the Rota. They like,' he added, smiling, 'a little proper respect.'

Alice did not know whether this priest was going to help or not. She would have preferred someone quiet and grave. They entered a large, long room with a balustrade running round it – the upper section was yet another ecclesiastical library. Below, the walls were hung with pious pictures. A crucifix dominated the far end of the room. The windows were of frosted glass.

Three priests, already at the table, stood up as Alice and Dominic Dogherty came in. He introduced them in turn, adding, 'You'll never remember their names. Rather like at a party.'

He settled her at the table and sat beside her.

The table was as enormous as one at Apsley House, the home of the Duke of Wellington where she and Matthew had dined sometimes. But there the table had been loaded with silver, candelabra, vases filled with roses three feet high, with fruit and glittering glass. Here there were only pads of paper and pencils placed in front of nine seats. More priests filed into the room.

The proceedings were opened by Monsignor Vicelli, an acquaintance of her father. He had come to New York after Alice had left for England, and she did not know him. He was small and grey, handsome in an ascetic way, wearing touches of Church Crimson and a small skull cap of the same brilliant colour.

Fran, surveying the dignitaries, would have called it quite a turn-out. They were all priests. Not parish priests, but theologians, in a way technicians. Their faces varied from Irish to Italian but their manner had a certain similarity – it was marked by reserve. Dominic Dogherty dropped his own raciness when the proceedings began, but remained matter-of-fact and at times ironic.

For three hours Alice, the only woman in the room, was scrutinised by nine pairs of priestly eyes. The questions began as in a court of law, establishing her name, nationality, place of birth, date of baptism, name of parents and godparents. And date of marriage.

One priest asked about the Leckfords and Dominic Dogherty spoke for her.

'They are one of the oldest English Catholic families. Much respected for having retained the Faith.'

'Yes, we know that, Father Dominic. But,' turning to Alice, 'do they practise it?'

'They do.'

'You do not sound quite certain, Lady Leckford.'

'My mother-in-law is very pious. She hears Mass every day in the family chapel.'

'And your husband?'

'Now and then. He – he is not exactly lapsed.'

'Did you try to get him to do more about his religious duties?'

'Often,' said Alice, and did not know that her tone was dry.

When she was questioned about her own practice of her religion, Alice's answers were tinged with impatience. Twice she unconsciously added 'Of course.' Of course she went to Mass and Confession. Of course.

Eventually they came to the point.

Alice plainly told them how she had attempted not to marry Matthew. She saw that they were unwilling to believe her. They looked at the graceful figure wrapped in furs (she hadn't taken them off, it was damply cold), and Alice knew that there was not one of them who considered what she was saying was even possible. How could this young woman have been such a dolt? How could they accept such a story? It was ridiculous.

Dominic Dogherty had saved Alice's two letters to Fran. He explained before they came into the room that he wanted 'to keep a shot or two in his locker'. He had told her to answer all the questions simply, and he would follow them up later.

Alice now saw that the questions she was being asked – there were many of them – were mildly spoken, gently phrased and all intended to trip her up. If she had not been speaking the miserable truth she would have fallen flat. When there was a pause she said.

'Monsignor, may I explain something?'

'Of course, my child. That is why we are here.'

Alice clasped her hands.

'Yes. You're all here to decide if I'm speaking the truth. I realise I'm asking for something nearly impossible – for the sacrament of matrimony to be rendered null and void. The dreadful thing is that I shouldn't be here at all. Should never put the Church to such trouble or myself to such pain. But I swear before God that I never wished to marry Matthew Leckford. I did not love him or any other man. I wanted to remain at home until – if I ever did – I fell in love and marrried in the way it was meant to be. My mother is very strong. She had ambitions for me and believed them to be right. She loved – still loves – the idea of an ancient, noble Catholic family. She thought Matthew Leckford a good man. And he is. But I was horrified when she told me what she intended. She is very severe; she dominated my childhood and girlhood. When we went to Europe and two men asked for my hand, she did not allow them to speak directly to me. She simply refused them. She told me later that they were not – not exalted enough.'

She paused. There was a dead silence.

'When we were all with Matthew, after my sister had said she would not marry him, Mother determined on me. Monsignor. Fathers. I tried. I tried to refuse. I begged her. She would not listen. I was a coward. I couldn't stand up to her. It is my fault that I am here.'

A pause.

'I would like to submit two letters which Lady Leckford wrote to her sister before the marriage,' said Dominic Dogherty, standing up and placing them in front of Monsignor Vicelli. 'And there is to be evidence from Miss Murphy, Lady Leckford's nurse,'

Half-an-hour later, after many other questions about the first year of her marriage, some of them needing much tact from Alice and the priests when dealing with what they called 'her conjugal life', Alice was released.

The moment that they left the room, Dominic Dogherty's humour returned. Could he give her some tea?

'We do a good line in buttered buns.'

'It is very kind of you, Father, but –'

'But you can't wait to get home to a good fire and a chat. Quite.' He saw her to the door, shouting to a young priest on the way, 'If you're serving my benediction, Charles, put on your skates. You should be in chapel by now.'

Going out into the snow without a coat, his black habit was immediately sprinkled with large flakes, he insisted on finding her a cab. He opened the door, and gave her a grin as she climbed in.

'Well done. In my book that was rather a good morning's work.'

CHAPTER NINETEEN

Old Lady Leckford heard the news that Lewis Shipton was an impostor without comment. It was Walter Smythe and not her son who came down to Dorset to tell her. When he returned to London he telephoned Matthew at Belgrave Square.

'Your mother looks very pulled down. And – ' He just stopped himself from saying 'as pale as death'. Matthew said he would go home at once.

The thought of his only parent, his old enemy, sick and alone, haunted him. On a spring evening of rough winds which bent the trees as if wanting to snap them his carriage turned through Leckford Court's gates. That morning he had received two letters which had arrived within hours of each other. One was from Alice. The second bore the coat of arms of the Vatican.

His wife's letter had been an utterly unexpected shock. She had asked for their marriage to be annulled and had already given her evidence. Priests whom he did not know, on the other side of the ocean, had judged that the marriage had been no sacrament. She would soon be cut free. Matthew found it difficult to accept and to bear. He had never imagined the repugnance she must have suffered, or known that the submissive girl who came to him in her young purity was given over to him like a slave. The thought disgusted him.

She wrote with a painful candour.

> You will be hurt and grieved about all this, and I *know* I should have come back to England to tell you myself. But for many reasons I could not. And

you will have to forgive me for that and for other things. The papers from the Vatican will explain the grounds on which they will grant what I've asked. They need a letter from you, and will tell you what they wish confirmed. I don't think, my dear Matthew, you ever knew how it all happened between us. You always behave to women – specially to me – with true consideration. I am so ashamed of my cowardice, it is all my responsibility that you will now be hurt. But I promise you I truly begged Mother not to make me marry. I did not – do not – love you. I am fond of you and that is all. In truth I know you do not love me. And since we have no children, it is best that we should part.

Again I ask you to forgive me. Perhaps at first you won't, but in the end I feel sure you will. You are so kind. My comfort when I think about you is that neither of us needs to pretend any more.

With my prayers,

Alice

PS. I am so very very relieved that the dreadful Shipton business is all resolved.

Reading the letter, Matthew did not think of the formally dressed young woman who had sat at the head of his table, or walked under a parasol in summertime. But of what he had known emotionally with Alice. The first time he had kissed her. The way she had accepted his proposal. Their wedding night and all the other nights when she lay under him without stirring. His nature, graceful to women and fond to indulgence of their soft company, considerate, gallant even, recoiled. He did not blame her. Why should she stay when she felt like that? He and her mother had made a captive of her. Now she was gone.

At Leckford Court, the servants were subdued. Old Hopkins had left Belgrave Square days ago and Matthew wondered, with a stab of guilt, if he'd known before Matthew did that Honoria was ill.

The old man opened the door. The house was very quiet.

'Her ladyship only took to her bed two days ago,' Hopkins said as if in comfort. 'Doctor Atkinson says she has a temperature, but it is not high. Only 100, your lordship.'

Matthew went up the staircase to the first floor and through the picture gallery to his mother's apartments. He had not entered them for so long it felt curious to go in. Her maid was sitting by the bed, sewing. The room was chill and the fire low. He put his hand gently on the elderly woman's shoulders.

'I'll take a turn, Keely. Make up the fire before you go. But quietly.'

'She said she was too hot and asked me not to, my lord.'

'People with a fever feel hot but must not get chilled. Make up the fire.'

She obeyed and crept out of the room.

Matthew took her place, leaning forward to look at his mother. She lay, small and shrunken, yellowish and old and ill. A little nightcap crowned her head, her hair was plaited and yellowish like her face. Her hands lay idle on the sheet and he saw with pain that her wedding-ring hung off the wasted finger.

She opened her eyes and slightly frowned.

'What are you doing here?'

'Sitting with you, Mama.'

The old name came without his noticing it.

'Where is Keely? I prefer Keely.'

'She won't be long.'

She shut her eyes and he resumed his pitiful study of the wasted face. He thought of the sunny portrait, a young Honoria with the baby Robert clinging to her skirts. He thought of when he himself had been small and how he could not remember her kissing him. He remembered her with his father, sharp and laughing, lit by male affection. He remembered her looking at his brother as if at a god.

'Are you there?' said the weak voice.

'Yes. Yes.'

He took her hand. It burned. But he could feel the flesh's reaction and knew she wished him to release her. In sheer humanity he couldn't hold her hand when she wanted him to let her go.

'Why isn't Alice here?' she said fretfully.

'She went to America for a while.'

'I remember. She must come back.'

'She will. Soon.'

Keeping her eyes shut she said, 'She's a good Catholic. Better than you deserve. That man,' she went on, 'wasn't the heir, it seems.'

'No. An impostor.'

'He looked like you.'

She turned as if the movement hurt. Longing to reach her, longing to do something for her, he said, 'Shall I move your pillows?'

'No.'

There was a long silence. The fire began to burn, the coal making spurting noises and the flames springing up, yellow and blue. She breathed so quietly that he could not hear her. Her eyes were still closed and he thought she was asleep. But they opened again.

'I must say goodbye, then,' she said, with a faint sign of the old contemptuous smile. 'You may kiss me, I suppose.'

He bent to do so. The cheek was as hot as her hand.

'You will be better soon, Mama.'

The smile, like a rictus, remained.

'I will not . . . see you again. It is my duty – to forgive you. I do. I have prayed for you as I pray for your brother – *you* need prayers. Yes. I forgive you for the sin you committed. Now go.'

'Have I your blessing, then?'

She made a sort of gesture, but whether it was assent or denial or a stiffening of some muscle, he did not know.

She died that night without him.

The day of her funeral the harsh wind blew again from

362

morning until night, trees were struck down, slates fell, animals were killed. Walking in the park after everyone had left, Matthew bent into the gale as if fighting against the sea. The weather raged, and when he went to bed that night the house groaned and shifted. He would not stay in this place. He would live in London, he thought.

On the morning of his departure, he went all through the house from room to room as if searching for something. He looked at the damask-covered walls, the ceilings like the lids of carved golden boxes, the screens embroidered by Leckford women in the past, the curious tapestries and intaglio tables set with blue and yellow and red. At objects collected, chosen for pride, kept for sentiment, at the myriad things which gave Leckford its own strong presence. Alice's portrait by John Singer Sargent hung in the gallery next to Honoria's. Beyond the two women, more Leckfords looked down at him. Sargent had not captured Alice, she appeared vapid and pretty-pretty. But a pastel by Paul Helleu was in his study, and that rang true. She wore one of her vast tip-tilted hats, her head, turned towards Matthew, was fixed for always in a delicate melancholy.

And he saw how the whole of Leckford sparkled with her money. She had served *his* past when she re-created this place. Not for love. Not for their children. She had wasted her generosity as he had wasted her. He could not bear to stay.

As he crossed the courtyard, Father McKenna came out of the chapel.

'There you are. I've been saying my goodbyes to the little place. I don't expect you'll be wanting me to celebrate daily Mass, will you, now?'

'I am going to London, Father.'

'Shaking the dust off your feet, eh, my lord?'

'You used to call me Matthew.'

It was painful to hear the young man repeat, almost word for word, what his wife had said.

'And will again, will again,' said Brendan McKenna heartily. 'But I hear more sad news of you from the Bishop.

An annulment. It is hard for a mere parish priest to grasp such matters.'

For a moment he debated whether to ask the son of his fierce old patroness whether he'd really known the little American lady never wished to wed him. He decided against it. The nobility were a puzzle. He had visited old Lady Leckford for twenty years and she had flummoxed him three or four times a week. A religious woman. A pious convert married into a family who'd been Catholics for centuries. Yet there were mortal sins in her nature like iron bars.

The tall man looked troubled, and Brendan McKenna said encouragingly, 'So you'll be making a new life, then?'

'I expect so, Father.'

'God bless and keep you.' The priest made a sign of the Cross, giving Matthew the blessing which Honoria had perhaps refused.

During the momentous days following Nelly's discovery, Matthew had seen her every day. They went to Walter Smythe's chambers, where Nelly made a long statement. As well as enormous satisfaction at the turn of events, the lawyer developed a penchant for Miss Nelly Briggs. Smythe moved fast over the affair, but apparently not as fast as Violet Lane. Goschawk/Shipton vanished into thin air. An extraordinary letter arrived at the Chambers. It was printed in ink, not handwritten, and said merely,

> I nearly won hands down. It was worth it for the laughs. Don't bother to look for me. By the time you get this I'll be – guess where, and how far, and indeed *who*.
>
> Alfred Goschawk.
> Or should I say Leckford?

'Actors,' remarked Nelly, unsurprised, 'like a bit of recognition.'

'But the effrontery, Miss Briggs. The fellow should be behind bars.'

'How can you be so cruel, Mr Smythe. Poor Alfie. Turned out such a good actor, too.'

Although Matthew and Nelly were united by their common purpose and absorbed in it closely, he felt a change in her. She was part of everything that happened and was always there when she was needed. But if he suggested meeting for any other reason, she refused.

'It's the rehearsals, Matt. I know you understand.'

At first he simply did not realise what she was saying. Apart from the breaking down of a marriage he had not cared about, he had never been rejected by a woman. He was sure of his power over them, of his sexual power over Nelly. He needed her and was certain she needed him. Buried in his thoughts, affecting his judgement was the memory of the Rue Saint-Sauveur.

Her silence while she was away in Ireland had only partly disturbed him. It was Nellyesque not even to scrawl him a postcard, although he had written twice to Dublin. It was true that when they met at the Temple she did not mention the letters. Matthew's tact stopped him from doing so.

The 'Canadian Claimant' story finally ended, to the fascination of the public when Goschawk dramatically disappeared into thin air. That night Nelly agreed to dine with Matthew to celebrate. They were both in high spirits. He had never seen her look so radiant. We are going to be together again, he thought. It is high time. We'll be lovers as we used to be, but differently. Differently.

He was moved and even nervous, something rare in him, when after the meal they walked to the door of Romano's.

Nelly said, 'Will you see me to a hansom, Matt?'

'But –'

'But I really have to go. You know how actors need as much sleep as they can get.'

It was difficult to hide his feeling of desolation when she

stretched out her hand to him and smiled. And he saw in her face that it was over.

A few weeks later he read the notices for *Twelfth Night*. The critics appeared to have fallen in love with 'this most captivating of our young players. Here is a new Nelly Briggs. Beautiful and young, intelligent, above all poetic. Among the illusory loves and quarrels, Miss Briggs's Viola has an exquisite genuineness of feeling. She is the very heart of the drama. When she is sad, so are we. Miss Briggs banishes sentimentality, makes love into an active passion. She brings us pure delight.'

He knew he would never go to see the play.

Recoiling against the idea of the London season, Matthew took a house in Chelsea not far from the studio he had used when Robert was alive, down a secluded road near the river. The house had a glass-roofed studio, an untidy garden and an ancient mulberry tree. He left most of the staff at Leckford with the task of caring for a mansion without a master.

Honoria's death in February and the mourning for her which followed gave him a respite from friends who supposed he had gone abroad. Nobody was given the Chelsea address except Leckford's agent, Henry Whitfield, who sent him muddled letters about the estate, requiring answers. Matthew replied with exasperated telephone calls and Whitfield promptly mishandled every problem. Matthew sourly recalled that Alice had shown, in a distinctly American way, that she thought Whitfield an incompetent fool.

Alone, thrown back into himself as he had not been for years, he found he wanted to paint again. He wondered if it was too late to take up the discarded mistress to whom he'd turned once before when his life was in ruins. Then he had been an exile. Now he was conscious of nullity and the death of love. I don't deserve to paint at all, he thought. But I'll try.

He began tentatively. Threw away his first attempts in disgust, then grew more absorbed. He began to paint for hours at a stretch, not bothering to eat, deep in the impossibly difficult seductive problem of paint as he hadn't been since he had lived on the Butte. On a sunny April day he gave the servants who had come from Leckford the day and evening off. He wanted solitude. He noticed vaguely that they were pleased, and had a moment of wondering what the devil they found to do in London.

He went back to his easel. The day shone but he never saw it. There was no sun here in the studio, only the cold paleness of a truthful light. He was painting Nelly. Not the star, but a girl who wore a raggle-taggle hat whose feather she licked to smooth it down, who came up the steep Montmartre road with wet violets in the bosom of her dress. He managed to catch her figure's vitality, the colour of skin and hair, the thick underlip, the angle of the snub nose. But her expression, was it right? Had she looked so? At last with a groan of annoyance he realised that the light was failing and the day was over.

He had a bath, changed into evening dress and went out into the tree-shaded evening, to a warmth surprising for spring. Finding a hansom in the King's Road, he gave the name of a restaurant in the Strand. He sat listening to the horse's hooves. Clip-clop. Trip-clip-clop. He was in the mood for somewhere busy and noisy, for the sight of pretty women. If they were acquaintances, he would dodge their invitations. Nobody yet knew where he was living.

The restaurant was as crowded as he could wish, and he was given a corner table by a *maître d'hôtel* who had a respect for *Debrett*. Matthew ordered his meal and some wine, and sat looking at the room. Its pink-shaded lights gave it a Frenchified air. There were large mirrors, reproductions of simpering shepherds and shepherdesses on the walls. But the place was far from Paris, a London copy and that was all.

Tired and pensive, he sat watching the scene. The doors of the restaurant swung open and two men came in, escorting a woman.

It was strange to see the very face he had been trying to paint all day long. She wore sea-green, the colour she had wrapped herself in the last time they had made love. The dress shone like the skin of a mermaid as she swept across the room.

367

Leon Seidl was with her and the other man, spidery, thin and fair, must be an actor. Matthew did not stir.

Happy to be with men she was fond of, Nelly settled at the table with a sigh of pleasure.

'Go on, Claude. Be a devil and do what Leon wants. You know he's the clever one.'

'Of course he is, Nell, but . . .' said Claude, not wearing the silly-ass face tonight.

'You'd be wonderful in the new play,' she said.

'Perfect for the part,' added Leon, ordering champagne. He enjoyed persuading actors.

'I've told you both over and over. Singin' and dancin' is the only thing I know how to do.'

'That's what I said to *you*,' said Nelly. 'But Leon – and you – changed it all. And, forgive the swank, look where I am now.'

The men smiled and Claude and Leon began to go over the subject for the twentieth time. Nelly left them to it and looked lazily into the huge mirror on the wall nearby. She liked big looking-glasses. There as in a painting were couples in intimate talk, glasses winking, pearls gleaming, waiters whisking past . . .

The voices of her two friends faded. She had seen him. How thin he was. His fair hair had fallen slightly across his forehead. She looked with a pang at the moustache which hid his promising mouth. Putting up her hand, she waved at a young waiter who skidded to a stop.

'Would you be very kind and bring me a pencil and paper.'

He hurried away and returned with both. She thanked him prettily.

'Who are you going to tease now?' inquired Seidl, breaking off his talk.

'Somebody new, of course,' said Claude with a slight edge. He was still a little in love with her now and then.

'You're both wrong.'

The waiter was asked to take the note to the 'fair gentleman alone over there.' Nelly pointed with her fan.

Matthew had not been looking towards her, he somehow couldn't, and he received the folded scrap of paper with surprise. Opening it he read in the huge childish scrawl, 'They say your wife's left and gone to America. Is it true? Are you divorced? N.'

Under the enormous writing he put, 'Yes. And yes.'

He did look towards her then. He saw her smile and wave. Then begin to talk to her companions.

When the meal was over, Matthew remained, an untouched brandy in front of him. As she was leaving, Nelly walked by his table, put another scrap of paper in front of him, and was gone.

'My telephone number's a private one now. Here it is . . .'

He did not telephone her that night. It was too eager and too soon. And where might she be? And with whom? Knowing that actresses slept late, he telephoned her from his studio at midday. The painting, still wet, looked at him from the canvas. The moment he spoke, her voice said, 'Ah.'

'May I see you?'

'Of course. Where are you?'

'In my house in Chelsea. But –'

'I'd like to see your house in Chelsea. I thought the one in Belgrave Square was yours.'

'It's to be sold.'

'Poor house. Shall I buy it?'

'It isn't very cheerful.'

'True.'

'I didn't know you knew it.'

'I went there once. You were out. Very well, Chelsea it shall be. When?'

'Now. This afternoon. This evening. Midnight. Dawn.'

'I'll be with you in an hour. I'm still in bed.'

He couldn't settle. He couldn't paint. He wandered about, getting in the way of the maid who was dusting the sitting-room, going into the scrap of garden to look at some white hyacinths, returning to the studio. He despised his own nerves. What a fool. He stood, arms folded, looking at the girl in the painting and thought – you won't think me a fool. Nelly never denied emotions, she bottled up nothing. Let love, sex, affection, the whole world rip.

At last he heard a carriage and the slam of a door. He ran out into the street, and there she was paying the driver and exchanging a joke. She wore clothes lovelier than the hyacinths and turned to him in all her friendly beauty.

'I say, I like your house. What an improvement. Show me everything.'

They went into a sunny house where the windows had been thrown open. The trees in the next-door garden seemed to be full of blackbirds. Nelly looked into rooms and exclaimed over staircases.

'You'd think I was going to buy it. Other people's houses always fascinate me. I've never seen Leckford Court.'

'Let me take you there.'

'It might be interesting,' was all she said.

When they went into the studio, her eyes went straight to the easel and the canvas. She unpinned her hat and threw it like a cartwheel across the room, then stood with her arms behind her back, studying the picture. She said finally, 'It's good.'

'Is it?'

'It tells the truth. That's how I was.'

She turned and looked at him, narrowing her eyes.

'You're a bit of a cheat, aren't you?'

'I don't know what I am.'

'That's funny. I do.'

She sat down on a divan heaped with cushions, dropping them and his portfolio on to the ground. Nelly was careless with objects and always had been. To the floor with them. Throw them across the room. Trip over them. Squash them sometimes. Not people, though.

'Come and sit down, Matt, and let me look at you. You're much too thin.'

'What do you suggest? Glasses of stout?'

He drew up a chair, took her hand and kissed it.

When he released her she said, 'So you're divorced.'

'Yes and no. The marriage is being annulled.'

'You're making some kind of upper-class joke.'

'Oh no. The Vatican are granting it. It will be official next month. When Alice went back to America she asked for an annulment. She gave evidence that her mother forced her into the marriage.'

'Good grief, Matt! Is that how it was?'

He shook his head slightly, and sighed.

'I don't know, Nelly. Alice says it's true and I have to believe her. The Church is certainly pronouncing the marriage null and void. There's already been a civil divorce in the States.'

She listened with sympathy.

'What goings on. You've kept it all very quiet.'

'There was a line in the newspapers. Nothing much. With the Russo-Japanese war so much in evidence.'

It was strange how that echoed. Wars, thought Nelly. Men pore over them and we hate them.

'And how is Alice?' she said, after a moment. 'Perhaps she's happier. Back in her own country and not set upon by snooty peeresses.'

'Yes, she didn't like that very much. How did you know?'

'I saw a play about it. Art imitating life. Often, you know, the theatre is a good way of learning how people feel.'

He picked up her hand again. It was rather plump, exquisitely pale. Her wrists were heavy with bracelets.

'Alice is marrying again. And –' He stopped, and then said, 'She is expecting a child.'

'But – but you told me the doctors said she couldn't!'

'They were wrong, weren't they? Her sister wrote to tell me. I imagine Alice felt she couldn't mention it. She feels badly about our marriage. And about this too, I daresay. I must take it,' he added with a bluntness he never used except to the woman eloquently listening, 'I must take it I am the sterile one. It was because of me she never conceived a child.'

'A good thing too as it turned out. The poor mite would have been pulled both ways.'

She looked at him, and said after a moment, 'Do you mind a great deal? About not having children.'

'I suppose I do. They are the future.'

'Oh Matt!' she exclaimed with an exasperated laugh, 'What a solemn old owl you've turned into. Cheer up.'

She stood up and opened her arms. He came to her, held her closely, pressed her to him. She leaned against him, closing her eyes. I believed I was free of you, she thought. Didn't I try? Didn't I almost succeed. She didn't know why it was that only Matthew had the power to turn her bones to water, to excite and wound her with his male weakness and his male strength. She was not the girl who had climbed the Butte and danced the *chahut* in a painted dress. Who had worshipped him, and cried herself ill when he walked away. Why then did she stand in his arms, leaning against him and feeling her heart would break?

When she drew away, her eyes swam.

'I have to make a confession,' she said, and gave a long sigh. 'Edith has been nagging me to do it for so long. I kept saying I wouldn't.'

'You are going to tell me you are married. To Seidl.'

'No. I wasn't. I'm not.'

'What, then?'

She sighed again.

'Here goes. You can just stop feeling you have no slice in the future. You've got a son.'

His arms dropped from round her shoulders. He literally took a step backwards.

'What the hell do you mean?'

'You've got a son,' she repeated. 'Tom is yours, you stupid, stupid man. Did you never look at him? Never suspect? Couldn't you see how like you he is? There you were brooding over these ridiculous newspapers and saying Alfie Goschawk was like you and all the time in the garden a few yards away was your own image, the very pattern of Matthew. Edith and I couldn't believe it.'

He said in a cold, flat voice, 'Why didn't you tell me?'

She wiped her eyes with the back of her hand.

'The question that comes into every badly written play in town. Why do you *suppose*? After you'd b— gone off and left me. That five pounds didn't last too long, you know. Wasn't I big with child and couldn't pose with a stomach bulging like a hot cross bun? I had the baby in a hospital in Pontoise. Madame Moréas was so good. She fixed for me to work in the bakery, and I kept Tom in his pram in the courtyard. And Edith, oh, she's one of the uncanonised saints, she is. Now we go on saying Tom's an orphan, a sort of second cousin of mine and her godson. It's for his sake as well as mine. But Edith disapproved of me not telling you. She said it was my duty. Well. I have.'

His face was white.

'Why did you stop seeing me? Get rid of me?'

'Don't you know that either? For a clever man you're so – ' she paused. 'You asked me to live with you, remember? Matt, we *did* all that. It's such a mistake to play a part for the second time. Either you repeat yourself or you mess it up. I couldn't cry myself silly on the Butte for two entire days all over again.'

'What a bastard I was.'

'Weren't you?'

She remembered the day she had lain on his clothes and kept saying aloud, 'Where are you? Oh please come back.' It had felt, it did now, as if her breast was filled with broken glass. This isn't being in love, is it? It hurts.

When he took her hands she pulled them away.

'Nelly, I wish to God you'd marry me.'

'Oh Matt. Have mercy.'

'I beg you. Be my wife. We'll adopt Tom. Have other children. A quiver-full.'

The splinters of glass hurt when she moved.

'I'm in love with you. I always have been and didn't know

it. The day I left you was the worst of my life and I've paid for it every day since. I adore you. Will you have me?'

'A Viscountess. All that stuff. Preserve me from it.'

'Yes,' he said passionately. 'Yes. I will.'

They stood looking at each other. They couldn't, for a moment, speak.

'I'll think about it,' said Nelly.